Forever Love

Wanda Y. Thomas

Indigo is an imprint of
Genesis Press Inc.
315 3rd Ave. N.
Columbus, MS 39701

ISBN: 1-58571-036-9

Manufactured in the United States

First Edition

This book is dedicated to the babies in my life. From them I learned patience, the true meaning of unconditional love and trust, enjoyment of the little things in life, and to see the world through the innocent eyes of a child again. So, to Shannan, Branden, Catherine (Sunshine), Jennifer, Leanndra, Morris, Joshua, Jarrett, Addison, Tanner, Jamie, and with a mother's love to my son, Marcel, thank you.

Gerald crouched down beside her and removed the plate from Leah's hand. "I'm sorry. I'll take care of the mess. Here, let me help you up."

His touch sent a tremor upward to reverberate against the walls of her chest and before Leah could engage her control mechanisms, her imagination took flight. Her hands were running over the close-cropped dark hair, her lips fluttering kisses along the chocolate-colored cheeks above the neatly trimmed, shallow beard that covered the bottom half of his face. Would she feel silky softness or piercing pricks if he pressed his full-lipped, mustached-mouth against hers? At the thought of her body aligned opposite the large frame in front of her, Leah's heart began a rapid palpitation.

Prologue

June 4, three years earlier

The air hummed with barely restrained anticipation. More people arrived, adding their mass to the large crowd already gathered on the steps. None noticed the dark clouds moving in to block the sun or the breeze that suddenly turned several degrees cooler. All eyes were riveted on the doors. A black limousine pulled up to the curb. The doors of the building opened and a hush fell over the crowd in the moment before pandemonium broke out and the gathering became a chaotic, jostling mob.

"Ms. Ellis! How do you feel now that the trial is finally over?"

"Ms. Ellis! What will you do now that Dupree is behind bars?"

Bushy white eyebrows lowered over the ice blue eyes of the large man whose presence dominated the courthouse steps. He quickly calculated the distance to the car, then faced the horde of reporters and photographers trying to gain the attention of the woman dressed in a crisp black linen suit. "Ms. Ellis has nothing further to say!"

Turning, he grasped the arm of the young woman at his side and moving forward, used his broad physique and alligator briefcase to force a path through the crowd.

The shouting mass dogged them. "Ms. Ellis! Is it true that you and Dupree had plans to marry today?"

Leah Nicole Ellis pulled the wide brim of her coal-black hat low, shielding her face from the flashing bulbs, and ducked inside the car. Sliding in next to her, the man with her rapped on the glass partition and the car pulled away from the yelling mob. He leaned back in the cushioned, leather seat. "Leah, you did just fine. It's finally over and your testimony will ensure Dupree receives at least five to ten. Though with the crackdown on drugs and the new laws, I'm betting his sentence will be a lot longer."

Her bottom lip trembled and Leah bit down on it, but said nothing. Instead, she trained her mind on the storm clouds outside the window and tried to direct her thoughts elsewhere. A flash of lightning lit up the sky and Leah shivered as she closed her eyes. Had it been just three months ago that she'd awakened from a heavy sleep and a dream warning her that her impending marriage would be a mistake? Sitting back in the seat, Leah looked down at the hands trembling in her lap. Her life lay in shambles and all because of her involvement with Michael Ray Dupree.

A tear spilled onto her cheek and Leah swiped it away. She hadn't cried since her ordeal began and she was determined not to start now. But she couldn't divert her mind from reviewing the horrible events of the past three months, beginning with the one that had started it all. She remembered walking down the hallway two weeks after the premonition and the sounds that had caused her to stop. She remembered her feelings of betrayal when she opened the bedroom door and walked in on her sister and fiancé rocking together in a passionate sexual embrace. Lastly, Leah remembered giving heartfelt thanks for the police who burst through the door and arrested Michael Ray Dupree three weeks later.

Turning to the window again, Leah watched the passing scenery and began placing each of the emotions that had brought her to this day behind an impenetrable wall. By the time the limo stopped in front of her new home, the old Leah was gone and a new, more realistic Leah thanked her lawyer and stepped from the car. Inside her apartment, she went directly to the bedroom. In her suit, she lay down on the twin-size bed. What her lawyer believed was irrelevant. Leah knew the system. Michael Ray would cut a deal and be back on the streets in a matter of months, not years, a thought she refused to let frighten her. She was going to rebuild her life in spite of the media circus it had become. Before Michael Ray, Leah had been very active in helping to effect change and progress for her people. Now that the craziness was behind her, she would direct her time and energies into doing just that again.

One

As the newly elected president of Project Spruce, I look forward to a banner year. Our former president set and fulfilled some lofty goals," Merri Taylor, said smiling at Leah, "and our agenda has not changed. The brothers and sisters still need our help and I thank you for your faith in electing me to head the organization and for the commitment and zeal you've shown in the past. With your continued support, PS will move forward in our efforts to clean up the South Side. Now," Merri said, moving her hands to the waist of an hourglass figure. Her eyes took in the people seated around her living room. "Let's get this party started!"

Leah rose and began to gather her things. She stopped when she heard the ebony-skinned Merri issuing orders with the authority of a traffic cop. Just completing her own two-year term, she was happy to turn the reins over to her best friend of thirteen years. They were initially drawn together because of their height-at five-three, Leah was an inch taller than Merri. Though the years, they had shared their hopes and dreams; weathered the storm of Merri's teenage pregnancy and rejoiced or commiserated on their various relationships with men. Merri had a bubbly personality and the energy of a hyperactive four-year-old. Leah had often wondered how she sat still long enough to have her hair woven into the thick, brown braids she wore hanging to her waist. Merri also had a reputation for getting the job done, and while some viewed her take-charge attitude as harsh, Leah knew that under Merri's leadership, Project Spruce would flourish. And with her in charge of projects and special events they would make quite a team.

Leah also knew that since she herself was one of the main catalysts behind the almost three-year-old organization, Merri expected her to act as co-hostess of the party being held in honor of PS and the new slate of officers. Slinging her briefcase on her shoulder, Leah picked up her things. She would fulfill that obligation, of course, but first she wanted to jot down some thoughts for the conference report she was preparing for work before she forgot them.

"I've just spotted my reason for living," Peter Jackson said, stepping through the patio doors. "Later, G."

Gerald Tyler Morris watched his friend walk away, then moved to the edge of the patio and surveyed his surroundings. Banners tacked to the fences proclaimed the excellence of something called Project Spruce. Red, green, and black balloons hung in bunches from every conceivable fence post and tree branch. A grill smoking by the back fence filled the air with wafts of the spicy sauce being seared into the meat, and several tables along the right fence held many and varied dishes of traditional barbecue fare. The soulful beat of music added to the party atmosphere being enjoyed by the more than forty adults and children circulating in the yard.

Except for Peter and his girlfriend, Gerald didn't

know any of the people or the organization being hon-
ored. He had let Pete talk him into attending the
party, but he'd had the foresight to bring along his
briefcase which he would retrieve from the car and
find a quiet place to work. Turning away, Gerald
came to an abrupt halt when his eyes spotted and
anchored to a pair of golden brown legs and a shape-
ly behind. When the woman straightened and a shag-
gy-styled riot of dark auburn curls tumbled down and
settled along bare shoulders, Gerald didn't think he'd
draw an even breath again.

The feeling only intensified when she turned to face
him and he treated himself to a visual journey that
started with the tiny feet encased in white sandals
and moved slowly over hips outlined by a bright yellow sundress. Hearing her soft sigh, Gerald lifted his
eyes higher and followed the graceful movement of a
slender arm and the hand brushing hair away from her
small, oval-shaped face. Naturally blushed cheeks
framed a small linear nose, and a sensually tilted and
full mouth sat above a rounded chin. Her thick and
curly lashes swept up and she scanned the area
around them. When her search included him, he
found himself staring into a set of the most stunning
gray eyes he'd ever seen. Gerald felt his heart shift
with something he'd never felt before, and when she
turned away, he felt a keen sense of disappointment.
She'd looked right at him, but hadn't seen him. He
watched her select and drag a white plastic chaise
lounge into a secluded corner. By the time he thought
to help her, she had settled in and buried her head in
paperwork. He wanted to go over and talk to her, but
she'd made it obvious that she didn't wish to be disturbed. Gerald reviewed his options and for the first
time in his life, felt a sense of uncertainty as he grap-
pled for a decision. Unable to choose, Gerald found a

seat on a nearby picnic bench and focused his stare on her.

"Leah! Will you give it a rest and come join the party?" Merri sat down on the end of the chair and snatched the brochure from Leah's hand. "This is the PS Summer Kick Off and you're being a real show stopper."

Looking up, Leah found hazel-green eyes snapping in annoyance at her. She retrieved the brochure and glanced around the yard. "By the looks of things, it doesn't appear that I'm having any effect on the party, and I need to finish this report."

"If all you're going to do is work, then you might as well go home," Merri replied, piqued.

"Is that what you would prefer?"

"No. What I would prefer is that you get with it. We have good food, good friends, good music and good men. Why don't you choose one of those and get out there and party hardy?"

"I will, Merri. I just need a few more minutes. Besides, we both know that any party given by you will last into the wee hours. I don't see how my taking a couple of those hours to do my own thing is going to make any difference."

"Don't you know it, girlfriend. Never let it be said Merri T. don't know how to throw down." Both women laughed, then Merri sobered suddenly. "The police called about the break-in this morning."

"What did they say?"

"They think it was gangs-some sort of initiation thing. And they sympathize with us, but said it would it be best if we thought about moving the office or hiring a security guard."

"Well, moving the office is not an option," Leah replied with indignation. "We have to be accessible to the people that need us. And we can't afford a security guard."

"I know. But if we raise the kind of money we're hoping for at the fundraiser, we'll have more options." Merri stood up. "But I didn't come over here to get embroiled in a conversation about PS, Leah. I came over to get you out of this chair. However, today I'll be reasonable about this. I'll even fetch you a glass of wine. Then you have thirty minutes to finish whatever it is you're doing before I send over the boys. Got it?"

"Yeah, yeah, I got it. And I won't even need all of your measly thirty minutes."

A bottle of sparkling spring water in hand, Gerald returned to his seat at the picnic table and resumed his observation of the woman sitting on the patio. Other than the few minutes she'd spent talking to another woman, she'd been completely immersed in her work. That disturbed Gerald. Why, he couldn't say. And while he admired her ability to focus, this was a party and it was something Gerald planned to mention just as soon as he worked up the nerve to approach her.

Leah looked up and scanned the yard. Someone was watching her. She'd had the feeling earlier and had decided to ignore it. Now it felt as if the eyes were touching her. Her eyes honed in on the man sitting at the picnic table. He wasn't looking at her and for a moment she permitted herself to admire the strawberry red suit and black tee covering his large frame. Caught unawares when his gaze swept back and seized hers, Leah's heart constricted with apprehension. She thought she'd grown accustomed to the furtive glances and bold peeps that suggested some people still wondered about her. This time though, Leah sensed that something was different. This man's face held more than curiosity and made her so

nervous, Leah had to mentally check herself from flee-
ing into the house.

Forcing her attention away, Leah continued her
scrutiny of the people in the yard. A guest, she
noted, had waylaid Merri. That meant she would
have to get her own glass of wine, and Leah left the
chair. She moved to the opposite end of the patio and
had just filled her glass when she heard a deep, bari-
tone timbre close to her ear.

"Lose the wineglass, gorgeous. Drinking, even for
social reasons, is a bad habit and you're way too pretty to need the booze."

Delicately curved brows rose in surprise. Leah's
first thought was that she could listen to that voice all
day and wouldn't care what he was saying. Her second, that it was rather presumptuous of him to tell her
what to do. She turned around and looked up, and
up, and up some more. When her eyes finally reached
his face, her mind reacted with total female apprecia-
tion. He was absolutely stunning. Stumbling back,
she swallowed hard. "Are you speaking to me?"

"Since you're the most gorgeous creature here, I
guess I am speaking to you."

Annoyance replaced the surprised expression on
Leah's face. With a demure smile, she raised the
glass to her mouth and drained it. Then she picked up
Gerald's hand and set the empty glass in it.
Dumfounded, Gerald watched Leah walk away and
again settle into the chair. By the time he recovered,
the 'do not disturb,' 'not interested' and 'stay away'
messages flashed around her like neon signs.

Gerald went back to the picnic table. What was it
about her that had drawn his attention and why, after
the rejection she'd just handed him, did she still hold
his interest? Before Gerald could consider the matter
further, a man approached her chair. That generated

another new sensation inside of him. It pulsated to life without warning, heating his blood and stimulating his heartbeat. Gerald observed their affectionate interplay for a few moments, then directed his eyes elsewhere and tried to convince himself that he couldn't possibly be jealous of another man's attention to a woman he hadn't even known existed until an hour ago.

"Hiya doing, babe?"

Leah flashed a smile as Anthony Wright lowered his long, lean body to the end of her chair.

"I'm fine, Tony."

Tony ran his eyes down her body and his tone turned half-joking. "That you are, angel face. That you are. But tell me this. If you're so fine, how come you're sitting over here when the party's over there?"

"I'm trying to catch up on some work."

Tony took a swig from the beer bottle in his hand. "Leah, we punched off the clock at five. Leave this stuff and come party with me. I want you to enjoy yourself this evening."

"I am enjoying myself, Tony."

"How can you be enjoying yourself when all you ever do is work?" When Leah stopped smiling, Tony sighed and picked up a brochure. He casually flipped through the pages. "So tell me. What bits of wisdom have you picked up so far?"

Although she did note the haphazard way Tony had slapped the brochure closed and tossed it back onto the pile, Leah replied, "I wish you had attended the session on new product demographics with me yesterday. It was very informative and we can use a lot of the data in the presentation you're developing for the Philly market."

"Real-ly," Tony quipped.

Leah leaned forward, her expression serious. "Yes,

really. Now, while the bric-a-brac and kitchen utensil business has sustained this company since it's inception, Americans are preparing for the twenty-first century. High tech is where it's at and I think it's time we updated our inventory to include computer hardware, ancillary components, software, compact discs and the like. You'll understand more of what I'm talking about when you read my report."

Tony's face displayed an attentiveness that had nothing to do with what Leah was saying. He had something else on his mind and knowing Leah would discuss anything as long as it did not pertain to matters of the heart made broaching the subject with her difficult. When Leah stopped talking long enough for him to get in a word, Tony tabled his thoughts. "I'm glad you found the conference beneficial, Leah. But, this is a party and as of now the sweatshop is closed."

He stood and reached down for her hand. Leah looked up into dark brown eyes that always danced with laughter. She'd known Tony for four years. For the last year, he'd been her boss. He was six-three, thirty-two, and wore his wavy, black hair brushed back from a face the color of melted brown sugar. Tony had an outgoing personality and he kept her in stitches with his dumb jokes. More importantly, he'd been one of the few who'd stood staunchly behind her when the press and other media had tried to vilify her. Leah allowed him to pull her up from the chair. "Yes, sir, Mr. VP. But when this report isn't ready on Monday, I want you to remember whose fault it is."

Tony squeezed her hand. "Leah, the last thing on my mind is that report."

"Hey, man."

Fixated solely on the woman and the man, Peter's approach caught Gerald totally unaware and the slap on his back startled him so much, he almost jumped off the bench. Peter rounded the table and sat across from Gerald. "See anything you like?"

Gerald lifted the water bottle to his mouth. Though he didn't drink, he was not in the habit of forcing his views on others. Still, that she'd thumbed her nose at his suggestion had pricked Gerald's ego. That other man now commanding her attention really bothered him, too. Resisting a strong urge to look over at Leah again, he asked, "Who is that woman?"

"What woman?"

"The one in the yellow dress." Gerald nodded his head at the patio.

Peter looked toward the house. "You must be talking about Leah."

Gerald tested the name under his breath. It had a musical quality that sounded good to his ears. "What is her last name?"

Peter gave Gerald a curious glance. "Ellis. Why? You interested in meeting her?"

"I don't know, Pete," he said slowly." He paused for a moment. Since he didn't know Leah, he didn't want to say something that might be construed as being derogatory. "She seems kind of...standoffish." Gerald looked at Leah again and felt a definite rise in his body temperature. Then he shrugged. "No, Pete," he said with an assurance he didn't really feel. "Definitely, not interested."

Peter pursed his lips in an effort not to smile. "Too bad. She's one heck of a lady."

"You sound as if you know her-well."

"I do." Peter grinned when he saw Gerald's cocked brow. "Not in that sense, buddy. Leah and Ja'Nise are tight. They're part of something they call Les Cinq Belles Noir."

"The five beautiful blacks? What is that supposed

to mean?"

"I don't know, man. I do know that five of the most beautiful women walking the face of the earth make up the group. Ja'Nise and Leah are two," Peter said, looking around the yard. "There they are, at that table over there. The little one is Merri Taylor. She's the one hosting this gig. The other two are Danye Taylor and Stacia Waters. Danye is Merri's older sister."

Gerald glanced briefly at the women as Peter pushed himself up and propped one foot on the bench. "I'm headed to the club. Ja'Nise needs to get to work. She also said Raymond has a new band and they're hot. I thought maybe we'd go and check 'em out."

When he heard the skeptical grunt, an embarrassed flush stained Peter's cheeks. "Right," Gerald said. "The only thing you want to check out at Raymond's is Ja'Nise Montclair."

Peter crossed his arms on his leg and leaned closer to Gerald. "G., this isn't about Ja'Nise. This is business, man. We're scouting new talent and this band is supposed to be good."

"Uh-huh. Are they as good as Ja'Nise?"

"Ja'Nise is good, my brother." Peter released an exaggerated sigh and swiped imaginary sweat from his brow. "And those legs. Man, I can still feel the fire. The lady's hot with a capital H. I think I'm in love, homeboy."

"And what, pray tell, would you know about love, Pete? You go through women faster than you change your socks."

"You're one to talk, my man. When have you ever felt crazy enough about a woman to take out any man laying his eyes on her?"

Gerald glanced at the patio and his heart blipped.

He looked back at his friend, sure Pete had no idea how close he'd come to hitting a bulls-eye. "You're right. I don't know a damn thing about love. I do know that I'm not in the mood for Raymond's tonight. I'll see you in the studio tomorrow."

"Okay, but don't look for me too early. I also plan to take Ja'Nise home."

For the next hour, Gerald watched Leah and her male companion circulate among the guests, his gnashing back teeth the only sign of his agitation. "Finally," he murmured when Leah moved alone to the buffet tables. He waited until she'd filled a plate and crossed to a lawn chair, then got up and went to the tables. He dumped an ear of corn and a rib on a paper plate and grabbed a chair. "Hello again, gorgeous." Gerald positioned his chair across from Leah and sat down.

She appraised him coolly. "Why are you bothering me?"

"Am I bothering you?"

"Yes, and I'd appreciate it if you'd go away."

"I guess that's better than not affecting you at all," Gerald replied, completely unfazed by her untoward remark.

His eyes began a lazy tour that lingered on Leah's breasts and left her heart pummeling by the time they met hers again. This man hadn't laid a hand on her and yet he had disrobed and caressed her body in a touch so intimate it took her breath away. What he wanted was so obvious even she couldn't ignore it.

When a warm flush began inching its way up her body, Leah tucked a lock of hair back into the yellow headband and lowered her hand to her cheek. That she was having this kind of reaction to a total stranger, and a meddlesome one at that, made Leah furious with herself. Not to be outdone, she angled

her chin and subjected Gerald to the same bold examination she had just received. Having been out of the
flirting game for so long, hers was brief and not nearly as thorough. When she looked into his face again,
Gerald winked.

"Like what you see?"

Chagrin added to the heat in her cheeks. "No."

A smile tugged at his lips. "Well, I sure do. How
serious are you about that man?"

Thrown by the sudden change of conversation,
Leah frowned at Gerald. "What?"

"The man who hasn't left your side for the last
hour. How serious is it?"

"I don't think that's any of your bus-"

Gerald interrupted. "I hope it's not serious because
I think I'm in love with you."

"That's it," Leah hissed between her teeth as she
rose from her chair. "Look, mister..."

He rose too. "Gerald Morris, and you've just lost
your dinner."

Leah looked down at the mess on the ground and
stamped her foot. "Now look at what you've made
me do." Idiot, she added. The silent derogatory title
was directed at Gerald, along with a glare before Leah
bent down, turned over the plate and began picking
up the spilled food.

Gerald crouched down beside her and removed the
plate from Leah's hand. "I'm sorry. I'll take care of
the mess. Here, let me help you up."

His touch sent a tremor upward to reverberate
against the walls of her chest and before Leah could
engage her control mechanisms, her imagination took
flight. Her hands were running over the close-cropped
dark hair, her lips fluttering kisses along the chocolate-colored cheeks above the neatly trimmed, shallow
beard that covered the bottom half of his face. Would

she feel silky softness or piercing pricks if he pressed his full-lipped, mustached-mouth against hers? At the thought of her body aligned opposite the large frame in front of her, Leah's heart began a rapid palpitation. Her head swept up and in the silence stretching into the expanding twilight, their eyes linked and held.

Gerald waited for the bells and fireworks he knew would ring and explode when he'd found the right woman. Instead, all he could hear was the loud pounding of his heart and a voice inside his head that said, "You've found her." He looked away first, then helped her stand. "I'll get another plate for you," he said, his voice strained.

Leah expelled a deep sigh. "Please, don't bother."

She turned away and left a deeply confused Gerald standing in the middle of the yard.

Two

June 5

When the words on the page began to waver, Leah looked up from the pamphlet she was reading, the intolerant frown on her face reflecting her irritation with the racket outside her window. After a fitful night filled with strange dreams starring Gerald Morris, she was doing her best to forget the man by working on the conference report and had been doing a good job of it until 'Soul Train' started in the street.

Leah dropped her pencil and rose from the chair. She padded barefoot across a beige carpet to the window, pushed aside sheer, beige curtains and looked down on the street from her third floor apartment. As a prelude to the long, hot summer ahead, a heat wave had moved into the city, bringing with it unusually high temperatures. Oak and maple trees lining the long city block drooped languidly in the sun. Flat-topped hedges fenced small yards where sprinklers attempted to ward off the damaging heat and give the romping children playing in the spray some relief. Her own building sat nestled amongst rows of red-bricked, white-roofed houses making up the middle class neighborhood.

Leah sought the source of the noise, and when she

saw the group of boys standing in the middle of the street, her eyes narrowed in annoyance. One of them carried a boom box and for some reason felt he had to share his music with the whole block. A white front door opened across the street and Merri emerged onto the cement stoop. Leah returned her friend's wave, then winced when Merri's loud, clear voice cut through the already deafening racket.

"Jimmy Taylor! Get in this house right this minute!"

Ten-year-old Jimmy, who had his mother's eyes and a skin tone several shades lighter, cast an indignant glance over his shoulder in Merri's direction.

"Jimmy Taylor! You have..." Merri hollered again.

Leah slammed the window closed with a force that had the glass pane shimmying in the box frame and returned to her chair. She had just situated herself again and picked up her pencil when she remembered the other thing that had been niggling at her. The PS flyers! She'd forgotten to pick them up and Project Spruce had a meeting on Monday at noon.

Leah looked at the clock. It was already 4:20 in the afternoon and the print shop closed at five. Leaving the chair, she ran to her bedroom and the closet where she slipped her feet into a pair of black slings. Turning away, she caught sight of her appearance in the mirror. The blue and white checked shorts set was old and faded, and usually reserved for wear around the house. Most of her hair was still secure in the clip, but errant curls had escaped to frame her face and remind her that she needed to make an appointment for a trim. In evidence of her lack of sleep, dark circles shadowed her eyes. Leah lifted her hand to brush the hair away from her face. Well, it wasn't likely that anyone in the print shop would care how she looked.

The sudden appearance of Gerald's image next to hers in the mirror had Leah jumping back. She shuddered through a deep breath and stepped closer to the mirror. She hadn't been able to get the man out of her thoughts for a more than a few minutes at a time since she'd met him, and while she did wonder why, Leah knew that she didn't want or need a man. And especially not Gerald Morris. He made her feel things-things Leah hadn't wanted to feel in over three years. For a fleeting moment though, her face saddened at the memory of how she'd once bought into the love illusion big time. Then she straightened her shoulders and turned away from the mirror. It had been her emotions that had gotten her into trouble and almost ruined her life. Love was a myth! And it was a painful lesson Leah would not forget, having learned it the hard way.

In the living room, she grabbed her keys from a wooden bowl sitting on a not-too-sturdy table by the door and left the apartment. On the street, she climbed inside her white Wrangler Jeep and turned the key. Glad to see the Cubs baseball cap she'd left lying on the seat, Leah slapped it on her head and pulled away from the curb.

She never noticed the black sedan that followed her down the street; nor did she know that its lone occupant had been following her every move for months.

∽

Pulling up to the curb, Leah grabbed her purse and climbed from the Jeep, rushing to get inside before the print shop closed. Entering the shop, Leah welcomed the aura of tranquillity that greeted her. She looked around at the long oak counter running to the center of a rather large room with light blue walls and dark blue carpet. Display racks of bookmarks and notepads sat on the counter beside a row of black binders. To her left were two desks with large white calendars and beige telephones. Toward the rear of the room, she saw an open doorway from which she heard the noise of a copy machine. Seeing no one in the outer area, Leah moved to the counter and tapped a silver bell. When no one answered the chime, she rang it again, this time twice. She saw the cuffs of the white overalls first and her eyes began a slow upward route until they stopped on the smiling face of the man advancing into the room.

Leah's eyes closed in a prolonged blink and when she opened them again, the force of his presence registered through her body like tiny zips of hot flashes. She stared at the counter top. What had she done to deserve this?

"Sorry. I didn't hear you come in. The employees have all gone for the day and I was in the back finishing a last minute rush job." He continued forward as he explained. "What can I do for you today?" Gerald asked when he reached the counter.

"I'm here to pick up the flyers for Project Spruce," Leah mumbled without raising her head.

"I'm sorry, miss. Will you please repeat that?"

"The flyers for Project Spruce, I'd like to pick them up." She looked up and a shot of exhilaration made her insides quiver. The killer smile stayed in place and sweeping dark lashes accentuated the lightest brown eyes she had ever seen. They were the color of raw sienna touched by hints of brown. Only the one-carat diamond glinting in his left ear surpassed their brilliance.

Nothing could have made the smile on Gerald's face any wider when he recognized Leah. For most the of night, he had contemplated the many missteps made with her and could only describe his behavior as out of character. He knew he had to make a better impression this time. He held out his hand. "Hello again. We met last night, though we haven't proper-ly introduced ourselves. My name is Gerald Morris."

Leah's heart pounded when his thumb aressed the back of her hand. "Leah Ellis."

Releasing her, Gerald reached for and flipped open one of the black binders. "Let's see now. That was Project Spruce. Oh, here it is. Fifteen hundred flyers. They're in the back. I'll be just a minute."

When Gerald disappeared, Leah released the breath she wasn't aware she'd been holding. His sudden return to the doorway had her catching her breath again. She was so busy staring at him, Leah missed most of what he said as he walked back into the room. "It's a good thing you arrived when you did. Says here, these flyers are needed before Monday and this shop's closed on Sundays."

Dry-mouthed and confused, Leah couldn't have responded if she'd wanted to. Where was the insuf-ferable man who had tried to make a move on her last night?

"Here you go." Gerald set three boxes and a mani-la folder on the counter. "That order total is seventy dollars and twenty-three cents."

"Um, will you take a personal check?"

Gerald observed the emotive display on Leah's face, a testament to her nervousness. She'd lifted her lips in accompaniment to the question, but the tiny smile seemed to take effort on her part. Her eyes, however, spoke volumes. There he saw a deep held sadness, something so palatable he could feel it. He wondered at its cause, but hoping to put her at ease, stuck to his professional manner. "Of course. As long as you have two pieces of identification, that is."

"Thank goodness," Leah said softly. She quickly wrote out the check and handed it to him, along with her driver's license and a credit card.

Writing down the information he needed, Gerald tried to think of a way to detain Leah. If he could get her talking, perhaps she'd loosen up a little. Unfortunately, his mind chose that moment to draw a blank. He handed back the license and card. With a smile, he said, "Thank you for using JetGraphics. Be sure to come back if we can help you again."

"Thank you." Leah grabbed the three boxes and headed for the door.

Gerald stayed at the counter watching Leah until she drove off. As he turned away, the manila folder on the counter caught his attention and he picked it up. Leah had rushed out of his shop like a frightened rabbit, and he knew his display of good manners had done nothing to convince Leah that the man she'd encountered the previous evening was not the real him. The folder in his hands made what he did next easier. Gerald punched the open key on the cash register and retrieved Leah's check. Returning the paperwork would save Leah a return trip to the shop. It would also give him another chance to somehow reverse the opinion she obviously held of him. Pleased with his plan, Gerald noted the address on the check, slipped it into his pocket and returned to the back room.

∾

At the three soft raps, Leah set her report aside and smiled, knowing who was at the door. "Come in, baby. It's open."

"Hi, Mama Leah."

Leah left the couch. She gave Jimmy a big hug, cleared a place for him on the couch and went to the kitchen. She filled a plate with cookies, poured a glass of milk and returned to the living room. Jimmy fell on the food. Leah waited until he had devoured five cookies and half the milk. "Okay, now tell me what's wrong."

With the milk mustache, the scowl on Jimmy's face looked comical, but Leah knew this was not the time for laughter. "It's Mom. She's always yelling at me and I don't know why. I'm not doing anything except hanging with my friends and every time she sees them it's like she goes nuts."

"Jimmy, you've been living with Merri Taylor for ten years. I'd think you'd be used to your mother by now."

"I am. But sometimes I think that she doesn't like me very much."

"Jimmy! Why would you say something like that? You know your mother loves you."

"I think it's because of my father."

Leah's antenna rose. "Has your mother said something that would make you think that?"

Jimmy's eyes filled with tears. "No, Mama Leah. That's just it. Mom never talks about my father, even when I ask her. She just gets this really mean look on her face and tells me to go and clean my room. You knew my father, Mama Leah. Was he a bad man?"

Leah took Jimmy into her arms. The time was coming, and soon, when Merri was going to have to deal with her son and his questions about his father. As much as she loved Jimmy, it was not her place to step into that role. "Baby, when I knew your father, he was a good person. Whatever your mother feels about him has absolutely nothing to do with you. I know sometimes it seems like Merri is being a little unreasonable, but that's when you have to remember that it is because your mother loves you that she acts the way she does."

Jimmy ate two more cookies. Leah knew the discussion wasn't over when he turned his sad hazel eyes toward her again. "I still want to know about my father."

Nodding shrewdly, Leah knew she needed something to distract him. "You know what I think?" Jimmy shook his head no. "I think that you and your mother need a break from each other. So why don't the two of us hang out tomorrow after church? It will be your day and we'll do anything you want."

Jimmy brightened at that suggestion. "Can we go to the park?"

"Uh-huh."

"And after that can we go to the arcade?"

"Anything you want to do, as long as it doesn't get us into any trouble."

"Okay."

Jimmy finished the cookies and milk and Leah walked him to the door. She watched him saunter down the corridor until he turned the corner. Raising a child by yourself had to be the hardest job in the world. As far as Leah was concerned, Merri was a saint.

Gerald parked his black Ford Bronco across the street from a white, limestone apartment building with dark green shutters. A painted sign hanging to the left of the entrance confirmed the address on Leah's check and a quick survey of the street yielded the white Jeep. Gerald stepped from the truck and crossed the road. He ducked under the dark green awning and climbed six cement steps leading to the glass door entrance. A few minutes later, he rapped on the wooden door of Leah's apartment.

"Who is it?"

"Gerald Morris."

Gerald Morris! What in the world was he doing at her apartment? Leah didn't move, unsure if she should let him inside.

"Leah?"

Then again, leaving him standing on the other side of a closed door was a little asinine, Leah decided. She reached for the knob and opened the door. "Yes?"

"May I come in?" Gerald asked. "Just for a moment," he added when he saw her hesitation.

Not wanting to appear completely inhospitable, Leah stepped aside. The small room seemed to shrink when he entered, and Leah's heart took up an irregular beat, impeding the flow of blood to her brain. She backed up a step. Sensing her anxiety, Gerald backed up a step, too.

"Why are you here?"

It was a good question and now that he thought about it, he really didn't have a good reason to be there. "You left the shop without your paperwork and I...well, I thought you should get it back right away."

"Thank you," Leah murmured, still baffled by the strange sensations his presence had created within her.

Gerald didn't release the folder when Leah tried to take it. He stared into her eyes and wondered at the deep pain they held. He'd noticed that same aura of sadness the last two times they'd met. Perhaps that was the reason he couldn't forget her. Gerald let the folder go and, acting on a sudden impulse, he opened his arms. Urged forward by the intensity of his gaze and without a thought as to what she was doing, Leah walked into them. A deep sigh left her lips when Gerald enfolded her and held her close to his body. For a few silent minutes, they stood holding on to each other.

Leah laid her head on his chest and snuggled closer. Gerald drew in a deep breath, inhaling the flowery scent of her hair and closed his eyes. The pleasure of her touch thrilled his senses and coursed through his body in waves that were almost overwhelming. This felt right, and in the back of his mind, Gerald knew that they were meant to be together. He squeezed Leah tighter, then stroked her back with his hands, wanting only to comfort her and to let her know that he was there, if she ever needed him. "Don't hurt anymore, sweetheart," he said in a voice that sounded whisper soft.

His words jolted Leah back into reality and she jerked herself out of his arms. The indignant toss of her head told him that she had dismissed her temporary lapse in judgement and that Leah was preparing for a battle.

Gerald's heart thudded against his chest and the discomfiture over his behavior showed plainly in his face. What in the world had he done? Leah was not his woman, and he had no business holding her as if he were her man. Unsure of what to say or do next, he cleared his throat. "I guess I'd better get going." He didn't move and Leah didn't respond. "Hope the job we did for you is satisfactory."

"I'm sure it is," Leah stated through clenched teeth.

The tone of her voice chilled the lingering effect of her touch and Gerald moved stiffly toward the door. "Well, I'd better get going," he said again. He reached for the knob and stopped. Turning back, he asked, "Leah, will you have dinner with me this evening?"

His question pushed everything else from Leah's mind. "Thank you for the invitation, Mr. Morris. But I don't date."

Leah thought it odd when a smile glossed his face. "It's okay this time, Leah. You'll come around." The smile broadened to one of supreme confidence. "I'll see you later."

Again, Leah did not respond and after satisfying himself with one last look, Gerald headed down the corridor. Leah rushed forward and locked the door, then leaned back against the hard wood, unable to believe that she'd walked into the arms of a stranger. She didn't know what was going on between the two of them, but she was sure that she didn't want to find out.

Three

wo hours, and he was going home. Gerald had this thought as he drove his red Porsche through the gates of the Country French estate his mother called her little home by the lake. He knew what was in store for him and figured two hours would satisfy his mother.

A parking attendant hired for the occasion opened his door and he stepped from the car. "Good evening, sir."

"Evening," Gerald replied. He retrieved his black dinner jacket from the back and had just pulled on the coat when the double rosewood doors opened and two caramel-colored children ran down the steps.

"Uncle Gerry," they yelled, flying into his arms.

Unmindful of his clothes, Gerald knelt on one knee to embrace both children. "Hey! How are my munchkins this evening?"

Reggie slid his hands into the pockets of his blue jeans. "Nana won't let us come to the party. She said we have to stay upstairs."

"That's how it goes sometimes, little man. Tonight's party is for grownups." Gerald rose and brushed his hands across the knees of his pants. "I'll let you in on a secret, though. I'm slipping out early and if you're good, I'll take you with me."

"Really?" Reggie said, perking up instantly.

Gerald looked down into eyes that matched his own. He stood six-four, and at nine, Reggie already showed signs of surpassing the six feet plus height attained by all the men in the family. "Really," he said. "But I'm depending on you not to say anything. If you do, we can't leave." Gerald held out his little finger. "Deal?"

Reggie hooked his finger with that of his uncle. "Deal."

Audrey reached her arms into the air and Gerald picked her up. If any female had his heart it was four-year-old Audrey, who had only to push out her bottom lip for her uncle to be like putty in her little hands. He kissed Audrey's cheek, hooked his free arm around Reggie's shoulders and started up the steps. Entering a two-story foyer, Gerald continued through the house until he reached the doorway of a spacious living room.

"Boy, it's about time you showed up. We've been waiting on you for over an hour."

Gerald set Audrey on her feet, then directed his eyes to the regal woman occupying a high backed chair with a floral print. She wore a floor length gown of pale yellow silk and a frown wrinkled her otherwise flawless, nut-brown face.

"I was tied up at the shop."

"The shop, huh? Why is it then that when I called the shop the telephone went unanswered?"

Gerald pursed his lips. He should have known she'd check on him, especially when it involved one of her dinner parties and she was playing matchmaker again. His father had died before his birth and Gerald had often wondered why his mother had never remarried. He'd always hoped she would marry Peter's dad, so they'd really be the brothers they always claimed to be. Instead, Linda Morris focused on his single state and her zeal on his behalf knew no bounds. "I had to run an errand."

"Humph," Linda replied. "Guess that cell phone in your pocket is running on dead batteries, too."

Gerald attempted to disarm his mother with a kiss. "I love you, Mama."

Linda pushed him away with a smile and stood up. She took hold of his arm. "Well, come on, baby. I have someone I'd like for you to meet."

Gerald sent his friend a look of desperation and Peter took the cue. "Mama. May I borrow Gerald, for just a sec?"

Clearly exasperated, Linda turned to the man she had helped rear when his own mother ran off to escape the strain of an interracial marriage. For a long moment, she appraised the tall, lanky man with high yellow skin, green eyes and hair so light it was almost blonde. "Why, son?" she finally asked.

"Um, I, um." Peter's eyes scintillated when he finally hit upon an excuse. "It's business, Mama," he said with a smile.

"Baby, can't it wait? Gerry's late arrival has already ruined my schedule."

"No, ma'am," Peter replied with respect.

Gerald stepped in to rescue his friend. "Mama, this will only take a minute, and your latest find isn't going anywhere." He grabbed Peter by the arm. "Come on, man."

In the library, Peter shoved Gerald's shoulder. "Don't ever do that to me again."

"What's the problem? Mama bought it, didn't she?"

"Yeah. She bought it. But I don't like lying to the 'Barracuda.'"

Gerald waved him off. "You better not let Mama hear you call her that."

"Man, you know it's meant affectionately."

"You know that and I know that, but Linda Morris may have a different perspective on the matter." Gerald sat on the velvety cushioned sofa. "Have you seen her?"

"Seen who?"

Gerald clenched his jaw. "Quit messing around, Pete. Have you seen her?"

Peter chuckled. "Yeah, I've seen her, but you're not going to like her. Her name is Rachel James."

"And?"

"And she's way too thin, a bit too uppity, and a little light in the brain department. But you know, Mama. Good luck, bro."

Gerald directed his stare into the room. His sister, Beth, had laid out the space with her usual flair, and the furnishings, in muted shades of sea foam green and off-white, gave the room an elegant look and appeal. Pillows and other decorator items accented in rust added spots of color. Gerald propped his feet on the oak cocktail table and looked across the room at Peter, who leaned against the beige brick bar. How was he going to get through this evening when his mind was still seeking answers to what had happened between him and Leah? "I have to get out of here," he grumbled.

They looked up at the knock and Gerald grimaced when he saw his brother-in-law. William Thompson walked to the middle of the floor, adjusted his black dinner jacket and cleared his throat. "I've been sent by the 'Barracuda' to break up this little meeting." A slow grin spread across his face when he looked at Gerald. "Time for dinner, boys."

❧

Mabel Ellis watched her daughter fork the potatoes into a small hill, mash it down and pile it up again. Not only was it about the fifteenth time Leah had done that, but she also had a faraway look in her eyes.

"Leah? What's wrong?"

"She's out of it, Ma." Sheila's lips formed into a smirk. "As usual."

"Hush up, Sheila," Mabel scolded her youngest. "Leah!"

Leah looked at her mother. "Huh?"

"What's wrong, baby?"

"Bet it's man trouble." Sheila sent a taunting look in Leah's direction. "Then again, Leah doesn't have a man, now does she?"

"I told you once to hush up, Sheila. Don't make me repeat it. Leah?"

"Nothing's wrong, Ma. I have a lot on my mind."

"Like what?"

"For starters, this evening I have to finish a report for work. It's due Monday and I'm spending the day with Jimmy tomorrow. Then there's PS. We have a house to fix up in a few weeks and we've been having problems with our supplies. An older couple owns it and they will be very disappointed if we don't show up. And it looks like PS may be losing Maxwell Corp. as a sponsor." Leah looked at Sheila. Her sister worked for Maxwell. Maybe she knew something. She shook her head. Even if Sheila did know anything, she would never tell her. "I don't know," Leah sighed. "Just a lot of things."

"Figures she'd be worrying about other people's problems instead of her own."

"And what problems would those be, Sheila?"

"Oh, Leah, please. When was the last time you had a man in your life or went out on a date, for that matter? But then considering your track record, I can understand why it's been so long."

Leah heard the mockery. A horn honking outside the house saved her a response. Sheila left the table. In the living room, she pushed aside the light peach drapes and looked out the picture window at the car parked in the driveway. "Anyway," Sheila continued, "at least one of us can get a date." She let the curtain fall and went down the hallway to her bedroom.

When she returned, Leah examined her sister. If it weren't for her scandalous behavior, Sheila might be a likable person. She was smart and pretty. No. Pretty wasn't the right word. Her sister was five-seven, model thin, and blessed with wavy, shoulder length auburn tresses. With her golden brown skin, round gray eyes and dimples, no one could deny that Sheila was beautiful. However, the red dress she wore could pass for skin and would put a miniskirt to shame. Her makeup enhanced her looks, but Sheila's features held no softness and the smile on her face stopped just short of her eyes.

"Bye, Ma. I'm off."

"Bye, baby. Have a good time."

"Sheila," Leah called from the table. Normally she didn't bother sparring with her sister, but Sheila's comment had been uncalled for. "Just so you know. I do have a man. His name is Gerald and he's very handsome. He is also smart, suave and successful. The exact opposite of those losers you seem to attach yourself to."

Sheila responded by slamming the door as she left the house.

Mabel stood and began clearing the table. "Well, now. That was an interesting exchange. But it would be nice, if on occasion, the two of you would at least try to act like sisters."

"I'm sorry, Ma."

"I know, baby, and I also know that Sheila initiated it."

Leah helped her mother clean up, then followed her into a living room so clean they could have eaten dinner off the floor. The surfaces of the dark oak tables gleamed. Even the leaves on the variety of green plants shone in the lamplight. Everything had a place and Mabel put it there. Leah took a seat on the ivory couch. Mabel sat in a peach and ivory-striped chair and faced her daughter across the coffee table. Her eyes drifted to a photograph of her husband and her smile saddened. Hamilton had died just over a year ago and Mabel missed him terribly. Who would have thought that after all the good he'd done, his life would end in a mugging outside his law office? Mabel turned back to Leah and jumped right in with the questions. "Baby, tell me more about this Gerald. What is his last name? When and where did you meet him? How long have the two of you been dating?"

Leah groaned. Mentioning Gerald had been a mistake and she regretted letting Sheila goad her into it. "Ma, please."

Innocent brows rose. "Leah, as your mother I have every right to ask questions."

Leah slapped her hands on her thighs and stood up. "You're right, but I really have to run if I want to complete my report. I love you, Ma, and thanks for dinner."

Mabel started to say something, then just shook her head. "Bye, baby. I love you, too."

She had wanted to voice her concern over the type of neighborhoods Project Spruce ventured into, but knew it would have been a waste of time. Leah never listened when it came to her causes. Her daughter was a nonconformist, though Mabel had reared her family in the suburbs to shelter her children from the lingering effects of the black power movement and civil unrest of the sixties and early seventies.

Mabel acknowledged her duty to the race by mailing an annual check to the NAACP and renewing her subscriptions to *Ebony* and *Jet*. Once a month, she attended the Colored Women's Auxiliary meeting where rousing discussions on issues affecting African Americans took place. That as an organization they had yet to do anything about the problems didn't bother Mabel. She was aware, and that was key in her book. In that way, Sheila Marie was like her. They were content to sit on the sidelines and root for the winning team. Leah was just like her father, always rushing into the game without regard for her own welfare. Mabel remembered the near apoplexy she had suffered over Leah's two-week suspension in high school. Her daughter had been one of the ringleaders that had organized a walkout to protest the school curriculum's lack of a black history class. Mabel shook her head. Leah was still very active for the cause, but that man, Michael Ray Dupree, had changed her daughter.

Rising from her chair, Mabel released a wistful sigh. Well, since Leah wouldn't listen, maybe God would. She prayed every night, asking that He end the friction between her daughters and draw them closer together. In church tomorrow she'd offer up an extra prayer to keep her baby safe. She'd also put in a good word for this Gerald, just in case he turned out to be the one who could capture Leah's heart.

Mabel saw the envelope and picked it up, then headed for her bedroom. Leah slipped the same white envelope on the table every month. Mabel didn't need the money and on Monday she'd add it to the special account. On her birthday this year, Leah would receive living room furniture, because Mabel had decided that if her daughter wouldn't decorate that sparsely furnished apartment she called a home, Mabel would do it herself, one room at a time.

Leah entered her apartment and went directly to her bedroom. Noting the mess, she shook her head. When made, a rose and black spread covered a light oak waterbed that matched the mirrored dresser and end tables. And the pillows on the floor belonged in the rose armchair, only it held her computer and briefcase. The furniture was a birthday gift from her mother and it did look better than the secondhand stuff previously occupying the space. The least she could do was keep the room neater. Her eyes strayed to the picture of an African water maiden hanging over her bed. It was the only new item she had purchased in three years; and it wasn't because Leah didn't have the money. With her salary, inheritance, and the money her father had invested for her before his death, she was quite well off. She just didn't care about material possessions and she preferred not to spend any money on herself, especially after—

Banishing the thought, Leah picked up a deep aqua skirt and after arranging it and the matching jacket on padded hangers, proceeded to straighten the room. Picking up her laptop and briefcase, she returned to the living room and stood unconsciously tapping her foot as her eyes moved back and forth between the kitchen table and the living room. Which room would she be more comfortable in? This was procrastination and Leah knew it. However, tonight she was going to triumph over the bad habit.

Leah loved her job, and could get totally absorbed in

manipulating and analyzing data. She also liked the brainstorming sessions with Tony and the marketing team often jumping into the middle of those discussions with enthusiasm. Writing, though, wasn't exactly her forte. Setting her things in a kitchen chair, Leah turned to the refrigerator. She filled a glass with juice and sipped at it, still eyeing the two rooms. Okay, she would set up shop in the living room. Retrieving her things, she snapped on the lamp and got comfortable on the couch. Pulling the computer into her lap, she set her mind to putting her recommendations down in written form. Within minutes, the words on the screen blurred and a dark face with awesome brown eyes appeared. Setting the computer aside, Leah pulled her feet under her and leaned back on the couch to reflect on the man it had taken only two days to stamp indelibly on her mind.

At his house, Gerald checked one last time on his niece and nephew, then tramped down the stairs, expelling a long and weary breath. At times his mother was a bit imprudent in her quest to get him to the altar. If he were in the market for a wife, the woman he chose would have to stir not only his loins, but his mind. She'd also need to be taller. Gerald paused on the steps. Then why the attraction to Leah?

A package sitting on the bar drew his eyes as he entered the den. Jeffrey Jones was waiting for his response and taking the kids to the zoo tomorrow meant he needed to deal with this tonight. Leah took a back seat in his thoughts as Gerald retrieved the box and sliced through the TyJo Productions label. He loaded the five tapes on a multi-player stereo system and, taking the paperwork and remote with him, lowered himself to a plush, dark gray leather couch. He picked up the first stat sheet and hit PLAY.

Hidden speakers filled the room with music and Gerald settled back to read the information on the first group. It wasn't until the fourth tape that a rush of adrenaline raced through his body. The format was rough, but he picked up on the hip-hop funk and old school harmony laced with just enough bass to add flavor to the mix. It was the signature sound of TyJo Productions. Gerald picked up the stat sheet. "Ebony Silk," he said, testing the name out loud. "Yep," he said with a definitive nod of his head when a quartet of voices blended in harmonic song. Listening to the smooth, melodic rhythms, he studied the group's photograph.

The four black men were young, good-looking, and would no doubt make the ladies delirious. When the demo concluded, Gerald placed headphones on his ears, jacked up the volume and listened to the entire tape again. Liking what he heard, he reached for the stat sheet and wrote down his comments. J.J. had found another winner.

He leaned back again and pushed PLAY. The thunderous drums and crashing cymbals blasting in his ears had Gerald jerking the phones off in a hurry. He grabbed the stat sheet. Chic-a-Boom? His aversion showed in his face as he flipped the page to the descriptive write-up. "NEW! EXCITING! OUT OF THIS WORLD! Chic-a-Boom's pulsating beat will send you to new heights of musical delight."

Gerald read no further as he hit the remote, stopping the din, and picked up his pen. On the stat sheet he wrote, "Jeffrey Jones, if you sign this group to a TyJo contract, you deserve to lose every dime you have!"

Gerald repacked the box, loaded jazz on the stereo and returned to the couch. He lay down and stretched out his two hundred and thirty-pound build in luxurious comfort. He had no sooner crossed long legs at the ankles than Leah entered his thoughts again. With her face on his mind, Gerald closed his eyes and, for the first time in months, drifted into a restful sleep.

Across town, a booming laugh rang out from the man watching television. Frowning at the interruption of the ringing telephone, he shoveled another forkful of Chinese noodles between his teeth before leaving the couch. "Hello," he mumbled over the food in his mouth.

"You were supposed to check in at seven! It is now ten after eight!"

"Man, I just hit the door. I was grabbin' a bite to eat, then I was gonna dial."

"I'm not interested in your damn excuses! When I say report by seven, that's exactly what I mean. You got that? Or do I need to make it clearer for you?"

"Yeah, I got it."

"Well?"

"Well, what?"

"Look, don't jack me around. I'll have your ass slapped back on ice so fast it'll make your head spin."

"Hey, calm down, man. There's no need for threats here. She went to a Project Spruce meetin' this mornin', a print shop, her mother's and after followin' her home, I left."

"That it?"

"Oh, yeah. A man came to her apartment."

"A man? Who?"

"How should I know? I ain't her keeper."

"Did you get pictures?"

"I'll get 'em to ya tomorra."

"Okay. Is that it?"

"Yeah, that's it."

"Keep your eye on her, and tomorrow, this phone better ring at seven. Understand?"

The phone slammed down in his ear and the man's lip curled as he replaced the receiver. Then he shrugged. As long as the money kept coming in, what did he care about some jerk drug dealer?

Four

June 6

At six-thirty the next morning, Gerald paused at the bay window in his sitting room. An immediate downward glide of extensive, dark lashes shielded his eyes from the sun's glare as he looked down on the three guest cottages and the roof of the enclosed pool house. He was thinking about Leah and the decidedly erotic turn his dreams had taken during the night.

Though he barely knew her, Gerald knew his captivation with Leah was genuine, and much more than a sensual temptation sparked by a look, wink or brush against the body. That kind of allure had nothing to do with any real feelings. What Gerald felt for Leah had substance. Their spirits had touched in a way that went beyond the spurious or superficial. Opening the doors, he stepped onto the balcony and stood looking out over the considerable expanse of his property. A breeze warmed by the morning sun touched his face and Gerald tilted his head toward the blue sky.

Could it be love at first sight? His sister believed it happened all the time and they had often debated the subject. Perhaps there was something to the old cliché. Otherwise, how could he explain the intense emotions he felt for a virtual stranger? This called for further study, which meant he would have to see Leah again. Gerald suddenly smiled, remembering his plans to take the kids to the zoo. With any luck, maybe he could talk Leah into going with them.

❧

Leah rolled from her side to her stomach and extended her legs. She wiggled her toes, then leisurely stretched her arms toward the headboard. Sighing deeply, she crossed them under her head and closed her eyes. She sank back into her dream and smiled when the large brown hands that had just given her the most erotic massage she'd ever experienced reached for her again.

Groaning at the intrusion of the ringing telephone, she fumbled around the nightstand and picked up the receiver. "Hello," she mumbled.

"Good morning, Leah."

Her eyes snapped opened and Leah bolted upright in the bed. Gerald! This couldn't be Gerald on the other end of her phone, and if it was, why was he calling her at, Leah squinted at the clock, 7:15 on a Sunday morning? She pushed hair from her face to the back of her head and lay back on the pillows, shaking her head in bewilderment. "Ger—Gerald," she finally stuttered.

In his den, Gerald settled back into the cushions of the couch. "I know it's Sunday and I apologize for calling so early, but I have my niece and nephew here and we were thinking that after church we'd spend the afternoon at the zoo." He paused to take a deep breath. He was talking a mile a minute and needed to calm down. "Leah. Will you come with me?"

She remained silent.

"Leah?"

"Hmmm," was all she could get out.

"I know this is last minute and that you may have other

plans today."

Somehow, Leah managed to find her voice. "Gerald, thank you for asking me, but I can't go with you. I do have plans today."

Several quiet beats passed while Gerald searched for a way to change Leah's mind. "Perhaps we can join you," he probed.

Fully awake now and thankful she had an excuse, Leah responded quickly, "No. That's not a good idea. Today is kind of special and I'd rather spend it alone with Jimmy."

Jimmy? If Leah didn't date, then who was Jimmy? The man at the party? Gerald tempered a flash of anger at her deliberate attempt to deceive him. "Okay, Leah. But know this. I'm a very persistent man. Sooner or later you will go out with me, though I'd prefer the sooner rather than the later."

What was she supposed to say to that? "Good-bye, Gerald," she said with finality.

"This is not good-bye, Leah Ellis. This relationship has only just begun and I will see you later."

Leah replaced the receiver slowly. Relationship? Gerald had said the word like it was a foregone conclusion. Well, he was sadly mistaken, because there would be no dates or anything else with Gerald Morris! She glanced at the clock again and left the bed. Since she was already awake, she might as well get ready for church. If she prayed hard enough, maybe she'd receive divine guidance on how to handle a man who didn't understand the meaning of the word no.

"Mama Leah, did you see that man?" Jimmy's voice sounded childishly loud.

"It isn't polite to point and please lower your voice,"

Leah chided, not looking in the direction of his finger. She had already seen Gerald and was hoping like heck they could get through the gate before he saw her.

A shadow fell across her body. "Hello, Leah."

She peeked at him over the rim of her sunglasses. "Hi, Gerald."

"Aren't you going to introduce me to your...date?"

Jimmy stuck out his hand. "I'm Jimmy Taylor, and you're supposed to go to the back of the line."

Gerald shook the small hand and hunched down. "My name is Gerald Morris. And you are right, Jimmy. You should go to the back of the line, unless you have a special pass."

"Do you have a special pass?"

"Yep." Gerald rose, pulled out his wallet and took out the pass.

Jimmy studied the document, then looked up at Gerald from beneath the brim of his baseball cap. "I guess it's okay then." He handed the pass back and looked up at Leah. "Why don't we have one of those, Mama Leah?"

Had Leah been looking at Jimmy instead of the red linen shirt molded to Gerald's chest and the black twill shorts outlining his thighs, she might have noticed that Jimmy hadn't stuck around for her answer. "Well, people who come to the zoo a lot find it's cheaper to buy a pass. We don't come that often, but I'm sure we'll be admitted—" Leah stopped when she heard the deep chuckle.

"Please. Do go on. I find your explanation fascinating even if Jimmy didn't."

"Excuse me," Leah said, looking around for her lost charge. "I need to find Jimmy."

Folding his arms over his chest, Gerald peered intently at Leah. Her confused expression and the rapid pulse at the base of her neck told him she was more nervous than angry. Although he had to work at keeping his adopted stance of nonchalance in place, there was a teasing light in his eyes as Gerald admired the lime midriff top and knee-length black leggings Leah wore. "Don't worry about, Jimmy, sweetheart. He's with my niece and nephew. But please, do continue with your explanation," he said, grinning.

"I don't see anything particularly funny about this situation, Gerald." If Jimmy hadn't insisted on coming to the zoo instead of the park, she wouldn't be in this predicament. Fate seemed determined to throw them together. Leah was just as determined to keep them apart. After Michael Ray, she'd had her fill of men—all in general and this one specifically. With a shake of her head, Leah turned to ask the person standing behind her to hold her place in line.

"Why don't you join us?"

"No!" She'd spoken the word rudely and to soften the response, Leah added, "Gerald, your offer is very nice, but no thanks."

"It's G. And why the no? We're both already here."

"Because Jimmy and I planned this day for the two of us and I'd just prefer not to, if you don't mind."

Gerald dropped his arms. "Well, I do mind." He picked up her hand and pulled Leah forward. "So let's go."

For the next two hours, Leah tried to stay angry with Gerald, a next-to-impossible feat when he insisted on holding her hand, his touch sending her blood pressure soaring. His eyes continually roved over her body and left her feeling as if she were a ship he was about to pirate and plunder. She sneaked another peek at him. Her eyes skittered away quickly when she found him staring at her again. Never had she met anyone as bold as Gerald Morris. And knowing that her resistance was weakening, Leah moved further down the railing and focused her attention on the antics of the grizzly bears.

A smile graced Gerald's face as he stepped closer. He curved his arm around Leah's waist and pulled her firmly against his side. He had the girl of his dreams, literally, in his arms. How many men could say that?

Reggie, who was tired of carrying the full picnic basket, tugged at his shirt. "I'm hungry, Uncle Gerry. Can we eat now?"

Gerald looked down at his nephew. He'd been so focused on Leah, he'd almost forgotten about the kids. With reluctance, he released Leah and took the basket. The grass under a large oak tree provided the perfect spot for lunch and Gerald ushered them into the shade, spread a blanket and began laying out the food.

Leah was cooler now that she was out of the sun and his arms, and remembering that breathing was a natural function, she made her lungs cooperate. She lowered herself to the edge of the blanket, as far away from Gerald as humanly possible without being in the grass, and continued to analyze the effect he was having on her, disturbed that after all her diligent work a man could still make her feel tingly inside.

Audrey's voice broke into her thoughts and Leah turned her attention back to the group. The child was in the 'why' stage and Gerald had shown a limitless amount of patience as he answered every question Audrey fired in rapid succession.

"I wanna a ice cream, Unca Gerwee."

"Later," he replied, tweaking her nose. "If you eat all of your lunch, that is."

"'Kay," she responded. "Unca Gerwee?"

"Yes, pumpkin."

"Why's cho'late brown?"

Leah hid a smile behind her hand when after receiving an answer to the chocolate question, Audrey continued until she had gone through all the flavors she could think of.

"Uncle Gerry, can we stay with you again tonight?"

"I don't have a problem with it, Reg. You have to ask your parents, though. If they say no, that's the end of it. Are we clear on that?"

"Yes, sir."

Gerald wiggled his brows at Leah. "How about you, sweetheart? Want to spend the night at my place?"

Her mouth fell open and Leah hastily snapped it shut. Gerald was baiting her again and she wasn't going to add to his enjoyment by responding to his teasing. He might have forced himself on her, but she didn't have to talk to him.

"You know, Jimmy," Gerald drawled. "I think there's something wrong with your date."

Jimmy looked Leah over and shrugged. "She looks all right to me."

"No, Jimmy. I think something is wrong. You see, I really like your date and I've been trying to talk to her, but she won't talk to me. It's probably her voice. Maybe if I kissed her, it would fix the problem."

Leah's face flamed as Jimmy examined her again. Before she could come up with a cutting reply that would knock Gerald down to size, Audrey spoke up.

"Is Jimmy your boy?"

"No, Audrey," Leah said, sending Gerald a look that promised retribution.

"Why did he call you Mama?"

She turned her attention to the child. "It's a special name. Jimmy's my godson."

Audrey studied Reggie and Jimmy. "Do you have some godgirls?"

"No, darling. I don't have any children."

"Why?"

"Well, because I have a very busy life."

"Why are you busy?"

"How do you feel about having children?"

Leah thanked Gerald with her eyes. Since he had been kind enough to rescue her from Audrey's 'why trap,' she figured she owed him at least one response. "I haven't really given it any thought."

"Why not?"

All right, she'd answer this one too, but only because she'd left herself open for his comeback. "Because I believe that if you bring a child into this world you should take responsibility for rearing it. That requires time I don't have and besides I-I'm not married."

Gerald started to tease her, using Audrey's mode of questioning, but hearing the catch in her voice, decided not to pursue the topic. He asked about her work instead. Leah told him she worked for a direct mail firm as the director of marketing. She tensed when he encouraged her to continue, and watched Gerald intently as she explained what the job entailed. She expected him to interrupt with more of his inappropriate sexual insinuations. The genuine interest she saw reflected in his face surprised Leah, and for the first time that afternoon, she allowed herself to relax.

Her voice washed over him like a sweet serenade and Gerald basked in the sound. All too soon, the dulcet tones stopped and he came out of his trance when he realized Leah had asked him a question. "I'm the owner," he responded to her query about his position at the print shop. "I own three others just like it," he added.

"That's nice." Leah picked up a plate and began filling it with food for Jimmy.

Gerald said very little during the remainder of the meal as he tried to discern what could have disappointed Leah so severely that unhappiness cloaked her like a blanket. A small bowl of fruit drew his eyes and as one hand picked up a knife, the other reached for a peach. Gerald carved the fruit and offered a slice to Leah. He cut another for himself and slid it onto his tongue, chewing slowly as he studied her. She took a bite of the fruit, rolling it around on her tongue to savor its sweetness before finally chewing and swallowing. Looking up, she caught Gerald's stare. "What?"

"I was just wondering what I'd have to do to trade places with that peach," he murmured.

Held hostage by his placid brown gaze, Leah's thoughts scattered. Gerald's constant surveillance and sexual innuendoes were unsettling. Hoping it would break his spell, she rose to her knees and began cleaning up the clutter from their lunch. She bumped into Gerald and mumbled an almost inaudible, "Excuse me."

His hands steadied but did not release Leah. He lowered his head, and as if willed by a mind of its own, Leah's head tilted back.

Five

At five that afternoon, Gerald stretched out on the couch in his den and cranked up the music. He was thinking about Leah and her reaction to their first kiss. She'd tasted of fresh air and peach juice and wanting more than one tantalizing sample he'd continued to taste her, reveling in the pleasurable vibes that had shaken his body. As soon as he released her, Leah had slapped him across the cheek, taken Jimmy by the hand and disappeared into the crowd. He had let her go only because he'd been stunned. Her response hadn't been what he'd expected, but it hadn't changed his feelings. If anything, it only made him more determined to find out more about the woman he'd held in his arms a few scant hours ago.

Chimes rang throughout the house and Gerald left the couch. Finding his sister on the porch, he stepped back to let her inside. "Hey, NayNay," he greeted her. "Didn't you get my message? It said I'd bring the kids home at six."

"I got it, but I've just come from Mama's. She's pretty upset that you spoiled her dinner party."

"I didn't spoil the party. I ducked out early to avoid becoming a fly in the spider's carefully woven web."

Beth trailed behind him when Gerald turned and headed back to his den. "I know how much you hate forced
introductions, Gerry," she said. "But it hasn't stopped
Mama from being mad at you."

Gerald sat on the couch. He turned down the music
and closed his eyes. Beth sent a covert glance in his
direction and braced herself for his reaction. "Monique
mentioned that the two of you are getting pretty close,"
she said, her voice full of innocence.

Gerald opened one eye. Beth Renee was thirty-seven
and stood a slender five-nine. She had just celebrated
twelve years of marriage and as the older of the two, also
tended to be excessively protective. Until recently, when
she'd joined his mother's campaign to find him a wife.
Beth maintained it was love on sight when she'd spotted
the six-foot-one, caramel complexioned William
Thompson at the mall and he'd turned his dark brown
eyes on her. Right, Gerald scoffed silently. He didn't
believe that story for a minute and he wasn't about to get
caught in the trap his sister and her best friend had
devised for him either. "Oh," he said, "and just why
would Monique tell you that?"

"Well, you have been dating her for over a month,
Gerry. And for you, that's a record," Beth replied,
relieved at his calm. "So, are you serious about her or
what?"

"Or what," Gerald responded, closing his eyes again.

Beth gave him a puzzled look. Then sat on the love
seat and crossed her arms in mild exasperation. "What
do you mean by, 'or what'?"

Gerald's voice rose a notch. "What do I look like,
NayNay? An idiot? I know what time it is and if you've
come to expound on Monique's finer qualities, forget it."

"Okay. Okay. I get the message, Gerry."

"Sure you do," Gerald replied. He picked up the
remote and turned up the music, curtailing any further

discussion, his brows drawn together in deep thought.
Beth sat back on the love seat and studied his face. The
dark smudges under his eyes were a true indication of
how exhausted Gerald really was, but Beth knew he
would never admit to being tired. He was like a demon
when it came to work and was almost fanatical about the
welfare of his family. She had hoped Monique would
help her brother appreciate another side of life, but it
looked like that wasn't going to happen.

"Where are the kids?"

"In the rec room. They want to spend the night again."

"No. I think I'll just go and get them and we'll get out
of your hair," Beth replied, refraining from voicing her
concerns. She rose and walked from the room.

Gerald followed. "They weren't any trouble, NayNay.
And you know they are welcome to stay any time."

Gerald saw Beth and the kids off and was on his way
back to his den when the front door opened and Peter
walked in.

"Man, you're never going to believe this! I just scored
an original Mahalia Jackson," he said excitedly.

"That's great, Pete. I know how much you like the
lady's music."

"Like? Like doesn't begin to describe how I feel, G.
Mahalia's in a class by herself, man. She was the great-
est gospel singer of all time and there will never be anyone like her again. I'm going to the studio. I have to hear
this right now."

"I'll meet you there in a minute," Gerald said.

Returning to the den, Gerald picked up the telephone,
but he didn't dial a number. After three hours of observing Leah, he had drawn some conclusions. Leah tried to
portray herself as a tough, unfeeling woman. He was
sure it was a front and her cold manner with him, a
defensive maneuver. With the children, she had been
tender and caring, almost to the point of being maternal.

For some reason, and only in regard to men, he guessed, Leah had built a fortress around her emotions and enclosed herself behind its walls. Kissing her had only forced Leah to entrench herself deeper. Gerald replaced the receiver and left the den. In the studio, he took his chair behind the console. "Sounds good, Pete."

"Yeah," Peter agreed with a grin. He carefully lifted the stereo needle and slid the album back into its case, then popped a tape into the machine.

Gerald leaned back in his chair and closed his eyes, his mind on Leah and what his next move should be. He again considered and rejected calling her, knowing that Leah would just use the telephone as a barrier against him. To get past her guard, he'd have to do so in person. The only way to get through the type of defenses Leah threw up was to storm them.

Peter glanced at Gerald. "What's up, G?"

"Nothing."

Peter shrugged his shoulders. When Gerald was ready to talk, he would. "These tracks Ebony Silk laid are smooth. Is J.J. going to sign them?"

"Probably. Susan will fax my notes on Monday."

"Does he have anyone in mind for EP?"

"I don't know. Why? You want a shot?"

"I'd love to produce these guys. Can't do it, though. Those boys are located in LA and I'd rather stay here with you and concentrate on SJB and the Mattise deal."

"Right," Gerald said. "The deal you'd rather concentrate on is called Ja'Nise."

Not rising to the bait, Peter sat in quiet reflection. Gerald, with his college roommate, Jeffrey Jones, had started with twenty-five grand and built one of the most successful recording labels in the country. He wouldn't mind being the executive producer for Ebony Silk, but the group would be under the TyJo umbrella, and except for giving his advice when J.J. asked, Gerald's day-to-day association with the company had ended.

Peter knew why Gerald had come home, but last year, when Gerald suggested they form a partnership to manage SJB, Peter had thought he was leaning toward going back to LA and TyJo. Gerald had changed his mind about coming to the club and after hearing Mattise now wanted to set up a meeting with their manager. However, in Peter's mind, Gerald's place was and always would be at TyJo. He picked up the *Billboard* magazine. "You have a chance to look at the charts?"

"Nope."

Peter tossed the magazine down in front of Gerald. "Well, check this out. TyJo just scored the number one R&B slot. They're number three on pop and have two more singles in the top ten. But SJB is giving J.J. a run for his money. Our single is number thirty and it's only been on the street for two weeks. The album's holding at forty-one. But if J.J. signs Ebony Silk, he's got another platinum group."

Gerald barely glanced at the charts. Energized at the thought of spending an evening with Leah and laying the groundwork for their relationship, he addressed his best friend since grade school and said, "Pete, how long have you known Leah?"

So, Gerald was finally ready to talk, Peter thought astutely. "A while now."

Gerald stood up and looked down at Peter. "Let's go shoot some hoops and while we're at it, you can tell me everything you know about Leah Ellis."

❧

Leah opened the door and Merri rushed into the apartment. "Sooo, who is he?" Merri continued to a brown vinyl couch. She picked up the Sunday newspaper and after folding it neatly, placed it next to a stack of papers on the table and sat down.

Leah closed the door and followed her into the living room. "Hi, Merri."

"Don't hi me, girlfriend. Who was the gorgeous guy at the zoo with you today?"

Leah gave her a somber look. She loved her friend, but after Gerald, Leah wasn't sure she could deal with Merri's effervescence right now. "How did you know about that?"

"Jimmy hasn't stopped talking about the man since he got home. From his description, I assumed he was gorgeous and there was the little matter of a kiss. So, what's his name?"

"Didn't you pump Jimmy for that, too?"

Merri rolled her eyes. "What's his name, Leah?"

"Gerald Morris," Leah replied, heedful of keeping her voice dispassionate.

Merri repeated the name as if testing a new flavor. "Hey, wait a minute! Isn't that the guy who came to the party with Peter Jackson?" When she saw Leah duck her head, she yelled, "It is the guy! Okay, start at the beginning and tell me everything."

"Merri, do we have to discuss this now?"

"Fine," Merri replied drolly. "Keep your little secret. I'll just wait patiently until you decide to tell me." She stood up. "Well, girlfriend, I've got to run. I know Jimmy's not cleaning that room and if I don't stay on top of him, it ain't gonna happen."

On the street, Merri watched the Jaguar come to a halt and the man inside skillfully back into a space just big enough to fit the sleek black sports car. This was interesting. Leah hadn't mentioned anything about going out with Gerald Morris again—and so soon, though it was exactly what Leah needed. Leah had wasted too many years condemning herself over Michael Ray Dupree. And a stick of dynamite couldn't get her friend to admit that she was lonely. However, Merri knew the truth, no matter how hard Leah tried to play it off, and the air of secrecy about Gerald had her inquisitive mind hopping. Maybe he was the one. She watched him pull a royal blue blazer over a black silk tee and loose fitting matching slacks. She stepped in front of him when Gerald reached the top of the steps and stuck out her hand.

"Merri Taylor."

"Gerald Morris," he replied, shaking the hand.

"Weren't you at the party the other night?"

"Yep. I didn't get a chance to meet you, but it's nice to meet you now."

Merri nodded. "Leah's upstairs. I don't believe she's expecting you though."

"She's not. I thought I'd surprise her. Think it'll work?"

"Oh, I think she'll be surprised all right. Only don't you be surprised if you come back downstairs alone."

"Why would I come back downstairs alone?"

"Because I happen to know that Leah doesn't date."

So, Leah had told the truth. Gerald filed the information away as Merri examined him quizzically. "Well, I think I can convince her to go out with me."

Merri laughed. "Not lacking in the confidence department, are we, Mr. Morris? But I have a feeling that you're an okay brother, so I'm going to give you a bit of advice. When Leah tells you to step off, and you can take my word for it she will, don't."

Gerald stifled a chuckle. Merri, he could like. "Don't you worry, Merri Taylor. I won't."

Merri started down the steps. "That's a nice car, by the way."

"Thanks."

"If you're planning to get serious about Leah, though, I suggest you lose the 'Swinger' plates. My girl won't give you the time of day if she thinks you're a player."

Gerald laughed outright. "Point taken. They'll be

gone tomorrow because I plan to get real serious about Leah."

"Well, good luck, Gerald Morris. You're going to need it."

Gerald watched Merri cross the road, then turned and entered the building. Merri Taylor was almost as beautiful as Leah. Almost, but not quite.

Deeply immersed in the process of dismissing all thoughts of Gerald from her mind, Leah rose from her chair and opened the door without inquiry when she heard the knock. Confounded when Gerald swept into her apartment, she stepped back and not knowing what else to do, closed the door.

Shoot! That was a really stupid move. Now she was alone in her apartment with him and she'd done it to her own self. Gerald had seemed like a nice man today, but what if he really wasn't? She glanced over her shoulder at him, then turned back and tried to remember even one of the self-defense maneuvers she'd learned two years ago.

She was thinking about opening the door again when she heard Gerald say, "It was okay to close the door, Leah. I really am a nice man."

Oh, good grief! Now the man could read her thoughts. When she turned around, Gerald held out a yellow rose. Leah shoved her hands behind her back. Feeling the doorknob raised her comfort zone. If Gerald Morris tried anything, she could open the door and run down the hall screaming at the top of her lungs. She stared at the flower. "Why are you here?"

Gerald didn't respond and he wasn't going to until Leah looked him in the eye. When she did, he took an electric jolt in his stomach and raised his hand to his heart as if he could somehow stop its rapid beat. "I enjoyed your company this afternoon, Leah, and decided we should share our evening meal together."

"No, thank you."

"Why not? We both have to eat, so why not do it with some pleasant company?"

"No."

"Leah, I'm hungry, and I know you are, too." The hunger he felt certainly wasn't for any food, however. "You didn't eat much at lunch today and I know you're not the type of woman who would throw a starving man out into the street."

Leah observed the smile most women probably found irresistible. Egotistical was the first word that popped into her mind, followed closely by arrogant and pompous. Gerald was a man used to getting what he wanted, when he wanted it. She watched him cross the room and sit on the couch.

"I'll wait here while you change. Oh, and don't dress up too much. I'm not planning to take you anywhere fancy."

A slow burn started in her chest. Telling a man like Gerald no had been tantamount to throwing down the gauntlet. Gerald had picked it up and meant to play by his rules. Well, he would be playing alone because Leah had taken herself out of the game. "Gerald, I'm not going anywhere with you."

"It's G. And why not?"

"Because I—" With him staring at her like she was a sheep being led to the slaughter, Leah couldn't think fast enough to come up with an excuse. "Just because," she said, stamping her foot for emphasis.

The gesture accomplished nothing more than to amuse Gerald. When he advanced, she backed up. He did not stop until she was up against the door. His fingers ran over her brow and down her face to cup her chin. "'Because' is not a satisfactory answer and unless you can come up with another in ten seconds, I'll wait while you get dressed," he said, letting his lips touch hers.

The peck he'd intended somehow turned into a mind-blowing caress and Gerald placed his hands on the wall behind Leah. His mouth cruised over hers for a minute, then hardened in a silent demand that she give in. Her arms came up to drape his shoulders. This isn't happening, Leah told herself, even as her lids sailed closed and she acquiesced to his request.

"So sweet," Gerald murmured, when she tentatively met the touch of his tongue. His circled hers, then moved on to continue his exploration. Gerald groaned deeply and lifting her, matched Leah's body to his. He wanted her to feel the full effect she had on him. Shivering with delight, Leah's hold around his neck tightened and she participated fully in the kiss until sanity returned. When she pushed away, Gerald set her down. Acutely aware of the position she had just placed herself in, Leah was mortified by her behavior.

Gerald raised her chin. "Your ten seconds are up," he said, his voice sounding hoarse. "Go and put on something pretty. I'll be on the couch."

Leah watched him walk away. He sat on the couch again and raised his brow. His eyes held a sheen of desire. Hers, annoyance and embarrassment over her inability to control herself around him. Gerald broke the tense silence. "Hurry up now, sweetheart. I really am starving."

Ten seconds or get dressed. Hurry up. Don't dress too fancy. Who did Gerald Morris think he was? God? Leah spun on her heel and marched to her bedroom. Her leaving, however, had nothing to do with concession. She was going to call the police. The man in her living room was a narcissistic nut and the cops would waste no time in removing him from her home. She gasped when he removed the receiver from her hand and hung it up.

"Leah, I am not a nut, and it won't do you any good to call the police. Once you tell them who is in your apartment, they won't come and if I were going to harm you, it would be done before they could get here. Why don't you get dressed, sweetheart?" Although Gerald's tone was humorous, his eyes held a plea. "We have a seven-thirty reservation."

Leah sank to the bed and covered her face with her hands. "I knew I shouldn't have gone with you today. I don't even know you. Why are you doing this to me?"

Gerald sat beside her. How could he explain what he was doing in her apartment, correction bedroom? For the first time in his life, Gerald was considering marriage. But how could he tell that to Leah when he didn't even know her? "Leah, I don't know if I can explain this to you so you'll understand. But I know you feel what's happening between us. We have a special connection and I think it would be to both our advantages if we tried to find out why."

Leah examined his eyes. She could see that Gerald really believed what he was saying. Looking deeper, Leah saw something else, something that had her scooting away from him. Gerald moved closer, as close as he could get without touching her.

Her lids came down, breaking the link. "No."

Gerald gathered her in his arms. "Leah, please. The only thing I'm asking of you is that you have dinner with me. That's all. Saying no only takes away any chance of our finding out what's going on between us. Can't we just go to dinner?"

Leah hadn't realized she'd said the word out loud. She knew Gerald was right. She had felt something, but she wouldn't tell him. He wasn't supposed to be here. Not in her home. Not after she had already told him no.

"Gerald—"

"I've asked you several times to call me, G. Indulge me."

"Okay. I will call you G, but I won't go to dinner with you."

Gerald lowered his head and kissed Leah with such power it left her head spinning. Then he rose from the bed and went into her closet. When he came out, he laid the pink sateen skirt and matching jacket on the bed. "I would like to see you in this, sweetheart. I'll wait in the living room while you get dressed."

Six

G erald pushed in Leah's chair and moved around the table to take his own. "If this is your first time at Tyler's Place you're in for a real treat."

"It is," Leah said quietly.

She was still trying to get over the deference accorded them upon entering the restaurant. They had the best table in the house and one would have thought Gerald a prince, the way the staff had all but rolled out the red carpet. The decor was ultra-modern, the atmosphere light and friendly and the jazz music playing in the background provided an extra bonus.

"Well, I'm a meat and potatoes man and the house specialties here are the prime rib and roast duck. But don't let me influence your decision on what to eat."

"I wouldn't think of letting you influence me in any way, Mr. Morris." What a crock, Leah thought before she remembered Gerald could read her mind. Girl, get control of your mind and shut it down. But her mind wandered on. He had coerced her into going to dinner with him. How had that happened? Why had she allowed it?

"You're crazy, " her mind answered.

Leah's face formed a slight grimace. Maybe she was crazy, but she wasn't a coward. She'd carefully considered her options and had concluded that Gerald wasn't leaving and she had no chance of forcibly removing him herself. She was also hungry, and having dinner with

him seemed a far better choice than being cooped up
with him in her tiny apartment.

Leah concealed the animosity she felt over his brazen
tactics. The man had come into her home, rifled through
her personal things and kidnapped her. Well, maybe
kidnap was a little strong, but was he this high-handed
with everybody? Or was it only women that sent him into
the Tarzanian district? As it stood, Gerald had won the
first two matches. That was because her defense was
weak. She needed to shore it up or come up with a good
offense that would get rid of Gerald Morris once and for
all.

Mentally working on a plan, Leah openly studied him.
The sexuality oozing from Gerald had the tip of her
tongue darting out in response to the hypnotic light
brown eyes. Licking her lips didn't pacify the lingering
effect of his kiss or the feeling that he'd somehow branded her. Gerald acted as if he owned her and she had the
feeling that what Gerald Morris decided he owned, he
kept. That thought had Leah wondering just how many
other women Gerald had branded. She lowered her
head when the notion that she was jealous sent a wave
of heat to her cheeks.

Gerald dispensed the waiter with their drink order and
suppressed the chuckle in his throat. He was skilled at a
lot of things, but reading minds didn't happen to top the
list. Leah was apparently unaware that her face mirrored
her thoughts. At that very moment, he could see the
wheels spinning; he just wasn't sure what she was planning. That she hadn't worn the outfit he'd chosen didn't
bother Gerald, but the royal purple halter dress was
wreaking havoc with his libido. Her response when he
had kissed her earlier and what he was seeing in those
timber wolf eyes confirmed that Leah had feelings for
him. He just had to make her realize it. "I apologize for
not consulting you on the drinks, Leah. But I don't con-

sume alcohol." Her look had him adding, "I'll be happy to call back the waiter if you'd like something else."

"What is G-Juice?"

"It's a little something I concocted a few years ago. Mostly, it's a combination of fruit juices and carbonated water."

"Then the juice will be fine."

"Good." Gerald leaned back in his chair. "So, baby girl. Tell me about yourself."

Baby girl? Shaking her head, Leah decided not to focus on that. To plan her attack, she needed information and this was just the opportunity she was looking for. "Didn't we do this bit this afternoon? However, since you seem to have a memory problem, I'll run through it again. I'm twenty-eight, single, childless and I don't smoke. I grew up here in Chicago. I have a widowed mother, Mabel, and a sister, Sheila, who is younger by two years. For the last three years, I've been a director in the marketing department of a direct mail firm. I'm a Democrat and my interest lies in issues affecting progress for our people. Right now, a lot of my time is spent as a volunteer for Project Spruce. My middle name is Nicole. I live alone. I don't have any pets. I love all kinds of music, except rap, because it gives me a headache, but my favorite is jazz. My favorite color is lavender. My favorite movie is *The Color Purple*. My favorite movie star is Billy Dee Williams, and my passion is for chocolate. That's about it in a nutshell. Now," she said, leaning back and crossing her legs, "tell me about you."

"Cute, Leah. Very cute. But since you've started this and the ball's in my court, I'm thirty-four, single and childless. I don't smoke and as I mentioned earlier I don't drink. I also grew up in Chicago, but I did pull a stint at LSU and spent a few years in LA. My mother, Linda, lives here. My father and an older brother passed before I was born and I have a sister who is older by almost three years, so I guess that makes me the baby. NayNay, a nickname she hates but lets me get away with, is married to William Thompson and they have two children. If you'll remember, you met Audrey and Reggie this afternoon."

"Cute, G. Very cute," Leah said, chuckling.

Gerald held up his hand. "Hold on. I'm not finished. Right now I'm the owner of four print shops, but I have other business endeavors. I'm a Republican and my interests lie in issues affecting our children, which I already know, is a direct conflict with my political affiliation. Their education is high on my list of priorities. My middle name is Tyler. I live alone. I don't have any pets. I love all music, including rap, but my favorite is also jazz. My favorite color is red. As far as movies, I have three: *Glory*, *Posse*, and *The Sound of Music*. My favorite actor is Wesley Snipes. But if we're talking turn-ons, then I'd go for Holly Robinson and my passion is basketball." Gerald frowned. "You'll have to help me out here because I can't remember. Did you mention any friends?"

Leah shook her head and let her laughter ring out.

"Why are you laughing? I'm trying to hold a serious conversation here."

"I know," Leah replied, bringing her giggles under control. "No. I didn't mention friends."

"Okay." Gerald settled back in his seat. "Now that we've dispensed with the general info, let's get down to the real deal. Leah, will you marry me?"

The humor left her face immediately. Leah didn't get a chance to respond as the waiter arrived at their table at that exact moment. She considered her menu while thinking about her response to his question. When she'd placed her order, she looked at Gerald. "What kind of man would ask a woman he doesn't even know to marry him?"

Not smart, Morris. He would drive Leah away if he didn't find a way to regulate his thoughts when he was around her. And if the look in her eyes were any indication, she was about to bolt. "Leah, I didn't mean to say that. If I promise to act like a gentleman for the rest of the evening, will you promise to at least consider giving the two of us a chance to get to know each other?" Gerald exhaled at her very hesitant nod. "Thank you. Okay, let's start over. How involved are you with this Project Spruce?"

That had not gone quite the way she envisioned and glad Gerald had moved on to a safer topic, Leah sat up. "I'm a founding member and this year I'm in charge of projects and special events."

"What does Project Spruce do?"

"Our main mission is neighborhood clean up and mostly we work the South Side. We paint houses, clean up the parks and the graffiti. We hope the clean up will incite undesirable people to move out of the area and attract others who will take pride in their neighborhood. In fact, a Project Spruce house just sold last week for twice its listing price."

Gerald had spent his early years living in a ghetto, and Leah's comment put him on the defensive. "Perhaps you can explain to me how spreading a few coats of paint will make people care about where they live or make 'undesirable people' move out."

"We do more than spread a few coats of paint, Gerald. The house is actually refurbished before it is painted. We also establish neighborhood watches, and have been known to provide assistance for people needing help cutting through government red tape or finding employment. We also put drug dealers and gang members on notice that we know who they are and PS has been responsible for the closing down of several crack houses. Once the people feel safe and take responsibility for their own lives, it is surprising just how fast the dealers and gangs clear out. They are the undesirable people I referred to, not the people who live in the neighborhood. We want them to stay."

Duly chastened, Gerald drank from his glass before asking, "Who funds your organization?"

"Businesses mostly. Maxwell Corp. is our largest sponsor. They import and export household goods. For PS, they supply people, paint, and very little money. But lately, their support has been tapering off." Leah sighed. "For a while, we thought Project Spruce might have to close its doors, but now plans are underway to hold a fundraiser in August. Why don't you come to one of our meetings and see for yourself what PS is all about?"

"I might just do that," Gerald replied, sitting back so that the waiter could place his plate of food on the table.

The conversation turned to lighter topics and after taking Leah home, Gerald drove through the streets in a thoughtful mood. It had been a wonderful evening and he'd never laughed so much in his life. Leah was not only beautiful, she was a smart, self-reliant woman with strong convictions. Somehow Gerald was going to find a way into her heart. But he'd pushed Leah enough for one day. If he didn't exercise some patience, he'd lose her before he had a chance to have her. Patience, though, was one of those virtues Gerald had yet to master. Nevertheless, if that's what it took, Gerald resolved to be the most patient man on earth, up to a point. Turning on the CD player, he focused his mind on thinking up phase two of his campaign to win Leah's affections.

∽

Moonlight spilled through the glass pane and cast its glow off the woman standing in the window. Chilled,

though it was hot enough to melt butter, Leah lifted
sweat-soaked hair off her neck and stood looking down
on a street now devoid of human activity. The light of the
street lamps left obscure silhouettes in the spaces
between the houses and cars parked along the curb.
The night held an unnatural, almost creepy kind of quiet,
which combined with the hollowed silence of her apartment to leave Leah feeling very uneasy.

She turned away from the window and made her way
to the couch. There was no storm, so why couldn't she
sleep? Actually, Leah knew why. She had what she now
termed as Gerald-itis. It was one o'clock in the morning
and officially one of the strangest days of her life was
over. She was tired, but restless, and unable to sleep;
she had left the bed and fixed a cup of hot milk, hoping it
would make her drowsy.

Sitting, Leah pulled her legs under her and used her
arms as a pillow for her head. Gerald had kept his word
and despite his bad start with her, she felt she could now
draw a more accurate assessment of him. He was intelligent, handsome, successful, well-mannered and had a
sense of humor that bordered on harassment. He was
also presumptuous, cocksure and possessed a gener-
ous dose of sensual appeal.

Gerald had said he was a record producer or at least
he used to be, but that was only one of the many businesses he'd explored. He owned extensive real estate
holdings, had dabbled in television and the movies,
owned several racing thoroughbreds, two radio stations,
a working ranch in Wyoming, Tyler's Place, and Leah
couldn't remember what all else. That he had accomplished so much suggested Gerald might be a workaholic, which, being one herself, Leah didn't consider a
fault. That he'd shown signs throughout the day of being
sexist, she did fault. Truthfully, she did feel a connection
between them, and sitting alone in her apartment she

could admit that now. Why, Leah did not care to explore.

She sat up when the next wave of thoughts hit her and fought to hold them back. She didn't want to think about Michael Ray or the foolish young girl she'd been just a few years ago. Leah still questioned her value system when she thought about how easily Michael Ray had seduced her with the money, the condo, the jewelry and the cars. He'd given her all the material things a girl could wish for, but none of the feelings that made up a true relationship. Michael Ray's so-called charmed life had been her downfall and his so-called love, her teacher.

Leah picked up and grasped the mug in both hands. Michael Ray was her past and it had taken too long to get her life back in order. She was no longer the naive girl she had once been. She was older, wiser and not as trusting. The last thing she needed or wanted was another man messing with her head. She had her job and Project Spruce. Both kept her busy and any remaining time was for family and friends. Leah finished the milk and headed for her bedroom. "Gerald Morris can be an acquaintance and no more," she muttered. And she would terminate any feelings she thought she had for the man, starting right now. With her decision made, Leah climbed on top of her bed and closed her eyes, determined to get some sleep before her alarm shrilled in announcement of a new day.

Seven

For the first time ever she was late. Leah hurriedly pushed through the crowd of people standing in the lobby. "Please, hold the elevator," she called out, arriving just in time to have the doors swish closed in her face. Leah stabbed her finger at the button and slumped against the wall. Not only was she late, she was also tired and grumpy. A hodgepodge of dreams about Gerald and Project Spruce had filled what little sleep she had managed to get last night.

When the doors opened again, Leah stepped on the elevator and stood with the same feeling of foreboding she'd had the previous night. She couldn't shake the feeling that her life was about to change, and not necessarily for the better. She stopped for her messages and glanced at the large white vase of long-stemmed, yellow roses sitting on her assistant's desk before turning in the direction of her office.

"Leah." Diane Rogers, her red-haired, blue-eyed assistant pointed at the vase. "These are for you."

Leah stared at Diane as if she were speaking a foreign language. "Those are for me?"

"As far as I know, you're the only Leah Ellis we have working at this company. So they must be and you must have had some great weekend," Diane intimated. "Or at least the man you were with did. There are twenty-four roses in that vase. I counted them."

Juggling her briefcase and purse, Leah wrapped her arm around the vase. In her office, she saw a request tacked to the front of her chair. Joe Carpenter and his daily requests, she was sick of. A rural market history on sales, revenue and buyer demographics would take some time to complete and, of course, he wanted it yesterday. The man had brown-nosed his way to his current position as a director in the sales and marketing department and had several major accounts, including Maxwell Corp., in his territory. Everyone knew his goal was to be an officer of the company, but when the vice president of marketing retired, Tony had gotten the nod.

Joe knew he couldn't touch Tony. So instead, he had identified every African American employee at the company, then planned contrived situations to make them look incompetent. In a company of 250 employees, there were only ten of them and two had already quit. Since she was a director and the second highest in rank, Leah was at the top of his hit list. If she didn't like her job so much, and if she didn't know his reign of abuse was about over, she'd tell Joe to shove it. Still, Leah smiled as she set the vase down on the desk and plucked the card from its holder:

Leah,

Just wanted you to know that I had a great time yesterday and at dinner. Please enjoy the roses.

G.

Leah's smile turned into a grin. She shook her head in awe, then buried her face in the large yellow blossoms, sniffing their aromatic fragrance. It was then that she noticed the long, curling white ribbon. She pulled and the ribbon came out with a little gold key attached. Other than a 1J stamped on the front and 18k on the back, there was no other clue as to the reason for the dangling object. Why the sudden mystery? Leah wondered. She had already pegged Gerald as the straightforward type and was planning a counter defense that was just as bold. Now he was switching gears. Now they were playing a different game.

Sending the key this way meant he wanted her to ask him about it. Well, maybe she would and maybe she wouldn't, but she should thank him for the flowers and calling Gerald would take only a minute. Before she could change her mind, Leah reached for the telephone directory. By the time she had decided which print store to call, dialed the number and waited for the telephone to ring, she'd almost decided that calling Gerald was not a very good idea.

"JetGraphics. How may I help you?"

Leah took a deep breath. "I'd like to speak to Gerald Morris, please."

"He's just heading out the door. Hold on a minute and I'll see if I can catch him for you."

Leah fiddled with the telephone cord and rehearsed the words she would say when Gerald came on the line. Mostly, she tried to slow her pounding heart.

"Gerald Morris."

Leah exhaled the air she'd been holding in. "Hi, Gerald. It's Leah Ellis."

Surprise lit his face when he heard her voice. He had expected the call, just not so soon. "Leah! How are you today?"

"I'm fine, Gerald. I called because I wanted to thank you for the flowers. They're lovely."

"You received them already. Good."

"And the key is nice, too. Is there some significance I should attach to it?"

"Only that it's very special and should be kept in a place of importance."

"And that's all you're going to tell me?"

"Yep."

Well, she had thanked him and he wasn't going to tell her about the key. Now what? "I've taken up enough of your time, so I'll let you get back to work," Leah said after a few moments. "Good-bye."

Good-bye? "Leah, wait a minute. How would you feel about having dinner with me tonight?"

After spending almost an entire day in her company, Gerald had spent the entire night planning phase two of his campaign. Despite having to contend with his obvious sexual attraction to her, Gerald was sure Leah had enjoyed herself at dinner and that she wouldn't say no again. He was so sure of her answer that incredulity sculpted his face a moment later when Leah knocked the wind from his sails.

"Tonight is not good for me. I have a PS meeting this evening."

"How about dinner after your meeting?" he suggested, recovering swiftly.

"I can't. After the meeting, I have errands to run and phone calls to make."

Gerald took a deep and calming breath. "Leah, I hope you are not holding my behavior yesterday against me. I've apologized and I will again if it will help."

"Yesterday has nothing to do with it. I truly am busy and I really have to go."

"What about tomorrow night? Can we get together tomorrow?"

"Gerald, I told you that I don't date and the reason is that I don't have a lot of spare time."

Gerald's tone resonated with the hurt he suddenly felt. "When can you fit me into your schedule, Leah?"

"I don't know." Leah flipped open her organizer. "Remember when I told you about PS. Well, coordinating the fundraiser is my responsibility. We've also scheduled a house for repair on the twenty-sixth. Both projects take time to plan and tomorrow we are meeting with two potential sponsors. Thursday, is another PS meeting. Friday, I'm having dinner at my mother's and Saturday I spend all day at the Project Spruce office and I have a meeting with the caterer for the fundraiser in the evening. To top it off, I've just been hit with a monster project at work and I'll have to use any remaining evenings to catch up on my normal workload."

The roster of activities floored Gerald, and busy wasn't the word that came to his mind. Leah's schedule read like that of a drill sergeant with one week to train a platoon of greenhorn cadets. "You're kidding."

"No, Gerald. I'm not, and I have to go. Thanks again for the flowers and the key."

"Leah! Please. I need to see—" Realizing he was on the verge of begging, Gerald gritted his teeth. "I'm glad you like the flowers." He hung up and for a few moments tried to decide whether Leah was really that busy or if she was trying to tell him to take a hike. Glancing at his watch, he knew he needed to go. In the parking lot outside the print shop, he climbed inside his Porsche. Leah had told him she led a busy life so it shouldn't disappoint him that she couldn't change her plans for him. Gerald knew this, but it didn't help him accept it any better. It wasn't until he turned into the garage at The Path building that Gerald realized that other than working, Leah hadn't mentioned anything specific for Wednesday evening. And that, work or not, was the evening he decided would be his.

∽

Leah rose from her chair and went the window in her office. Situated fifteen stories up in a thirty-six-story, shimmering, green glass structure, she looked down at the Chicago River and tried to get her mind back on business. Gerald had sounded like a little boy who'd lost his puppy, and now she felt bad for turning him down. No, Leah admonished herself. There was no reason for her to feel bad. She had warned Gerald and she didn't want to be in the dating game anyway. Men were a problem she could live without.

"Hiya, Leah," Tony called, stepping into her office. "I heard this great joke." His voice trailed away and he frowned at the flowers on her desk. "Boyfriend?" he asked.

"No. Just a friend," Leah replied as she returned to her desk.

"Must be some friend," Tony remarked, closely examining her face. "Those are some expensive buds."

"Yeah. But aren't they beautiful?"

"If you say so, Leah," he sighed wearily. "Is the report ready?"

"Almost. The write-up's done, but I'm still working on a couple of the graphs. I'll need about twenty more minutes."

"Twenty minutes! The staff has already gathered downstairs. What are we supposed to do for twenty minutes while you're up here doing...?" Tony just stopped himself from waving his hand at the vase. "God knows what," he sputtered.

Evidently she had missed something. Otherwise, Tony would not be ranting at her over something so trivial. "First of all, Tony, I got a late start this morning or the report would be finished. Second, weren't you the one who insisted I party the other night instead of working on this report? Third, I believe I said I would have the report to you on Monday and by my calendar it is still Monday. If you wanted a tighter deadline, then you should have said something."

Tony took a fighter's stance and interrupted her. "If

your love life is going to interfere with work, Ms. Ellis, perhaps you should send a memo to the staff the next time."

Leah leaped to her feet. "This is a business discussion, Mr. Wright. Just how did my love life enter into it?"

"If you had been working instead of staring at a bunch of flowers, the report would have been ready on time."

Leah could not imagine what had set Tony off, but she was already weary of the battle. "Tony, I cannot believe that the world of marketing is going to fall apart if you do not have my report right this second. Start with something else on your agenda. When the report is ready, I'll bring it downstairs."

Leah sat and turned to her computer. Tony stood for a minute, then spun on his heel and left her office. An angry stride took him down the hallway. Already, he regretted yelling at Leah in the office. He should apologize to her. When he'd calmed down, maybe he would.

Gerald ran up the ten marble steps and pushed through the revolving doors of the building housing The Path. Talking to Leah had him running about fifteen minutes behind a schedule he usually followed rigidly. Susan probably had the woman he was to interview sitting in his office.

"Hey! Slow down there, big guy," the man in the janitor's uniform called out. "That floor just got waxed."

Gerald looked down at the red and white checkerboard floor, realizing that the man had probably just saved him from breaking his fool neck. "Thanks."

"You Gerald Morris, ain't cha?"

"Yep."

"Heard a lot about you, Gerald Morris. Seems you're a pretty important man in this city."

"You're new here, aren't you?"

"Yep. Just started today. Name's Malcolm."

The man stepped back into the shadows when Gerald

peered at him. "It's nice to meet you, Malcolm. One day we'll have to sit down and chat, but right now I'm running a little late."

"Didn't mean to hold you up, son. Know an important man like you must be pretty busy."

"I'll see you around, Malcolm." Gerald lifted his hand in a wave and headed for the elevators. That man had the same name as his father, he thought, punching the button. When he looked across the lobby again, the janitor had disappeared. Gerald stepped into the elevator and forgot about Malcolm as he focused on his meeting.

The throb at the base of her skull started again and Mabel rubbed at it as she turned away from the window. The exchange between daughters still bothered her and she knew she'd have to speak to Sheila about it. Hamilton had always been the disciplinarian; she, the soother of hurt feelings. And Sheila's feelings were easily hurt; she'd have to choose her words carefully.

Mabel pulled on her robe and headed down the hallway. She stopped and knocked on Sheila's door. "Time to rise and shine, baby."

"Okay, Ma," she heard her daughter say.

Mabel stopped to get the paper, then continued to the kitchen where she poured a cup of coffee and sat at the table. She opened the newspaper and became immersed in reading an article on homeless shelters, and mentally disagreeing with the position Linda Morris, as President of the Colored Women's Auxiliary, had taken in regard to the group becoming more involved in helping to solve the problem. She'd just finished the article and decided that she would confront Linda at the meeting later that morning, when Sheila entered the kitchen.

"Mornin', Ma.

Mabel looked up from the paper. She'd been awake when Sheila returned from her date, and the late hours were starting to show on her daughter. "Are you going to work this morning?"

Sheila fluffed her hair, a nervous habit, and crossed to the refrigerator. "I haven't decided yet."

Mabel folded the paper and laid it aside. "You've missed a lot of days this month."

So what, Sheila thought, glancing at her mother. "It's all right, Ma," she said. "The boss is okay with it."

"The boss might be okay with it, but I don't think it's fair to the other employees. Anyway, didn't you say that you were looking for another job? I'm sure your new employer will expect you to show up for work and on time, so you might as well get in the habit starting now."

Sheila grimaced at the reprimand. "Don't worry, Ma. I've got everything under control."

"I'd also appreciate it if you would stop the arguments with Leah."

Here we go, Sheila thought, scowling as she poured herself a glass of orange juice. Leah, always Leah. She sat at the table across from her mother. "Maybe you should talk to Leah about stopping the arguments with me."

Mabel took a deep breath. "Sheila, what transpired last night was started by you, and I don't think your father, rest his soul, would be happy seeing his daughters constantly at each other throats."

A chill rolled down Sheila's back and she jumped up from her chair. "My father didn't care about me when he was alive. So it hardly matters what I do now that he's dead!" She ran from the room, and Mabel shook her head wearily. Well, she'd tried.

Inside her room, Sheila threw herself across the bed. She rubbed at her eyes and willed her mind blank, but couldn't stop the memory of the night her father had found out about her and Michael Ray Dupree, and it had all started with Leah and that damn organization of hers...

❧

"Who made you the savior of all people, Leah? What do you get out of it anyway?"

Hamilton peeked around his evening paper. "Project Spruce is a worthwhile organization, Sheila. Today, a woman came into my office praising the group for helping to get her child support checks started. You'd do well to join that group. They have a big future ahead of them."

"Sheila, why don't you attend a meeting with me? We're always looking for volunteers and if you like what you hear, maybe you'll consider joining."

Sheila narrowed her eyes at her sister. If she never, for the remainder of her life, heard another word about Leah and her accomplishments, it would still be too much. "Maybe if you had stayed home occasionally, Michael Ray wouldn't have had to go elsewhere for some company." Sheila leaned back on the couch, her face full of insolence as she waited for her sister's reaction.

Shaking with rage, Leah stood up. It was all she could do not to slap her sister. "How dare you, Sheila? How dare you sit there and throw your affair with Michael Ray in my face?"

The paper rattled to the floor when Hamilton leaped from his chair. "What! Is what I'm hearing true, Sheila? You had an affair with Michael Ray Dupree!" Hamilton shot across the room. His powerful grip had Sheila shaking like a rag doll.

"It...it wasn't an af—affair. It was only one time. And anyway if Leah—"

"SILENCE! Don't you dare try to blame this on Leah! Your name should not even be spoken in the same sentence as your sister's. How can you stand to look at yourself in the mirror, Sheila? How? I cannot believe that a daughter of mine would do something so despicable. To have an affair with your own sister's fiancé! Why, I just can't believe it!"

"Daddy, it was a mistake."

"I SAID SILENCE! Don't you dare 'Daddy' me, and don't you dare stand here and tell me you made another mistake. A mistake is adding a column of numbers wrong. A mistake is putting a red sock in with the whites. This was not a mistake. You knew exactly what you were doing when you climbed your hot-to-trot ass into Dupree's bed."

"Hamilton, please."

"No, Mabel. It's about time someone told this daughter of yours exactly what she is." He turned back to Sheila. "You are a whore, Sheila. A tramp and a slut. You have the morals of an alley cat and sleep with every Tom, Dick and Harry that crosses your path. We have tried to raise you to know right from wrong. We have tried to instill in you a sense of ethics, but you take every opportunity to throw it right back in our faces. Get out of here! Get out of this room! I can't even stand to look at you anymore..."

Sheila sat up, dried her eyes and went into the bathroom. It didn't matter what her mother said; she knew exactly how her father had felt about her. And she had stopped caring what Hamilton Ellis thought a long time ago. But somehow, some way, she would show them all that she was as good as her father's precious Leah.

∾

Linda Morris patted the powder puff against her face, then stood back to view her handiwork. Satisfied, she moved into the bedroom and slipped into the scallop-trimmed jacket matching the rose-colored skirt she already wore. She picked up a tube of lipstick and moved to the mirror to survey herself.

To some in the Colored Women's Auxiliary, the image she projected was more important than any skills she brought to the table. After twenty years in the real estate game that was something Linda already knew how to deal with. It was often her image and projected confidence that helped a buyer make that all-important decision to purchase a home.

Turning to the side, Linda ran a critical eye over her figure. For fifty-seven, she wasn't a bad looking woman and men asked her out all the time. Since Malcolm though, she had no interest in anything remotely resembling a relationship.

In the middle of outlining her mouth with the lipstick, Linda stopped and stared into brown eyes that were suddenly bleak and hollow. Sometimes when she looked in the mirror, she saw the broken woman she had become when her husband walked out the door and she'd realized that he wasn't ever coming back. Sometimes, she still felt shame over the years she had spent living on welfare.

Linda's shoulders reared back and she shook off her despondency. It had taken eleven years to complete her education and move herself and her children out of that ghetto. While she might have been a welfare mother once, today she was the owner of Morris Estates, a multi-million-dollar real estate firm. Today, she was a respected member of the community, and today she had to preside over a meeting as the president of the Colored Women's Auxiliary.

Taking up her keys from the dresser, Linda headed down the stairs and for the front door. Seconds later, she was leaning against the doorjamb, her heart hammering against her rib cage

"Malcolm!"

Eight

Gerald stopped in the doorway of his personal assistant's office. "Hey, Suse."

Susan Hill looked up from her computer and quickly masked the look of love shining in her eyes. "Hey yourself, G."

Susan's office and desk were always neat, and the many plants and other touches of home gave the space a coziness that made anyone entering feel immediately at ease. Gerald settled his frame in a brown leather chair and set a box on the desk. "Fax this to J.J. And you can send the box back, too."

Susan scanned the notes on the stat sheet. "Liked them did you? I knew you would."

Susan might have sounded like she was joking, but Gerald knew there was more behind her statement. Susan had been with him for the last nine years. He had hired the dowdy looking woman in large horn-rimmed glasses on a gut feeling. From day one, she had been attuned to his likes and dislikes, and when he'd left LA, Susan hadn't hesitated to pack her belongings and relocate with him to Chicago. He knew she missed the glamour and glitz of the business. He also knew she was in cahoots with J.J., who'd made it no secret that he wanted Gerald back at TyJo.

Gerald looked at Susan now. When had she replaced

her bun with that profusion of long, thin braids? Her glasses with contacts? And the grandmotherly clothes with a style that could only be classified as haute couture? Gerald shrugged. Whatever had happened, he knew that he depended on this intelligent, organized, and highly efficient woman to run his life. She kept his schedule, ran his office at The Path, managed his print shops and anything else he had his hands into, including his dealings with SJB.

"If you knew that, then why were my ears assaulted by the sound of pounding drums and crashing cymbals?"

Susan grinned at her boss. Not many men could pull off wearing a suit the color of dandelions. "J.J. wanted to make sure he still had your attention," she replied. "By the way, the woman interviewing for the tutor position is sitting in your office and you're late. See you later, boss man."

Gerald rose from the chair. "When you talk to J.J., remind him that I run print shops now. Later, Suse." At the door, he turned back. "You like her, Susan?"

"Yeah. She seems nice and her credentials are in order."

Gerald flashed a grin. "That's good enough for me."

Susan watched him cross the hall to his office and sighed in dismay. She had moved across the country and gone through a complete transformation, hoping that Gerald Morris would notice her. However, his taste ran to the lofty, long legged, full-bosomed women that graced his arm from time to time. She was five-six, had a flat chest and didn't stand a snowflake's chance in the sun with Gerald Morris. Susan sighed again and picked up the phone. She had to call J.J. and let him know that his latest ploy to lure Gerald back to TyJo with Ebony Silk hadn't worked.

∽

"I apologize for my tardiness," Gerald said, stepping into his office. The woman rose from her chair and met him with her hand extended. Gerald took the hand and just kept himself from grimacing when he saw the brown-haired, reed-thin woman, whose round black eyes fairly shined at him. Susan would have to like her.

"Hello again, Ms. James. I wasn't aware that you were a teacher."

"Yes, Mr. Morris. I've taught in the Chicago Public School system for five years."

Gerald moved around the large antique desk and fell into his chair. "Have a seat, Ms. James." Studying her, his manner held a hint of intimidation. "Why are you interested in a tutoring position at The Path?"

Rachel jumped when the deep voice finally broke the silence. "I-I love teaching and I love kids. I mean, I like helping to further the education of our youth. If they are going to become productive members of society, then someone needs to educate them. I've read about The Path and its mission. I think it provides a necessary service to our community."

"Then you are also aware that we have forty students, ten of whom are taking college preparatory courses, who come here every afternoon for help with their studies and that this position is for an English tutor."

"Yes, Mr. Morris." Rachel handed over her résumé. She aligned her rust-colored jacket with her skirt and smiled modestly. She had to make a good impression. She really needed this job. "As you can see, I was an English major and I've recently completed the required refresher courses. Here in Chicago, I've taught at both the junior and high school grade levels."

Gerald's eyes skimmed the page. He knew it was an

exercise in futility. Susan had already checked Rachel out and it would be unfair to deprive the kids of a perfectly qualified teacher based solely on personal reasons. He leaned back and made a temple of his fingers.

"The ages of the forty students I mentioned earlier span from ten to seventeen and their GPA's range from a low of 2.4 to a high of 4.1. The children are all from single parent homes and all, except one, attend high school. That one, Carlos Ramirez, is our ten-year-old. "It is our intention to see that these students graduate from high school and that they pursue a college education, for which The Path will pick up the tab."

What Gerald didn't mention and what only a few select board members knew was that he was the creator and total financial resource behind The Path.

"These children will finish school because that is our top priority. In addition, two hundred or so other children descend on our doorstep every Saturday. We induce them here, with parental permission, with our speakers. The roster includes entertainment and sports personalities, prominent professionals and community leaders. They lead the children in discussions on self-worth, community pride and abstinence from drugs and alcohol. After that, we turn them loose to participate in fun activities. The programs are free and we provide transportation. Are there any questions so far, Ms. James?"

"No, sir."

"If you are hired, this job also requires that you lead a discussion with the children from time to time. Would this be a problem for you?"

"Oh, no. And it might be of interest to note that I, too, am a member of an organization that is community-oriented. While we don't deal specifically with children, we do try to instill community pride."

"And what organization might that be, Ms. James?"

"Project Spruce."

Gerald raised his brows. "Well, Susan will discuss salary and benefits with you," he replied, hitting the intercom. "Susan, Ms. James is hired and I'm outta here. Call the studio if you need me." Gerald stood up. "Welcome on board, Ms. James."

"Thank you, Mr. Morris," Rachel replied, shaking his hand. "I look forward to working with you and the children of The Path."

"It's Gerald, and I look forward to working with you also."

❦

Her eyes stayed glued on the man across from her as Linda pinched her leg to make sure that her mind was not playing tricks on her. The pain felt real and she winced. When the man didn't disappear, she knew that he was not an apparition. Malcolm Morris was in her house and sitting on her couch as comfortably as if he'd been doing it for years.

The telephone rang, but Linda was oblivious to the sound. She sat mystified by the fact that Malcolm looked so calm and relaxed when she was quite possibly losing her grip on reality. As the enormity of their situation penetrated, she struggled to keep her mind functioning. But her head still reeled with the astonishment she'd felt after she'd opened her front door and found her husband standing on the other side. A soft moan escaped her lips and Linda dropped her head to her hands. Oh, my Lord. How was she supposed to deal with this?

The telephone rang again. Linda did not move.

"Your phone's ringing," Malcolm said.

Her head snapped up and she blinked slowly as if awakening from a dream. "W-What?"

"The telephone, it's ringing."

Linda nodded and rose from her chair. Feeling woozy,

she stood for a moment to get her balance before moving to the desk and the phone. Her eyes didn't leave
Malcolm's face as she lifted the receiver. "Yes,
Leslie...No, no. I didn't forget about the meeting, but I
have crisis on my hands and I won't be able to
attend...Yes, please apologize to the other ladies for me
and shift the agenda items to next week. Good-bye,
Leslie," she said quickly before her friend could begin on
another topic.

On wobbly legs, Linda returned to her chair. The
waves in her stomach pitched and rolled again as soon
as she sat down and Linda fought desperately to hold
back the nausea. She closed her eyes and shook her
head in disbelief. Oh, my Lord. This was not something
she could deal with right now.

Malcolm sat nervously on the couch and watched his
wife. He hadn't meant to cause the shock he saw in
Linda's face. He also hadn't meant to show up on her
doorstep unannounced. He had meant to find a way to
enter her life again slowly. However, seeing his son this
morning had hastened those plans. Malcolm smiled
when he thought about Gerald. Linda had done a fine
job raising his son.

"W-would you like something to drink?"

"No, thank you, darlin'."

Darlin'! The old endearment had Linda's head swoon-
ing and she examined her husband through the airy
vapors. Malcolm was a lot older now, but he was still a
good-looking man. The hair at his temples had grayed,
but the color gave him a more cultured look. Looking at
him, Linda couldn't stop her heart from beating faster at
the thought that she still had feelings for the man she had
fallen in love with and married at the age of eighteen.

However, Malcolm Morris had walked out on her. He
had left her in that slum with a small child and another on
the way, and the humiliation, pain and anger Linda felt

pushed its way to the surface. She sat up straight and stuck out her chin. "Then what do you want, Malcolm?"

Malcolm shrank under the hostile glare. He had gone over and over his speech, but looking into the glacial face of his wife, the words he planned to say seemed woefully inadequate and died in his throat. What could he say to this woman that would make any difference now? If he were in her shoes, would he want to hear anything she had to say? Hell, he wasn't even sure if Linda was still his wife. Malcolm directed his gaze to the room. Linda had done all right for herself, too, and knowing that she'd done it without him had the old feelings of failure rushing Malcolm. He scooted to the edge of the couch. "Linda, I'm sorry."

Her brows raised when he didn't say anything else. "You're sorry. That's all you have to say to me after thirty-four years. You're sorry." Linda's voice rose to a loud shrill. "Well, Malcolm Jamal Morris, you can take your 'I'm sorry' and your sorry butt and hit the door like you did thirty-four years ago!"

Malcolm stood up and Linda watched him begin a pattern with which she was very familiar. Her son always paced whenever he needed to calm his emotions. Linda's eyes enlarged, then sank in a face gone pasty with fear. Oh, my Lord. Her son! How in the world was she going to tell Gerald that his father was not dead?

Nine

June 8

Leah caught herself gawking at the flowers again and turned back to her computer. She had to stop thinking about Gerald Morris and get back to work. She typed only a couple of lines before swiveling her chair around. Her face had a dreamy look as she gazed at the vibrant burst of wild flowers on her desk. A yellow rose with two more gold keys, marked 2P and 3B, had been in the center of the arrangement. She reached in the desk drawer and took out all three keys. There was a message in there somewhere and since she couldn't decipher the code she'd have to wait until Gerald decided to tell her. She had sent her thanks by way of his assistant, disconcerted to learn that she was a coward after all.

She reached for the telephone. "Diane."

"Leah, I was just getting ready to— Hey! You can't just walk in there."

Leah was frowning at the receiver when she heard his voice. "Hello, Peaches."

Her eyes lifted slowly and she looked into the face of the man responsible for shattering her views on love, marriage and relationships.

Diane moved to stand in front of Michael Ray. "I tried

to stop him, Leah."

"It's okay, Diane. Mr. Dupree was just leaving."

"Oh, I don't think I'll be leaving just yet, Diane," Michael Ray said, leaning down over Leah's desk. "I have some business with Ms. Ellis."

Diane backed out of the office. She ran to her desk and picked up the telephone, keeping her eye on Leah's door. She didn't know what was going on, but she knew Leah needed help.

Leah trembled inside, terrified by the thought that Michael Ray had barged into her personal space. Outside, none of the fear showed as she rose to her feet and faced him. He hadn't changed much. At forty-two, he was older and tiny wrinkles around his still sexy black eyes fanned out over raven skin. His hair had always been his crowning glory and he still wore it in a ponytail. His sudden appearance had shaken Leah more than she cared to admit, but she would never let him see how scared she was. She put her hands on her hips. "What do you want, Ray?"

"It's been over three years, Leah. Is that all you have to say to me?" When his eyes dropped to her breasts, Leah shivered, but quickly brought her body under control.

Michael Ray smiled a wide, toothy grin. "I've missed you, Peaches, and I dropped by to take my best girl to lunch."

Leah watched Michael Ray saunter to the couch in her office. He held out his hand. "Sit with me."

Leah marched to the door and opened it wider. "I don't know why you think I'd go anywhere with you or that I'd have anything to say to you, Michael Ray, but I would like you to leave."

Michael Ray was at her side before Leah knew what happened. He wrenched the door from her hand and slammed it shut. "Oh, I'll leave all right. But first I have something to say."

His head lowered and Leah turned her face away. His lips skidded off her cheek. Michael Ray straightened and smiled. "Just kidding around, Peaches. What I really have is a message. There are some people, people in high places, who don't like what Project Spruce is doing. They don't want those ghettos cleaned up and they want the gang-bangers left alone. In short, they want Project Spruce off the South Side. And my advice to you, pretty lady, is that you listen."

"Is that a threat, Ray?"

His knuckle skimmed over the surface of her breast as he leaned closer. "Hmmm. Threat? Now isn't that an interesting way to look at this situation. No. I wouldn't say it was a threat. I'd say it was more of a recommendation."

"I'm not afraid of you, Ray, and if you think you can scare me, you are wrong."

Michael Ray's eyes crackled with anger; his voice turned ice cold. "Stay in suburbia where you belong, Leah. I wouldn't want to see anything happen to that gorgeous body of yours."

"Ray. You can take your recommendation and—"

Michael Ray grabbed Leah by the shoulders and pinned her against the door. "Back off, Leah. And tell that organization of yours to back off, too. Or next time it might not be supplies that turn up missing." Michael Ray released her and slipped a piece of paper into the bodice of her lavender jacket before standing straight. The paper felt cool against her skin and Leah held her breath as he opened the door. "Oh, and that little fundraiser you're planning to hold in Adams Park. Well, let's just say if I were you, I'd cancel it." He backed out of her office, rubbing his hand along the front of his pants. "Hmm. Hmm. Hmm. That body of yours still does wild things to me."

Leah gasped and closed the door. She went back to her desk and slumped into her chair. Michael Ray had just threatened PS and Leah knew the warning had also been a personal one directed at her. She reached for the telephone and stopped when the paper beneath her jacket crinkled. Pulling it out, her hands shook as she read the message. "My number. I'll be waiting for your call, Peaches." The note fluttered to the desk as Leah grabbed for the telephone. She needed to talk to Tony. He would know what to do.

She jumped when her office door crashed open, then breathed a sigh of relief when she saw Tony stride in.

Tony snatched the receiver from her hand and slammed it down in the cradle, then pulled Leah up from the chair. "What did he want?"

Leah flinched when he shouted at her and tried to move around him. Tony stepped in front of her. "I said, what did he want, Leah?"

"He came here with a message."

"Why would you let that piece of scum in here?"

"I didn't let him in," she snapped. "He came in on his own. Michael Ray said that Project—"

Tony glowered at her and crossed his arms over his chest. "I don't want you talking to him. On the telephone or anywhere else. Got that?"

Her eyebrows elevated. What was it about her that made men think they could tell her what to do? "Tony, will you please listen? Michael Ray said there are peo-ple—"

Tony dropped his arms and sighed. "I don't want that guy hanging around you, Leah. Michael Ray is, and always will be bad news." Tony pulled her close and hugged her.

Leah removed herself from his arms. She took his hand and led him to the couch. "Anthony Nolan Wright, will you please listen to me! Michael Ray didn't come here to see me. He came with a warning for Project Spruce and I want to know what you think we should do about it."

Sheila stepped to the reflective glass in the window of the print shop. She used her finger to rub away the red lipstick in the corner of her mouth. They knew how much she hated being sent on little errand runs for the company. It had been a year since she'd passed the CPA exam and she was getting damned tired of playing girl Friday at Maxwell Corp. She checked her reflection again and straightened the skirt and matching jacket of the red leather mini outfit.

It, along with a few others, was about the only thing she had left to show for the inheritance her father had left her. The rest she'd spent on lavish parties, cruises and indulging the whims of her friends. Friends who wouldn't even return her calls now that the money was gone. Sheila grimaced. If she'd invested her money like Leah, she probably wouldn't have to work and she certainly wouldn't have to supplement her income by moonlighting. What she needed was a man, preferably one with a lot of dough so that she could quit both jobs. Only her luck in the man department was worse than her choice in friends. With a sigh, Sheila adjusted her shoulders and pulled open the door.

"Well, hel-lo there."

Sheila glowered at the tall, skinny dark man with marked dislike. Early twenties. Bald headed. Broke, she surmised. "I'm here to pick up the reports for Maxwell Corp."

Stung by her spurning tone, a crestfallen look replaced the young man's grin. "Your order's in the back. I'll be just a moment."

He, however, no longer had Sheila's attention. Her eyes had spotted and zeroed in on the handsome brother in the yellow suit and black tee who had just entered the shop through the back door. Watching his lithe movements, her eyes wandered all over his body before she looked at his face again. Now, he was a brother she could definitely get next to. "Hello," she called.

Gerald set the box he was carrying on a table and crossed the room. "Hello. Have you been helped?"

Gerald frowned, and, thrilled with the attention, Sheila fluffed her hair. Brothers didn't study a woman with that kind of intensity unless they had an interest and if he was interested, then she was more than ready. She smiled and fluttered her lashes. "Yes, but not in the way I'd like."

Gerald cleared his throat. "Pardon me for staring, but you look a lot like a woman I know."

"Do I? This woman isn't a wife or a girlfriend, is she?"

"No. She's not."

Sheila's eyes glowed with excitement. "I'm Sheila Ellis."

"Ellis? Maybe you do know her. Her name is Leah Ellis."

Sheila crinkled her nose in distaste. "Leah is my sister."

"She is. That's great! I'm Gerald Morris," he replied with a smile.

"Here's your order." The young man dropped a small box on the counter.

Gerald stepped away. "Sheila, I'm glad we met. This is Rick McNeil, one of my best employees. He'll take care of you." He turned from the counter and paused after taking a few steps to face Sheila again. "When you see Leah, tell her that I had a nice time Sunday and look forward to seeing her again."

Sheila placed a manicured hand on her hip. She hadn't believed Leah, but here, standing right in front of her, was living proof that her sister did have a man. "You and Leah are dating?"

"At the moment," Gerald replied. "But I have other plans for your sister." He turned and headed for his office.

Sheila's eyes narrowed at his back. Leah, huh? Well, we'll just have to see about that.

Though reassured by the mass of nine-to-fivers also heading toward their cars, Leah nevertheless scanned the parking garage and inspected the inside of her Jeep before she climbed inside. Michael Ray's visit had unnerved her, and Tony had advised her to call the police or at least get some sort of protection. He'd even offered to pay for a bodyguard. Leah had rejected both suggestions. She refused to live in fear of Michael Ray Dupree. He'd almost ruined her life once and she would not give him the power to do it again. Besides, she told herself, Michael Ray wasn't a stupid man. And it would be stupid for him to try anything that would return him to prison so soon after his release.

Parking the jeep, Leah approached the entrance of the hardware store. Project Spruce needed plumbing supplies for the house project on the twenty-sixth. The store's owner, while a supportive sponsor of PS in the past, could be a tough old bird at times. She needed to focus on getting him to donate what they needed, rather than waste her time thinking about a man who had no respect for women and who issued vague threats and warnings to get what he wanted.

"Malcolm! What are you doing here? When I told you to leave, I meant forever." Linda attempted to close the door, but his foot prevented the action. He pushed his way into the house, knocking Linda off balance. Malcolm caught her around the waist, breathed in the scent of her perfume and let Linda go quickly. He turned away to close the door. He just needed a few moments to get himself together. He turned to face her. "Linda, I just want to talk to you, darlin'."

Linda ran. Malcolm followed and entered the library just as she picked up the telephone. "I'll do it, Malcolm," she stated. "If you don't leave my house, I'll call the police."

Malcolm closed the doors behind him and walked into the room. Linda pushed the buttons, but he was there to lift the receiver from her hand before the call connected. He hung it up.

Linda made a dash for the fireplace and picked up a poker. If Malcolm Morris thought to harm her, he was in for a shock. There would be a knock-down, drag-out up in this here house before that happened.

Malcolm contemplated Linda's reaction for a minute, then he crossed to the bar. He selected a decanter and poured a splash of brandy in a tumbler. He carried it back to Linda and held it out. "Here, darlin', drink this. It will help to calm you down."

Linda looked at the glass, then at the closed doors. She wouldn't be able to get them open before he caught her. She released the poker and took the glass. Malcolm led Linda to a chair and after seating her, lowered himself on the couch. He swallowed hard as he watched her chest heave up and down. Linda's breasts had been beautiful and very sensitive to his touch. He wondered if they were still as firm as he remembered.

Linda raised the tumbler and took a large gulp of the liquor. The brandy burned a slow path down the back of her throat to her stomach, where it sparked into a tiny flame. She knew he was staring at her breasts and couldn't stop the tingling sensation from swelling them fuller. She leaned over and set the glass on the table, hoping the movement would suppress her body's response to him.

She sat back, and Malcolm, pushed beyond his ability to control himself, left the couch. On his knees, he fumbled with the buttons of Linda's blouse.

"Mal-Malcolm, stop!" She tried to slap his hands away.

He ignored her and when he'd gotten the blouse open, he removed the brassiere. His mouth came down on her and Linda exploded. Malcolm's lips nuzzled her neck. "How long has it been since you've lain with a man, Linda?"

An embarrassed heat crept up her neck and Linda focused her eyes on the oil painting on the wall beyond his head.

Malcolm's grip on her shoulders tightened. "How long, Linda?"

"Not since you left, Malc."

Malcolm closed his eyes, feeling pride in her answer. If Linda hadn't had sex since he left, that meant that he had been her only lover. He rose to his feet and held out his hand. "Then I think it's about time we changed that, darlin'."

Ten

The enticing aroma of someone's evening meal filled the corridor, and it wasn't until Leah reached her door that she realized the smells were coming from inside her own apartment. She removed the folded piece of paper taped to the door and read it.

"I'm here. G."

Gerald tilted his head around the kitchen corner when he heard the key in the lock. "Welcome home, sweetheart," he greeted, crossing to her. He kissed her and removed the briefcase and purse from her shoulders. "This way. Your bath is getting cold."

In a zombie-like state, Leah stood in the middle of the floor surveying the room. Something was different and she couldn't quite put her finger on it. Then she realized that her apartment was clean. The furniture shone; the windows gleamed; the rug bore groove marks of being vacuumed; even the walls looked less dingy.

She opened her mouth to speak. Nothing came out, and when Gerald took her arm and walked her to the door of her bedroom, she offered no protest. He waited until she entered, then went back to his pots and pans. Leah removed her clothes, knowing there were a zillion questions she should be asking Gerald. Only her mind wouldn't let her think of a single one. She found another note on the bathroom door.

"Don't question; enjoy. Don't worry; relax."

When she opened the door, the strong, steamy fragrance of wild strawberries assaulted her senses. With her face still reflecting her baffled state of her mind, she gaped at the tub full of bubbles and the lighted candles sitting around its edge, and on every counter and shelf. A brass stand, within arm's reach of the tub, held a crystal pitcher of juice and a glass filled with ice.

"Don't question; enjoy." Taking the advice, Leah removed her wrap and slipped into the tub.

Standing in the bedroom doorway, Gerald smiled when he heard the slosh of water. He moved to the stereo.

Phase three had begun.

Her gaze flew to the wall. Who had installed those? She sat in the tub, dumbfounded, with the strains of a romantic ballad flowing from the speakers on either side of the mirror. Leah shook her head in despair. How in the world had she ever thought she could play this game? She was no match for Gerald Morris. He not only marched to the beat of a different drummer, but he played the instrument himself and every note he hit was an original. In a blitz of moves so rapid she had no time for recovery, Gerald had stormed her castle and all that remained was taking the princess.

"Don't worry; relax."

When the words of his note came to her again, Leah accepted that she was waging a losing battle. She lay back in the tub and conceded the game.

Twenty minutes later, a gentle hand on her shoulder awakened Leah. She opened her eyes and squinted into the smiling face of the man who had been the focus of her dreams.

"You're supposed to be bathing, not sleeping." Gerald

reached for the washcloth and bar of soap. "Unless, of course, it is your intention to become a raisin."

Leah couldn't talk. Her vocal cords had fallen victim to the sensual movements of the hands stroking the cloth over her body. She closed her eyes and rested her head on his chest.

Sheer mental will!

It was the only thing keeping Gerald Morris on track. He forced a downplay in his body's reactions to the hills and valleys making up hers. One day soon, he would cherish Leah and savor the feel of her exquisite womanly shape in his hands. But he couldn't break now. This was too important, and it was not about physical satisfaction. Until Leah acknowledged her feelings for him, he would try to arrest his own desires for as long as he could.

When he'd completed the task, Gerald helped Leah from the tub, wrapped her in a fluffy, white towel and carried her into the bedroom. He sat on the bed with Leah on his lap and dried her with the towel, following each swipe with a kiss. Then he placed her on the bed, went to the dresser and returned with a bottle of lotion.

His chest labored for air. Hers did too when she saw the fight he was waging to keep a firm grip on his emotions. Her panic rose. If Gerald wanted to make love, what was she going to do? Leah had never lain with a man, and without that knowledge, she'd never be able to satisfy the level of desire she saw rising in him. She tried not to flinch away when his hand reached out and stroked the side of her breast.

"Lie down, please," Gerald requested.

Minutes later, Leah was squirming on the bed, the recipient of an erotic massage surpassing her wildest dreams. Gerald's hands moved over her skin and left a trail of heat she thought would never cool. When his lips followed, Leah muffled her moans in the pillow. Unable to take anymore, she twisted on the bed and reached for him.

He kissed her. "You are so beautiful," Gerald murmured. Then he stood up and crossed the room, returning with a lavender silk nightshirt. He dressed her and held out his hand.

Flabbergasted, her breath coming in erratic puffs, Leah stared at the hand. "You're not...I mean, aren't you...?" Leah stopped and took a deep breath. "Gerald, aren't you going to make love to me?"

"Nope."

"Why not?" she gasped.

"It's time to eat."

Eat! In a daze, Leah looked up at him. Gerald expected her to eat? Now? "Eat?" she repeated.

"Yeah. I'm starving and my dinner's getting cold. Come on, sweetheart."

A short while later, Gerald laid down his fork. He thought that the angel hair pasta and clam sauce was one of his best dishes. Apparently Leah didn't share his opinion. She hadn't taken even one little bite. Gerald's heart constricted when he saw the tears in her eyes. He'd upset her and that had not been his intention. "Why don't you eat something, baby girl?"

Leah was miserable. She didn't understand Gerald or what he was trying to do, but she did know that being rejected again hurt. Michael Ray hadn't wanted to make love to her either. "Gerald, what's wrong with me?"

He rose from his chair and moved around the table. Crouching down, he said, "Leah, there isn't a thing wrong with you. You're an intelligent and beautiful woman."

"Then why don't you want to make love to me?"

"Not want to make love to you! Girl, I'd take you on this floor right this minute, if I could."

"If you could? Why can't you? Isn't that what this

evening is all about? I come home to find you in my
apartment preparing a fabulous dinner. There is a bub-
ble bath already drawn for me and you give me a massage that would make Mount St. Helen's top blow again
and when I'm lying there all hot and bothered, all you
want to do is eat. I don't understand. What kind of game
are you playing with me, Gerald?"

Gerald pulled Leah up from the chair. He took her to
the couch and sat them both down. His warm brown
gaze caressed her face for a long moment before he took
her hands in his and said, "Leah, let me assure you, I am
not playing a game. I am very serious about you and I
mean to have you. All of you: mind, body, heart and soul.
This evening is a preview of what it will be like to love me
and when the time is right, you and I will take a journey
you can only imagine. But when that happens, it will be
because you have given your heart to me and not
because you are wallowing in a heated lust any man can
make you feel." Leaning forward, he placed his mouth at
her ear. "When I am the only man who can ignite your
fire and only my lips can cool the burn of your skin, when
I'm sure that only my touch can give you pleasure and
only my body can fulfill your needs, then I will know it is
time."

Gerald worked tiny kisses around her face, then
placed his lips on hers. Leah returned the caress. His
speech sounded wonderful. Leah just didn't know if the
degree of love Gerald sought was possible. It would
require total commitment from both of them and could
prove very elusive. Of that Leah was sure, for she had
once believed and had been badly burned. Saying yes
to Gerald would mean opening herself up to the possibil-
ity of being hurt again. Was she ready to take that
chance?

Lifting his head, Gerald saw the inner conflict mani-
festing itself as distrust and knowing why Leah might be

afraid, he said, "Take a chance with me, Leah. You have my word that I'll make our voyage of love one of happiness."

Leah placed her hands on his shoulders. "G?"

He kissed her again before answering. "Yes, baby girl."

"I hope you aren't expecting me to clean up that mess in the kitchen."

〜

A coke head will do anything for a hit.

Michael Ray grabbed the hair of the woman on her knees and grunted as he leaned forward. Satisfied, he zipped his pants and turned to retrieve his jacket from the chair. He pulled a bag from his pocket and tossed it on the table.

Rachel stared longingly at the cocaine, then back at Michael Ray.

"Go ahead, babe. Hit it."

Rachel crawled to the table and snatched up the bag, crying out in frustration when her clumsy fingers wouldn't allow her to undo the knot. Okay, just take your time. It's only a plastic bag, she told herself. Clearing her throat, Rachel grimaced when she felt an abrasive shaft of pain. She hadn't had a hit in three days and if she didn't get this bag open she was going to scream.

"Let me get that for you," Michael Ray offered. He took the bag and Rachel watched his fingers deftly untie the knot. When he didn't dump the contents on the green-flowered tray, she squeezed her eyes shut. What now?

Michael Ray sat on the couch and glowered at the smeared mascara and lipstick of the trembling woman on the floor. Waste of skin, he thought. People with no backbone turned his stomach, and Rachel was weaker than most. She was nothing like his Leah. Leah would never let him get away with the crap he'd pulled tonight. His eyes softened as thoughts of their relationship overcame him.

For the first time in his life, he had known how it felt to love and be loved. Leah had been so special, he'd put her on a pedestal and given her everything a woman could want. He hadn't even touched Leah, because he wanted a virgin bride, and he hadn't meant to do what he did to her. But after all those years of grooming her, the thought that Leah could so easily dismiss everything they shared had made him crazy. That she had been responsible for sending him to prison didn't matter either. It only confirmed what he'd know all along. Leah was a strong woman; the type of woman he needed; the type of woman he wanted at his side.

A barbarous scowl settled on Michael Ray's face. If Gerald Morris thought he was going to move in on his territory, the man was sadly mistaken. No one took Ray Dupree's property and lived to talk about it.

Rachel saw the look of pure evil that entered his eyes. She gasped in horror when she saw what he did next. After coating himself with the coke, Michael Ray tossed the bag on the table.

"You need a hit real bad, don't cha, baby?" He grinned when she nodded. "Then I suggest you get busy again." Michael Ray chuckled when Rachel crawled over to him and laughed outright when she lowered her head to his lap. He pushed her away after a few minutes and dumped the rest of the coke on the tray. Rachel looked at the tray with tears in her eyes. "It's okay. Go ahead, Rach."

Rachel eagerly grabbed up the little silver spoon. She dipped it into the powder and, raising it to one nostril, snorted deeply, then quickly repeated the action with the other. Buoyed by the drifting sensation, she rose from her knees and flopped down on the couch. She was smiling until she glanced at the man who treated her worse than a whore.

Ray was the one who had gotten her hooked on the stuff in the first place. Introduced by a mutual friend at a party, he had gotten her high on cocaine and wine and taken her to bed that same night. Over the years, she had learned that his prostitute mother had kicked him out at age ten. Ray had obtained his education in the streets and his eyes had never seen the inside of a church. He cared about no one but himself and he used people as stepping stones in the pursuit of his god, the almighty dollar. Rachel had never understood how she, a preacher's daughter, a college graduate and a schoolteacher had fallen in love with him. She shook her head sadly. She was a cocaine addict and in love with a drug dealer. Could her life get any worse? She watched Michael Ray pull on a condom and quickly took another a hit of the coke. Knowing what was next, she lay down on the couch. A few minutes later, Rachel closed her eyes on tears of humiliation when Michael Ray yelled Leah's name in her ear.

Eleven

June 10

The streaks of sunlight bouncing off Leah's face the next morning were bright, but they weren't the reason she opened her eyes. It was the loud pounding on her door. She left the bed and grabbed her wrap. "Who is it?" she asked at the door.

A knock answered.

"Who is it?" No response, and Leah turned for her bedroom. The knocking began again. Exasperated, she marched back to the door and yanked it open. "What?"

Gerald sailed into the room. "Good morning, sweetheart." He dropped a kiss on her nose and continued to the kitchen. Leah followed him with her eyes as she closed the door with her foot. Gerald set his bags on the counter and began unloading their contents.

Leah sat in a kitchen chair. "Gerald, do you have any idea what time it is?"

He glanced at his Rolex. "Yep."

She examined the assorted array of foodstuffs littering the counter top. "What are you doing here, G?"

"You don't have any food," he replied, bending to peer into the cabinet beneath the kitchen sink. When he found what he was searching for, he turned on the cold water tap, then went back to his bags.

"So?"

Gerald finished arranging the flowers and crossed to the table. "So, if you're going to feed me, then you need to have food." He set a vase of white lilies on the table and went back to unpacking his bags. Leah pulled the ribbon from the yellow rose in the center. A 4HF marked the gold key.

"Gerald, in case it has escaped your notice, this is a weekday and I need to get ready for work."

Gerald closed the refrigerator, moved to the table and bent down to eye level with Leah. "Then go and get ready for work. Breakfast will be ready by the time you're dressed."

Leah left the kitchen and wasn't in the shower two minutes when Gerald pulled the curtain back. "Where is the coffee pot?"

"I don't have one."

"Why not?"

"I don't drink coffee."

"Leah, that's un-American. Everyone has a coffee pot."

"Well, I don't," she replied, flicking water at him. The gleam in his eyes had her backing up. "You wouldn't."

He pulled the curtain closed and left the room. Leah finished her shower and had just turned off the faucets when a downpour of cold water doused her from above. Sputtering, she looked up and found Gerald holding a large pot and grinning down at her.

"Always expect a payback," he said.

Twenty minutes later, Leah was slicing her fork through a crepe covered with a freshly made blueberry sauce and a dab of whipped cream when she heard the whine.

"I need coffee."

She picked up her cup of tea and tried not to laugh at the woeful expression on Gerald's face. "Then the next

time you come barging into my apartment at six in the
morning, I suggest you bring a coffee pot with you."

"Is she in, Diane?" Merri asked, walking up to the
desk.

"She is, Merri. Go on in."

From the doorway, Merri observed the head bent over
a report on her desk. She firmed her shoulders and
walked into the office. "Hey, girlfriend."

"Hi, Merri," Leah said, looking up. She came around
the desk and hugged her. "Did we have a lunch date?"

"No. I was in the neighborhood and decided to stop
by."

"You work across town, Merri, which is nowhere near
my neighborhood."

Merri sat on the couch. "Okay. So I didn't just stop by.
I was at the PS office."

"And?"

"And, there was a message from Marjorie Masters.
She sends her regrets, but she's already accepted a
speaking engagement on the same date as the fundraiser."

When Merri saw the look on Leah's face, she went
over and hugged her again. "I know how hard you're
working on this, Leah, but this is a minor setback. We'll
find somebody to speak for us."

Leah's fingers rubbed her temples to forestall the tension she felt building inside of her. "You don't understand, Merri. I've been through the entire list and
Marjorie Masters was my last hope. What am I supposed to do now?"

Leah saw a sheen enter Merri's eyes. Wariness
crawled across the back of her neck when her friend
grabbed her by the arm and led her to the couch.

"Now, Leah. Before you say no, hear me out on this, okay? I know you don't have any experience as a public speaker. Lord knows, I'd be scared to do this myself, but we don't have a speaker and we are running short on time."

Leah jumped up from the couch. "Oh, no, Merri. Don't even go there!" She went to the small refrigerator in her office and took out a bottle of water. She was twisting off the cap when she felt Merri behind her.

"Leah, you know this organization like the back of your hand and you know what we're trying to accomplish. You're the past president and a founding member. Who is better than you to speak for us?"

Leah's took a sip of the water and replaced the cap. An agitated hand placed the bottle back in the fridge. "There's you and there's Tony. Both of you are founding members, too."

"Leah, as president, I have too many other responsi-bilities and I don't have the time to be messing with a speech. And Tony." Merri pursed her lips as she frowned in annoyance. "Well, let's just say I don't think he'd treat the subject with the seriousness it deserves."

"No, Merri. I can't. I'll keep looking; I'm sure I'll find someone."

Merri had known Leah long enough to know when to back off. Leah wasn't going to agree to anything today, but at least she had planted the idea. "Well, I have to run," she said, crossing to the office door. "But you at least think about what I said."

Tony was leaning against the wall with seeming indif-ference when Merri approached the elevators. "Hiya, Merri."

"Hi, Tony."

"You here to see Leah?"

"Uh-huh. We just lost Marjorie Masters for the fundraiser."

Briefly, Tony considered her statement, then smiled. "Here today, gone tomorrow and life, it do go on," he wisecracked, with a snap of his fingers.

Merri's expression showed her distaste for the comment. "I don't think this is anything to joke about, Tony," she stated sharply, stepping into the elevator.

The smile dropped from his face when the doors closed. Tony stood for a moment, then shrugged his shoulders and went down the hallway to Leah's office.

"Hiya, Leah," he called out, stepping inside. When Leah waved him in, he moved around the desk and leaned over her shoulder, peering at the computer screen.

Leah continued her telephone conversation. "Has Houston faxed their numbers?" She covered the mouthpiece as she listened to the response. "I'll be just a moment, Tony." To Diane she said, "Get them on the phone and tell them to fax those numbers now and no more excuses, and please bring in the file for Maxwell...No, call Houston first, then bring in the file. And Diane, thanks." She turned to Tony. Though still waiting for an apology, she had chalked his little outburst on Monday down to having a bad day. "How was the trip?"

"We got the account. What's up with Maxwell?"

Leah looked pensive. "I don't know. I thought I'd review their numbers and see if their sales are on target with our projections. If there is a problem, I was thinking it might be the reason they're pulling their PS support." She shrugged. "It's a shot in the dark."

"If you're reviewing the Maxwell account, why is Joe's Atlanta deal on the screen?"

"Because there's a problem." Leah pointed to the research report on her desk. "Look at these numbers. I've entered them several times using a different set of criteria for each run. Any way you look at it, we had less than a five-percent response. If these figures are true, then something is very wrong, because sales, revenue and inventory aren't jiving. I'm still waiting for Houston's numbers and a report from inventory control."

"Tough break, kid," Tony replied, putting his hands on her shoulders. "But hang in there and make sure I get a copy of that Atlanta report, the one from Houston and anything else. Joe's number is just about up. The management conference is in September. When it's over, I'm putting his bigoted butt on the street. If it gets to be too much for you though, let me know."

"Okay, Tony." He began a gentle massage of her shoulders that eased the tension from the back of her neck. "Mmmm. That feels really good," Leah moaned. She leaned her head back to look up at him.

Tony's hands stopped moving. "Do you have plans for lunch?"

"I do if you're inviting me."

"Then consider yourself invited," Tony replied.

When he left, Leah turned to gaze at the vase of purple lilacs sitting on her desk. Two more gold keys, 5HB and 6SDB, had been attached to the yellow rose.

Six gold keys—no clues. An incredible massage—no sex. A surprise breakfast—no coffee, and all with the man who, she knew, just as surely as she knew her name was Leah Nicole Ellis, had become the focal point of her world.

∽

Sitting in the black leather chair, Sheila surveyed the chrome and smoked glass office. She turned apprehensive eyes toward the man across from her when he sprang forward in his chair and began shouting into the telephone.

"What? What do mean you haven't gotten to the partner in LA? Up the offer...You tell Montgomery, I don't give a damn if the man no longer owns it. I want that company and I mean to have it...Look, don't jack me around, boy. Montgomery has his own reasons for hating the man and you're both paid to do what I tell you to do. Now, you get back to LA. And while you're at it, put word in the street that TyJo Productions is going public and has plans for expansion...I know what I said, damnit! I want those boys spinning in so many circles they won't know what hit them. And when you get back, I have another little job for you...Just do it, and don't ask me no goddamn questions."

Sheila cringed when he slammed down the phone and directed angry, coal black eyes at her. "Where's my money?"

Sheila leaned forward and tried to keep her voice steady as she made her explanation. "The guy you set me up with on Saturday stiffed me."

Though a muscle ticked in his cheek, his voice remained calm. "You're supposed to get my money first."

"I did," Sheila implored. "Only, he took it back afterwards."

A sound of disgust left his lips as he rose from his chair and moved around the desk to the couch. "You're worthless, Sheila, and the son of a bitch who stole my money will be meeting his maker sooner than he expected."

Lowering himself, he reached into the teakwood box sitting on the glass table. Sheila followed him to the couch. She watched him remove a pen-shaped lighter from his pocket and fire the tip of the joint. Her heart beat an anxious pitter-pat under the red jacket she wore. She was working up her courage to ask something and wasn't sure how he would react. If she was correct, he would help. But she had to play it cool and time it right. She licked her lips and touched his arm. "I have this problem and I need your help."

Michael Ray stuck the joint in the corner of his mouth. He squinted one eye closed against the smoke and leaned forward to lift a crystal brandy decanter. He filled two glasses and offered one to Sheila. Sitting back again, he drained his. "Considering that you came in here empty-handed, why are you wasting my time?"

Sheila gulped at the liquid in her glass before responding. "It concerns Leah."

She smiled inwardly when she saw the muscle jerk in his cheek. Ray still had feelings for her sister. The smile turned to fear when he left the couch and his black eyes glittered down at her. Knowing Michael Ray was astute at spotting and using a weakness when he saw one, Sheila swallowed her fear with another drink from the glass.

"Why would anything that has to do with Leah concern me? And why do you think I would help you since you are the reason she left me?"

"I don't think our sleeping together had anything to do with that, Ray. Leah is so soft-hearted she probably would have forgiven you that little mistake. I think it was your career choice that clenched it for her."

"And what career choice would that be, Sheila?" Michael Ray's eyes pinned her to the sofa. "I'm a respectable Chicago importer. My products are legal and the US postal service distributes them to my customers."

Feeling a bit braver, Sheila rose and sauntered over to him. She rested one hand on his chest and rose to her toes to whisper in his ear. "Sure you are, Ray. And I'm a perfectly respectable CPA who happens to know where your money really comes from."

Michael Ray pushed her away and went back to the couch. "Let's cut the bull, Sheila. What do you want?"

"I told you. It's Leah. There's this man that she's involved with and I want them uninvolved."

"What's the man's name?"

"Oh, I don't think you need to know that."

Michael Ray propped an elbow on his arm, inhaled deeply on the joint and released the smoke into the air. He watched the smoke curl its way to the ceiling. "Oh, I think I will need to know, if you expect my help."

Sheila took a deep breath and exhaled. "Okay, Ray. His name is Gerald Morris and I want him."

Michael Ray pulverized the joint in the ashtray. "Well, he apparently doesn't want you, if he's involved with Leah."

Sheila cringed behind that remark. "Oh, he'll want me all right—as soon you do your part and get Leah away from him."

Michael Ray laughed. "My part! In case you haven't noticed, Leah and I aren't exactly on speaking terms. So, I don't see how I can help you with your little problem." He opened the box again, reached into a velvet pouch in the top of the lid and pulled out another joint. "But you can help me with mine." Sheila leaned away when he held the joint out to her. "Take a hit."

"No thank you, Ray. You know I'm not a user," Sheila said, rising. "I'll just be on my way."

Michael Ray brought her forcefully back down to his lap. "I said, take a hit. Then you and I are going to have a little fun."

That evening, Leah entered her apartment, flipped on the lights, and burst out laughing. Sitting on her living room table was not one, but two coffee makers, and on the floor nearby were four cartons of coffee. She moved into the room and found a place to sit among the other gift-wrapped packages littering her couch and chair and began opening them. When she finished, Leah sat back.

On her floor was a set of china, crystal glasses, silver cutlery, various-sized pots and pans, mixing bowls and assorted kitchen utensils, a state-of-the-art mixer, a juicer, a toaster and a stack of cookbooks.

A dwarf Bonsai tree sat on the table. Leah picked it up and removed the gold keys. Turning them over, she found them stamped: 7PF, 8PW, 9PH, 10PS, 11PD and 12PB. Even with the other six, they made no sense and after a while of trying to figure out the message, Leah began to wish that she were on *Wheel of Fortune* so that she could buy a vowel.

Giving up, she gathered them up and after stashing the keys in a little box in her dresser drawer, removed her clothes and headed for the bathroom. She soaked in the tub for an hour, then dressed in an ivory silk chemise and matching wrap, she lay on the bed and waited for the telephone to ring.

An hour later, Leah reached for the receiver. Since Gerald hadn't called her, she'd call him. She hung up a few minutes later when his home and cell phone both went to the answering service. Where was Gerald and why hadn't he been here when she arrived home? Leah glanced at the clock and slipped down on the bed. It was already ten-thirty, but she would give him another hour. She focused her eyes on the red numbers of the clock in a bid to stay awake.

Two hours later, Leah was sitting up in the bed with tears streaming down her face. She picked up a pillow and tried to use it as a shield against the searing pain lodged in her chest. The dream had been frightening and caused her to relive the anguish she'd suffered at the hands of a man who had claimed to love her.

Determined to stop the tears, she grabbed a tissue and dabbed at her eyes. After expending all of her ener-gy pushing the harrowing images from her mind, she lay down again but didn't close her eyes. The rain and thunder booming outside her window scared Leah almost as much as the dream. She gripped the covers in her hands and had to steel herself to keep from leaving the bed. And yet Leah felt foolish. Here she was about to turn twenty-nine and she was afraid to go to sleep in her own room. If the situation weren't so pathetic, Leah might have laughed at herself.

Deciding that Michael Ray's visit was the probable cause of the nightmare, she sat up and left the bed. In the kitchen, she pulled a pan from the cabinet and the milk from the refrigerator. Standing at the stove, Leah waited for the milk to heat and shook her head sadly. She couldn't have made a worse choice in a man than Michael Ray. After the trial, she'd put on her mask, gone on with her life and everyone thought her so strong the way she'd handled herself. However, the last few days in Gerald's company had underscored just how lonely Leah really was and seeing Ray again had caused her front to slip.

Now she would have to rebuild the façade so that everyone's perception of her remained intact. Merri was the only one who knew how much Michael Ray had hurt her, but not even Merri knew how hard she had to push herself just to get through each day.

Twelve

June 18

Lost in their own worlds, the three women sitting at the kitchen table were unusually silent. Mabel studied each of her daughters, then focused on her youngest. Sheila had done some outrageous things Mabel had long suspected were all in a bid to gain her father's attention. Knowing how much Hamilton had loved his children, Mabel didn't understand why Sheila believed her father didn't love her. She looked at Leah, who seemed to be somewhere other than with them at the table. As involved and outspoken as Leah was with her many causes, her daughter was a very private person. Mabel was convinced that Leah had not revealed all that had happened between herself and Michael Ray. Likewise, Mabel had never told her daughter of the visit she'd made to see Michael Ray in jail. Or that the only reason he wasn't dead, and Mabel serving time instead, was because of the young cop who had stopped her from pulling the trigger and Hamilton's connections with the court.

Though her daughters were both adults, and in their own way, strong and independent women, she was still their mother and as long as there was breath in her body, she would do everything in her power to protect them.

Mabel rose from her chair and picked up a knife. And, as their mother, she would continue to try to help them resolve their differences so that her daughters would again become the loving sisters that they had once been.

Sheila held back a sob and pressed her eyes shut on unshed tears. Going to see Michael Ray had been a terrible mistake. This was the second time he had drugged her and she'd found herself in his bed. Only this time she had fought Michael Ray, at least until she felt his hands close around her neck and heard his threatening voice in her ear. Michael Ray had fondled her breasts while whispering Leah's name. Sheila shuddered and the glare she sent her sister could have shaved ice. What was it about Leah that drew men to her like bees to honey?

Leah heard the soft sob and glanced at her sister. Sheila looked so dejected she wanted to reach out and comfort her. Leah didn't, knowing the gesture would be not only unwelcome, but rejected. Their relationship was strained at best, malicious at its worst. Leah had tried to understand why Sheila detested her so much, and couldn't remember doing anything to warrant such keen dislike. Still, Leah loved her sister; the strong sense of family instilled in her by their father made it impossible for her to feel otherwise. With all the problems she had on her mind, she really didn't need take on whatever was bothering her sister, too. But she would, if Sheila would only ask.

When her eyes turned misty, Leah willed herself not to think about Gerald Morris. She hadn't heard from him in a week, and she missed him more than she could have thought possible. The man had blown into her life, caused mayhem with her emotions, and now couldn't take the time to make a simple phone call.

Stop it, Leah told herself. She silently commanded the tears in her eyes to dry up and the pain in head to go away. After all, Gerald was a busy man. If he couldn't find two minutes to call her, it was no big deal. And if she was going to do this with Gerald, and by this, Leah really meant have a relationship, she had to learn to trust him. But after Michael Ray, Leah was short on trust and wary of the games people played. She couldn't help thinking that Gerald might be trifling with her emotions. If it turned out that he was, this time, Leah promised herself, she'd be ready.

Mabel pasted a smile on her face and sliced the knife through the cake. "Happy birthday, baby."

"Thanks, Ma," Leah replied, her voice a cheerless whisper.

"Have you people lost your damn minds?" Fred Hays shouted. "Why are you all sitting here acting like this is nothing? This organization has just received a fu—"

"Chill out, man. There are ladies present," Tony chided.

"Yeah," Bobby McVey spoke up. "Besides this isn't the first threat we've received and PS don't back down for nobody."

"PS might not back down, but Fred sho' do. I joined PS to help the brothers and sisters out, not lay down my life for 'em."

"That's enough," Merri stated. "Now, I will admonish you people again. We will discuss this situation like the professionals we are or this topic will be tabled." She looked at Leah. "Tell us again what Michael Ray said."

All eyes turned to Leah. She had already related her conversation with Michael Ray and the reaction had been like an atomic bomb going off at a Nevada testing site. She examined the faces staring at her; none stared more intently than Rachel James. What the woman had against her, she'd never know. Leah decided to focus on

Tony. He gave her a slight nod of encouragement. "Michael Ray warned us to cancel the fundraiser and implied that if we didn't, something might happen. He also intimated that he might have had something to do with our missing supplies."

"That's all I need to hear," Fred said, jumping up. "I say, let's call for a vote."

"You cannot call for a vote, Fred. You are part of the membership, not an officer," Merri replied with irritation in her voice.

"Hey, I paid my dues just like everybody sitting in this room."

"Yeah," Merri responded, "and that entitles you to one vote. Now sit down!"

Tony stood up. "Look. Why don't we all take a minute and relax? Now, I think we should ignore Dupree and his threat. He's nothing but a small time hood."

"A small time hood with large connections," Fred called out.

Tony turned to him. "Fred, if you want to step off, hit the door, man. We have serious business to discuss here and if you don't have anything productive to add, then just be quiet."

Merri sat back. So far this evening, Tony had stood up four times and brought calm into the meeting. Normally, he would have tried to mollify Fred with a stupid joke. Tony hadn't told one joke or amusing anecdote the entire night. She smiled to herself. It seemed that the man had a serious side after all.

"Now, as I was saying," Tony continued, shooting a cautioning glance at Fred, "Michael Ray just stepped out of prison a few months ago. So, I doubt he's had the time to make any so-called large connections. Right now, he's so hot only a fool would go anywhere near him. We also know Leah was partly responsible for putting him behind bars. I think it's possible he's just trying to rattle her cage."

Heads turned in her direction again. "It is possible his words were aimed just at me," Leah said. "I just thought the membership needed to know what's going on."

"Aimed at you, huh? Then why are you scaring the hell out of the rest of us?" Fred yelled, jumping up from his chair again. "If Leah is putting Project Spruce in danger, then I say she's out!"

Bobby's chair hit the floor when he leaped up. "Sit yourself down, man, before I do it for ya!"

Merri blew out a breath. "This discussion is now tabled."

"Why don't we just table Fred?" Bobby remarked with a glower.

"Bobby, please. Let's not degenerate to that level again." She turned to look at Fred. "First of all, Fred, Leah has done more for PS than anyone sitting in this room, certainly more than your lame butt, and telling us is exactly what she should have done. Now, if you don't like the way this organization is run, there's the door. Otherwise, shut up because I'm tired of hearing your mouth." Merri surveyed the others. "And if any of the rest of you hear anything, I'll expect you to bring it before this membership. Now, we have a fundraiser to plan and a project on the twenty-sixth and I say, let's call for the vote."

When the meeting was over, Leah laid her head on her arms. The headache had intensified and she felt much like a piece of metal being pounded on a smithy's anvil. If she didn't take something for it she was going to have to skip the night out with the girls.

"Lele? Don't let Fred's comments upset you," Bobby said. "His bark is worse than his bite."

Leah looked up into eyes that were watching her with concern now, but had once pleaded with her to help him. Bobby had been fifteen when she first met him. She didn't know what had made her tell the police that he was with her when they'd raided that crack house. She just knew those big, Bambi browns had melted her heart. As soon as they were away from the cops, Bobby had run off into the night yelling, "Thanks, lady!"

The next morning, she couldn't shake the feeling that Bobby needed her and she had gone back into that neighborhood to search for him. Two hours later, she had finally found him in an alley. He was on the ground behind a dumpster and he'd been shot.

She had stayed through his surgery, sat with him in the hospital while he recuperated and listened to his story. Abandoned at twelve, Bobby had survived the streets. How he had kept himself out of the gangs, off drugs, and alive, still amazed Leah. Bobby had, at first, rejected her offer to find him a foster family until she'd whetted his appetite with stories of her own childhood. For the last three years he'd lived with the McVeys and had set himself up as her knight in shining armor.

Leah kneaded her temples. "Fred doesn't bother me, Bobby. I just have this awful headache."

"Don't move. I'll get something for you and be right back."

Leah laid her head back down. She lifted it again when Tony sat on the table beside her. "Happy birthday, angel face."

"Thanks, Tony."

He examined her face and the lines around her mouth. Poor kid. Michael Ray really had her worried. "You don't sound like someone who's celebrating a birthday. How are you really doing, Leah?"

"I'm fine, Tony."

Tony heard the sadness in her voice and puckered his lips. "Know what you need?"

"Yeah. A speaker for the fundraiser."

"No. What you need is a break, and I'm just the man

to give it to you. How about having a birthday dinner with
me?"

"Can't, Tony. I already had dinner at my mother's and
I'm planning to head home and hit the phones for an hour
or so. We still need supplies for the project on the twenty-sixth and I'm waiting to hear back from the Chicago
Bulls. Their PR man promised to let me know if any of
the players can speak at the fundraiser. And if I can rid
myself of this headache, the girls are taking me out for a
birthday celebration."

Tony rolled his eyes. "Tonight isn't what I had in mind,
Leah. I'm leaving tomorrow for meetings in Atlanta and
Houston. I'll be back in the office on Friday. I was thinking maybe we could go somewhere after work." Tony
picked up and rubbed the back of her hand. "Tell me
something, Leah. If you could choose any restaurant in
this city to have dinner, where would it be? And I don't
mean a fast food dive either; I mean a really fancy place."

She smiled meditatively. "There is this restaurant
called Everest on LaSalle. I've been told that that they
serve the most heavenly French cuisine and if you're
lucky, you can sit by the window and look out over the
city. But it's very expensive and you're not really serious,
Tony."

Tony squeezed her hand. "I am serious, and don't
worry about the expense, I can afford it. Now, here's
what I want you to do. Forget the phones, go out with the
girls and celebrate your birthday. Next Friday night, it's
you and me at Everest." When he saw Merri struggling
with a box, Tony patted Leah's shoulder and slipped off
the table. He hurried across the room. "Hey, pres! Let
me help you with that."

Leah watched Tony relieve Merri of her burden and
walk with her from the room. Gerald entered her
thoughts and Leah momentarily questioned the wisdom
of going to dinner with Tony, then shook her head.

Gerald was out of town and she had no idea when he'd be back. She'd only known him a few days, so it wasn't like they had a real relationship anyway. Besides, Tony was her friend and if he wanted to take her out for a birthday dinner, who was she to complain? And since tonight was her birthday, for once she'd place everything on a back burner. She was going out with the girls.

Gerald pulled one of the two boxes on his desk forward. His brows rose when his saw his sister's return address. Now, why would NayNay send a box to him at The Path? It couldn't possibly be anything good. More likely, it was in retaliation for the three dozen black roses and champagne bottle full of vinegar water delivered to her office on her birthday last week, courtesy of him. His lips edged up. The game of pulling practical jokes on one another had started when they were children. As they had matured, so had the complexity of the jokes.

He'd do well to exercise a little caution opening this box. Leaning away, he ran the knife through the tape on top. Surprised when nothing happened, he sat up and lifted the carton lids. That proved to be a mistake when two tiny water pistols sprang up and fired. Gerald looked down at the dripping mess, his mouth set in a firm line. He rose and went into his private suite. Thirty minutes later, he was back at his desk dressed in a teal colored suit and black silk tee. The sky blue suit was in the trash. Those ink stains were not coming out and he owed his sister big time. "Yeah," he said, when the intercom buzzed.

"J.J. on one, boss man."

"Thanks, and Suse, go home. I know you must have something better to do on a Friday night than hang around here."

"I'm just finishing the supply requisitions for the stores."

"Go home, Susan."

"Okay, G. See you Monday."

"Good night." Gerald hit the blinking light, leaned back and propped his feet up on the desk. "What's up, Money?"

"G-man! How was the flight back to Chi-town?"

"It was fine, J.J."

"Listen, homes. Did a little research on that Chic-a-Boom thing and I'm sorry to say that it's on me. I gave it to my assistant by mistake." J.J. laughed heartily. "Can you believe that garbage, man? Meant to fly that tape out the win'da."

"What I can't believe, Mr. Jones, is that you wasted good money having that tape put into a box."

"It was an honest mistake, G. Hey, wait a minute! I hope you're not planning to sweat me over this. 'Cause if you are, I'd suggest you remember who's got your back while you're out there in La-La Land, buddy."

"I wasn't planning to give you a hard time, but don't think I'm ever going to let you forget."

"Didn't think you would," J.J. replied with a chuckle. "Did the box arrive?"

"Yep. I was just about to open it."

"Cool. The tracks we talked about for Ebony Silk are inside and I'd appreciate your comments. But here's the real scoop, G. I know you just left, but I'm ringing to find out if you could schedule another trip to LA."

"Why, J.J.?"

"After you left, Ebony Silk's people called. They're ready to move forward and I've set a meeting for the first week in August. I'd like to have you sit in on this one, G."

J.J. was really starting to push the buttons now. However, if memory served him correctly, the fundraiser for Project Spruce was scheduled that same week. "I won't be able to make it," Gerald replied. "You have my comments. I'd keep it clean with this group. These boys are talent, and I'd make sure the listening public focuses on that. Put them in suits on the first video. No trend-setting outfits, dreads, tattoos, bare chests or gyrating women. They don't need the hype."

"Sorry you can't make the gig, G. But I agree on the Ebony Silk assessment," J.J. replied. "Check you later, man. Peace out."

"Peace." Gerald hung up the phone and swung his feet to the floor. He hadn't planned the trip to LA and had only gone as a favor to J.J. He had wanted to see Leah's reaction when she came home and discovered his surprise. All-day meetings and late nights had not given him many chances to call her and the few times he had, he hadn't gotten through.

Lord, how he missed that woman! Over a week of not seeing Leah had Gerald feeling like a candidate for the loony bin. He picked up his keys and headed for the door. He needed to see Leah and at nine o'clock at night she had to be at home.

Thirteen

The chicken wings and baby back ribs were hot and spicy. The potato salad cold, the rolls warm and buttery. Besides enjoying the food, a mass of men and women bopped on a crowded dance floor to the beat of the latest jams being spun by a local DJ. It was Friday night, ladies' night, and the party at Club Raymond was on and in full swing. Outside, Club Raymond looked no different from the other older brick buildings lining the docks of the Chicago River. Inside, Club Raymond was a world of elegance.

The delicate wrought iron railing surrounding a large parquet dance floor also lined the walkways and the spiraling staircase leading to a second level. White marble-topped tables and black velvet, cushioned seats were placed so that patrons could walk without bumping into one another, and the padding under the black shag carpet provided a pillow for the feet. Decorative fixtures dispensed plenty of light. Original deco art hung from the walls and the air circulated at a pleasantly cool temperature. On the bottom level, the club had two bars built entirely of black marble slabs. Raymond's customers expected the best and every conceivable label, heavy on those from the top shelf, stocked both. The waiters and waitresses could have stepped out of *GQ* and *Vogue*, and they, as well as the rest of Raymond's staff, had been well trained to cater to his upscale, thirty-something guests.

"Happy birthday, sister-girl."

"Thanks, Merri," Leah replied.

Five of the six women at the table clinked their glasses together, hampering the efforts of the attractive black waitress. She waited until they sat back, then continued removing the plates and a few of the glasses on the table. The waitress dumped an overflowing ashtray and set down her tray. "Okay, ladies. These drinks are courtesy of the two handsome gentlemen at the bar to your right." The ladies turned and waved their thanks. Three hours at the club and this was the sixth set of drinks delivered to their table. The women were having a good time and all were somewhat tipsy.

Danye removed the cigarette from her mouth and leaned back in her chair. "Watch it, girls. Here they come."

"Beautiful lady, will you please dance with me?"

"Yes," Leah replied, drunk enough to let her inhibitions down.

That unleashed a flurry of men rushing the table. When it was over, all of the women, except Rachel, were on their way to the dance floor.

Danye's partner curved his arm around her waist and looked back over his shoulder. "If you're still here when I get back, I'll kick it with you, too."

Rachel responded with a withering glare. She grabbed her purse and made her way across the club to the bathroom. Inside the stall, she sat on top of the toilet seat and removed a small amber vial from her purse. Being invited to join the Les Cinq Belles Noires clique for a night out was a rare occurrence, but she'd rather be anywhere other than here with this shallow bunch of bitches. She had come only because the alternative was even worse.

She had copied the information Ray had requested from the Project Spruce files and not wanting a repeat of last week's performance, had left the folder outside her door. Instead of going home after the meeting, she had accepted Stacia's invitation. Had she known it was to celebrate Leah's birthday, she would have skipped the party. Michael Ray shouting out Leah's name every time they made love was enough of a reminder of how much she hated the woman.

Rachel screwed off the cap, dipped the burgundy tone nail of her pinkie finger in and lifted it to her nostril. Sniffing quickly, she repeated the action on the other nostril and threw the vial in her purse. She had to get out of here. Club Raymond had a strict policy regarding the use of illegal narcotics on the property. If they caught her, the consequences would be very embarrassing. Leaving the stall, Rachel stopped at the mirror to wipe away any trace of her indulgence and returned to the table.

Ja'Nise offered a smile. "Where have you been?"

"In the ladies' room."

"Well, that man I danced with has been here twice looking for you. And if the way he was rubbing up against me is any indication, the boy's got a definite love jones happening."

Rachel shot an annoyed glance at Danye. "Well, that's too bad 'cause love don't live here tonight."

"Right on, sister," Stacia said, slapping a high-five with Rachel.

Leah returned to the table and plopped down in her chair. She slipped off her shoes, plucked a napkin from the holder and used it to mop up her neck.

"Your butt was sure shaking out on that floor," Danye remarked. "Where did you learn to move like that?"

"Girl, pleeze. I've been doing those same moves since high school. I don't have the time to go around learning the latest dance crazes."

"Now that I think about it, Leah," Ja'Nise said, "you haven't been to the club in months. What's got you so occupied that you can't spend a little time with the girls, besides PS that is?"

"Dealing with a jerk on the job."

"That's not the reason," Merri commented, winking at Leah. "Homegirl's got a homeboy who's hot to trot."

Ja'Nise leaned forward. "Merri, you've got to be kidding. Leah Nicole Ellis has a man. Our Leah, who can send a brother packing in five seconds flat?"

Danye laughed. "Yeah. Leah has elevated turning down a brother to an art form."

"If you've got a story, get to telling it, girl," Stacia said.

Leah picked up her glass. Ja'Nise, a long-legged, nutmeg beauty, wore her brown hair in a silky cap that curved around her face, and her coffee brown eyes gaped in wonder at Leah. Danye was a replica of Merri, down to the braids, except Danye was five inches taller, three years older and she chain smoked. Elegantly tall, Stacia had light brown skin, brown eyes and long black hair hanging to the middle of her back that had come from her Native American mother.

Why is she here? Leah wondered, directing her eyes to Rachel. Rachel didn't like any of them. That wasn't quite true. The woman did seem to like Stacia. Leah picked up her glass and took a healthy drink. "There is no story."

"Oh, Leah. That's not true," Merri said. "I'll tell you about him. His name is Gerald Morris and he's one of those tall, dark and handsome brothers. Reeeally handsome, now that I come to think of it."

A man approached the table and Leah gladly accepted his request to dance. The very last thing she wanted to hear was Merri expounding on the man she was trying to forget. On the dance floor, she threw herself into the song's rocking beat, her movements deliberately seductive. Her partner locked his eyes on the gyrating body, sure he had hit the jackpot. Because she was upset with Gerald, but mostly because she was drunk, Leah offered no protest when her partner pulled her closer and even tipped her head back when his came down and his lips met hers. Leah was pressing herself closer when she realized what she was doing and that it wasn't Gerald she was doing it with.

Stifling a sob, she pulled away and ran from the floor. She pushed her way through the crowd, climbed the stairs to the second level and found a quiet place on a couch. She either needed to take her tired butt home or pull it together. Leah used the back of her hands to dry her eyes. If Gerald had decided to leave her alone, it was something she would accept. Ten minutes later, she returned to the table where Merri was still going strong.

"That man is too fine. And he drives a black Jag, too," she finished with relish. She leaned toward Leah. "On the cue-T, girlfriend, I told Gerald to lose the 'Swinger' license plates."

Leah's eyes widened in surprise. "And just when did you have the opportunity to tell him that?"

"I could tell you it was during the conversation we had outside your building the Sunday before last, but I won't. I wouldn't want you to think I was butting into your business or anything."

Leah forced a smile to her lips. "Now, why would I think something like that about you?"

"Merri, you did say the guy was cute, didn't you?" Stacia asked, wiggling her eyebrows.

"As a bed bug. Which is exactly where I'm betting he'd like to be with sister-girl here."

Grimacing, Leah picked up her glass and downed half the contents.

"Oh pah-leez," Danye spoke up. She took a drag of

her cigarette and blew the smoke into the air. "You two need to quit. Merri, you wouldn't know cute if it bit you on the rear end. The last time you let a man near you was what, ten years ago? And you," Danye huffed, crushing her cigarette in the ash tray as she turned to Stacia, "are just plain pi-ti-ful. I guess you've already forgotten how cute little ole David left your butt high and dry. How many times has he called since you gave out your digits?"

Stacia squirmed uncomfortably in her chair. "None. But it has only been a week, Danye."

"Get real, girl," Danye said, puffing to light another cigarette. "That man ain't going to call you, Stacia. It's a line. Men say that crap just to get you off their back. But do you listen? No, you don't. Your silly butt will be sitting there, right by the phone, waiting for a call that's never going to come."

"Shove it, Danye."

"Back at you, babe. If you had any sense you'd know these Chicago brothers are a trifling bunch and I'm through with the lot of them," she said, blowing smoke out the side of her mouth. "I plan to cross the line for my next man. I'm getting me a white boy."

"You're the one who needs to quit, Danye," Merri said. "You ain't no more going to lie down with a white man, than I'm going to be President of these United States."

"You're probably right. I do prefer my coffee black, but haven't any of you ever wondered what it would be like to try some cream?" When none of the women concurred, Danye sat back and crossed her legs. "Well, I have."

"Then take your silly talking butt to the African American Book Center and pick up some reading material on slavery," Merri retorted.

"Listen here, girlie. I already know about slavery and for your information..."

Knowing how much Merri and Danye liked to spar,

Ja'Nise interrupted. "I know Gerald Morris. He's the best friend of the guy I'm dating or rather was dating. Those boys come in here all the time."

"What else do you know about them?" Stacia asked.

"Only that they have money to burn. They're starting a record label and they come to hear the bands. Damn, I wish I could remember what else Peter said, but as I recall I was little tipsy then, too, and Peter didn't give up much info."

"A little tipsy hell," Stacia commented. "Your butt is drunk."

"Don't even let me get started on you, Miss I-can't-hold-my-liquor Waters. Anyway, Gerald is the executive director of that foundation that's been in the news so much lately." Ja'Nise's brows furrowed as she tried to remember the name. "You guys know the one I'm talking about. They work with children and send them to college."

"You mean The Path?" Stacia asked.

"Yeah, that's it." Ja'Nise shrugged her shoulders. "Anyway, that's all I know."

Rachel had been staring at Leah throughout the conversation. Envy colored her features and her eyes glazed over in fury. It was inconceivable that Leah had not only Michael Ray Dupree panting after her, but also another rich and attractive man who wanted her, too. She narrowed her eyes and leaned forward, resting her elbow on the table. "Tell us some more about Gerald, Leah."

Puzzled, Leah looked at Rachel. "I've already said there's nothing to tell. We had a couple of dates. End of story."

"Real-ly." Rachel sat back, crossed her legs, her gaze unwavering. "Now, I wonder if that would be because he found out about you and Michael Ray Dupree."

"Oh, oh," Ja'Nise whispered to herself. Stacia's eyes

grew round, then lowered to the wineglass in her hand. Danye puffed on her cigarette. Merri's green eyes flashed fire.

Leah stood up. "You know, Rachel, I usually make it a point to try and find something good in every one I meet. But I can see it would be a waste of time to try and find something nice about a bitch like you."

When Leah picked up her purse and walked away from the table, Merri jumped up. "Lady, I suggest you call it a night, because if you're still here when I get back, we'll be throwin' down in Club Raymond this evenin'."

"That goes ditto for the rest of us," Ja'Nise added.

In the bathroom, Merri went over to Leah. "I'm sorry, sweetie. I don't know why Stacia invited that puttin'-on-the-Ritz, ain't-got-a-clue, much less the manners to go along with those my-daddy-was-rich-airs, which every-one knows is a lie, bitch."

By the time Merri stopped to take a breath, Leah was laughing. "Are you finished?"

Their eyes met in the mirror and Merri laughed, too. "I don't know. How about if I add this? If Rachel's still there when we get back to the table, we'll kick her butt."

"Merri, that's absurd. Three grown women rolling around on the floor in Club Raymond would look ridicu-lous."

"Yeah, you're probably right. It might be fun though. We haven't had a good rumble since high school. Remember big Bertha?"

"I do. But I still don't know why you jumped her. That girl was four times your size."

"I jumped her because of what she said about you."

"Me? I didn't hear Bertha say anything about me."

"I know. But I did, and I didn't appreciate her calling my best friend a skinny butt, light-skinned Negro with good hair who had no business trying to lead a rally for black folks and saying that you should take your half-white butt on home. And that's the cleaned up version."

"Merri! You mean to tell me that we were suspended from school because you started a brawl over a comment someone made?"

"No, Leah," Merri replied patiently. "We were suspended because the principal thought we were the radical element, and he wasn't having no militant Black Panthers in his 'skool.' Anyway, Rachel's not worth it, so don't let her ruin your birthday."

Leah turned from the mirror. "People like Rachel don't bother me anymore, Merri. I just don't understand what the woman has against me." Then she smiled. "But then, I don't really care, now do I?"

"Good for you."

Leah checked the time on her watch. "It's still early. Let's get back out there and get this party started again."

"Lead the way, girlfriend; I'm right behind you."

Looking over her shoulder at Merri, Leah stumbled back when she ran headlong into a very large and hard body. Her gaze traveled upward from the strong hands keeping her on her feet to light brown eyes that were blazing.

"Gerald!"

"It's time for you to go home."

Leah shrugged off his hands. "You can't tell me what to do, Gerald Morris. Why don't you just go away, again?"

Gerald noted the slurred words and watched Leah try to stand straight. "I'll repeat this only once, baby girl. It's time for you to go home."

"Leave me alone," Leah responded.

"Yeah, leave her alone," Merri added. "Come on, Leah, let's go back to our table."

Both women found themselves hauled up against Gerald's sides. Peter's look was a question when he stopped at the bar. "I'm taking Leah and Merri home and

I'd suggest you go and get yours. If these two are any indication, Ja'Nise is just as loaded. And have Raymond call a cab for the others."

∽

Sitting in the middle of the bed, Leah dabbed at the tears in her eyes and snuck a peek at the man standing off to her left. Gerald's anger was very apparent and she bit her down on her lip to stop a giggle, then swiped at a tear on her cheek. This was the reason she didn't normally drink; she couldn't control her emotions when the liquor began to wear off.

"Thank you for bringing me home, Gerald," she whispered. Actually, Leah wasn't at home. At least, she was pretty sure she wasn't, because she didn't recognize any of the things in the room. When Gerald didn't respond, she leaned back on her hands and surveyed the immense space. It was almost twice the size of her entire apartment and he seemed to favor mahogany furniture. She fingered the boldly-striped hunter green, gold and maroon silk spread covering the giant four-poster bed. Matching end tables sat on both sides and a twelve-drawer dresser with gold handles sat off to her left. Pictures covered the top of the wardrobe sitting across the room to her right. Those, she would like to see more closely, and Leah contemplated leaving the bed. She changed her mind when she looked at Gerald again. He hadn't moved and looked as stiff as one of those guards that stood outside Buckingham Palace.

She turned her attention back to the room. State-of-the-art electronic equipment filled mahogany shelves built into a wall covered in pale gold cloth, narrowly striped in hunter green. Trees, in massive pots, sat on the maroon-carpeted floor on either side. She couldn't see anything in the sitting room except a large mahogany table and the green drapes hanging from a window. It was an elegant bedroom and bespoke a man with sophisticated tastes.

Leah glanced at Gerald again and fell back on the bed in a fit of giggles.

"Why were you in that club tonight, Leah, and what were you drinking?"

Leah stopped laughing and sat up. She scooted to the edge of the bed, hopped down to the floor and weaved her way over to Gerald. "Because, silly boy," she said, "today is my birthday. And you," she added, waving her finger around in the air, "didn't come to my party."

Gerald caught Leah around the waist when she lost her balance and kissed the top of her head. "It's time for bed, little one."

Gerald fed Leah aspirin and orange juice to help ease the hangover he knew she'd suffer in the morning. By the time he'd removed her clothes, dressed her in one of his pajama shirts and tucked her under the covers, Leah was asleep.

He sat on the edge of the bed and studied the oval face with its delicate, brown skin and shock of dark lashes. The tip of the tiny nose was red, the cheeks rosy and her mouth seemed to form a slight pout. She looks like an angel, Gerald thought, kissing her temple. He left the bedroom and went downstairs to his den. Shaking his head, Gerald toppled to the couch and turned on the music. He hadn't known it was Leah's birthday. If he had, his baby wouldn't have had to celebrate by drinking herself into a stupor. This was the last year that would happen.

Gerald leaned his head back on the couch and closed his eyes. The trip to LA and his exhausted state brought the reason for his sudden departure from the city to mind, along with the memories of Hunter Reece, the motivating force behind the establishment of The Path. A major talent under the TyJo umbrella at eighteen, Hunter's first album had shot to the top charts. In the middle of laying tracks for the second, Hunter hadn't shown up for a scheduled recording session. He'd missed so many sessions there was no way the album would meet its announced release date. Fed up, Gerald had gone to his condo and found Hunter dead in his bed, a crack pipe in his hand.

That had been the turning point for Gerald. The music he loved. Widespread acceptance of drug use in the business, dealing with the egos of rising young stars, parties that lasted into the wee hours of the night, and the city, he hated. Gerald had stayed as long as he could stand it. Then needing to get away from the insanity, had handed full responsibility for the day-to-day operations of TyJo Productions to J.J., and left LA. That was two years ago. The print shops, while therapeutic, were nowhere near as satisfying as the thing he loved most. Making music was as natural to Gerald as breathing and he missed playing a direct role in TyJo. Locally though, he was back on the scene and for now, that was enough. And as of right now, even that would take a back seat while he focused his attention on the woman upstairs in his bed, the woman Gerald had acknowledged on the plane ride home as the one he wanted at his side for the rest of his life.

Fourteen

The next morning, Leah awoke and sat up in the bed. Still groggy, she rubbed her aching head and tried to get her brain to focus. This was not her room and certainly not her bed. The last thing she remembered was encountering Gerald in the club. Something beside her moved and Leah was stunned to find him in the bed with her.

Oh, no! What had she done last night? She couldn't remember and frustrated, Leah lay back against the pillows and covered her face with her hands. How had she ended up in bed with Gerald Morris? Gerald awoke a few minutes later and smiled when he saw Leah's shaking head and covered face. Then he narrowed his eyes. Watching Leah kissing another man had made him so angry, he'd wanted to punch the guy and give her the spanking she deserved. That she was drunk was no excuse. It was payback time, and the little minx deserved this. Gerald pushed himself up and tugged Leah's hands down. He kissed her on the cheek. "Good morning, baby girl." The soft whisper of his voice fanned over Leah like a seductive breeze. Gerald lowered his hand to her breast. "You were very good last night, Leah. I hope that we can continue where we left off." He lifted his body over hers and lowered his head.

Leah didn't see the mischief dancing in his eyes as she bucked beneath him and thrashed her head from side to side to avoid his mouth. Gerald used his hand to hold her face still. "Nothing happened last night, Leah. However, I think it would be best if you left the booze alone in the future."

She gawked at him when he shifted to his side of the bed and noting his bare chest, grabbed the spread and pulled it up to her chin.

"How's that head of yours this morning?"

"Fine," she replied. His brow rose skeptically. "Well, it does hurt a little."

Gerald left the bed and returned with aspirin and a glass of water. Leah took the items, making sure she kept her eyes on the legs of his pajama bottoms. Through her lashes, she peeked at his full frame and suppressed an involuntary moan. Power, confidence and charisma radiated from Gerald. It was so magnetic, Leah felt like an iron plate being drawn to him against her will. Desire began to simmer and Leah diverted her attention from the hard physique in front of her, realizing that while Gerald might not have made love to her last night, she wouldn't mind if he did this morning. Shocked by the train of her thoughts, Leah closed her eyes and swallowed the pills.

Gerald took the glass. "Are you hungry?"

Just about to respond no to his question, her stomach chose that moment to growl, loudly.

"I guess that answers that." Gerald picked up his robe and turned for the door.

"Where are you going?"

"To the kitchen."

"If you'll give me something to wear, I'll go with you."

"It's not necessary. You stay right where you are, woman. I'll be back shortly."

Leah's mouth formed a lazy smile. Until Gerald, never before had a man cooked for her or served her breakfast in bed. She had to admit that Gerald was spoiling her big time and that she enjoyed the attention. Having forgotten most of what she'd seen last night, Leah inspected the room again. When Gerald returned carrying a bed table, she sat back against the pillows. "This is a lovely room, Gerald."

He smiled and crossed the floor. "Thank you. I'll give you the nickel tour later."

He placed the table across her lap and Leah looked down at the tray. The pineapple boat had cubes of honeydew and cantaloupe, strawberry halves, raspberries and whole green grapes. The fruit dish had a creamy yogurt topping sprinkled with slivers of almonds. The slice of nut bread had a smiley face drawn with orange flavored butter. There was also a glass of freshly squeezed orange juice, a pot of tea and a small white vase filled with red geraniums.

She lifted her head and his heart jerked. Gerald sat on the edge of the bed and gently wiped away the solitary teardrop on her cheek. He winked at her and encouraged her to eat. Leah picked up a piece melon with her fingers, then looked at him. "Aren't you having anything?"

Copper and silver orbs linked, united by the electrified currents drawing them into a sexually energized web. Staring at Leah, Gerald reached for the melon in her hand. Popping it into his mouth, he chewed slowly, swallowed, then abruptly left the bed. A few minutes later, Leah heard the shower. Drained and enervated, she began to eat the food he'd prepared.

Gerald came out of the bathroom wiping the side of his face with the towel hanging around his neck. Very aware of the physical tension still flowing between them, he resisted its pull and removed the table from Leah's

lap. The cold shower hadn't helped and if Leah continued to lie in the bed staring at him with those vivacious,
gray eyes, he knew what was going to happen. They
needed distance. He needed distance or Leah, who
seemed innocently unaware of her feminine allure, would
be ravished. "Now, might be a good time for you to take
a shower, then I'll give you that tour, sweetheart."

Leah studied him, silently debating whether to leave
the bed. She had a clue about her effect on him all right
and wondered what she should do about it. What would
Gerald do if she left the bed and kissed him on the lips?
Seeing the smoldering embers his eyes had become
gave pause to that thought. Lifting her shoulders in con-
sent, Leah left the bed for the bathroom and greatly disturbed by his scrutiny, moved quickly to the door and
slipped inside.

Closing the door, she turned around and stopped.
The room was large and two of its walls were windows.
The others were lined with mirrors, but everything else
had been constructed in green marble. It was everywhere, from the raised Jacuzzi and wet bar to the walls
and floor. She was even more surprised to see her
things laid out on the marble counter. Her white denim
dress hung on a rack and a pair of white sandals was on
the floor. When had Gerald gone to her apartment? She
was never getting drunk again. Though she looked longingly at the whirlpool tub, she stepped into the double
shower and after finishing her toiletries and dressing,
returned to the bedroom.

Gerald, dressed in an aqua polo shirt and a pair of
white shorts that emphasized his long brown legs, held
out his hand. "Ready?"

Leah could feel Gerald's excitement as he led her
through the house. He was like a kid getting his first
glimpse of the presents under the tree on Christmas
morning. To cover her own agitation, she made the

appropriate noises as he opened the door to each room. Besides his suite, there were five other bedrooms on the top floor. Two belonged to Audrey and Reggie; the other three were mini suites with full baths, walk-in closets and window seats. The rooms differed only in the dominant colors of rose, beige or teal used in the decor.

Leah fingered the hand-carved oak banister as they moved down the stairs to the main level. At the bottom, Gerald turned to his left and opened the doors to a sunken living room. Inside the black and white setting were a wall of windows, a black lacquered baby grand piano and a massive white marble fireplace. The formal dining room, paneled in African mahogany, had Baccarat crystal chandeliers, and gold satin covered the seats of the chairs at the mahogany table. The deep wine and ivory family room was a gadget lover's dream. The copper-accented kitchen, a chef's delight, and the colorfully decorated recreation room had a walk-in dollhouse with Audrey's pink Corvette parked out front.

On the lower level, Gerald led Leah around the video arcade, the private gym complete with bleachers, the sauna and weight room. Then he took her back up the steps for a tour of his glass-enclosed office center and the backyard. Now they stood outside another door and when he opened it, Leah took in the consoles, microphones and sound booths. She turned to Gerald. "If you no longer make records, why do you have a recording studio in your home?"

"I still dabble in music." He took her hand "We'll talk more about that in a few minutes. Come on. There's one other room I'd like to show you."

Gerald led her back through the house to his den. Leah sat on the couch and surveyed the vaulted ceiling, mahogany paneling, massive grey stone fireplace, dark gray leather furniture, steel gray carpet and jazz mural taking up the entire wall behind the bar.

Gerald took her hands in his. "Leah, anything you don't like in this house can be changed. This is my sanctuary. I like it the way it is, but even in here you are free to do what you like."

Leah frowned in confusion. "Why are you telling me this?"

"I love you, Leah. And when you're ready to become my wife, this will be your home, too." Concern darkened his eyes when Leah left the couch and went to the windows. "What's wrong, sweetheart?"

Leah fixed her gaze on the trees at the far edge of the property. Gerald's home was a palace, fit for a queen, and filled with all the lovely things a queen would want. Only, she wasn't that queen. She turned to face him. "Gerald, you have a beautiful home and I thank you for the tour. But I could never live here with you."

Taken aback, Gerald's mouth fell open. "Leah, why?"

"This house represents everything I've been trying to get away from for the last three years. Will you please take me home now?"

"I just told you that I love you, Leah, and I think I deserve to know what is going on. Why don't you come away from the window and sit over here by me?"

"No! I want to go home!" Leah ran from the room and didn't stop until she was sitting in the Jaguar.

Bewildered, Gerald watched her go. He retrieved her purse and followed her out to the garage. "Leah, I'm going to take you home, but only because you're so upset. But one day, and soon, you're going to talk to me and tell me what that was all about."

"Thank you," she whispered when he started the car.

∾

Right on her heels when she opened her apartment door, Gerald bumped into Leah when she stopped abruptly. He moved her aside and stopped himself, then curved his arm around her shoulders. His eyes assessed the damage as he waited for Leah's reaction to the trashed apartment. All she owned had been tossed about, smashed, shredded, ripped, slashed or turned over.

Leah wiggled free of his arm and ran to the bedroom.

"Leah! Don't go in there," Gerald yelled, following her. He stopped in the doorway and a sick ache pounded his heart. Her bedroom was worse. The bed and dresser mirrors were shattered. Her clothes from the closet and dresser drawers, scattered about the room. He wasn't sure, but it looked as if someone had used a sledge-hammer on the waterbed frame and a knife to slash and stab holes in the mattress. Water still leaked and every-thing on the floor was sopping wet. The perpetrators had been thorough in their destruction.

Leah was on her knees searching through the items on the floor. Gerald tried to pull her up from the mess. "Leah, we have to call the police."

"The keys! I have to find the keys!"

"Whoever did this didn't need any keys."

Leah grabbed him by the front of his shirt. "No! Your keys! The keys you gave to me. I have to find them." She scrambled away again.

Gerald couldn't believe it. Her apartment lay in ruins and all Leah could think about were the keys he'd given her. Watching Leah where she sat in a puddle of water, Gerald regretted ever sending them to her. He sighed. "Okay, Leah. If those keys are still here, we'll find them together. Then we'll call the police."

∾

A few minutes before sundown, Gerald sat on the beach and watched Leah stroll through the surf. She was back in his home, but he knew she didn't want to stay, especially since she had asked him to take her to her mother's and he had refused. He wanted Leah here, where he could keep his eye on her.

He felt bad for Leah. One kitchen chair had somehow escaped the destruction and he had put Leah in it while she called the police. Everything else she owned was destroyed, not that she'd had much. The bedroom had been fully furnished, but except for the kitchen table and what he considered stick furniture in her living room, Leah's apartment had been virtually empty. No pictures had graced the walls, not a green plant in sight to take away the barrenness, no decorator touches to make the place a home.

Concerned that she needed money, he'd asked about it. Her explanation that since she was never there it hardly mattered just didn't ring true. He knew she'd lived in the apartment for a while. Surely, in all that time, Leah could have done something to make her surroundings more comfortable and inviting. He hadn't pressed her after her reaction this morning, but Gerald had every intention of bringing up the subject again in the near future.

"Leah!" he called when a large boulder threatened to take her from his view. "Come and sit with me, woman." She ran over to him and the tiny keys tinkled on the bracelet on her wrist. Gerald settled her between his legs and kissed her cheek. "Everything you lost today can be replaced, Leah."

"I know," she replied somberly.

They sat together quietly, watching the sun set in all its fiery glory and a flock of screeching gulls diving into the lake for their evening meal. At twilight, with the first sprinkling of stars dusting the sky and the breeze from a rising wind cooling the air, Gerald turned Leah in his arms and hugged her so tight she couldn't move. "I am so thankful you were here with me last night. I don't know what I'd do if I lost you."

He released her and Leah asked, "If that's true, then why didn't you call me last week?"

"A friend and business associate needed my help. Back-to-back meetings and late nights kept me tied up most of the time. When I had a few minutes, I did try to call, but I couldn't get through to you. I left messages with your new secretary. By the way, I've been meaning to ask you, what happened to Diane?"

"Nothing. Why?"

"Well, when I called yesterday, a man answered your line. He told me that that you would be in meetings all day. I left the message that I was on my way home. He said he'd make sure you got it."

The name Joe came to Leah's mind immediately "If you ever call my office again and a man answers, do not under any circumstance leave messages with him, and make sure you tell me about it. Ask for Diane, she's still my assistant."

"Okay, sweetheart. But it sounds like this man might be giving you some trouble. Tell me about him; perhaps there is some way I can help."

"It's nothing I can't handle on my own.

"Okay," Gerald replied as he wondered how long it would take to have the people in Leah's office checked out. Basking in the glow of having her in his arms, Gerald looked up at the darkening sky and began counting the stars. Leah's voice broke his concentrated effort.

"The police think the break-in was a random hit, but I'm not so sure it was."

"That's probably because two other apartments were also broken into, and none of you were at home last night." However, while the other apartments had merely been burglarized, Leah's had been destroyed, a fact Gerald hadn't overlooked, though the police hadn't seemed to make the connection. In his mind, that made the matter very personal.

"That's true, but..."

"Gerald! Dinner is ready and I'm going home."

Gerald waved to Mrs. Melcher, his housekeeper, and pulled Leah to her feet. "Stop worrying about it, baby girl. You're safe and that's all that matters. Let's go in now and have our dinner."

Fifteen

Surrounded by darkness and the sweet sounds of Kenny G, Leah lay on the couch in the den. She had already taken a bath and wore the silk jacquard gown and matching mint wrap she'd allowed Gerald to purchase. After talking to the police, he had driven her directly to Oakbrook Center, an open air mall on the outskirts of the city that while perhaps not as celebrated or upscale as the Magnificent Mile, held a charm all its own. There they had engaged in several verbal skirmishes over who was going to buy what in the various stores where they had stopped. Gerald had wanted to purchase an entire new wardrobe, but Leah, sure some of her things could be salvaged, had bought only a minimum of clothes. She was thinking about the break-in and was sure Michael Ray was involved somehow. Only there was no way she could prove it. If only there had been some sort of clue connecting him to the crime. She frowned when the lights came on and Gerald walked into the room with something under his arm.

"I thought you might like a little entertainment to take your mind off, other things." He placed a backgammon board on the table and set up the game. "And just so you know, I have no intention of being beaten by a woman."

Leah swung her feet to the floor. She had thought to tell Gerald that she was an expert backgammon player. Now, she was going beat those sexist pants right off of him. "Okay," she replied. "Let's give it a go."

Seven games later, Gerald threw up his hands. "What are you—some kind of hustler? Why didn't you tell me you were so good at this game?"

"Because you needed to learn a lesson. You're a male chauvinist, Gerald."

Gerald placed his hand over his heart. "I am no such thing. I'm a happenin' kind of guy and I'll have you know I can cook and clean with the best of them."

She rolled her eyes. "Right."

"Leah, I love women."

"Sure you do," she smirked. "If they're in the kitchen. Those little goodies you left in my apartment last week were good clues as to your thought process regarding the female gender."

"I cannot believe that you of all people would say something like that to me."

"Protest all you want, Gerald Morris. But let us not forget who just beat whom seven times."

Gerald laughed and packed up the game. He stretched out on the couch and Leah settled against him. It was a few minutes later that she felt a thud on her stomach.

"Even though you ran a scam on me at backgammon, I want you to know I'm not the kind of man who holds a grudge."

Leah sat up. "What is this?"

"Your birthday present. Open it."

She turned the gift over and untied the red ribbon. After removing the gold foil wrapping paper from the red velvet jewelry case, Leah looked at Gerald, who, not sure of her reaction, had moved to the fireplace. He cocked his brow at her.

Leah popped the latch and slowly lifted the lid. The bracelet was exquisite, a 24k gold band encircled by eight rubies and ten pear-shaped diamonds. Several minutes passed before Leah snapped the box closed. Rising, she crossed to Gerald and held out the box. "Thank you. This bracelet is beautiful, but I can't accept it."

Gerald jammed his hands into his pockets. "It's a birthday present, Leah."

His stare pierced her back when Leah moved to the couch. She tossed the case on the table. "My birthday was yesterday and letting me stay in your home is present enough."

At the mall, they had clashed every single time he had tried to buy something for Leah. Most of what she did buy, she'd purchased with her own money. He had tried to understand her rationale, but Leah had talked in circles and after the day they'd had, his patience had run its course. Gerald strode over to her and held Leah by the shoulders. "Why can't you take anything from me without an argument?" he blasted.

Leah twisted from his hands and moved to the window to escape the line of fire.

Gerald attempted to rein in his temper as he watched her. "This wouldn't have anything at all to do with Michael Ray Dupree, would it?"

Leah turned around slowly. It didn't surprise her that Gerald knew. Everyone in Chicago knew about her and Michael Ray. What did surprise her was that it had taken Gerald so long to mention it. Her spine stiffened in defense. "Michael Ray has nothing to do with this. The bracelet is very nice, but I don't want it."

"Why?" Gerald asked with deadly calm.

"Look. I don't need you or any other man to buy things for me. I can take care of myself."

"I can tell. Your house of sticks was lovely."

Her bottom lip trembled. "That remark wasn't necessary, Gerald."

He sighed wearily. "You are right and I apologize, but

I don't understand why you find it so distasteful to accept a simple gift from me."

"Simple, Gerald? Ha, that's a laugh. There is nothing simple about a bracelet that cost hundreds of thousands of dollars. Those rubies and diamonds are flawless. I know. I used to own a lot of them."

"Used to own?"

"Yeah, Michael Ray had me fairly dripping in jewels and every bit of them were purchased with drug money. I don't want anything that reminds me of that time in my life." She turned back to the window. "It makes me feel…it just makes me feel so guilty."

"Why should you feel guilty—unless you knew all along about Dupree's line of work?"

"I didn't know he was a drug dealer until after I broke up with him."

"After you broke up with him? I thought that was why you broke up with him."

"No. It wasn't."

"Then why?"

"That's something I'd rather not go into now."

"Okay. But how could you not know Michael Ray sold drugs for a living? When someone is involved on a scale as large as he was, there are usually some outward signs."

Gerald waited through a lengthy silence before he walked up behind Leah and turned her to face him. He picked up her hand and placed it on his chest. "Do you feel that?" Leah nodded. "That's where you are, Leah. In my heart. Nothing can ever change that. I am not going to hurt you and I am not going to judge you, but there is something I need from you, Leah. I need you to trust me."

Trust? Gerald didn't know what he was asking. She had trusted Michael Ray and for the last three years she had been living under a cloud of shame for allowing her-

self to be played for a fool. But Gerald was not Michael
Ray and hadn't she told herself the very same thing just
last night? "I was sixteen when I met Michael Ray
Dupree, and against the advice of everyone around me,
I jumped headlong into a relationship with a man thirteen
years my senior. I never knew about the drugs because
Michael Ray successfully kept it hidden from me, and he
wasn't a street dealer, he was a trafficker. He received
the shipments and dispensed them to the people who
sold them locally. I thought I was engaged to a real
estate developer. He told me his parents were killed in a
plane crash and that most of his money had come from
their life insurance policies.

"I saw Ray on the weekends or on breaks because for
most of the relationship I was away at school. When we
did see each other, he would fly me out of town to attend
some business function or vacation in the islands. Ray
and the circle of people he introduced me to were rich
and powerful and very overwhelming to a young girl.
Ray dominated my life. He decided the course of the
relationship. He decided what we would do, what I would
wear and who I would meet. The man had total control
over me and the sad part is, I let him." Tears filled Leah's
eyes, but she steadfastly held them back.

"But I liked the clothes, the jewelry, the trips, and I no
longer cared about the people or issues that had once
been very important to me. That's why I've tried so hard
to change and that's why there was nothing in my apartment that I cared about. I don't like the person I became
when I was with Ray."

Gerald pulled Leah into his arms. The self-recrimina-
tion she felt showed in her face. His finger lifted her chin.
"Leah, you were a teenager and a grown man used your
age to his advantage and swept you off your feet, knowing that he could influence a child. But that was long
ago; inside, where it matters most, you know what kind

of person you are. You are not someone who cares more about material things than people. If you were, then you couldn't devote the time and energy you do to helping others."

His head lowered and Leah melted into his arms, returning the kiss. She tightened her arms around his neck when Gerald tried to pull away, drawing him deeper into her embrace. Placing his hands on her waist, Gerald didn't raise his mouth from hers as he lifted Leah and took her to the couch. The wrap was off before he knew it and the gown soon followed. His heartbeat accelerated and lusting hunger gripped his body at the sight of her breasts. He grazed the pads of his thumbs over the nipples, then bent his head.

"I love you, baby girl," Gerald murmured, trailing wet, hot kisses down the column of her neck. He moved lower until his lips encountered a stiff peak and he took her into his mouth.

"Yes, Gerald. Yes," Leah sobbed in short, jerky pants.

She raised his head and her mouth moved with feral intensity over his face, memorizing each feature. She teased the tip of her tongue at the diamond in his ear and her teeth nipped at the skin on his neck. His hands glided down and pushed the full, luscious mounds of her breasts together and his mouth moved back and forth between the two. Lost in the mystic pleasure of having Leah beneath him, Gerald latched onto one and suckled greedily.

Leah gasped and arched, then rode the explosive tide of pleasure in a long, drawn-out moan. On her descent to earth, the urge to feel Gerald was so strong Leah tugged desperately at the shirt covering his back. She wanted to feel the taunt, rippling muscles beneath her hands, lie against him skin to skin. "Let me...Help me," she whimpered.

Gerald sat up and removed his shirt, allowing Leah

the access she craved, then again took her breast into his mouth. Her soft cries set fire to his loins and his full arousal threatened to burst through his shorts. Leah took his head in her hands, pulled him up and attacked his mouth. "Love me, G. Make love to me and help me forget."

It took several moments before Leah's words penetrated his passion-induced fog. When they did, Gerald wrenched his lips away and sat up. Breathing harshly, he battled to bring himself under control.

Leah leaned up on her elbows. "Gerald, please. I want you to make love to me."

Gerald's heart stopped and his head snapped up. It only took a moment for him to discern that while Leah's eyes held a passionate plea, it was not in response to any feelings she had for him. She hadn't offered herself to him to satisfy a passionate need only he could fulfill. Leah needed him to help assuage the guilt she felt over her involvement with Michael Ray Dupree. And Gerald refused to let her use him for that purpose. He wanted her love and he would settle for nothing less. Leah drew back at the austere set of his features. He exhaled deeply. "Do me a favor, Leah, and go upstairs to bed."

He saw the hurt that flooded her face at the tone of his voice and watched Leah try to repair the emotional wall around her feelings. Gerald looked away from the rapid rise and fall of her unclad chest.

With each breath the sharp pain pinching her heart increased. What had she done? Leah tried to catch his eye, but Gerald wouldn't look at her. What had she done to make him act this way? She pulled on her gown and rose from the couch. "Okay," she said, her voice faint.

Gerald didn't move until Leah left the den. Earlier that day, while Leah talked on the phone with the police, he had searched through the rubble of her apartment. Finding the note had been a shock; seeing the TyJo stationery it was written on had shaken Gerald to his very core. He withdrew the piece of paper from his pocket.

"Responsibility for your apartment lies with the man at your side. Gerald Morris is dangerous and not who you think he is."

Leaving the couch, Gerald opened a safe hidden in the mural and tossed the note inside. His shoulders slumped as he turned away and moved back to the couch. Gerald knew he had made enemies in LA, and one in particular had sworn to take him down. Montgomery Wallace! A drug-addicted, sexually-perverted, two-bit player in the music industry. Montgomery Wallace had made most of his money from bootlegging the tapes of his artists. Gerald had exposed Montgomery and been influential in shutting down his label. Gut instinct told Gerald that Montgomery was somehow connected to the destruction of Leah's apartment. But he had to be sure. If it turned out that he was, Gerald wanted to deal with the man before he told Leah about the note or TyJo. Until then, all he could do was make sure that at all costs, Leah was protected.

Sixteen

June 23

Feeling better than she had in over thirty-four years, Linda stretched her arms lethargically above her head and looked down at the man snoring softly at her side. She smiled as she ran her hand lightly over Malcolm's broad chest. For thirty-four years, she'd thought that she hated Malcolm for the pain and humiliation he'd caused her. After only one night in her husband's arms, Linda now knew differently. Now she knew that she'd always held on to the hope that Malcolm would return. And now that he had, everything would be right again. Malcolm could again be a husband to her and a father to their children.

Their children! Linda suddenly pulled a shaky hand back into her lap, a frown of worry lining her face. Her children still didn't know about Malcolm and that was because Linda had yet to work up the courage to face her son. And she couldn't tell Beth without telling her baby. Though she'd repeatedly played out the scene in her mind, Linda knew that her imaginings didn't come anywhere close to what would really happen when she told Gerald about his father.

She slipped from the bed, donned a robe and headed for the kitchen. The coffee had just finished brewing when

Malcolm's still strong arms surrounded her waist.

He dropped a kiss her on the cheek. "Mornin', darlin', he said.

Releasing her, he picked up a mug and poured himself a cup of coffee. He carried it to the kitchen table, sat in a chair and watched Linda move around the room. He'd tried several times to talk to Linda over the last few days, but her irate outbursts kept putting him off. So far, the only connection they had made was in the bedroom. Linda had always used anger as a shield when she didn't want to deal with something, but he wasn't going to let her stop him this time. The time had come for him to speak his piece. Malcolm leaned back and Linda set a plate holding a cheese omelet in front of him. "Looks good, darlin'," he said.

Linda seated herself. "Let's eat before it gets cold," she responded, bowing her head. After the blessing, she picked up her coffee cup and gazed warmly at her husband. It was good that Malcolm was back. There were times after he'd left that Linda had lost hope and more than once she'd almost given up. She'd survived because of her children. They, especially Gerald, had helped her through the bleakest of times. She remembered the dimes and nickels he'd worked so hard for and gladly handed to her. Though her son still continued his role of taking care of his family, things were vastly different now. But Linda could pretend things were the same, and that Malcolm had never left her.

Malcolm picked up his cup. "Linda, when I came here two weeks ago, I came to talk to you. I wanted to explain why I left the way I did."

Linda's world of pretense shattered like crystal and she set her cup down on the table. Why did Malcolm have to say that? Why couldn't he just leave it alone? "I don't want to talk about this, Malcolm. Not now. Not ever!"

Malcolm shook his head no. "Linda. Please. I understand your feelings about this, but I would appreciate your listening to me."

Her chair scraped back on the shiny wood floor and Linda crossed her arms in front of her. "Okay, Malcolm Morris. You want to talk. Then talk! You talk, and you tell me why you left your pregnant wife and two-year-old daughter alone in that place."

"I never meant to hurt you, Linda, and I didn't plan to leave. I left for work that morning with every intention of coming home just like I had every day for five years. But do you have any idea how it felt to walk day after day through those trash-filled streets to that run-down building? Then enter that raggedy apartment and see your smiling face, knowing this was the best I could do for the woman I loved—and that it wasn't going to get any better?"

"Malcolm, I never complained."

"I know, darlin'. You never did." Malcolm sighed. "It was me. When Damon died, I couldn't handle it anymore. I tried, but the thought that I had killed my son ate away at me until there was nothing left."

Linda's eyes filled with tears. After a short illness, their son had died at the age of three. "Malc, you weren't responsible for Damon's death. We did everything we could to save him. It was pneumonia."

"I am responsible, Linda! Our son died because I didn't provide for him. Damon would be alive if I had been a better father. I was a failure, Linda. A failure as a husband, as a father and as a man. That day, I couldn't do it anymore. I just couldn't make myself walk up those steps to that apartment." Malcolm hung his head and set his cup back on the table, letting his arm fall to his lap.

"So, what you're telling me—is that you left me alone in that god-awful place because of your pride. Is that what you're saying to me, Malcolm? The woman who loved you so much I left a home in the suburbs to live with you in that ghetto."

This time Linda was the one who left the table to pace the floor. "The woman who bore you three beautiful children, one of whom you didn't stick around to welcome into this world, and who took what little money you did bring home and stretched it so that you always had heat, water and three meals a day. Is that what you're saying to me? Well, you want to know how I felt, Malcolm? Do you want to know what it felt like to work your fingers to the bone for the man you loved, only to find out that he didn't love you enough to stay by your side?"

"That's not true, Linda. I did love you! It was because I loved you that I left. Because of me, we couldn't even qualify for government assistance and when that hospital turned us away because we didn't have medical insurance and my son died, I knew I had to get out of your life." Malcolm dried his face with his hands. "I had to give you a chance, Linda. I had to give my children a chance. When I walked away, I knew they would have to help you. I also prayed you would find someone else. Someone who could get you and my children out of that place."

Linda whirled around with an astounded look on her face. "And just how many men do you think came knocking at my door, Malcolm? How many men did you think would come into the ghetto looking for an abandoned woman with two small children?"

When he didn't answer, Linda's face crumpled with pain. "Well, I'll tell you, Malcolm. None! No one came to help me. I got my children out of that place. Me! Alone! By myself!"

When Linda dissolved into tears, Malcolm tried to take her in his arms. She knocked his arms away and went back to the table.

"Linda, I'm sorry. I was wrong to leave you, but at the

time I couldn't see any other way. I know nothing I do now can make up for the past, but I'd like a chance to try. I love you, Linda, and I'd like to get to know you again and let you get to know me."

Linda raised her head. Her eyes glowered at him. "I don't want to get to know you, and I don't want your love."

"What about our children and Reggie and Audrey? Don't they have a right to know their father? Their grandfather?"

Linda's entire body shuddered with the intensity of her emotions. She picked up her cup and sipped from it before responding. "Yes, Malcolm, they do. I'll even arrange for you to meet my children. But understand this. If Gerald and Beth don't want you in their lives, that is the end of it. And if by some miracle they do, if you ever hurt my children the way you've hurt me, I'll make sure you regret it for the rest of your life."

Leah stood in the window of her office looking down at the river with vacant eyes. When the view turned foggy, she turned away and moved stiffly back to her desk. The strain she felt had etched itself into every plane in her face and her jumbled emotions churned in her stomach.

One day. That's all she could take being near Gerald after what had happened between them on Saturday. On Sunday, he had apologized and professed his love over and over. On Monday, Leah had taken a couple of days of vacation, packed her bags and returned to her apartment. The service had done a thorough job cleaning up the mess. She'd found her clothes hung up in the bathroom and while the cleaning bill would be huge, most were undamaged. Sleeping on the floor last night had proved uncomfortable, but Leah didn't care. She would have slept in a tree to get away from Gerald Morris.

She had just finished sorting through her clothes when her mother's birthday present had arrived. It had been welcomed. Returning from the cleaners and finding Gerald sitting on the front steps had not. She had let him inside and even managed to say 'thank you' when a furniture truck parked in front of her building and Gerald had the men unload a new bedroom and dinette set. They had worked in near silence while arranging the new furniture to her liking. Then Gerald had asked her to change her mind about staying with him, and she had asked him to leave. Leah never knew a man could rant and rave for so long, but she had stood her ground. And she wasn't going to back down. She might love Gerald...

Her mind stopped and Leah brought tremulous hands to her face. Oh, God! She couldn't possibly be in love with Gerald Morris. It was too soon! Her chair was suddenly under her and Leah wasn't sure how it had gotten there. The idea that she loved Gerald was so astronomical her mind took the thought and began an in-depth study. During the evaluation, the phone rang and Leah's hand perfunctorily picked up the receiver. "Leah Ellis."

Gerald heard the wooden tone and his spirits sank lower. "Leah, it's G. How are you, sweetheart?"

The resonant timbre set her heart to fluctuating. Not now. She couldn't talk to Gerald now. "I'm fine. How are you?" Was this her voice? How could she sound so calm?

"Not so fine, baby girl," Gerald said. If he were going to have any chance at all, he had to keep it in check this time. "Leah, would it be all right if I picked you up for lunch today?"

Her stomach did a somersault and Leah grasped the phone. She couldn't see him. Not after the realization she'd just had. Her eyes lit on the Houston folder on her desk. Joe had already been in her office twice this morning. She couldn't go with Gerald, even if she wanted to.

"I can't go to lunch today. I have a deadline."

His temper began a moderate simmer and determined not to let it reach the boiling point, Gerald counted to ten, then twenty. Satisfied with his effort, he continued, "Okay, sweetheart. I know how busy you are. What about having dinner with me on Friday?"

Leah almost said yes, then remembered her birthday dinner with Tony. Thank you, Lord, for the small blessings, she prayed. She relaxed her hold on the phone. "I'd like to, but I already have dinner plans with a friend on Friday."

His temper returned immediately. "Leah, I know what you're doing and I'm not going to let you push me away. You're busy on Friday and I accept that. But on Saturday, I want to see you. Cancel any prior commitments and I'll plan something for the two of us."

Leah stood up and pulled the telephone cord across her body as she tapped her foot. It sounded like Gerald had just issued an order. "I'm busy on Saturday, and I have to go. I'll talk to you another time."

Leah heard the sharp intake of breath and held the telephone away from her ear just as Gerald Morris detonated. "Leah Ellis! Don't you dare hang up on me!"

"When you learn to speak to me in a proper tone, I won't have to hang up on you." Leah dropped the receiver into its cradle.

Gerald hung up and shoved his body back into the chair in his office. No matter what she'd said, he was going to see Leah on Saturday. He never should have allowed her to leave his house. Persuading her to come back now would be like pulling teeth. Gerald sighed dismally. Leah needed him and if she wasn't so obstinate, she would see that. She was right though. He did need to stop yelling at her. It wasn't helping and only made her more determined to defy him. Well, he wasn't sure how he was going to handle this situation with her yet, but at least she was being protected. In the meantime, he needed to work off this tension. Gerald looked toward the doors of his suite, then at the telephone on his desk. Dousing his desires with another freezing spray of water was not an ordeal he was willing to put himself through right now. He'd rather call Pete and meet him at the house for a game of B-ball.

Seventeen

June 25

Tony, you have to stop making me laugh. I'm not going to be able to eat and I've been told the food here is really good."

Tony tucked her hand beneath his arm. "Okay, Leah. I won't tell any more corny jokes. Let's go. Our table is ready."

Entering the establishment, Gerald's head came up when the sound of a euphonic voice reached his ears and vibrated through him. His eyes glinted as they traveled Leah's backside. Then lifting a shoulder, he quickly dismissed the notion forming in his mind. Leah had said she was meeting a friend for dinner and that's all it was, he assured himself.

"Mr. Morris, if you'll follow me, I'll take you to your table. Your guests have already been seated."

Gerald followed the hostess across a cat paw-print carpet to his table. When he found it located directly across the room from Leah, his stomach began to churn.

Peter stood up. "G, I'd like you to meet, Marcus Wilkins, manager of Mattise."

"It's good to meet you, Marcus." Gerald shook the offered hand, but his mind was across the room. When he sat down, the churn in his stomach turned to twinges of apprehension. He's just a friend, Gerald told himself again, even as he felt a stab of pain in his heart. But why did the friend have to be the man from the party? Was he the reason Leah didn't want to see him? No, Gerald thought, answering his own question. They had fought and she was upset. Tomorrow, though, he'd apologize again. Leah would forgive him and they would be all right. Wouldn't they?

"Your club soda with a twist should be here any moment, Mr. Morris," the hostess said, drawing his attention. Diverting his eyes to the hostess, Gerald pushed his doubts aside and took the menu she held out. Though calmed somewhat by the talk he'd given himself, the ache in his heart hadn't gone away completely and he glanced at Leah again.

When Gerald's drink arrived, Marcus raised his glass. "Boys, let's talk record deal."

❧

Tony pushed in Leah's chair and leaned over her shoulder. "You look very pretty, Leah," he whispered in her ear.

Leah set her evening bag on the table and faced him. That was his fourth compliment of the evening and he had been acting a bit odd all night. "Thank you, Tony."

He placed a chaste kiss on her temple and moved around the table, unbuttoning the jacket of his black pin-striped suit to take his seat. Tony ogled the midnight blue, baby doll dress canopied in a glittering mesh. Its shine competed with the curls on Leah's head. A gold bracelet with little keys, circle drop earrings and a watch sufficed as her jewelry. Leah wore very little makeup; then again she didn't need it. Tony smiled. If he wasn't already in love, he'd swear he could fall all over again.

Leah looked down on the shimmering lights of downtown Chicago from forty stories above the Chicago Stock Exchange. She turned back to Tony and found him staring at her with that look in his eyes again. She liked Tony and was having a good time, but she had never had any romantic thoughts about him because Tony was...well, he was just Tony.

Tony picked up his menu. "So Leah. How long have you known Merri?"

"What?"

"Merri Taylor. You've known her for a long time, haven't you?"

Leah studied his face. When realization hit, she smiled. Tony didn't have any feelings for her. Tony liked Merri. She decided to let him spill the beans in his own way. "I've known Merri since junior high school. Why?"

"She has a little boy, doesn't she?"

"Yes. His name is Jimmy."

"What kinds of things does Jimmy like to do?"

Leah put her elbow on the table. "I think that's something you should ask Merri." Then unable to hold on to her new found knowledge a moment longer, Leah asked, "Tony, do you like Merri?"

Tony grinned. "No, Leah. I like you." Leah slumped back in her chair. This was the second time this evening that she'd misread his signals. She sat up straight at his next words. "I love Merri."

Leaving her chair, Leah moved around the table and punched Tony playfully in the arm. Then she threw her arms around his neck and hugged him. Tony hugged her back and Leah returned to her seat. "Anthony Nolan Wright, you've been toying with me all night. Why didn't you just say you liked Merri? Better yet, why don't you tell Merri?"

Tony leaned forward on the table. "Leah, I've tried to tell Merri, but every time I go near her, the words stick in my throat and I end up telling a dumb joke. She scares me to death."

Stunned, Leah sat back in her chair. She never would have pegged Tony as unsure of himself. Tony did like to tell jokes, but, Gerald excepted, she had never known a man with so much confidence. How many times had she watched him schmooze a client, put them at ease with a joke, then move in for the kill? Leah couldn't believe this was the same man. "But, Tony, there's no reason for you to be afraid of Merri. She's as nice and kind as they come. Merri is a good woman. She needs a good man and you, Mr. Wright, fit that bill."

Tony picked up her hand and placed a kiss on her knuckles. He continued to hold her hand when he lowered it to the table. "Thanks, Leah. But will you help me out? I want to get next to that woman so badly, I can hardly sleep at night."

Did she have any choice? Tony and Merri were her best friends and they deserved to be together. "Of course, Tony. I'll do everything I can to help."

The jealous rage roared so suddenly it almost knocked his breath away, and Gerald couldn't stop the thoughts scurrying into his mind. That man wasn't Leah's friend. He was her lover! All this time he had been laying the foundation for them and Leah was in love with someone else. Now he understood why she refused to take anything from him and why she didn't want to live in his house. As the chasms of pain widened, hurt male pride washed his face with angry heat. Gerald blew out an indignant breath and tried to bring himself and his temper under control.

"Our lawyers will draft a contract and we can have something for you to look at on Monday. Right, G?"

"Yep."

Peter leaned toward Gerald. "You okay?"

"I'm fine," Gerald muttered darkly.

"You don't look fine. You look like you're about to explode."

"Gentlemen, let's have a toast," Marcus said, raising his glass. "Mr. Morris, I am aware that you are no longer associated with TyJo Productions and though we won't have the backing of the label, Mattise and I look forward to working with the G-man of Music. Here's to a long, healthy and profitable relationship."

Gerald raised his glass and glanced at Leah. A long, healthy and permanent relationship, he silently modified.

Gerald had been sitting in his car for over an hour when he finally saw headlights turn onto the street. Turning off the music, he tried to cap the wild fury threatening to erupt when he saw Leah sitting in the car. When she stepped out, burning emotion crystallized the light brown gaze following Leah and her escort as they made their way up the walk. Gerald watched the clock. Two minutes was about all the time that man had to come out of the building or Gerald wasn't sure what he would do. Tony left a few minutes later and Gerald stepped from the Jag. He saw the light in Leah's apartment go out.

"Oh no, sweetheart," he said, crossing the street. "Tonight you deal with me."

Leah had stripped to the lacy blue teddy she'd worn under her dress and was standing in the closet when the racket started at her door. She reached for a kimono, and wrapping it around her body, rushed into the living room.

"Tony, did you forget some—" Her voice trailed away when Gerald straightened and faced her.

"Obviously, you were expecting someone else."

Gerald moved into the apartment and closed the door quietly behind him. Leah backed up when she saw the inferno in his eyes. Disillusionment shone in hers. Not you, too, she thought, pulling a hand through her hair. Her eyes skittered to the left, then to the right before she turned and headed for the bedroom.

"Did you enjoy yourself tonight?"

Leah stopped so suddenly she almost tripped. His question told her Gerald had seen her with Tony. His insinuating tone implied that he had drawn the wrong conclusion. When she turned around, Gerald stood so close his woodsy cologne filled her senses. Leah inhaled deeply to control the harsh breaths rushing her lips. "Tony is my friend and he's also my boss."

"Yeah? From my vantage point the two of you looked really friendly. In fact, a little too friendly. So, why don't you try again."

Leah thought she could have been mistaken, but it sounded as if Gerald was accusing her of telling a lie. No one called her a liar. Especially not Gerald Morris, to whom she owed no explanations. "My personal life is not up for discussion. Please see yourself out. I'm going to bed."

Two steps were as far as Leah got before strong, tapered fingers on her forearm spun her around. "I asked you a question and I want an answer." Gerald towered over her like a large brown bear awakened prematurely from its winter's nap. "Who is that man and what is he to you?"

Leah jerked her arm from his hand and focused a hardened glare on him. "What are you doing, Gerald Morris? Following me around? We had a couple of dates and a couple of kisses. And I believe I did remember to thank you for letting me stay at your place. But my personal life is just that, personal, and none of your business."

A stony gaze appraised Leah. She was beautiful, standing there with her hands on her waist facing him down. His eyes fastened on the mound of golden flesh visible through the open robe. Leah looked down and gasped. She tried to close the robe, but only succeeded in making the garment fall completely open.

Gerald sucked in his breath. "Did he touch you?"

With fumbling fingers, Leah finally closed the robe. "You have no right to ask me that."

"You will never see him again," Gerald stated emphatically.

His remark had her fuming and Leah impaled him with her eyes. "Just who do you think you are, Gerald? I am a grown woman and I do not have to explain anything I do to you." Once she got going, Leah didn't stop. She wanted to hurt Gerald, just like he had hurt her. "But you know what, G? If I did decide to sleep with Tony, at least he would take what I offered. He is not a boy playing at a man's game. And that's what I need, Gerald. A real man."

The dauntless speech was not what he had expected and respect and admiration lit his face. It was only there for a fraction of a second and did not stop the anger that ignited at her combative stance and recalcitrant attitude. A second later, a pair of sturdy hands had Leah dangling several inches from the floor.

"So. You need a real man, huh?" Gerald mimicked. "Well, baby, you've got one!"

His lips crashed against hers and within moments, a battle ensued in a kiss that was as hungry as it was punishing. With their mouths pushing, tugging and tussling, each vied for mastery over the other. Leah gave as good as she got until she surrendered to the flames licking at her body and moaned into his mouth.

Sensing victory, the kiss of anger swiftly became a kiss of passion. Gerald mated his tongue with hers, then caressed the inside of her cheeks. He raised his head and set Leah on her feet. His hands tunneled through her hair to the back of her head as his eyes bore into hers. "You already have a man, Leah Ellis. Me! And tonight I'm taking what you're offering. Then we'll see who is a boy playing at a man's game."

His mouth closed over hers again and Leah stood stock still in her awareness that she'd pushed him over the edge. When images of what was about to happen flickered, she immediately began flailing her arms and hitting out at Gerald, grappling to free herself from his arms. At first, Gerald ignored Leah's struggles, intent on making her see reason. Then the thought of what he was doing broke free and Gerald lifted his head. Seeing the fear in her eyes, he eased his hold on her body and buried his face in her hair. "Oh, God, Leah. I'm so sorry. I didn't mean for that to happen."

Leah hit out at him again; her hand landed on the side of his face. "Let go of me," she shouted. He released her and she stood in front of Gerald, her chest heaving in shuddering gasps. She wrapped her arms around her body. "Get out of my house."

Gerald moved slowly toward her. "I am sorry, Leah. And all I can say is that I lost my head for a minute and that it won't happen again."

Leah backed away. "No! You get out of my house and don't you ever come back!"

Gerald kept advancing until she hit a solid mass and slid down the wall. He knelt down in front of her. "Please, Leah. Can't we talk about this?"

"No!" She placed her hands over her ears.

Gerald took them down and held them. "Leah, I promise it won't ever happen again."

Leah lifted tear-soaked eyes to look at him. "Why, Gerald?"

He examined her tortured face. While he felt guilt over

his own actions, he couldn't help noting that Leah's reaction seemed a little out of proportion to what had amounted to little more than a kiss. But he knew she deserved an answer. "Because I saw you with Tony, and I didn't like it."

Eighteen

E yes bright with unshed tears stared back at Leah
from the bathroom mirror and her hand shook when
she reached for the tap. She lowered her head to
splash cold water on her face and tried to clear her mind.
It had been wrong to fight Gerald, but looking at him, she
had seen the same emotions in Gerald's eyes that had
once fired Ray's, and afraid for her life, she'd fought him.
She would never stand passively in the wake of a man's
anger again.

Gerald sat on the bed and waited. His mind wouldn't
let him erase the accusation he'd seen in Leah's eyes.
But even through the magnifying remorse, his heart
hammered inside his chest. Leah was his and he'd do
whatever it took to keep her. He stood up when she
entered the room and walked to meet her. She held up
her hand and he stopped. Leah examined him from
head to toe.

Gerald wasn't Michael Ray and he hadn't done the
things Ray had done to her. She had to learn to set aside
the past. That meant accepting Gerald for the man he
was and leaving behind her distrust of men. He opened
his arms and Leah walked into them. Holding her tightly, Gerald hooked his arm under her knees and carried
her to the bed. Kneeling down in front of her, he held her
head in both hands. His mouth wandered over her face

and he groaned when he reached her soft, fleshy lips. Gerald devoured her mouth. "I need you, Leah."

The intensity of his kisses weakened her; the plea in his voice lured her and Leah reached for him. She needed the solace Gerald offered and she dissolved under the pressure of the mouth hungrily possessing hers. Desire rose from the pit of her stomach, erupting like hot lava. She wrapped her arms tightly around his strong neck. "I need you, too," she said before joining Gerald in the fiery furnace melding them together.

Her words fanned the flames torching his body and he couldn't remember ever wanting a woman more than he did right that minute. Gathering her closer, Gerald deepened the kiss. Not wanting a repeat of what had happened earlier, he gently worked his lips against hers until Leah relaxed in his arms. With a deep moan, she pulled back and laid a small hand along the side of a bearded cheek. "Gerald. Make love to me."

Reaching deep down inside himself, Gerald found the will he needed to momentarily suppress the wild desire teeming his body. Leah needed comforting. She needed to be held and cuddled. What else did she need beyond that? Did she really need him, as she'd said? With these thoughts running through his mind, Gerald rose to his feet. For a few moments, he gazed down lovingly at Leah, then turned away.

Through her lashes, she watched him remove his clothes and return to stand in front of her. She took in the full majestic sight of him. Gerald was everything Leah had envisioned him to be. Formidable in his stance, her African lover was ruggedly handsome, dynamically impressive, and distinctly, hugely male.

Butterflies skirted her stomach and Leah took a concentrated interest in the floor. Her hands fidgeted with the folds of her wrap as panic set in again. Sensing her anxiety, Gerald lifted her chin. "I love you, Leah," he said, his voice a delicate whisper against her lips. "As long as you believe that, nothing else matters."

Gentle hands helped Leah to her feet and slid the robe off her shoulders and Gerald turned Leah away from him. She drew a steadying breath when his large brown hand swept her hair to one side. He placed a scalding kiss on her nape and the air whooshed from her lungs. Gerald fluttered kisses along soft shoulders. He tilted his head, trapping a fleshy earlobe between his teeth. He suckled for a moment, then let it go. "Do you know how long I've wanted to do that?" he whispered.

"N-n-no." She stuttered the word in a rush of emotion.

"Since the party," he breezed in her ear, sliding the straps of the teddy down her shoulders.

Gerald cupped Leah's breasts in the warmth of palms and tenderly kneaded the soft full mounds until they grew taut and heavy. He caressed the stiff, sensitive tips with the pads of his fingers. At her throaty response, his hands slid sensuously down her body.

Leah moaned and closed her eyes in acceptance of the spinning sensations floating her away. Pure, sweet agony. Gerald's kisses had only been a prelude to this night. Her skin was on fire and only his lips could cool the feverish intensity of his tantalizing touch.

"Gerald," she cried out breathlessly a moment later, when the feathery touch of his beard and his firm lips scorched her backside.

"Yeah," he answered through lips that continued moving down her body. Gasping sobs poured from her throat and Leah tried to turn her body toward him. His hands encircled her golden brown shoulders and his mouth followed the lacy blue undergarment he inched over the mounds of her hips, down her legs and all the way to her feet. Gerald laid kisses on her buttocks, then retraced his path at a torturously agonizing pace back to her shoulders where he spent an inordinate amount of time buzzing his lips along her shoulders. He nuzzled the side of her neck and tilted his head toward her ear again.

"Do you know how long I've wanted to do that?"

Erratic whimpers answered him. Succumbing to the spasmodic convulsions rocking her body, Leah couldn't respond. At her yielding, Gerald panted in her ear. "Ever since you sat across from me at the dinner table."

Turning Leah into the circle of his arms, he raised her soft body against his rock hard masculinity. Her arms draped his neck and Gerald laid her reverently in the middle of the bed, before quickly joining her. Her arms encircled his waist and her hands roamed the muscular back and chest above her. He caught and held the roving hands at her sides and charted a path down her front to her belly. Gerald didn't stop until he'd reached the heart of her womanhood. At her convulsive tremors, he blazed a new route back up to her breasts where Gerald feasted. He lovingly laved each velvety surface as if he were enjoying the smooth creamy taste of an ice cream cone until Leah called out his name. At her cry, he took the nipple into his mouth and nurtured it lovingly before paying the same homage to its companion.

Leah arched against him. Why didn't he just take her? He had filled her with a white hot need, led her to the edge, then pulled her back before she could cross over the border to utopia. She wanted him so badly she thought she would die. When Gerald released her arms, her frenzied hands explored the downy softness on his face and the tightly strained muscles of his back.

"No more, Gerald, please. Please make love to me," Leah finally begged, shutting her eyes against the tidal waves of bliss surging her body.

Gerald unlocked her arms and raised himself from the bed. Her face blushing with desire, Leah sat up and watched him retrieve a small silver packet. She gulped and watched in fascination as Gerald slipped on the latex covering and rolled the condom over his long hard length. He moved back to the bed and kissed the frown of worry on her forehead.

"Don't worry, baby girl. I am not going to hurt you."

"I know," she whispered.

Laying Leah down on the bed, Gerald took her mouth in a demanding kiss and positioned himself at her center. He began his entry into her body, stopping when he felt not only her resistance, but her body's as well.

No! She couldn't be.

Gerald scrambled off Leah and pulled her up. "Baby girl, are you untouched?" Leah lowered her chin to her chest. "Answer me, Leah. Are you a virgin?"

She nodded her head and moved to leave the bed. Gerald's hands gripped her around the waist. "Where do you think you're going?"

"I thought you didn't...I don't know."

"You're not going anywhere, sweetheart."

He laid her down on the bed again. "Leah, when I told you I wouldn't hurt you I didn't know that you had never before made love. Now you listen and do exactly what I say. When I come into you I want you to hold onto me and relax. I promise this will be over in a few minutes."

Gerald slipped between her legs and his lips began an amorous excursion over her body that left Leah limp and wet with the heat of desire. Knowing she was ready, Gerald's hands glided down to raise her hips and he pulled back. His mouth descended to cover hers right before he thrust forward.

Leah squeezed her eyes closed and reflex had her fingertips digging into his back when Gerald entered her body.

"Relax, baby girl," he whispered. He eased himself inside, allowing her body time to adjust. "Hold on to me and relax."

When he had filled her, his burnished brown gaze got

lost in a passionate gray sea. "I love you, Leah," Gerald growled as he withdrew. "I am yours and you are mine!"

In minutes, Gerald had laid claim to Leah and established what would become their rhythmic harmony. He stroked her gently at first, then more fiercely as he lost the battle to control his desires. Leah stayed with him, accepting each powerful thrust of his relentless pace that branded her as belonging to him.

Waves of pleasure washed over them both and teetering on the brink of ecstasy Leah began her ascent to the summit. His mouth covered hers and they exchanged feverish gasps. His breathing became harsher; his jaw clenched tighter and grasping her hips, Gerald accelerated his tempo until he heard the cry of his name from her lips. With one final drive into her fiery softness, he propelled them both into a dizzying haze of blinding, euphoric rapture.

Gerald picked up a curl, rubbed the tendril between his fingers and let it fall back to the head of the woman asleep on his chest. The carnal tension in his body was gone, but his face held a different kind of stress. He looked down at Leah, who purred like a kitten as she slept on top of his chest, remembering how soft and pliant she'd been in his arms and the sweet sound of his name on her lips. He hadn't allowed Leah many rest breaks last night and by all rights he should be exhausted, but his mind was in turmoil.

How had Leah come out of an eight-year relationship with Michael Ray Dupree, a virgin? It was one of the questions keeping him awake. From what Gerald knew, the man didn't strike him as the type who would refuse to take a woman, especially when she was his for the taking.

The other question though, bothered Gerald much more than the first. Leah had just given him the most precious gift a woman could give. In the heat of passion, she had said she needed, even wanted him. But she hadn't spoken of loving him. That she waited so long and that he'd been the recipient had to mean something. And if it wasn't love, then what exactly was it that Leah felt for him? Gerald wanted answers. He knew they would have to wait. With tender hands, he moved Leah to the bed and got up.

An hour later, she stirred. Gerald watched Leah stretch her body and cross her arms under her head. When her lids drifted open, she squinted up at him and smiled. It was a knowing smile, and one that acknowledged her new status as Gerald's woman.

He scooped her from the bed.

"Wait," Leah gasped. "Where are you taking me?"

He brushed his lips over hers as he walked across the bedroom. "It's time for your bath, beautiful lady."

"It's four in the morning, Gerald."

"I know, but you'll sleep better after a soak in the tub."

Leaning over the tub, Gerald's movements were gentle and his eyes thoughtful as he ran the cloth over her body. Leah reached up a hand and laid it on the side of his face. "What are you thinking about?"

"Leah, how did...? Why haven't you...?" His brown eyes glazed over her face. "It's nothing," he finally said, standing up. Taking two fluffy white towels from the rack, he wrapped them around Leah as she stood and lifted her from the tub.

Back in bed, Leah snuggled her body against Gerald, her fingers playing in the hairs on his chest. "I want you to know that I like making love to you. And that I plan to do it often."

Gerald smiled softly and stilled her hand. It wasn't an admission of love, but it warmed his heart nonetheless.

"That's good," he said, nuzzling the side of her breast. "Because I plan to fulfill that request."

Her body reacted immediately and under Leah's guidance, Gerald navigated the course over her body. "That's it, baby," he murmured softly. "Show me what you want me to do."

Dissolving in the currents of liquid pleasure flowing through her limbs, Leah sank into the pillows, luxuriating in the things Gerald made her feel. At her urging, he lay on his back and Leah spread open-mouthed kisses over his face before she kissed her way down his upper torso. She took one of his nipples into her mouth and circled it with the tip of her tongue.

Gerald's stomach formed a concave when her hand found him and began toying with him. A blast of raw lust tore through him when her lips replaced her hand. "Enough!" he shouted a few minutes later, his voice a strangled cry. Leah glanced at him and continued her ministrations. "Baby girl, please," he implored in desperation a minute later. Leah raised her head and climbed on top of him. Gerald gripped her to his chest tightly. "Marry me, Leah."

Surprise stole over her face as she considered his request. "You don't really mean that, Gerald. This is just a reaction to…to our being together."

"No, baby girl. I do mean it. I want to share my life with you. Marry me, Leah."

Rather than respond, Leah lowered her head and kissed him with all the passion she could find inside. Aching with need, Gerald gripped her hips and thrust upward. Leah sucked in a gulp of air, then smiled sensuously as she set the pace that had him convulsing in a shuddering climax in a matter of minutes.

∽

June 26

The next morning, Leah moved with care from Gerald's body. She propped her head on her hand and observed him at rest. In sleep, the planes of his face lapsed into a docile repose that was never there when he was awake. Gerald Morris liked to rule and he'd been in control of their relationship almost from the moment they'd met. That did cause Leah some concern, because she'd vowed never again to let a man run her life. She had to find a way to make Gerald see her as an equal and capable of more than being an ornament for his arm. Remembering all they'd shared the night before, she resisted the urge to run her hands over the moving broad mass of his chest, and looked at the clock. It was already nine and she needed to get up. Making sure not to wake him, Leah left the bed and headed for the shower. It wasn't long before Gerald pulled back the curtain.

"I missed you."

"I was hoping you would rest a little while longer. How did you sleep?"

"Perhaps you should look up that word because I don't believe what we were doing would qualify as sleeping," Gerald said, lifting her against the wall.

Leah wrapped her legs around his waist when he moved into her and was soon whimpering through another rushing tide of explosive glory.

Sometime later, Gerald walked up behind Leah and dropped a kiss into her curls. "I'm looking forward to spending the day with you."

Leah finished pulling the shirt over her chest. "I can't spend the day with you."

A baleful look kindled in his eyes. "What do you mean,

you can't spend the day with me?"

"It's the twenty-sixth."

"So, it's the twenty-sixth."

"The house." His expression remained blank. "For Project Spruce," she continued to explain.

"I don't care about that house. I want you here with me."

"I told you about this project, Gerald. It's been on the calendar for months and I have an obligation to be there."

He brought her down on the bed beside him. "What about your obligation to me? I'm clearing my schedule to spend time with you and you should be willing to do the same."

Is this what it would be like? The question was like a light bulb turning on in her mind. Did Gerald think she was going to change her plans just because he told her to? PS was a part of her life and she had a commitment to see this project through. And it wasn't something she planned to argue with him about either. "I'm going to pick up Merri and head downtown. Now, this project will not take up the entire day. When we're done, you and I can get together then."

In the blink of an eye, the forbidding look changed to confrontation. "I am sure that just this once Project Spruce can paint a house without your supervision, Leah. In any case, they will have to get along without you today because you won't be there."

"What did you say, Gerald?"

He rose from the bed and crossed to the dresser. "I said, you won't be there."

Leah's chest heaved with congested fury. "Gerald Morris, by what right do you stand here and dictate to me?"

"The right of being your husband."

"Perhaps you would care to enlighten me as to exactly when we got married."

Gerald turned from the mirror. An alarm went off in his head when he saw Leah's furious face. "Baby girl, I know we aren't married, but we will be soon, and I don't want to argue about this. I just want us to spend some time together."

Look at the two of us, she thought. One night together and already the sparks were flying. One of them was going to have to compromise, and by the look in his eyes it was not going to be Gerald. "This project will not take the entire day, G. We are meeting at ten o'clock and if all the volunteers show up, I figure we'll have this house refurbished and painted by three or four at the latest. Then I will come home and you and I will have the rest of the day and night. Don't you think this is a reasonable solution?"

Gerald sat on the bed and pondered her offering for a minute. "You said three, right."

"Or four, at the latest."

"Okay, sweetheart," he said, rising and walking to the dresser again. "I will expect you at four."

With relief, Leah finished dressing. Turning, she surreptitiously studied the play of muscles in his shoulders and back as Gerald stood at the mirror. There was power in those arms. The power to hold her in a gentle embrace or lash out at her in anger. Going over to him, Leah wrapped her arms around his waist. She placed a kiss in the middle of his back, then picked up her hairbrush.

"Here, let me," Gerald said, taking the brush from her hand.

Their eyes met in the glass. His were clear and full of self-assurance; hers tinged with apprehension and doubt. Leah hoped they could resolve all their disagreements as easily. Frankly, she hoped they would have no further disagreements.

Gerald laid the brush on the dresser and leaned over her shoulder. He kissed her on the side of the mouth and stood straight. "You'd better get a move on or you'll be late."

When she reached the door, Gerald asked, "How would you feel about going to the beach this afternoon?"

"At the house?"

"No, I was thinking we'd go to Fullerton." Fullerton was the locals' beach and Gerald wanted to show Leah off. Unlike North Avenue, with its sand and tourists, grass and concrete rimmed Fullerton Beach's shore line and there was a wooded area where they could find privacy, should their thoughts turn romantic. "We could catch a show afterwards." He wiggled his eyebrows. "Unless you'd rather be alone with me?"

Leah smiled. "Doesn't matter to me. I'm sure I'll like either one. See you later, baby."

Ninteen

L ater that afternoon, Gerald walked into a yard that
was more rocky, brown dirt than grass and knew
immediately that something was wrong. Every face
looked disgruntled and their dissonance grew with each
passing second.

"I don't know about the rest of you people, but I'm
outta here," a male voice yelled.

"Please don't leave," Leah shouted, trying to make her
voice heard above the griping crowd.

Egged on by the group, Fred continued. "Leah, this is
the third time I've given up a Saturday only to find you
don't have anything organized."

"Things were organized, Fred. I don't know what happened. The supplies were supposed to be here," she
replied. "But if you'll give me a few minutes, I'll send
someone to the office to find out what happened."

"Forget it," Fred shouted. "I'm gone, and if the rest of
you were smart you'd be leaving, too."

In a scene reminiscent of Moses at the Red Sea,
Gerald crossed the yard, moving through a throng that
parted with haste. Perhaps it was the volatile tempest
they saw in his face that divided them so quickly.

"And the next time you need volunteers," Fred bellowed, "don't even think to dial my number!" In the next
instant, Fred was stuttering over his tongue. "Wh-who

are you?"

"G!" Leah jumped down from the porch and ran over to him. "Gerald Tyler Morris! You release that man."

Gerald continued to glare at Fred. "I will not. This man owes you an apology and I intend to see he gives it."

The people who had been so intent on leaving turned back and gathered in a circle for a better view of the showdown. Leah felt the hard, taut muscles when she placed her hand on Gerald's back. While she appreciated his need to protect, she did not appreciate that he had one of Project Spruce's best volunteers in his hands. Fred was just blowing off steam and since this was the third time something had gone wrong, he had every right to do so. She knew if they needed Fred tomorrow, he would be there.

"If anyone owes an apology, Gerald, it is you. Now you let Fred go. Now!"

Gerald glanced down at her and with a grunt let his hand fall.

"I'm sorry, Fred. Mr. Morris is laboring under a misconception. Why don't you get a cold drink from the cooler and take a break? I'll let you know when I find out about the supplies."

"It's okay, Leah," Fred replied, still shaking. He glanced up at Gerald. "And I am sorry for yelling at you."

Leah grabbed Gerald by the arm and led him away from the crowd. She folded her arms over her chest and fixed him with a glower. "What are you doing here?"

He stared down at the little moppet in front of him. This morning he had thought she looked cute. Now those gold overall shorts were just a bit too scanty, the turquoise tee a bit too tight, and the sunlight glinting off the shining curls further added to his distraction. He took a quick survey of the yard and felt the gauge on his temper rise when he encountered the lascivious gawks of

the men making no pretense of their interest in the bare
legs Leah had stuffed into a pair of turquoise socks and
gold high top tennis shoes.

Gerald had a hard time quelling the urge to pick Leah
up and take her away from those lecherous looks. He
pushed his hands into the pockets of his cacao shorts
and instead of answering her question, asked his own.
"Why was that man yelling at you?"

She tried to focus on the question and not the little
hairs peeking from the opening of the canary polo shirt.
The color enhanced his spectacular build and some of
the women were practically drooling. The competition for
a good black man was fierce and she knew most of them
would have no qualms about moving in on her.

Knowing that, Leah probably could have made a case
that the heat she was feeling came from the hot sun
beaming down on them, but she'd be lying. The heat she
felt emanated from three things: Gerald, his titillating
effect on her and her mistrust of the women. Leah did
her best to keep her voice composed when she spoke.
"The supplies aren't here, and we've already repaired the
house, cleaned up the yard and fixed the back fence and
the porch. I thought by the time we were finished, Bobby
would have the supplies here." Her voice rose several
octaves and Leah paused to take a breath. "Bobby left
over two hours ago. He's usually so dependable, but
he's not back and the volunteers are leaving and I..."

Gerald pulled her to him. "Calm down, sweetheart.
I'm sure Bobby is on his way."

Leah stepped away. "No, the office is only fifteen minutes from here. I think something's happened to him."

"Okay, let's not blow this out of proportion. Right now,
you need paint."

"And I suppose you have some paint up your sleeve,"
Tony said, walking up. He put his arm around Leah and
drew her to him.

The dark brow arched, but Gerald offered his hand. "Gerald Morris."

Tony ignored the hand. "Anthony Wright."

Sensing the friction, Leah moved away from Tony and stepped closer to Gerald. "What were you saying about paint?"

"That I'll take care of it and whatever else you need. On the way, we'll look for Bobby."

Her eyes lit up. "Do you really mean it?"

Gerald looked down at her with a smile. "Yep."

Leah almost restrained herself from hugging him, then wrapped her arms around his waist. "You stay right here. I want to tell everyone to stick around and get my purse."

"You drive." Gerald held out the key to the Jag. His thought was that it would give Leah something to concentrate on instead of sitting in the passenger seat letting her imagination run wild over Bobby.

Her eyes went to Gerald, the key, the car and back to Gerald. Leah took the key. "Okay."

A minute later, he was having second thoughts when Leah adjusted the seat and the mirrors, then shoved the car into gear and floored the gas pedal, throwing Gerald back against his seat. "You might want to ease up on that foot," he suggested.

Leah laughed. "And you might want to hold on."

Gerald made no further remarks. He sat back and relaxed as Leah easily handled the car. Having her here gave him pleasure. He had tried to find something to do after she left the apartment and had even gone and conducted a session with the children at The Path. But for the first time in his life Gerald found he didn't want to work. He wanted to enjoy life and he wanted to do it with Leah. "Sweetheart, what are you doing on the Fourth?"

"The fourth of what?"

"July, silly. It's next week, you know."

"Is it? I hadn't realized it was coming so soon. Merri hasn't said anything," Leah replied, frowning. "But we've been so busy planning the fundraiser, it's possible it just slipped her mind. Then again maybe she's decided not to do anything this year. I don't know. I guess I'm going to have to ask her about it."

"Leah, what are you talking about?"

Realizing she had been rambling, she looked at him. "I'm sorry. It's just that Merri usually throws a big party at her house on the Fourth of July."

"Leah, I want you to spend the day with me, not Merri."

"But the party. It's almost a tradition."

"Sweetheart, the reason I want you with me is that I'm taking you to meet my family."

"What!" Merri threw a one piece black number back onto the pile of swimsuits. Leah had tried on all of them and was not satisfied. "What do you mean you're not coming to the party? You come every year. It's tradition."

From the dresser where she was bent over a drawer searching through clothes, Leah peered over her shoulder at Merri. "I'm spending the day with Gerald. He's taking me to meet his family." She walked to the bed, picked up the black suit and gave it a crucial once-over, then tossed it back on the pile and returned to the dresser. "I have to find something to wear."

Merri picked up a red bikini and tossed it to her. "Here. Wear that."

Leah caught the suit, but didn't look at it. Her friend was upset and knowing the reason, Leah said, "I know what you're going to say, Merri, but this is different."

"Still the trusting soul, aren't you, Leah?" When the

teeth came down on the bottom lip, Merri crossed to her. "Gerald Morris seems like a nice man, but if you'll recall, Michael Ray seemed like a nice man, too."

"Gerald is not like Ray."

"How do you know? Michael Ray's front was good. But I never liked him and I used to hold my breath and pray every time you went off with him."

"You don't know what you're talking about, Merri!"

"Don't I, Leah? Look at you. You're running around like a chicken with its head cut off searching for something to wear to the beach when any one of these suits will do. You used to do the same thing when you were with Michael Ray."

Leah's body shook with anger. "Gerald is not like him!"

Merri expelled a breath and hugged her. "Leah, if Gerald is truly the one, you know I'm the happiest person in the world for you. But you just met him a few weeks ago. Now you're considering a marriage proposal. Don't you think you should really get to know the man before you make up your mind?"

Leah returned the hug. Their friendship had no conditions and the choice was hers to make. Merri had voiced her opinion and that was that. She would have done the same thing had it been Merri in the same situation. If it worked out with Gerald, Merri would be happy for her and if it didn't, Merri would still be there to help her pick up the pieces. "Okay, sweetie. I promise I'll try to slow it down and get to know Gerald." Leah stepped away. "Now, are you going to help me find something to wear or not?"

Merri folded her arms over her chest. "There is nothing wrong with the suit in your hands."

Leah looked at it and tossed it on the bed. She wanted something different, something that would knock Gerald's socks off and make him proud to be seen with her at the beach. She brightened and went to the dresser again. When she stood up, she held in her hands a hot pink bikini and silk sarong that tied at the hip. Big aqua, lavender, yellow and pink flowers made up the sheer print. Though she wasn't overly modest, the suit didn't leave much to the imagination and Leah hesitated before she turned around and held up the outfit. "What do you think?"

Merri shrugged. "I think it's fine." She gathered up the suits on the bed and tossed them in the closet. "Now that you've decided what to wear, I'm leaving. I'm off to the grocery store to pick up some things for the party." At the bedroom door Merri turned back. "I'm sorry I mentioned you know who. I love you, Leah, and you take care. You're way too pretty to have that face of yours bruised."

An hour later, Gerald knocked.

"Come in, G. It's open."

He did, and a second later his jaw plummeted. He used his foot to close the door. Leah looked stunning, but no way was he letting her out of this apartment in that outfit. He'd be fighting men off all afternoon, and Gerald was pretty sure he hadn't packed a baseball bat amongst his things. He moved into the living room and began to pace. He couldn't just order her to change. He needed a way to make his wishes clear that wouldn't set Leah off. "Baby girl," he began cautiously, "I'm a bit early, so take all the time you need to finish dressing."

"I am dressed." Leah picked up a pink straw bag from the chair. "And I'm ready to go."

His hand came up to rub the back of his neck. "Are you telling me that you intend to wear that outfit in public?"

"What's wrong with it?" she asked, looking down.

Leah turned around and Gerald sucked in air in a hiss. When she faced him again, he took in the mounds of breasts visible above the top. "Leah, you are not leaving this house in that getup." Gerald sat on the cream leather couch and crossed his legs. "I'll wait while you change."

She firmed her jaw as her lids came down in a squint. She had been right about the suit, and she probably would have changed clothes if it wasn't for his attitude. "Then you'll be waiting until the sun turns blue, Gerald, because I have no intention of changing."

He leaped up. "Then the beach is out! Go and put on something else while I decide what we'll do for the rest of the afternoon."

Her brow rose in a camber. "I want to go to the beach."

"I don't care what you want. I said the beach is out." He sat back down and opened the paper. "Hurry up now. By the time you're dressed, I'll have narrowed our choices and you can pick the movie."

Leah shook her head. Gerald was acting like a macho maniac and Merri was right. She really didn't know him. She moved and stood in front of him. "You know, Gerald, it's funny how this relationship works. I talk and you don't listen."

He peeked around the paper. "I hear you, Leah. But I'm not going to be talked into letting you wear those clothes out of this house."

Leah removed the paper from his hands and sat in his lap. "Gerald. When you look at me, what do you see?"

Gerald hugged her to him. "I don't know, baby girl. All I know is, I can't stand to see other men gaping at you knowing you're still free to be with them. But there is a way to fix it."

"What way?"

"Marry me, Leah."

❧

Merri was standing in the fruit and vegetable section considering the tomatoes when someone tapped her on the shoulder. Rattled, she turned, then relaxed when she saw Tony. She smiled at him.

Tony stepped back and returned her smile. "Hiya, Merri," he said. "Seems we both had the same plans today."

"I guess," Merri responded. "My refrigerator's empty and I'm also picking up a few things for the party. You are coming, aren't you?"

"Yeah. I'm planning to be there. How is Jimmy?"

"He's his usual hardheaded self," she replied, selecting five tomatoes and twisting a tie around the plastic bag. She placed the fruit in her basket. "It was nice running into you, Tony. I'll see you at the next PS meeting."

Tony surprised her by falling in step beside her. "So what's next?"

Merri looked into his empty shopping cart. "Tony, I only have a couple more things to get and it looks like you're just starting."

He grinned. "Yeah, but I'll walk along with you, if that's okay?"

Merri shrugged and pushed her cart forward. In the cereal aisle, she looked up. Jimmy had been very specific about what he wanted. It would have to be on the top shelf, she thought.

Tony glanced down at Merri, reached for a box of the cereal and handed it to her. "See how handy I can be to have around," he told her.

Merri thanked him and took the box. Normally, she felt comfortable around Tony. But something was different today and she was beginning to feel kind of weird. She placed her hands on the handle of her shopping cart and looked into his empty cart again. "Shouldn't you be starting your own shopping?"

Tony regarded her for a moment. "No, Merri."

He didn't add anything to the statement and starting moving his cart forward again. Merri stared at his back.

Tony stopped and turned back to her. "What's next?"

Merri shook her head. "I only have tuna left. Then I'm headed for the checkout counter," she replied quietly.

"Let's go," he said, pushing his cart. Merri chewed the insides of her cheeks. Why was he acting so strangely? When she turned down the aisle, Tony was already there. He held two cans of tuna in his hands. "I assumed you wanted the kind packed in water, but I'm having a hard time deciding which brand." He studied the cans as if making a decision of momentous importance.

"I'll take that one," she finally said, pointing.

Tony smiled and handed her the can. "That's the one I was just about to choose," he chuckled. "All done now?"

Merri looked around the aisle, then at Tony. "Where is your cart?"

"Lost it," he replied. He took the shopping cart from her hands and began walking. He glanced over his shoulder. "Let's go."

In the parking lot, Merri took the car keys Tony held out and tried to absorb what had just happened inside the store. Tony had unloaded her cart, paid for her groceries and had just finished packing them in her truck. To break the tension, she said the first thing that entered her head. "Did you hear? Bobby's okay. He wasn't hurt in that car accident."

"I know. I called him at home. He also said that when he got to the office, the door was open and the supplies were gone."

"I know. I've already called the police. They said the same thing they said the last time. It's probably gang-related. Anyway, after what happened today, I think we should purchase cell phones for PS. If we had one, Bobby wouldn't have been rushing to get back."

"Good idea, and an expense well worth the cost. Bring it up at the next meeting and I'll second the motion." Tony pushed his hands in his pockets and shifted his feet as he studied her. He exhaled. "You ever go on dates, Merri?"

Her heart slammed against her chest. What was going on? She tossed the keys from hand to hand as she considered his question. She lifted her head. "Why are you asking me this?"

Tony strove to keep his voice steady. "Well, I was wondering if you'd go out with me?"

"Go out with you?"

"Yeah," Tony replied. "Are you busy on the ninth?"

"No," Merri replied before she could stop the word.

"Hmmm." Tony regarded her again. "Then would you like to attend the Soul Revue with me?"

When Merri didn't answer right away, Tony's nervousness rose.

"Do you have to have an answer right now?"

Tony hid his disappointment. It was only natural for Merri to want to think about his invitation. Their relationship was about to undergo a major change. "No," he replied. "But while you're deciding…" He bent his body, wrapped his arms around Merri and kissed her. It was a modest kiss and did not convey any of what he really felt. He sighed when he raised his head. "Think about that, too." Then he grinned, turned and walked away.

Merri watched him leave with a puzzled look on her face. When he'd driven off, she sat in her car and stared blankly out the windshield. It was a while before Merri started her car and backed out of the space.

Twenty

July 3

Gerald perched the Ray Bans on his nose and turned the key in the ignition. The Porsche roared to life and conscious of the children leaving The Path building, he drove slowly out of the driveway. On the street, he turned in the direction of the freeway and hit the gas pedal when he reached the exit. In a matter of seconds, the elegant red machine was cruising down the road at a little over eighty miles an hour.

He was on his way to see his mother. She had sounded so upset on the telephone, Gerald had immediately left his desk. He might be the male head of the family, but nothing came before the needs of Linda Morris, the matriarch. He would take care of the problem, then head over to Leah's.

The past week with Leah had been like a balm to his soul. She had again turned down his marriage proposal and had seemed amazed when he hadn't gotten upset, but to his mind it was reasonable that Leah would want to slow things down for a while. He only hoped it wouldn't be that long a while. Gerald suddenly chuckled out loud. Maybe he'd finally caught a clue as to how that patience thing worked.

He left the car parked in the circular drive and ran up

the steps as thoughts of his mother returned. The worry
on his face only escalated when he entered the library
and found Linda in tears. He rushed to her and drew his
mother up from the chair. "Mama, what is it? What's
wrong?"

Linda clung to her son and continued to weep. Gerald
heard another sob and looked toward the couch. When
he saw Beth's wet face, anguished eyes and the crumpled tissues she twisted in her hands, his temples began
to throb. Something had happened to one of the kids.
His eyes searched the room. Or William! Oh, God, no!
Gerald thought. Taking his mother with him, he went to
his sister and took her in his arms, too.

"Beth, tell me. Is it Audrey? Reggie? William?" He
wanted to shout out his frustration each time Beth slowly shook her head no. "Jesus!" Gerald exploded. "Will
one of you please tell me what happened?"

Linda lifted her head from his chest. "Baby, you need
to sit down."

Gerald's imagination spun out of control. "Mama,
please just tell me!"

Gaining control over her emotions, Linda stepped
away from her son. "Gerald Tyler Morris, the kids are
fine and so is William. Now, you sit on that couch and
calm down," she ordered.

"Yes, ma'am," he muttered. In light of the seriousness
of the moment, Gerald thought it peculiar when it came
to him that the women in his life were starting to make a
habit of telling him what to do. He drummed his fingers
on his thighs. "Okay, I'm seated. Now, tell me what's
going on?"

Linda sat beside him. "Are you calm?"

"Mo-ther."

"Okay, Gerry. I have something to tell you. But when
I do, I want you to remember I only did it for your own
good. You see, baby, I only told you this because we

were living in that awful place and I didn't want you to grow up thinking there was something wrong with you. I wanted you to be the best you could be. Otherwise, I never would have told you that your..."

They both looked up when Beth gasped. Gerald glanced at his sister, then at the man who had entered the room. Linda drew Malcolm forward. "Gerry, I'd like you to meet Malcolm." Gerald rose from the couch and automatically held out his hand. "Your father."

His arm fell to his side like lead. Father? He looked at the man, his mother, his sister and his mother again. The corkscrews in his stomach turned and Gerald backed away. When his legs hit the couch, he dropped, his face a paradigm of bewilderment. Father? "Mama?"

The poignancy of that one word ripped through Linda's heart. She had to go to her baby. He needed her. She turned to Malcolm. He had caused the pain in her son's face. "Please leave."

"Linda, I want to talk to Gerald."

"This is not the time," she snapped sharply.

Malcolm looked at his family, and at his son in partic- ular, and his shoulders sagged. "You're right, Linda. This is not the time. Tell Gerald I love him and that if he needs anything, anything at all, to please call me."

Linda's body stiffened with indignation. "Gerald does- n't need you, Malcolm. He needs me. His mother. The one who fed and clothed him. The one who changed his diapers and taught him how to walk. The one who taught him how to play baseball, ride a bike, catch a football and drive a car. He needs the parent who calmed him when he had nightmares and sat up with him with he was sick. The one who helped with his homework and scrimped and saved for his college education. He needs the par- ent who explained the birds and bees to him, and lis- tened and helped with his problems. He needs the one who held him in her arms and comforted him when he came home crying because he didn't have a father like the other boys." Linda crossed her arms and sent a glare in his direction. "So. Tell me, Malcolm Morris. Just what did you do for Gerald that would make you think my son would need anything from you or care whether or not you love him?"

Without another word, Malcolm left the library. Linda rushed Gerald.

"Mama?"

Rather than answer, Linda sat beside him on the couch, took Gerald in her arms and rocked her baby, just as she had so often in the past.

∾

For a week, Merri had been thinking about Tony. She'd had no idea Tony liked her and wasn't sure how she felt about it now that she knew. For ten years it had been her and Jimmy. She set the rules and she called all the shots. Letting a man, into their lives now, would change everything. Merri didn't think that was something she was willing to allow.

"What about your son? Doesn't he deserve to have a man in his life?" her subconscious asked.

"He has his father," Merri answered out loud.

"Jimmy only sees that bum once in a blue moon. Doesn't he deserve a full-time father?"

Merri left the couch and was looking out her kitchen window when she saw Leah climb from the Jeep. She left the kitchen and headed for the front door. "Jimmy, I'm going across the street to Leah's. I'll be back in a few minutes."

Merri stepped onto the stoop. Besides, she thought, she couldn't possibly go to the concert with Tony. She already had tickets. "Hey, Leah."

Leah stopped and waved. "Hi, Merri. What's going

on?"

"Nothing but waiting on you, girlfriend."

"Well, come on up. I want to get out of these clothes."

When they entered the apartment, Merri followed Leah into the bedroom. "Can't stay long. Jimmy's home by himself."

Leah dropped her lemon yellow suit on the bed and changed into pink lounging pajamas. They returned to the living room. As soon as they sat, Merri started waving her hands in the air excitedly. "Remember the concert we wanted to attend next Friday and we couldn't get tickets? Well, girlfriend, I got us two," Merri said, thrilled with her accomplishment. When Leah didn't respond, she added, "Sinbad. The 70's Soul Revue. Remember?"

"I remember. I just can't go," Leah replied, a secretive smile on her lips.

Merri frowned at her. "Can't go? Are you serious? This is the Soul Revue we're talking about here. Why can't you go?"

"I can't go, because I already have a date. And I believe you will, too."

Merri scooted to the edge of the chair. "How did you know?"

"Tony told me. That man is crazy about you, Merri, and he wants to take you to the concert. He asked me to ask you to go with him. I think that you should."

"Leah, Tony's already asked me to go himself."

"Get out," Leah said, her eyes wide as saucers. "I can't believe it! He asked me to ask you because he was scared to ask you himself."

Puzzled, Merri shook her head. "Why would he tell you something like that?"

Leah paused for a moment, then decided to plunge ahead. "Merri, do you know people refer to you as the Dragon Lady?"

Merri left the couch. When Leah followed her to the window, she quickly ran her hands over her eyes.

"Merri, I didn't say that to hurt your feelings. It's just that sometimes you come on a little strong, though that's not necessarily a bad thing."

"I know you didn't, Leah. I just never realized I was projecting such a negative image. But sometimes, I get the feeling people are all the time staring at me, just waiting for me to fail. You have no idea how many times Jimmy and I have gone somewhere and people look at us, then at my hand. I can see them thinking. Another welfare mother. Another loose woman taking up my tax dollars to support herself and her child. Well, I'm going to prove them all wrong, Leah."

Leah curved her arm around Merri and turned her around. "I know how you feel." She began again when she saw the look in Merri's eyes. "Okay, so maybe I don't. But you have nothing to prove, Merri. You have a good job and you have always taken care of Jimmy and you're the president of an organization that will be big news one day. So, you just put all 'them' people out of your mind and keep on stepping, my friend." Leah went back to the couch. She sat down and crossed her legs. "Now, back to Tony. You did tell him yes, of course."

"No."

"Why not? That man is in love with you."

Merri turned back to the window. "How do you know? Besides, you can't take anything Anthony Wright says seriously."

"Don't dismiss Tony so easily, Merri. He's a good man," Leah said, wisely. "Why don't you call and tell him you'll go to the concert with him."

Merri faced her. "I can't."

"Why not?"

"You know I haven't had a date in ten years."

"Call Tony, Merri."

"Leah, look at me! I don't even have anything to wear."

Leah hid the smile that remark caused. Merri's closet contained enough clothes to open a fashion boutique. "What were you going to wear when you thought I was going to the concert with you?"

"These jeans and a clean shirt."

Leah tsked her tongue. "Call Tony, Merri."

"I can't. Why can't we just go together like always?"

"Because I have a date with Gerald. If you need a date, then call Tony."

"Leah, please!"

Leah sighed and left the couch. "Okay. What are you doing tomorrow?"

"Nothing."

"Then it's you and me at the mall, and we're going to find you an outfit that will knock Tony's socks off. Now go home and call that man and tell him you'll be happy to go to the concert with him," Leah instructed, walking Merri to the door.

"Leah, are you sure about this?"

"Very sure, and don't you dare forget about tomorrow. I know how you tend to let this sort of thing purposely slip your mind."

"Okay. And, Leah. Thanks."

Leah watched Merri walk down the corridor. Tony, she thought, closing the door. The ball's in your court now, bro.

The wet sand flicked off his feet and hit the back of his legs as Gerald ran through the surf. The footprints left in the dirt were deep and took the surging waves several passes to erase. He had been running for over an hour, and finally exhausted, Gerald fell to the ground. His

lungs labored with his breathing and he didn't wipe away
the sweat pouring down his face. Gerald rested his head
on the rock behind him and tilted his head upward at the
deep blue sky. His body suddenly went limp as the
thought of what he'd been running away from filled his
mind.

His father was alive! And his mother had lied to him.
She had been lying to him his whole life. Why hadn't she
told him the truth? His hands balled into fists as the
answer she'd already given rose in his mind.

"I did what I thought was best, Gerald. How would you
have felt if you knew Malcolm had walked out on us? I
loved you too much to let you grow up thinking that you
were the reason your father left."

Gerald tried, but he couldn't stop the tears stinging his
eyes. He had a father. How many times had he wished
that he had a father like the other boys? Pete had needed a mother. He had needed a father. Jackson and his
Mama had teamed up to raise the two of them. If it had-
n't been for Jackson, Gerald didn't know what he'd be
today. In his heart, he knew his mother had only tried to
protect him and he loved her too much to continue to
place blame on her. He had known his mother was a
strong woman. Now he knew she was stronger than
even he had imagined. She had raised two children
while living with the knowledge that her husband had
abandoned them.

With that thought came rage. Rage so hot, Gerald
struck the rock behind him with his fist. Malcolm Morris
had left his mother and sister in the lurch, and hadn't
cared enough about him to see him born! Now the man
was back trying to weasel his way into the family. Well,
that wasn't going to happen. Not in this life, Gerald
thought. He'd take care of Malcolm just as soon as he
found out what the man really wanted. Thinking it might
help him calm down, Gerald jumped to his feet and

began racing through the surf again.

The man staring at the television wasn't paying any attention to the stock quotes running across the bottom of the screen or the beeping computer letting him know that his requested information was available. Malcolm closed the folders, removed his glasses and rubbed his eyes. He couldn't give his clients good advice if he couldn't concentrate and his mind was on the chaos he'd caused within his family that afternoon.

Malcolm left the table and stretched out on the hotel bed. How was he going to fix this? All he wanted was his family back and so far nothing he'd planned had worked out. Linda was angry. Beth upset. And his son? Gerald had looked like his world had just crashed around him.

Gerald's world, Malcolm thought, smiling a sad smile. He remembered when he'd first read about the twenty-five-year-old music maverick taking LA by storm. The G-man of Music. That's what they called his boy.

The picture of Gerald on the cover of *Rolling Stone* had been taken on the fly and wasn't very clear. But he'd recognize his son anywhere. He'd shown that picture to everybody in the bar and proudly told anyone who would listen that he was the G-man's father. Of course, no one had believed him because, at the time, he had been in his usual soused state and drunks could pull any numbers of claims from the bottom of a gin bottle. That article though, had been the catapult that had impelled him to finally get himself together.

Malcolm's face crinkled in misery when his thoughts took him back to the night he'd left his family. He remembered standing outside the apartment building with raindrops pouring down on his head and staring at the two drunks lying on the stoop. In the two hours he had watched them, they had never moved. When he saw the light come on in the tenth floor apartment and Linda's form in the window looking for him, he had prayed harder than he had ever prayed in his life for guidance. He'd received no answer and had concluded that his family would be better off without him. Believing that, Malcolm had scurried back down that sidewalk and into the nearest bar where he spent the next twenty-five years in and out of a drunken stupor.

Malcolm left the bed when the telephone rang. "Morris."

"Magic! Where you been hiding, blood?"

"I'm not hiding. I'm on leave. Got some business to take care of."

"This business wouldn't happen to include raking in more of them greenbacks, would it?"

"This business is personal," Malcolm snapped tersely.

"Hey, cat. This is Stevie you're shouting at. If you say it's personal, then it's personal. But, my brother, we all know you got the Midas touch, and I didn't want to be left in the dust. But look-a-here, dude, we've gotten wind of a possible new venture and the cats want to know if it's for real. Seems there's this company called TyJo Productions and word on the street is that there is merger in the works and the company's going public. Now, we've already heard the news, and there's no tellin' how many others have, too."

TyJo Productions? That was Gerald's company and Malcolm hadn't heard about any changes in its ownership or financial structure. His son was music personified and TyJo was the preeminent and most successful recording label in the country. Any release from the house of TyJo was certified gold and more often than not, platinum. If TyJo was going public, it would be one of the hottest stocks on the market, and anyone getting in on the initial offering would make a killing. He had to check this out. "Stevie, you cats hold up on this buy. I'll look into it and get back to you."

"Right on, Magic. I'll spread the word to the brothers. Well, gotta jet, dude. Got me a hot filly lined up for the evening."

"Yeah, Stevie. I'll talk at you shortly."

Malcolm hung up the telephone with a feeling of uneasiness. That he hadn't heard about TyJo bothered Malcolm because it meant that someone was possibly spreading bogus news. Now he had to see his son. If it were true no problem, but if it wasn't...

Several times, Malcolm made a tour of the entire room before he finally came to a decision. Tomorrow was the Fourth of July. Linda had always thrown a party on the Fourth and Gerald would probably be there. It wouldn't be a good idea to attend the party, but if he arrived late in the evening, he might be able to get a couple of minutes with his son.

Yeah, Malcolm decided. He would again try to see Gerald by going through Linda. Sitting at the table, Malcolm hit the remote and opened the financial folders. With his mind pulled out of its melancholy funk, he paid close attention to what was happening with the stocks on the computer screen.

Twenty-One

July 4

With one eye, Gerald peered at his watch. Three a.m.? He needed to get out of here. He switched off the monitor in his office and glanced at the telephone. There wasn't any point in calling Leah now, he thought, picking up his keys.

He entered the apartment quietly and found Leah asleep on the couch. When he crossed the room and lifted her, she opened her eyes and gave him a sleepy smile before snuggling her face in his neck. Gerald stopped to catch his breath. Maybe this wasn't such a good idea. He should probably just tuck her in bed and go home. He looked down at her and started for the bedroom again. Tonight, he needed to be near his woman. Gerald deposited Leah on the bed and undressed.

As soon as he hit the sheets, she crawled on top of him. "How was your day, baby?" she asked tiredly.

His chest began to expand in anger; Gerald forced himself to cool down. "It was fine, sweetheart."

Hearing the tightness in his voice, Leah blinked her eyes open. She made a thorough search of his face before she asked, "What happened, G?"

How was he supposed to answer that? In one day, his entire life had been spun on its axis. That wasn't quite

true, Gerald thought, looking at the woman he loved.
Had it only been thirty days ago that he had met Leah?
His hand brushed the curls away from her face and
moved to the back of her head. Bringing her toward him,
he kissed her tenderly, then steered her to his chest
again. "Nothing happened," he said. "Go back to sleep,
baby girl."

Gerald glanced down at the hand lying on the seat
next to him and picked it up. He turned it over and
placed a light kiss in the satiny palm. "How are you
doing, sweetheart?"

"I'm fine, Gerald."

"If you're so fine, then how come you're way over
there when you should be over here next to me?"

Leah moved closer and when he heard the soft sigh,
Gerald squeezed her hand. "Leah, stop letting your
imagination run away with you. It's going to be okay."

Of course it was, Leah thought. For him. In Gerald's
mind, he was simply taking Leah to meet his family. No
big deal, no reason to worry. After several days medita-
tion, however, she had concluded that it was a big deal,
and felt as if she were on her way to an inquisition, where
grilling, evaluation and judgement would take place as to
her worthiness for the male head of the Morris family.
And the closer they got to the site of her trial, the faster
Leah's heart raced.

"Gerald, do I look all right?"

He stole a peek and turned his eyes back to the road.
She looked all right, though he really didn't like the ivory
pants suit. It was a nice enough outfit. It just didn't have
any color and Gerald liked the vibrant colors Leah always
wore. "You look beautiful," he said, driving through the
gates.

Leah's stomach plunged when she saw the sprawling estate. Did everyone in Gerald's family have money? She looked at the line of cars not yet moved from in front of the house. Their friends? It wasn't the money that had Leah so uptight, though Gerald had so much, it made her uncomfortable at times, especially after Michael Ray. No, what had Leah so overwhelmed was the thought that she was about to enter his world, that is, if she passed inspection.

She gave her hand over to the valet and stepped from the car.

At the door, Gerald said, "There is one small matter I forgot to mention." He kissed her when Leah's eyes grew big. "Calm down," he said with a chuckle. "It's only that we sometimes refer to my mother as 'the Barracuda.' Don't take it seriously and don't let her hear you say it."

Shaking now, Leah tried to calm her nerves. She didn't know what to expect when they stepped into the foyer, but it wasn't to be pulled into an immediate hug.

"Welcome to the family, Leah," Linda cried. "I'm Linda Morris, Gerry's mother."

"Mama," Gerald warned.

"Hush up, Gerry. It's just a matter of time." Linda hugged Leah again and passed her on to the next set of arms.

"Hello, Leah. I'm Beth Thompson. Sister and general recipient of nasty little pranks pulled by my baby brother."

"What! How can you say that, NayNay? You know you're worse than I am. And by the way, I owe you big time for the suit."

"That's another thing," Beth said to Leah. "My brother has a really bad habit of not calling me by my given name."

"Hello, Leah." William took her from Beth. "I'm William, husband of the sister and general referee of the little forays those two enter into." He looked down and smiled. "I believe you've already met our two rug rats."

"Hi, Miss Leah," Reggie said, sticking out his hand. "I'm glad you could come with Uncle Gerry today."

Having had no opportunity to speak, Leah crouched down to the children's level. "Thank you, Reggie. I'm glad I could come, too." She turned to Audrey. "Hi, lovey. Do you remember me?"

Audrey nodded and removed the thumb from her mouth. She brought her other hand from behind her back and held out a daisy, then hugged Leah around the neck. When she was released, Audrey ran to Gerald, who promptly picked her up.

Leah heard a loud booming voice as she rose to her feet. "Let me at her!"

Her brows elevated when she saw the dark, rotund giant headed in her direction. A huge pair of arms enveloped Leah, picked her up and squeezed the air from her body.

Peter took her next. "That," he said in her ear, "was Jackson, Randall T., my father." He held her away from him for a moment. "How you doing, girl?"

"Other than being scared almost out of my mind, I'm fine, Peter," she replied.

"Well, don't let this bunch scare you. They're really quite harmless. I know. I've been subjecting myself to them for over twenty-eight years. So, when you feel the need to be rescued, just give me a wink."

Linda removed Leah from Peter's arms. "Get your own girl, son. This one belongs to Gerry. Let's go into the library, Leah."

"The barracuda has spoken," Peter mumbled.

Linda stopped in mid-stride. "What did you say, son?"

The stain tinting Peter's cheeks told Leah there would be no help from his corner. "Nothing, Mama," he replied, just as the sound of running footsteps could be heard.

"Mr. G!"

Gerald set Audrey down when a pair of skinny brown arms wrapped around his legs. He looked down into shining black eyes and a wide full mouth. "Hey, Carlos."

A harried looking Mrs. Melcher rushed into the room. "I'm sorry, Linda," she apologized. "Carlos heard Gerry's voice and took off. I couldn't stop him."

"Carlos," Linda said. "Come here." He slowly made his way over to her. She bent down and ruffled the full head of glossy black curls. "I thought we agreed that you would wait for Gerald in the backyard." Biting back her smile when Carlos capriciously poked out his lip, Linda persevered in her gentle scolding. "It's okay this time, Carlos. But I want you to go out to the yard and wait for Gerald. He will be out soon."

"Come on here, boy," Mrs. Melcher said, taking his hand.

Linda started forward with an arm around Leah and looked back over her shoulder. "What are y'all waiting for? Let's go."

In the library, she pointed to the couch. "Leah, you and Gerry sit over there. The rest of you sit anywhere." Linda took her chair. "Your mother's name is Mabel, isn't it?"

Stunned by the question, Leah stammered, "Y-Yes, but h—how did you know?"

"Your father was my attorney. Though you resembled Hamilton a great deal, Mabel's there, too, especially when you smile.

"Oh," Leah murmured. "Have you met my mother?"

"On many occasions. I'm too much of an activist for Mabel, and we've established a pattern of disagreeing on every issue at the Colored Women's Auxiliary's monthly meetings."

Leah chose not to respond. If it didn't directly affect her life, Mabel would choose passivity over action every time. This was something Leah accepted about her mother.

Linda continued. "Don't worry though, my relationship with Mabel has nothing to do with you and Gerald." Linda leaned forward and smiled. "Tell me how you and my son met."

Leah recognized that the exchange had been meant to put her at ease. Now the official inquiry had begun. She related the story.

"You're kidding." Beth grinned at Gerald. "I could have sworn you said you weren't a believer in love at first sight."

"I'm not. It was more of an extreme wanting at first sight," Gerald replied, taking Leah's hand in his.

"Time out!" William laughed, pulling his wife back against him. "Don't you two get started."

As the joshing between her children continued, Linda considered Leah. Having been unsuccessful at her own matchmaking attempts, she realized the importance of the occasion. This was the first time Gerald had brought a woman home to meet her, which meant that her son was in love. And that was something she didn't take lightly. "Do you love my son?"

The room immediately grew so quiet you could hear a pin drop.

Leah directed her gaze first at Linda, then turned to stare into Gerald's eyes. "Yes. I do."

For a moment his grip on her hand tightened to the point of being unbearable. Then Gerald stood and drew Leah up with him. "That's it, Mama. The grilling is over."

"But I have a few more questions."

"Linda, let the poor girl out of the fish bowl," Jackson said. "We have a backyard full of guests."

A few hours later, Leah, deciding to take a breather before dinner, found a place on a boulder near the lake bordering Linda's estate. The Morris clan was active and the day had passed quickly. Ongoing activities included touch football, volleyball, basketball, croquet and swimming in the Olympic-sized pool. For those less inclined toward sporting endeavors, tables for checkers, bridge, chess and chair clusters for chatting had been arranged. The Path children were a wild bunch and they worshipped Gerald. She'd learned that The Fourth of July bash was an annual event, celebrated at the home of Linda Morris.

Leah gasped, then looked down in horror at the muddy water soaking into her clothes. A swimsuit clad Carlos, who having witnessed her face, stood paralyzed before her with a bucket in his hands. "Why did you do that?"

"I—I. It—it wasn't my idea," the child stammered.

Leah pulled Carlos down into her lap. "Then whose idea was it?"

"I can't tell you," Carlos replied. "We made the pinkie pledge."

Leah narrowed her eyes. "Oh, you did, did you? Carlos collapsed in a fit of giggles when her fingers began to tickle him. "Who put you up to it, Carlos? Could it have possibly been Mr. G?"

"Leah, stop torturing that poor child."

Released, Carlos ran off and Gerald's mustache twitched as he tried to control his amusement over her appearance.

"Why did you do it, Gerald? Look at me. I'm a mess, and my new suit. You know I didn't bring anything else to wear!"

Gerald pulled her up from the rock. "You need to take a shower and I'll have the suit cleaned. Up the stairs, third bedroom on your right."

Leah knew the room had been Gerald's as soon as she entered. She walked around fingering the sports trophies, scholastic awards, musical instruments and other mementos that had been a part of his childhood. She smiled when she saw the picture on the wall of two small, gap-toothed boys with their arms thrown around each other. Gerald Morris and Peter Jackson had been good-looking boys and they had grown into handsome men. Her smile widened when she saw the clothes on the bed. Gerald had been in her closet again.

Leah showered, dressed and went back down the stairs to join the party.

She halted just outside the patio doors when everyone stopped what they were doing and turned to stare at her. Feeling self-conscious, Leah's eyes sought out Gerald. Heartened when she saw the smile he broadcast, she took a couple of steps forward.

Now, this was his baby, Gerald thought proudly, taking in the deep coral chemise stopping a few inches above her knees and the matching heels. Yellow, lime and turquoise appliquéd shapes bordered the low cut, vee shaped neckline and Leah had pushed the sleeves up to her elbows. The key bracelet adorned one wrist, a wide, gold band watch the other and gold door knocker earrings hung from her lobes.

Gerald stepped forward and took her hand. "Ready for dinner, sweetheart?"

At the assigned family table, it was Jackson who got the rest of the family started. He took the crystal bowl of potato salad being handed to him and as he heaped a large helping onto his plate, said, "So, Leah. Tell us how Gerry managed to get a beautiful woman such as yourself to fall for him?"

"I've been wondering about that myself," William added. "It can't be him, so it must be the money."

"How much did you get when you went out with him the first time?" Peter asked. "And how much is he paying you to stick around and tell everybody that you're his woman."

"You do know, Leah," Beth interjected, "Gerry's reputation with the single women in this city is just about rock
bottom. He has persistently asked and been turned
down by all of them."

"That's right," William concurred.

Linda said nothing. She watched Leah place some of
each entree, no matter how little, on her plate and nodded her head in approval when Leah declined to have
her wineglass filled.

The members of Gerald's family were a bunch of char-
acters. But they were all also natural, warm, funny and,
most of all, loving to the other members. They had
accepted Leah as one of them, and as such, she was fair
game.

Before she could reply, Audrey piped up from her chair
positioned beside Gerald's. "She liked Unca Gerwee
'cause he's pretty."

"Uncle Gerry's not pretty," Reggie disputed. "He's a
man and men can't be pretty. Right, Dad?"

"That's right, son."

Audrey's bottom lip trembled. "He is so pretty! And
when I grow up I'm gonna marry Unca Gerwee."

Gerald bent down and kissed Audrey's cheek, then
leaned toward Leah. "See. I'm a good catch. So, you'd
better hurry up and marry me or I might decide to take
this offer waiting in the wings."

When night spread its cloak of darkness, Gerald took
the children across the lake for the fireworks display.
Leah had declined to accompany them and was relaxing
in a chaise lounge enjoying the quiet.

"Hello."

A large form blocked the light shining from the porch,
and because the light was behind him, she couldn't see
his face. "Hello," she replied, sitting up.

The silhouette moved and sat down in a chair near
her. "I'm Malcolm."

"It's nice to meet you, Malcolm. I'm Leah Ellis. I'm a friend of Gerald's."

"Friend, huh? Well, I guess you young people would have another name for it than us oldsters. But I believe my wife has a different understanding of the situation. Mrs. M. is under the impression that a wedding is imminent."

Though somewhat surprised the housekeeper would be discussing her and Gerald, Leah chose not to remark on the comment. "Your wife certainly is something," she replied. "Without her here today, I think the children would have run all over us."

"Yeah. Linda always was a whiz at organizing things. Ran our household like a general, she did."

Linda? Before Leah could switch her brain back on, the subject just introduced into their conversation walked up.

"Oh, good. I see you've met Gerry's father," Linda said, taking a seat. "Malcolm couldn't be here earlier and I was just coming to introduce the two of you."

"Father?"

"I can see by your face, Gerry hasn't told you," Linda observed.

"N—no." Leah took a deep breath. "No. He didn't." And Leah couldn't help wondering why.

"Well, he just found out himself yesterday and is probably still working through how he feels about it," Malcolm said.

"But—but I thought you were…"

"Dead? So did Gerald. But as you can see, I'm alive and well."

"I'm afraid this is all my fault," Linda said. "You see, I told Gerald his father had died."

"No, Linda. It's not your fault. It's mine. I never should have left."

"But I'm the one who didn't tell Gerald the truth."

"You did what you had to do under the circumstances," Malcolm replied.

Leah's head moved back and forth as if she were at a tennis match. Seeing her shocked expression, Linda said, "We shouldn't be having this discussion now, Malcolm." She scooted her chair closer to Leah. "I'd like to know your intentions regarding my son."

Leah answered Linda's questions as best she could, but her mind wasn't on the conversation. Why hadn't Gerald told her about his father? She had known something was wrong with him last night. He was the one who'd said that she could trust him. Why didn't he feel the same way about her? The sound of laughter interrupted Leah's musing and Linda's questions. Gerald and the children had returned.

As soon as he saw Malcolm, Gerald reached for her hand. "Let's go, Leah."

Linda and Malcolm followed them to the front door.

"Thank you for having me today, Mrs. Morris. I had a really nice time and enjoyed meeting you and the rest of Gerald's family."

"It was lovely to meet you, too, dear," Linda replied, but her eyes were on her son. "And please, call me Linda."

"Mama, it was great as usual," Gerald said, kissing her on the forehead. "I've already said goodbye to the kids and we have to run. I'll call you tomorrow."

He hustled Leah out the door and down the steps.

"Happy Fourth of July, son."

Gerald opened the car door and assisted Leah inside. "Your father is speaking to you, Gerald. Aren't you going to respond?"

Her heart leaped when she saw the naked fury in his face. "That man is not my father!"

He closed the car door, and Leah watched Malcolm approach Gerald. She couldn't hear what he said, but did see Gerald angrily shove Malcolm's hand off his shoulder and walk away.

A short while later, strained silence filled the car as they drove through the streets of Chicago. Gerald's teeth were clenched so tightly together, his jaw hurt from the effort. Leah was hunched against the door, as far away from him as she could get. Gerald hadn't responded to any of her questions and had finally yelled at her to shut up.

He had hurt Leah. Gerald knew that and he was sorry. It wasn't her fault she didn't understand, but he couldn't talk to her about this. He didn't understand himself, so how could he explain it to Leah? At her sigh, Gerald squeezed the steering wheel in a death grip and intensified his gaze through the windshield. Well, here's something else you're responsible for, Malcolm Morris, he thought. Why couldn't you have just stayed dead?

Satiated, and still glowing from the aftereffects of making love to Gerald, Leah adjusted her position on his chest and settled down again when she found a more comfortable spot. Gerald had been unrestrained in his lovemaking, almost as if he were seeking a kind of solace in her body he apparently couldn't find by sharing his thoughts and feelings with her. And while his apology had been heartfelt, it had done little to take away the ache Leah still felt in her heart. She tried to concentrate on the music floating around the den, but she couldn't get over how much his rebuff had hurt.

Sitting up, she snapped on a lamp and reached for her gown. She pulled it over her head and turned off the music. "Why didn't you tell me about your father?" When he didn't answer, Leah stood up and moved to the bar, her body rigid with anger. "Is this the way it's going to be between us, Gerald?"

Annoyed, he sat up, too. "What do you mean?"

"What I mean is, are you going to answer my question?"

Watching him leave the couch, she tried not to pay attention to the effect his magnificent bare form had on her body. Gerald didn't go anywhere near Leah. He rounded the corner of the bar, removed a bottle of his juice from the fridge, then stood, fist on waist, drinking it down. Leah gritted her back teeth together in an effort to keep her blood pressure from rising. "Are you going to answer me?"

"What do you want me to say, Leah?"

"I don't want you to say anything. I would like you to share what you're feeling about your father."

He set the empty bottle down on the bar top and went back to the couch. "Leah, I'm not feeling anything except a real need not to have this conversation with you right now."

Chilled by the coldness in his voice, Leah moved to the window. She shivered when she saw the trees bending in the wind. It had been a beautiful sunny day and she hoped a storm wasn't blowing in off the lake. She turned away. "G, don't shut me out," she requested. "Talk to me. You just found out that the father you thought was dead your entire life is alive. I know you must have some kind of feelings about that."

Her comment initially brought a scowl to his face. Then relenting, he said, "I don't want to talk about that man. I can't."

"Well," Leah said, moving toward the door, "when you can, Gerald, let me know. I'm going to bed."

Twenty-Two

July 6

Six very quiet people sat in the library at the home of Linda Morris. She glanced at Malcolm, who fidgeted on the couch. "I don't know where that boy is," she said apologetically.

"It's okay, darlin'," Malcolm replied. "I'm free for the whole evening."

"Can we go upstairs and watch TV?" Reggie asked.

From the couch, Beth glanced at her mother. "Mama, is it okay?"

"Yes, baby," Linda responded distractedly, staring at the doorway.

Beth nodded her head at Reggie and Audrey. The children jumped to their feet and hurried from the room.

William shifted on the couch. "Maybe I should call him."

"No," Linda answered. "Gerry knew the time."

"Mom! The television's not working," Reggie called from the top of the stairs.

Beth rose, sneaking a peek at Malcolm as she left the room. She climbed the stairs slowly. She already knew Gerald wasn't coming to the house and wondered why she had. It had been an agonizing decision, with her curiosity about the man claiming to be her father winning out.

She vaguely remembered a big man who used to come through the door with kisses and hugs for her. For a while, she had been upset when he didn't come anymore. But that had passed when her mother brought home a new baby and she had given him lots of hugs and kisses. She couldn't remember if she had cried when her mother told her that her father had died, not that it mattered since the man was sitting downstairs.

Beth stood in the doorway and watched her children at play. What would make a person abandon their child? Reggie and Audrey were her reason for getting up every morning. Nothing they could ever do would make her leave them. She walked into the room, gathered them in her arms, and laid a big, sloppy kiss on each of their cheeks.

"Mooom," Reggie cried, wiping his off.

"What's the matter? Can't a mother give her son a kiss?"

"Yeah, but not like that."

"I liked your kiss, Mommy," Audrey said.

Beth hugged her children again.

"Are you going to fix the TV, or what?" Reggie asked, squirming away.

Beth sighed. "Okay, little man, lead the way."

Used to the attention, Gerald ignored the bevy of beautiful women when he entered Club Raymond. Dressed casually in black slacks and a banded collar black shirt, he made his way through the crowd, headed for his usual table at the front of the club. He wanted to give Mattise another listen and find out if his first impression still held true. At least that was the reason he'd given himself for being there.

Sitting, Gerald crossed one long leg over the other and picked up the glass of juice already on the table. He took a sip while checking his watch and focused his mind on anything other than his mother and Malcolm, who were waiting for him to show up at the house.

His mind turned, as it inevitably did, to Leah. For two days, they had been walking on eggshells around each other and Gerald hated the tension he saw in her face every time he came near her. Malcolm be damned. He needed to resolve this thing with Leah. He couldn't stand having his woman upset with him.

"Everything okay here, G?" Ja'Nise asked.

Gerald returned her radiant smile. "Just fine, sweetie. Thanks."

Ja'Nise looked around. "Peter with you tonight?"

His brow rose. "No. But I'm sure the brother will roll up shortly. I thought I'd check Mattise out on my own tonight. That is allowed, isn't it?"

"Of course, G. Why would you think otherwise?"

"Well, it wouldn't be because of the moony-eyed looks the two of you throw at each other from across the room, now would it?"

Ja'Nise sat down at the table. "Is it that obvious?"

"Only to someone who knows the two of you. I think you've cut my main man off at the knees."

Ja'Nise reached across the table and laid her hand on his arm. "G, you know how much I like Peter." She stopped and shook her head sadly. "Damn, I'm so in love with the man I don't know what to do. But he doesn't seem like the marrying type."

"He's not." Gerald pursed his lips when he saw her face sag. "Unless we're talking about you, pretty lady. Don't worry, I'm sure Pete will make a move on you soon."

"You really think so?" Ja'Nise asked, her eyes lighting up.

"Yep. But if you tell him I said anything, I will, of course, deny it."

"Thanks, G."

"You're welcome."

Ja'Nise left and Gerald turned his attention to Mattise. By the end of the first set, he knew his decision to work with the talented group was correct.

Peter arrived just as the band started the second set. He took his chair and sat back. They couldn't talk until the loud music died down.

"How are you holding up, man?" Peter asked, when the band laid down their instruments.

"About as well as can be expected, considering I've just met the father who didn't give a rat's ass about me."

Peter straightened in his seat at that remark. "G, listen. If anyone knows how you feel, it's me. I know exactly what you're going through. However, Malcolm's showing up again changes nothing. And it doesn't take anything away from who you are. Three days ago, you were Gerald Morris and you're that same Gerald Morris today." Peter signaled for a drink. A waitress brought him a scotch and water.

Gerald picked up his juice. "That man looks just like me, Pete. I can't help wondering what else we have in common."

"Nothing, outside of some shared genes. Jackson and Mama raised us. They are the ones who shaped us and gave us our values. They are the ones who helped us become the men we are today. Malcolm Morris had nothing to do with that."

"I realize that. But what would you do if your mother showed up tomorrow?"

"I don't know," Peter replied truthfully. He drank from his glass while he thought it over. "For a long time, I wanted to know why she left. Now I don't care."

"You might not care, but her leaving had a lasting influence on you."

Peter looked across the club at Ja'Nise. "Yeah. I guess you're right. Anyway," he said, raising his glass, "here's to us, my brother. Regardless of what happens around us, you and I remain constant." They clinked glasses and drank. Peter lowered his and asked, "What did Leah have to say about it?"

"I don't know."

"You don't know? You did tell Leah about Malcolm, right?"

"She knows. He showed up at Mama's after you left the other night. We just haven't discussed it."

"Why? That's your lady, man. Leah will help you deal with this."

Gerald considered the statement, then said, "You're probably right, Pete."

"Heard anything from those detectives about the break-in yet?"

"Nope, and I'm tired of waiting. I'm thinking of calling in Watts."

Bill Watson was an ex-marine turned PI and a friend of Gerald's from the old neighborhood. After seeing countless friends die, Watts' beef was with the United States of America. Guns, drugs and crime seemed more prevalent in ghetto neighborhoods and Watts truly believed the government had a plot to wipe out all African American males. And after a couple of major scrapes with the law, he had taken his family and left the country.

"The big gun, huh? Well, Watts wouldn't step a foot in this country for anyone but you. If anyone can solve this mystery, it's him." Peter pursed his lips before continuing. "Now, I understand, based on what you've told me, why you haven't said anything to Leah about TyJo, but I do think that you should sit down with her and discuss your feelings about Malcolm."

❧

Merri looked up from the note she'd just finished reading. "Comments?"

There was a lot of foot shuffling, squirming and throat clearing, but no one said anything for a minute.

Bobby stood up. "Well, I don't know who these people are or why they would be interested in what we're doing, but I think we should go ahead with the fundraiser." He sat back down.

"You've been quiet tonight, Fred," Merri said. "Do you have anything to add?"

Fred looked down the table at Leah. She'd found the note in the stack of mail delivered to Project Spruce's office. "No," he responded.

Tony rose. "I agree with Bobby. Now, we could turn the note over to the police and tell them about the threats Michael Ray has made against the organization. But nothing has happened and we don't have any proof that it is Michael Ray Dupree, except Leah, and it would be her word against his. If we do go to the police, it's a sure bet we'll have to pull out of the festival, which will mean that Project Spruce is finished. I think the fundraiser should go ahead as planned."

"Are there any opinions to the contrary?" Merri asked, surveying the faces of the people seated at the table. "By your silence, I will assume we are all in agreement and that the fundraiser will go ahead. Tony, your report."

"I received a written response from Maxwell and it did not address the request I made for money at our last meeting. When I called, I was told that the company is reorganizing and all charitable contributions are under review. I asked for a meeting with someone in charge over there and was told that they will get back to us. We have only a few weeks left and we need some cash, so

I'll keep trying. Meanwhile, we're taking advantage of the community bulletin board on the cable system to publicize the event. The radio spots will start in another week and Danye's station will give us maximum exposure during their peak listening hours, including the five o'clock drive time. Per Leah, JetGraphics will print as many flyers as we need, so don't be shy about blanketing the city. Except for the booth, most of the other expenses have been paid. Right, Bobby?"

"That's right. I'm still waiting to hear from Stacia and Ja'Nise about the equipment. Ladies?"

"Club Raymond is lending us everything they have," Ja'Nise said, "and Stacia did get a verbal commitment for anything else we need from a supplier."

"That's good," Bobby replied, "because we only have about five thousand left in the account and Leah needs just about all of it."

"Why are you giving her the money?" Rachel asked with ire. "If that's all we have left, then I'd think you'd want to be a tad more frugal."

Leah rose from her chair. "The money is for the deposits to caterers and for the booth space, Rachel. My committee has managed to get most of everything else we need donated, including the items you wanted to decorate the booth."

"And you've all done a good job," Merri added. "What about a speaker, Leah?"

"I should hear back from the Bulls in a couple of days."

The remaining committee heads gave their reports.

"Okay, everyone," Merri said, closing her binder. "I guess that's it for tonight. When we come together next week, please bring your reports in writing. Rachel needs them for the files. This meeting is adjourned."

Rachel gripped the head of the man lying on top of her. "Ray," she began. "Please. When you make love to me tonight, don't call out Leah's name."

Michael Ray raised his head and fixed her with a vacant stare. "Rachel, I have no idea what you're babbling about." He left the bed and crossed to the dresser. He picked up one of the joints, lit it and turned to the mirror. Swinging his hair back over his shoulders, Michael Ray studied his profile.

Rachel reached for the green-flowered tray. Ray couldn't be serious. He had to know what he was doing every time he made love to her. Or else the drugs had really messed up his mind. She lifted the spoon and inhaled deeply, and continued to watch Michael Ray primp at the dresser.

"Listen, Rach," Michael Ray said, turning to face her. "Here's what I need. I understand that a few years back, there was an article written on Gerald Morris."

Rachel finished her hit and chuckled. "There must be at least a hundred articles written about Gerald Morris. The man is the executive director of The Path."

She stopped laughing when she saw an irate look enter his eyes. "I understand the man doesn't allow his photograph to be taken, but that this particular article had a photo accompanying it, and if I'm not mistaken, it was published by one of those music trade rags."

Rachel lounged back against the pillows. "Why are we talking about Gerald Morris when we could be doing something much more pleasurable?"

"I want that article," Michael Ray replied, turning back to the mirror.

"And what do you expect me to do about that?"

He finished the joint and crossed to the bed. "I expect you to bring it to me."

Rachel laughed again. "Ray, if there is such an article, it would be in the files. I'm not allowed near the files. They're locked and Gerald's assistant is the only one with the key."

Michael Ray rolled his body back on the bed. "You know, Rach, I'm forty-two and lately, I've been thinking a lot about getting married. And I was also thinking it might be kind of nice to have a kid."

Rachel perked up. Ray wanted to get married?

"But," Michael Ray with a sigh, "if I did get married, it would have to be to the right woman."

"And have you found this woman, Ray?"

Michael Ray stacked his hands beneath his head and focused on the ceiling. "Well, I thought I had and I'm in love with her. But I'm a little short on trust. Of course, if I have found this woman and she were to do me a little favor, I'd be a lot more sure of her loyalty."

Ray was talking about her. Finally, after all this time. "What would this woman have to do?"

"Bring me the article with the photograph of Gerald Morris."

Rachel hit the coke again; her mind already buzzing with ideas on how she could get into the files at The Path. "Okay, Ray," she said, sliding down in the bed. "But when I bring you this article. I'll expect you to keep your promise and make that marriage proposal."

A wily smile appeared on Michael Ray's face. "Don't worry, Rach. I will."

By the time Leah finished relating what had happened at the PS meeting, and the message warning them to cancel the fundraiser, Gerald's heart was lodged in his throat. All manner of thought ran through his mind, mainly Leah's safety. "Sweetheart, maybe you should think about distancing yourself from Project Spruce," he suggested, striving to remain calm.

"But why? The note didn't really say anything specific. It just said that someone is watching us and that they don't like what we're doing."

"Did you call the police?"

"No. We decided not to involve the police, at least until after the fundraiser. If we do, we'll probably have to pull out of the festival and that will be the end of Project Spruce. Tony's going to check it out though. The note was written on stationery from a company called TyJo Productions and he's going to try to find the person or people behind this." Leah shook her head. "Company stationery is so easy to get, anyone could have sent that note. I don't think he'll find out anything that will help us."

Gerald's thoughts spun as he held back his reaction. No way could he tell Leah about TyJo now. At the same time, he wasn't sure if not telling her was the right thing to do. Though talking, they were still at odds over his dilemma with Malcolm. Could he reveal his connection to the company involved with the threats against Project Spruce without increasing the strain already pulling at their relationship? Gerald had made his decision before he'd asked the question. He couldn't tell Leah, not until he found out who was trying to set him up. Then he would sit down with Leah and talk. Right now though, he had another priority. Leah had a fierce loyalty for the organization, but he had to get her away from Project Spruce. "If someone is out to harm this organization, I don't want you involved."

Leah didn't respond for a moment. "I am involved, Gerald. As a founder, I could never turn my back on PS."

"Leah, I know how committed you are and I applaud your efforts and the progress the group has made, but we can find another organization where you can fulfill your need to help the community. In fact, we have an opening at The Path where I'm sure your talents can be utilized."

Gerald was talking, but Leah wasn't listening. She leaned back on the couch and bit down on her thumbnail.

"You know what, G? I think Michael Ray is doing this.
The note mentions previous warnings and when he
came to see me..."

He grabbed her arm. "When!"

"Gerald, let me go."

His hold on her arm relaxed. "When did you see that
man, Leah? And why haven't you told me before now?"

"It was a few weeks ago and you and I had just met.
We discussed it at PS and decided Michael Ray was just
trying to intimidate us, well, actually me. But Michael
Ray hasn't done anything. He was just paroled from
prison and if he did try something, the police would pick
him up and toss him right back in that cell," Leah said bit-
terly.

"Have you told the police that Dupree has been
harassing you?"

"No. And except for that one time, I haven't heard
from him again."

Gerald's jaw worked convulsively. Leah hadn't said
anything to him about Dupree and this was the second
warning she had received with a TyJo connection. If it
was Dupree, how was he getting inside the company? If
it wasn't, it had to be someone connected to the TyJo's
LA office. J.J. wanted him back at TyJo, but that had
nothing to do with Leah. And besides, J.J. would never
do something like this. None of it made sense. In over
three weeks, the local detectives hadn't come up with
anything or anyone responsible for the break-in of Leah's
apartment. Given Chicago's crime statistics in relation to
population, Gerald suspected that they were no longer
actively working the case. It was time to make the call,
he decided. First though, he needed to take care of
Leah. If something happened to her... Gerald cut off
that thought. Nothing was going to happen to Leah, and
he quickly composed himself. "Sweetheart, I know how
important Project Spruce is to you, but this is serious.

You're putting yourself in danger and that I cannot allow."

"I know how serious this is, Gerald. But I will not allow Project Spruce to be shut down. We've worked too hard and it has taken three years to get to this point. The fundraiser will make sure we can continue our work."

"No, Leah."

Leah leveled her gaze on Gerald. "What do you mean, no?"

"I mean the others can do as they wish, but you're pulling out."

Outrage fanned through her body and Leah sat up. "Gerald, I thought we could discuss this like adults and make some rational decisions, but what I'm hearing has the distinct ring of parental authority and I don't like it. If this is the reaction I'm going to get whenever something doesn't please you, then I'll deal with this myself."

"You can't just push me away, Leah. You have to trust me enough to tell me what is going on in your life and know that any decisions I make are made only to protect you."

The look Leah slanted at Gerald held a lot of resentment. He had his nerve telling her to trust him when he wasn't willing to do the same. "I don't need to be protected and I think maybe you should follow your own advice."

"What are you talking about?"

"When are you going to talk to me about your father?" She felt and saw his guard come up and knew she was trying to climb a brick wall. Every time she tried to scale it, Gerald just added another layer.

"Malcolm Morris is not the subject of this discussion, Leah. You, and why you're not going to continue working with Project Spruce, are."

"Gerald, let me explain something that apparently hasn't been understood. I am the only one who runs my life and I decide what I'm going to do. If you have a problem with that, then perhaps we should be discussing the course this relationship is going to take."

"What are you trying to tell me, Leah? That you don't love me?"

Leah wasn't sure if Gerald was being obtuse on purpose or if he really didn't understand what she had just said to him. "This has nothing to do with love, Gerald. This has to do with behavior. I refuse to let you or anyone else control my life."

Control her life? He wasn't trying to control her, only to protect her. "Leah, I don't want to control you. I only want to keep you safe."

"Believe it or not, I've managed to live twenty-nine years without your protection. Now, don't get me wrong. I love you and I am very happy that you love me, but I can't be suffocated. And that's what you're trying to do. Either we love each other on an equal basis or we won't be together."

His expression turned lamentable. "Leah, if I could tell you how I feel about Malcolm Morris I would, but I'm not ready to talk about him right now and I wish you'd leave it alone. At least for now."

She shook her head sadly, knowing they hadn't made any progress this evening. "I'll leave it alone, Gerald. But the road runs both directions and I'll expect you to accord me the same distance."

Later that night, Gerald rose from the bed and went downstairs to his den. He picked up the telephone and dialed a number.

"Watson."

"Watts, it's G. I need you, man."

"I'm wrapping up a case now and I can be there within the week. Is that soon enough?"

A week, Gerald thought. That was probably okay. Starting tomorrow, Leah would be under twenty-four-hour guard and he would keep a closer eye on her, too. "Yep,"

Gerald responded. "But if you can get here any sooner, do."

"I'm on it, G. Later."

"Later," Gerald replied, hanging up the phone.

Twenty-Three

July 10

Not today, Gerald thought when he saw his mother's car parked in his driveway. He knew why she was there and the idea that he should just keep going crossed his mind. He pulled the Bronco into the driveway beside her car.

"Hi, Mama," he greeted her, climbing from the truck.

"Son," Linda responded.

Gerald led the way to the front door. He entered the house and kept walking until he reached his den where he slumped to the couch.

Linda followed. "I don't suppose you're planning to give me an explanation."

He considered his mother for a minute. "You're right. I wasn't."

She pursed her lips in vexation and sat on the love seat. "Gerald Tyler Morris, just when did you decide that it was okay to be rude?"

"I'm sorry, Mama. But if this is about Malcolm, I really don't wish to hear it." Agitated, Gerald stood up.

Linda rose, too. "And why not, Gerald? Malcolm is your father and he only wants to know his son."

"That's his problem."

"His problem?" Linda moved to stand in front of him.

"No, Gerald. It's your problem and ignoring him is not the way to deal with this. If you don't want Malcolm in your life, then you be the man I raised and tell him that."

Gerald snorted and put his fists on his waist. "You mean like he was a man when he walked out on you?"

Linda winced at the sneer in his voice. "Gerald, Malcolm came to the house specifically to see you."

"Did I ask him to come?" Gerald walked out of the den.

Linda followed him to the kitchen. "Okay, son. So you didn't invite Malcolm to the house, but why can't you at least sit with him and give him a chance to explain his side of the story?"

Gerald removed a pitcher of juice from the refrigerator. "I'm busy," he finally responded.

"Busy! This is ludicrous, Gerald. I know you can arrange your schedule to at least have a meal with the man."

His hand trembled, spilling juice on the island counter. Gerald set the glass pitcher down very carefully. "I could. But I won't."

"Well, if you won't, then I will. I'll just plan another dinner and I'll expect you to be there. Linda nodded her head definitively. "How's next Saturday?"

Gerald walked around the island and draped his arms over her shoulders. "Mama, if you feel the need to have another dinner, then go ahead. Malcolm can move into the house for all I care. But I won't be there. And if I find out his intentions are anything other than what he says they are or if he hurts you or any of the family again, he'll answer to me this time."

She watched Gerald return to the island and finish filling his glass. Her son was as stubborn as a mule, and Linda knew that as far as Gerald was concerned the conversation was over. She picked up her purse. "Gerry, will you at least think about what I said?"

"Mama, what would be the point? I've given my answer and it's not going to change."

He walked his mother to the door and kissed her. "See you later, Mama."

"Bye, baby," Linda said, heading for her car.

∾

"Did you ladies see that gold lamé dress Rachel wore to the concert?" Danye asked, laughing. "What was she supposed to be, a curtain?"

Les Cinq Belles Noires were sitting in Merri's living room discussing the concert of the night before. Merri entered the room and set another bowl of popcorn on the table, which also held several glasses, two opened bottles of white wine and a half-eaten box of chocolates. She plopped down in one of the plaid tan chairs and directed her gaze at Danye, who was seated on the matching couch. "Can we please not discuss that woman?"

Danye took the cigarette from her mouth. "Oh, Merri, chill. We're just having some fun."

"You have to admit," Stacia said, leaning forward to refill her glass. "She did kind of stand out in the crowd."

She sure did, Leah thought. And she'd stood out on the arm of Michael Ray Dupree. Until last night, she'd had no idea Rachel even knew Michael Ray. Not that it mattered. She had G now, and Gerald was worth a million Michael Ray Duprees.

Her mouth curved downward as Leah continued to think about Gerald. They had been tiptoeing around each other for six days and the rift between them was widening. Their conversations were stilted and cool. In the morning, they each went their separate ways. At night, they were nothing more than polite strangers. They had attended the concert together and put on a good show of being a loving couple, but at home, they had slept on separate sides of the bed.

"Forget Rachel. I want to know the scoop on Merri and that cute as hell Tony Wright. How long have the two of you been dating and why didn't you tell us?"

Leah put her thoughts aside and looked at Stacia who had made the comment.

"Cute is not the half of it," Danye remarked. "That man is too fine for his own good. And that blue tux he had on last night... Girl, that man wouldn't have to ask me to do nothing twice."

Leah turned to Merri for her reaction. Merri dipped her head. "Not long," she said. But Leah saw the diminutive smile on her lips.

"You're looking kind of peaked today," Danye remarked, carefully observing Leah's face. "Are you feeling all right?"

"Uh-hmmm," Leah responded. "I'm just tired. The concert ran kind of late."

"Well, let me tell you ladies about David," Stacia said.

"I was glad to see he finally figured out what a telephone is for," Danye stated.

"Humph. You're telling me," Stacia responded. "But we had a great time at the concert. He's a lawyer, divorced and has a little girl. Apparently, the divorce was pretty messy. I think that's why he was so gun-shy about calling me."

"So do you think he'll call again?" Danye asked.

Stacia drank from her glass. "I don't know," she said thoughtfully. "I certainly hope so. What's wrong with you, Ja'Nise?"

"Nothing." Ja'Nise hadn't said anything all afternoon. Her voice sounded flat and they could see that she was obviously distressed about something.

"Then why are you so quiet today?" Danye asked.

Ja'Nise looked at each woman in turn. She was quiet

because she was hurting. After what Gerald had told her, she'd been sure Peter would call and ask her to the concert. Instead, Peter had shown up with another woman. "I'm just getting tired of involving myself with a man and committing my heart only to have him walk all over it on his way out the door."

~

"Well?"

The others had left and Leah's question was directed to Merri.

Merri didn't bother pretending that she didn't know what Leah was talking about. "Tony's nice." She did pretend not to see the annoyed look Leah shot at her.

"Would you care to expound on that?"

Merri stood up and began gathering the glasses from the table.

"I'll help with the dishes later so you can stop avoiding the question and sit down. What happened between you and Tony last night?"

Merri flopped down in the chair and crossed her arms over her chest. "Nothing happened, except that we had a very good time."

"Why would that upset you?"

Merri sat forward in the chair. Leah could feel the nervous energy flowing from her. "Because Tony asked me out again," she snapped. She jumped up from the chair, stood for a moment then slumped back down, staring straight ahead of her. Her eyes were hard and resembled green jade.

Leah gaped in wonder at her friend and the unexpected response. "Merri, what's wrong?"

"Leah, Tony is wonderful. He was a gentleman last night and didn't try to pressure me or anything. When he brought me home, he left after kissing me on the cheek."

"I think you've lost me here. If Tony is so wonderful, why are you sitting over there looking like Evil-lene?"

"Because I can't let Tony into my life. Everything is working perfectly and a man would just cause problems I don't need."

"Even if that man loves you?" Merri's face crumpled and Leah opened her arms. Merri moved to the couch and leaned her head on Leah's shoulder. When the tears spilled over, Leah hugged her friend tighter and nodded her head in understanding. Tony didn't know what he was up against. Merri had been pregnant when she'd found out Jimmy's father had another woman and that she was also carrying his child. The discovery had devastated Merri, and Jimmy still didn't know he had a half brother or sister somewhere in the city of Chicago.

"Leah, you've been with Gerald for a while now. Is it what you expected? Does he make you happy?"

Leah thought about how to respond to Merri's questions. She and Gerald had problems. But didn't every relationship? And if they loved each other enough, surely they could work through them and get their relationship on an even keel again. "Merri, the only person who can make you happy is you. But being with Gerald does bring a happiness into my life. As for expectations, I don't know that I had any. If I did, I'm sure they were very negative, based on my prior relationships. But, if I didn't have G, I'd want a man who was thoughtful, sensitive, kind, romantic, loving, goal-oriented, handsome, athletic, an outstanding lover, and he'd need to have flair for cooking."

Merri sat up. "You sound like one of those 'what I want in a perfect man' personal ads."

Leah laughed. "And those are Gerald's good qualities. He also has a temper and a tendency to be controlling, as well as sexist. I'm too self-reliant, which sends Gerald over the edge. I'm also a workaholic, have

a tendency to rush into things without thinking first, am
not the neatest person in the world, and I have a stubborn streak."

"Is there a point, Leah?"

"Yes, and the point is, there are no perfect men or
women, and no such thing as a perfect relationship."

The look Merri sent Leah was dubious. "Then tell me,
Leah. Why be with a man if it's not going to be perfect?"

"Everyone has faults, Merri. You have to decide which
faults you can accept and which you cannot. Every relationship has its ups and downs, and both people have to
make adjustments. If you truly love each other you can
work through the downs and the relationship will be
stronger."

Merri still wasn't showing any signs of optimism.
"What if you can't get over past hurts? What if you're still
afraid?"

"Merri, do you think that I'm not afraid? After what
happened to me? I love Gerald so much; I'm afraid all
the time. Then he wraps me in his arms and I feel safe
and warm. But you know what makes it all worthwhile?"
Merri shook her head no. "Love. I have someone who
truly cares about me and I care about him. All that other
stuff fades in comparison to that. If you'll give Tony a
chance, I think it's possible that you'll experience the
same feelings."

It wasn't until Leah crossed the street to her apartment
building that she realized that the talk meant to help Merri
had actually helped her. Her step took on a bounce as
she bypassed the elevator and took the stairs. She did
love Gerald and she did feel safe, and tonight she
planned to do something about the tone their relationship
had taken. She had promised to cook Gerald a meal,
and cook she would. Once she had his attention through
his stomach, they were going to talk.

Her meal plan was simple. They would begin with a

small dish of orange sherbet, followed by a deep-dish hamburger and black olive pizza, a cold, crisp salad and G's juice served in fluted glasses. Then she would bring out the chocolate soufflé. It was certainly nothing fancy, but all would be prepared from scratch, and by her. Leah also planned to lay the food out picnic style on a blanket where they would consume the meal in the glow of candlelight.

So, it was understandable when she slumped against the counter three hours later, extremely perturbed over what had just occurred in her living room...

Leah looked up when Gerald entered the apartment. "I'll be just a minute, baby," she said, covering the mouthpiece with her hand. "We're finalizing the food order for the fundraiser."

Flagrant umbrage descended on his features and Gerald began trekking the carpet. When Leah finally hung up the telephone fifteen minutes later, he turned on her. "This morning, I thought you told me that this would be our evening and that you weren't going to work on that fundraiser."

Goosebumps covered her arms and chills rolled down her back. To steady her nerves, Leah jammed her hands into the back pockets of her shorts. "What was I supposed to do, Gerald? The woman called because she misplaced our order."

Gerald glowered at her. "I don't care what the problem was, Leah. When you make a promise to me, I expect you to keep it!"

Leah tried to hold in the anger. She didn't want to fight with Gerald tonight. "What is this really about, Gerald? If you're upset because of your father, we can talk about it, but please don't take it out on me."

Leah cringed when he strode over to her. "This isn't about my father. This is about you and Project Spruce!"

"G, I think—"

Her voice fell silent when the telephone rang. Both sets of eyes turned to the kitchen. Leah moved to the phone and glanced worriedly at Gerald as she reached for the receiver.

"Hello," she huffed into the phone. "Hi, Bobby. No, I need the check tomorrow." She glanced at Gerald to see him even more incensed. "Bobby, I'll have to call you back later." She hung up the telephone as the sound of the slammed door echoed around her living room.

Tentatively, Leah reached for the oven door, knowing what she would find inside. Sure enough, her soufflé was flat as a pancake. Infuriated, Leah turned to the cupboard and grabbed the largest tumbler she could find. She filled it with cold water and left the apartment. When she saw Gerald in front of the elevators, she strode over to him and flung the water in his face. Leah crossed her arms, her foot tapping as she waited for Gerald to clear his eyes.

"Why did you do that?"

"Because you need to cool off," Leah ground out. "Now, you just march yourself right back up that hallway where I will precede you into my apartment. You will then enter, greet me with a kiss and tell me how much you missed me today. Then we are going to eat the meal these hands prepared for you. And you are going to damn well like it!"

Gerald opened his mouth to reply.

"I said, you are going to damn well like it," Leah repeated. She left Gerald standing at the elevators.

A few minutes later, she heard a key in the lock. Gerald peeked around the door and entered. Humbly, he went to Leah and kissed her. "Hello, baby. I missed you today." He kissed her again.

Leah held his head in her hands. "I missed you, too." She moved her arms around his waist. "Was that so hard Gerald?"

His arms pulled her closer. "No, baby girl, it wasn't and I really did miss you today."

"I didn't know you were a little fireball," Gerald said, picking up his glass. "But, I still love you in spite of that one flaw."

"Flaw! Mister, I'll have you know that what you see before you is perfection, and that's with a capital P."

After moving the dishes from his path, Gerald rose on his hands and knees in front of her. "Well, I don't know about perfection," he said. "You have that awful temper. And when you're smashed, your nose gets red," he chuckled, kissing the tip. "And these lovely cheeks get really rosy," he continued, sliding his tongue over each one. "And these knock-out legs can't seem to hold you up very well." Gerald lifted one leg and starting at the ankle began moving his mouth upward. Leah held her breath when his mustache and beard tickled the inside of her thigh. Quivering slightly, she removed her leg from his hand and began to clear the floor.

Gerald sat back. "What are you doing?"

"Making room for dessert," Leah replied. She took the things to the kitchen and he frowned when she left the room. She returned shortly and moved to the edge of the blanket. She dropped the towel and stood before Gerald au natural.

"Dessert?" Gerald asked, reaching out his hands.

Leah dodged him, her face ponderous as she tapped her finger against her chin. "Well, I do believe there is some chocolate ice cream in the fridge." She went back into the kitchen and opened the freezer.

Gerald came off the floor. His lips found her neck, but his eyes didn't stray from her breasts. In the condensation blowing from the freezer, the tips had formed hard pebbles. He placed his mouth at her ear. "I'll need that ice cream, the whipped cream, and you. I'll make my own dessert tonight."

Twenty-Four

"Enter," Gerald said, his eye still on the SJB video on the monitor. Malcolm opened the door and walked inside the spacious office. He watched Gerald make a note on his clipboard before looking up.

Gerald turned off the television set and stood up. "What do you want?"

Malcolm shoved his hand in his pocket and moved further into the room. "The family missed you at dinner the other night, G."

Gerald walked to his desk. Air whooshed from the cushion when he fell into the chair and the black mark left on the desk by the heel of his boot was probably permanent. He turned frigid eyes to Malcolm. "First of all, the name's Gerald. Only those close to me may call me otherwise, and you are not one of those people. Second, if my family did miss me, what does that have do with you?"

Malcolm sat in a chair across from him. "Look, G."

Gerald swung his feet to the floor. "My name is Gerald!"

Malcolm leaned away, patting the air in a conciliatory manner. "Okay, Gerald. Okay. But listen, son..."

Malcolm paused when the brow quirked. This was

going to be difficult. "Gerald," he started again, "I want to explain why I left you the way I did."

Gerald propped his feet back on the desk. "You didn't leave me. You left my mother."

"Okay, Gerald. I don't want to get into a game of semantics with you. I only came here today to talk."

"Then say what you have to say and get out of my office."

Feeling his own anger rising, Malcolm swallowed. "Gerald, as your father, I ex—"

"You are not my father."

Malcolm stood up. "Why are you being so obstinate about this, Gerald? All you need do is pick up a mirror and you'd see that statement is not true."

"Why don't you get out?"

Malcolm released a breath. "I can see this is not a good time for you, Gerald. Can we arrange another time when we can talk?"

Gerald's feet hit the floor. "Well, my schedule's pretty tight right now and I don't see how I can fit you in right now. But why don't you give my assistant a call in, let's just say never and leave it at that."

Gerald rose from his chair and went back to the couch. He turned on the monitor and picked up his clipboard. Malcolm watched him. They were more alike than his son knew. Gerald was full of pride and stubborn just like him. Though he had left Linda for what, at the time, he'd thought were valid reasons, Malcolm knew it had been no more than arrogance. And that arrogance had taken him, scraped away the man he was, and returned a much older and wiser man. He only hoped his son wouldn't have to learn the same lesson.

"Gerald, I had another reason for stopping by today." Malcolm continued talking though Gerald ignored him. "Word on the street is that TyJo is going public. Now, if this is true that's fine, and I'm not trying to get into your business. But if it's not, I thought you'd want to know."

Gerald didn't respond and Malcolm moved to the door. He observed his son for a minute, then stepped into the hallway and closed the door quietly behind him.

When Gerald heard the soft click, he threw the clipboard on the table and lowered his head to his hands.

Later that morning, Sheila slid over to the passenger side in her car and flipped down the mirror. She retrieved a tube of lipstick from her purse. Red, a sure winner, she thought, touching up her mouth. Since Ray had declined to help her, she was going to have to do this herself. She stepped from the car and adjusted the red skirt. Then shook her head until her hair floated around her shoulders, inhaled and pushed out her chest.

"Well, Gerald Morris. Here I come." Sheila put on her most feminine smile and glided through the door.

Rick rushed to the counter, his grin wide until he recognized her. "Mr. Morris, it's for you," he called sarcastically loud as he walked back to his desk.

Sheila flashed a seductive smile when Gerald came out of the back room. Too little sleep was beginning to take its toll and after Malcolm, this he was not in the mood for. Moving forward, Gerald's total apathy towards Sheila showed in his face and was reflected in his voice when he spoke. "Sheila."

"Hi, Gerald."

"Something I can do for you today?"

"If you mean a printing job, then no," she answered. "I was hoping to take you to lunch."

"I've already eaten. Thanks for the offer though."

Sheila sighed. "All right, then how about having dinner with me tonight? If you're free, that is." Sheila raised her brows expectantly.

Gerald crossed his arms and assessed Sheila for almost a full minute before he responded. "I'm not," he stated bluntly. Then tired of playing the game, Gerald abruptly dropped his arms. "Look, Sheila. Is there something on your mind? I'm kind of busy today."

Sheila fidgeted with embarrassment, but regained her composure in a hurry. "Well. When will you be free, Gerald Morris? I'd really like to get to know you better."

"I'm already involved," he replied dryly. "And you might as well know that I've asked Leah to marry me. Therefore, even if I was interested in a relationship with you, which for the record I would never be, I'm already taken. So, why don't you go and work your magic on someone else?"

Her face contorted with rage and Sheila drummed her nails on the counter. "Why Leah, Gerald? I'm prettier than she is and I know how to treat a man." A sneer tainted her face as she continued. "Leah, gullible fool that she is, has no idea what life is about and she certainly doesn't know anything about men. That's why she was stupid enough to get herself engaged to a drug dealer."

A perilous look, screened by Gerald's lashes, fired at Sheila. He had been around enough women to know a self-absorbed, vindictive viper when he saw one and he didn't have the time or inclination to deal with this one. He walked around the counter, seized Sheila by the arm and escorted her to the door. "Look, Sheila. I would appreciate it if you didn't come by my store again."

Gerald opened the door and pushed Sheila into the street. Heaving a sigh of relief, he turned for his office, wondering if Leah and Sheila had really come from the same family.

That afternoon, Gerald hit the panel on the wall and a dark, rectangular-shaped, soundproof glass was revealed. He hit another button and turned on the audio, then stood watching and listening to Rachel as she interacted with the children.

Rachel was still on probation and would be until Gerald was satisfied that she was the right person to work with the children. Watching her, it came to him that he had more concern for the welfare of The Path children than his own father had for him.

But that didn't matter. Bill Watson was due to make his appearance in a couple of hours and Gerald was just waiting for the plane from the Bahamas to land. Watts would find out what Malcolm really wanted. Which, Gerald believed, was to get into his mother's bank account. When he knew for sure, Malcolm could return to wherever he'd been for the last thirty-four years.

Gerald hit the panel to restore the wall and headed for the elevators. The ice cream had proven to be a chilly but interesting aphrodisiac and had melted quickly in the sizzle of their passion. Leah had said she wanted to talk, but her eyes had drooped closed almost in the middle of the sentence. He was very concerned about Leah. She was wearing herself out and the stress they were under was threatening to take them both out. Yesterday, Leah had seemed so listless and had looked so tired this morning, Gerald had tried to get her to stay home.

With the fundraiser, the threats against Project Spruce, and Joe Carpenter's tricks, having to deal with him, too, was something she didn't need. This weekend, Leah had taken care of him and today, if he could convince her to leave work, Gerald would spend the rest of the afternoon and evening pampering his woman.

Leah hung up the phone and sniffed. She grabbed a tissue just in time to catch the sneeze she emitted. Rising from her chair, she moved to the window. The call she'd just completed had come from the Bulls' camp.

They were very apologetic, but Leah couldn't believe that
not even one player could help them out. She shook her
head and wiped the tears from her eyes. She was out of
options. It looked as if she was going to have to write
and give the speech after all, a thought that unnerved her
tremendously.

"Leah?" She turned and Tony rushed over. He put his
arms around her. "What's wrong, Leah?"

"I just received a call from the Bulls'. No one is available."

"Why would that make you cry?"

Leah drew back. "Tony, I'm not crying. I think I've
caught one of those summer colds."

He held her away and examined the flushed face and
watery eyes. "Leah, if you're sick you should go home."

"If you knew how much work was piled up on that desk
over there you wouldn't make that statement."

"So. This is what you people do when you think no
one is watching?"

Tony released Leah and stepped in front of her. He
focused a lethal glare on Joe Carpenter. "Would you
care to explain that?"

Joe shoved one hand into his pocket, the other inside
his suit jacket and casually walked into the room.
"What's to explain, Mr. Vice President? It's against company policy for officers to fraternize with their subordi-
nates and Leah reports to you. I knew she had to be
spreading her legs for you. Otherwise, she wouldn't
have gotten that promotion to director." Diane had followed Joe into the office and he turned and curved his
arm around her shoulders. She shrugged it off. "Now
I've seen it with my own eyes and have Diane here as a
witness."

Diane's blue eyes sparkled like diamonds. "You can
forget about me helping you, Joe. If I say anything, it will
be about your impersonations as Leah's assistant and

how you're always in her office when we're away from
our desks."

Joe glared at her. "Why are you siding with them?
You're one of us."

Diane frowned in annoyance. "One of us? And what
us would that be, Joe?"

He snorted in disgust and turned to Tony again. "It
doesn't matter. I saw it and I think the president will be
very interested in what I have to say." He started backing toward the door.

"While you're in talking to the president, Joe," Tony
said. "You can also explain what happened to the
money."

"What money?"

"The Atlanta account is missing over $50,000.
Houston another $100,000. What other markets do you
have, Joe? Oh, yeah. Leah, hand me those reports on
St. Louis, New Orleans, Birmingham, and anything else
that has Joe's name by it. And we haven't even begun
looking into the rural markets in your territory or talked
about that sweet, little side deal you cooked up with
Maxwell Corp."

Joe starting shaking. "I have no idea what you are
talking about."

"You don't?" Tony walked over to him. "Well, let me
spell it out for you, Joe. I'm talking about embezzlement,
fraud and just being an over-all jackass. If the company
decides to prosecute, I'm also talking about a jail sentence."

"You can't pin anything on me! And if you think I'm
going to let a couple of nig—"

Tony grabbed Joe's tie and jerked him forward. "Say
it, Joe. Say the word and give me a reason to kick your
racist, white ass."

Joe closed his mouth and looked at Leah. She
smiled.

Tony released him and straightened the front of Joe's jacket. "Now, here's what you're going to do, Joe. You're going downstairs to type out your resignation, which you can place in the middle of my desk. Security will meet you down there. They'll help you pack your things and escort you to the front exit."

Joe stuttered, stepped backwards to the door. "You haven't heard the last of me, Tony Wright or you either, Leah."

"Oh, I think we've heard the last of you, Joe," Tony responded. "Because if you're not gone in twenty minutes, you'll be leaving in a police cruiser. Call security, Diane, and tell them to meet Mr. Carpenter at the elevators."

Merri walked up to the door and was almost knocked down in Joe's hurry to get out of Leah's office.

Tony went back to Leah. "You okay?"

"I feel great, Tony—now that Joe's gone."

He eyed her critically. "Joe was only one of your problems. You're sick and you're outta here."

Leah moved to her desk and sat in her chair. "Tony, I have too much work to do."

Tony crossed to the desk and leaned down. "Then let Diane handle it! You're always telling everybody how great she is. Now, are you going to get your purse and walk out the door or am I going to pick you up and carry you over my shoulder?"

"What's going on?"

"Nothing, Merri," Tony responded. "Except that Leah's sick and she's going home."

"Tony, I can't go home now."

"And I said, get your purse."

Merri observed the dispute with interest. She had never seen Tony so in command. She stopped the smile from breaking on her lips as she watched Leah make one final charge only to have Tony knock her back down.

"Anthony Wright, please leave my office," Leah said with a sniff. She reached for a report on her desk. "I don't have time for this."

Tony strode around the desk. He was on a roll, and after dealing with Joe Carpenter this should be a snap. He removed the report from Leah's hands, retrieved her purse from the desk drawer and pulled her up from the chair. "You're right, babe. You don't have time for this. You're going home."

It was time to intervene, and Merri walked further into the room. She placed her arm around Leah's shoulders. "Come on, sister-girl. I'll follow you home." Merri looked back over her shoulder. "That man looks like he means business."

"Sweetheart?" Gerald called entering the apartment. "Leah, where are you?"

Receiving no answer, he went into the bedroom where he found Leah moaning and writhing beneath the sheets. He knelt at the side of the bed. "Leah, I stopped by your office and they told me you came home sick." Leah forced her eyes open and Gerald placed his palm on her forehead. Sticky, moist heat met his hand. "Leah, wake up. I'm taking you to the doctor."

She tried to sit up and flopped back down. "I don't need a doctor."

"Yes. You do and we're going right now."

"I don't want to go to a doctor. I want to go back to sleep."

He sighed and gave in. "Okay, sweetheart. Go back to sleep."

Gerald left the bedroom and picked up the telephone. He had just finished brewing the tea when he heard the knock on the door. Ten minutes later, Gerald walked the doctor to the door.

"Leah has the flu. Give her one of these every four hours, lots of liquids and make sure she gets plenty of rest."

"Thanks for coming."

"Any time, G."

An hour or so later, Gerald heard Leah moving around. He left the couch and went to the bedroom. He watched her stagger her way back to the bed and sit on the edge. "I'm sorry my baby is so sick," he crooned, picking her up. He carried her to the living room and lay down on the couch with her.

"G?"

He directed her head back to his chest. "Go back to sleep, baby girl," Gerald interrupted softly. "I just want to hold you for a little while."

The loud crash careened its way through Gerald's dream and his eyes snapped open at the sound of shattering glass. Gerald looked down at Leah, asleep on his chest, then at the large rock still rolling across the carpet. He glanced down at Leah again. She hadn't moved or awakened at the noise, and she was shivering. He raised himself with Leah in his arms and laid her down on the couch, then bent over and kissed her temple. Anxiety clouded his eyes. Leah was still burning up!

Taking the rock with him, Gerald crossed to the window and looked down on the street. There were a few children playing in the yards, but nothing else looked out of place. Still, his eyes were sharp as they searched the block several times before he removed the note wrapped around the rock. It was typed on TyJo Productions stationary.

"Miss Ellis. You've been warned several times to cancel the fundraiser. You will not receive another written reminder. Next time, we will take a more direct approach and you are the first target."

If Gerald's skin hadn't been so dark, it would have been colorless as every bit of blood drained from his face. What kind of organization was this? Gerald crushed the note in his hand. He didn't care what Leah said. As of this moment, her affiliation with Project Spruce was over!

Her coughing drew his attention and tender concern filled his eyes. He hurried to the couch and knelt down. He examined Leah's heat-flushed face. The grating cough she emitted jarred his nerves. His hand touched clammy skin when he brushed the hair away from her face and his tension mounted. He glanced at the broken window. Leah was sick and she couldn't stay here. "It's okay, baby girl. I'm getting you out of here," he whispered near her ear.

Leah coughed again and huddled her arms around her body. Gerald retrieved the spread from the bedroom and wrapped it around her, then did three things: he filled a suitcase, called to get the window fixed, and over Leah's hoarse protests bundled her up and took her to the car.

Her harsh coughing had him clenching his jaw. Gerald let go with an expletive and punched out a number.

"Watson."

"Watts, at the house. One hour."

"I'm on my way."

Gerald hung up the telephone. "It will be okay," he said, more to calm himself than Leah.

At the house, Gerald didn't stop moving until he'd tucked Leah snugly under the covers in his bed. With that done, he adjusted the temperature on the wall panel and went to the kitchen. He returned to the bedroom with a hot flu medicine and gently shook her shoulders. After helping her up, he placed tissues in her hands when she sneezed. She squinted at him, trying to focus on his face through the cloud in her head. A twitch of a smile shadowed his mouth at her scrunched-up face. Gerald picked up the cup.

"Sip this, sweetheart," he told her.

The only thing Leah wanted was to lie back down. She firmed her lips and refused to drink. Intransigent, Gerald held the cup at her mouth until Leah finished the medicine. When she had, he let her slide beneath the covers again and drew them up around her shoulders.

Gerald sat beside her on the bed. Stubborn, he thought, tilting his lips in a semblance of a smile when Leah closed her eyes and fell asleep almost immediately. He had wanted to take her temperature, but he'd wake her later after the medicine had a chance to work. In the meantime, he had bigger fish to fry.

The doorbell chimed just as he reached the bottom of the stairs and Bill Watson followed Gerald down the hallway to the kitchen. Watts poured a cup of coffee and sat at the table. Gerald stood at the sink washing the dishes Leah had used. He didn't register the force of his pressure until the cup broke in his hand. Completing his task, he poured himself some coffee and carried it to the table.

"One, I want a full report on a man named Malcolm Jamal Morris. He is fifty-eight and lives in Chicago. I want to know what he's been doing for the past thirty-four years and what he's up to now."

"Understand," Watts responded, not bothering with a notepad.

"Two, I'm being set up and I want to know who's behind it. It will probably have something to do with three," Gerald said, handing over the crushed note. "There is a group called Project Spruce, based here in

Chicago. I want everything you can get your hands on, including the person or persons out to harm the organization. Start with a Michael Ray Dupree." Gerald looked at his friend then and his eyes searched the dark, bearded face. "And Watts, this one's important."

"I'm on it, G," Watts said, rising from the table.

Gerald saw him out the front door and went to his den. He sat on the couch and turned on the music. Too antsy to sit still, he got up and journeyed the room. He would admit it to no one, but the note had him scared. For now though, Leah was in his home, and she was safe. Gerald bridled his anger and left the den. In his bedroom, he stood at the edge of the bed staring down at Leah. She was resting peacefully and that made him feel a little better. Laying his hand on her forehead and feeling coolness instead of the blistering heat he'd felt earlier comforted him even more.

He turned from the bed, changed into a pair of silk pajama bottoms, and climbed in beside her. He wasn't tired, he told himself as he wrapped his arms around Leah. He just needed to be near her. "I love you, baby girl," Gerald whispered in her ear, "and no one's ever going to harm you. I promise." The pledge was repeated over and over until fatigue finally sneaked up on him. His eyes closed and Gerald and fell into an exhausted slumber.

One eye opened in response to the soft chimes beside the bed. Gerald glanced at Leah and picked up the receiver. "Morris," he mumbled.

"G! Where have you been?"

"With Leah."

"Well, I've been catching hell from J.J. all day. I don't know what set him off, but the man totally tilted on me.

He mumbled something about a TyJo takeover. Call him, G. He sounds like he's losing it."

"I'll take care of it, Pete," Gerald replied, glancing at the clock. It was 9:00 p.m. He had been asleep for over four hours. "Anything else?"

"Yeah, I need to bend your ear. When can you give me some time?"

"Leah's sick and I'll be here taking care of her. If it's important, you know the address. If it can wait, I'll hook up with you in a few days."

"It can wait," Peter responded. "I'll check with you in a couple of days. Later."

"Later." Gerald hung up the telephone and turned to face Leah. He pulled the covers over her shoulders and closed his eyes. Opening them, he muted the phone. Leah hadn't coughed in a while and she seemed to be resting comfortably. It was the last thought Gerald had before falling into a deep sleep again.

Twenty-five

July 15

The loud clap of thunder had awakened her and Leah sat huddled against the headboard with a pillow clutched against her chest. Wide, terrorized eyes searched the darkened room and when a figure loomed in the doorway, Leah sprang from the bed and crouched in a corner.

The lights came on as Gerald entered the room.

"No!"

He came to a standstill and his eyes riveted to the woman on her knees hugging the wall. "Leah?" he said, moving forward again.

"No! Please don't! I can't take any more."

The frigid wind that blew through Gerald's body felt very real. It turned his blood to shards of ice that prickled his skin. His heart pumped at a furious pace as he focused totally on getting to Leah. He inched forward in half steps. "Leah. It's Gerald," he said soothingly. "Do you know where you are?"

Leah's eyes never left his face. When they dropped to his shirtless upper torso, she screamed, "Don't touch me!"

Almost to her now, Gerald continued to speak softly. "It's Gerald, Leah, and you're in our bedroom." A few

more steps and he was close enough to grab her hands.
They felt as cold as ice. Gerald hauled Leah up into his
arms.

On the bed, he sat with her on his lap. Jesus, he
thought, holding her quaking body. What in the world
was going on? What could have happened that was so
horrifying Leah would act like this? A shudder rippled
through him and gathering her closer, Gerald rocked
Leah, crooning words of calm in her ear and rubbing her
small back until he felt her relax in his arms.

"Are you all right?" he asked, his voice husky with
emotion.

Leah nodded and snuggled closer. This was where
she belonged and he would protect her. She turned her
face into his chest, breathing in his male scent, breathing
in Gerald. Succumbing to the wild craving whipping
through her, Leah ran her palm over the hard density of
his chest.

"Sweetheart," Gerald said, catching her hand.

More interested in the arms that had her wrapped in
paradise, Leah cut him off. "Gerald, it was just a nightmare and I'm sorry if I scared you."

There was something she was not telling him and
Gerald wanted to know what. His gaze dropped to her
face and his heart stepped up its pace when he saw hot
desire shining in her eyes. Gerald squashed the groan
in his throat. He couldn't think about that now. He needed to get her talking. "I think it was more than that,
Leah."

Using his shoulders, she pulled herself up, headed for
the sweet, full lips above her. He solidified his hold
around her back and raised her to within reach. He
placed a soft, silky kiss at the corner of her mouth. "Is
this what you want, sweetheart?" His mouth continued
to move lightly over her lips. "Tell me what you want."

Leah placed her hands around his face, stopping his

teasing movements. Staring deeply into his eyes, she fastened her mouth on his with a hungry urgency. His hands burrowed under the nightgown and explored the smoothness of her back. He laid her on the bed. Moaning deeply, he returned the kiss, matching Leah's ardent fervor. She was pulling him under and Gerald went willingly.

His mouth suddenly stopped moving. He couldn't do this. Leah was suffering an emotional crisis and all he could think about was sheathing himself deep inside her. He sat up. "Leah, we need to talk."

She placed a warm, wet kiss in the middle of his spine, causing him to shiver. Reaching behind him, Gerald pulled Leah into his lap. "Later," he growled, kissing her. "Right now I want to talk, and I want to talk about what just happened."

It was like a douse of cold water. Leah shoved at Gerald's chest. Expecting the move, he held her still. "Leah. You know I'd do anything for you, but I can't help unless you talk to me. I want...no, I need to know what's going on with you."

Leah remained deathly silent, her face distorted by a misery so dismal Gerald knew he'd never understand. A steel-like band compressed his heart and feeling her slipping away, he secured his grip on her body.

Leah lowered her head to his chest and burst into tears.

"It's okay, baby girl. Tell me and I'll take care of it."

She'd held everything in for so long that once the dam broke, Leah couldn't stem the flow. She nestled against Gerald, weeping for all she was worth. Her gut-wrenching sobs ripped at his heart, but Gerald let her cry. When she finally stopped, he asked, "Feel better now?"

Embarrassed, Leah's eyes remained downcast. "I'm sorry, G. I didn't mean to use you as a Kleenex."

"It's okay. I'm yours to use any way you see fit,"

Gerald said, brushing her lips with his. "Can you talk to me now about what happened?"

Leah stepped out of his arms and moved across the room. "It was a combination of things, Gerald. The storm, my problems with Project Spruce. Just a number of things really and, if you'll recall, I have been sick."

Gerald moved to her side. "Yes, you have," he agreed, more in an effort to keep her talking than anything else. "But I don't think what happened tonight had anything to do with your being sick. Do you?"

A crash of thunder had Leah hugging herself to keep from jumping. Gerald's eyes narrowed. "Is it me? I know you've been upset with me lately. Project Spruce? Your job?" His jaw hardened in frustration. He was running out of guesses and Leah hadn't responded or made any indication he was on the right track. "Does it have something to do with Dupree?"

Leah's body tensed. "Michael Ray is a drug-pushing loser. I was stupid to ever get involved with him and I certainly don't want to talk about him."

Bingo, Gerald thought. And now that he had hit on the cause of her distress, he wasn't about to let the conversation go that easily. "What does Dupree have to do with this, Leah?"

When Leah walked back to the bed, Gerald followed. She sat in the middle and crossed her legs Indian-style. She didn't look at him but knew he'd sat, too when she felt the dip in the bed. She began talking.

"About a week after breaking up with him, I realized I'd left some of my things in Ray's condo. Clothes, albums and other stuff like that. So I called and asked if I could come by and get them. Michael Ray readily agreed, which probably should have been a warning to me." Leah looked at Gerald to gauge his reaction so far. Except for the slight rigidity of his posture, he seemed perfectly composed.

"Go on."

"Well, I had to work late that day and by the time I got to the condo it was dark. In hindsight, I know it wasn't smart to go there alone. My things weren't really valuable and I've asked myself a thousand times why I felt the need to get that stuff. But I wanted a finality to the relationship," Leah said, waving her hand as if the words were unimportant. "Anyway, at the house, I followed Michael Ray into the living room and I found my things. He had destroyed everything and left it in a pile in the middle of the floor.

"I couldn't believe it and I was angry, but I didn't say anything. I decided it would be best to just leave. Michael Ray let me get all the way to the door before he pulled me back. I had no clue when he turned me around that he would hit me in the face with his fist. I hadn't recovered from that shock before he punched me in the stomach. I don't know how many times he hit me because I blacked out. When I woke up, at first I didn't understand why my body felt so sore or why I couldn't move my mouth or open my left eye. There was a dresser in the room and it wasn't until I looked in the mirror that I saw what Michael Ray had done."

Leah stopped when Gerald left the bed. He moved like a caged animal and she could hear his soft rambling. "It shouldn't have happened, not to you."

"It did happen and I survived."

Gerald went back to the bed. "But the storm. What does the storm have to do with this?"

"I was locked in that attic for three days while a storm raged outside. Michael Ray's mood seemed to ebb or flow with the ferociousness of the weather and when he wasn't conducting a drug deal in that room, he continued what he'd started on me. Most of the time he just slapped me around, but at times he seemed more crazed. I spent several weeks in the hospital recovering from his attack."

Gerald sat mute. He held Leah to him in an embrace of comfort, but couldn't stop the frenzy of rage rippling through his body. It took several long minutes before he could bring himself under control. "How did you get away, Leah?"

"Merri," she answered matter-of-factly. "When she couldn't reach me at home or at work, she called the police. They had been watching Michael Ray for some time and when they broke down that door I was never so thankful in my life. Luckily, I was conscious and aware enough to show them where the drugs were hidden."

Gerald rose and resumed his pacing. Leah observed his tightly drawn features. "Gerald, what's done is done, so let's just forget it." Leah would have said more if not for the boom of thunder that froze her body with fear.

Gerald looked down into the wide, petrified eyes. Enough, he thought. He pulled up the covers on the bed and Leah climbed in. He removed his clothes and joined her in the bed. In the dark, he fitted their bodies together.

"G."

"Yeah."

"I've never told the whole story of what happened in that attic to anyone but Merri."

"Then I'm glad you trust me enough to have share it with me."

Gerald broke the quiet after a few minutes. "Leah."

"Yeah."

"What I feel for Malcolm...is anger."

Leah didn't respond. If Gerald was ready to talk, she wanted him to do so without interruption from her. But she smiled with happiness that he was finally opening up and maybe, just maybe, she would get her G back. She laid her hand on his chest just to let him know she was listening.

Gerald wrapped his arms around her and Leah snuggled closer. "He left my mother and my sister in that ghetto. He just walked away like he didn't have a responsibility or care in the world and every time I think about what he did, I get angry. My mother struggled for years to get us out of that place and she shouldn't have had to. She had a husband! A husband who made a promise to take care of her. He had an obligation to do that for her and that man just got up one day, left the house and never returned. Men are not supposed to do that, Leah. Men are supposed to take care of their women and children."

"But what if he had a reason, something that made Malcolm think he had to leave?"

"There is no excuse for what Malcolm did. But I've been taking my anger at him out on you and I'm going to stop doing that. I'm trying to find a way to deal with this, Leah, but I don't know what to do. I always know what to do and for the first time in my life, I don't. That's why I couldn't talk to you about this. I didn't want to shut you out, but at the same time I didn't want to bring you into my state of confusion. Do you believe me?"

They were so close his mustache tickled her nose. "I believe you, Gerald, and I won't try to tell you how to feel, because that's something you have to work through for yourself, but have you talked to Malcolm?"

"No, and I don't plan to."

"What if he did have a valid reason for leaving?" When he tried to pull away, Leah held onto Gerald and kept him close. "Baby, I'm not saying Malcolm was right to do what he did, but I know you are a fair man and I think it would only be fair to give him an opportunity to explain."

Everyone was telling him the same thing. His Mama, NayNay, and now Leah. Talk to Malcolm. They were giving him sound advice. Gerald just wasn't ready to take it and he wouldn't be until he could get rid of the anger. "I don't know if or when I'll be able do that, Leah."

"Well, I think it bears thinking about, G. It hurts me to know that you're in pain and there is nothing I can do to help you."

Gerald puckered his lips and touched the soft lips next to his. "I don't want you to hurt over this, baby girl. And don't add it to the list of things you're worried about. Just know that I would never do what he did, Leah. I would never leave you or our children."

"I already know that, G." She framed his face with her hands and joined their lips firmly together. She poked her tongue inside his mouth and teased the inside of his upper lip. When he tried to capture her tongue, she slipped it out and sucked on his lip. She kept up the game until she felt the muscles in his body ease into relaxation.

His palms began to stroke and caress her body, stoking the fire that always simmered just below the surface and Leah let him take control of the kiss. When he let her up for air Gerald asked, "Leah. Do you love me?"

Intuitively, Leah knew Gerald was asking a totally different question that had nothing to do with love. He wanted confirmation that she would not compare him to his father. But she would never to do that. Gerald was his own unique, highly temperamental, wonderful self.

"Yes, Gerald. I love you, and it is not conditional on anything or anyone else. Only you, and the man that you are."

Gerald hugged her tightly, then raised himself over her. Leah welcomed him into her body. They loved each other fast and hard, both trying to take away the other's hurt at least for one night.

"I love you, Leah," Gerald said when he moved to his side of the bed and she crawled on top of him. "And no matter what happens, my love is forever."

Twenty-Six

Gerald was smiling as he pulled the Porsche into the garage. The last six days away from home had been rough and he hadn't been in the best of moods on this trip, but at least J.J., who had been about to bust a gut over the rumors and proposed offer, had been calmed. Since he was there, J.J. had also pushed up the meeting with Ebony Silk and Gerald had sat through round one of the negotiations. Pete had gotten SJB's latest video off to BET and he had the revised contract for Mattise in his briefcase. Everything else could wait until tomorrow. Six days away from Leah was too long.

The nightly phone calls had served only to make him want to come home. Their conversations had been long, flowery, often silly, statements of how much they loved each other. At times though, Leah had seemed distracted, almost as if he were keeping her from something more important. The fundraiser loomed before her and as focused as she was on Project Spruce and her job, the last thing Leah needed to add was writing a speech. It had aggravated Gerald to no end when she refused to let him hire someone to write the thing and be done with it. But that was his Leah, intractable and independent to

the end, two qualities he cherished in her that also
caused him the most grief. One thing he couldn't fault his
baby for and that was her consistency: Leah was consis-
tently stubborn.

Gerald went to the trunk of the car and retrieved his
suitcase. Whether or not Leah had missed him, he had
missed her desperately. After so long apart, tonight was
their night, and Leah was going to cook!

A figure moved from the shadows and into the light.
"Glad to see you got home safely."

"Anything happen while I was away?"

"Nope. She never even noticed that I was around. By
the way, I had a chat with a fella who seems real close to
Dupree." Watts lifted his lips in what could almost pass
as a smile. "The man should really exercise a little more
caution in choosing his confidantes. This one has an
affinity for booze and cocaine. Both of which I'll carefully conceal in your bill."

Gerald impatiently waved away the statement. He
wanted to know who was behind the buyout attempt of
TyJo and the identity of the person setting him up. "Did
he give us anything we can use to connect Dupree to
TyJo?"

"Not directly. But he did drop a couple of hints. I'm
heading to LA tomorrow. I'll let you know what I find out."
Watts held out a manila folder.

"Malcolm?"

"Malcolm," Watts confirmed.

"Well, that's something at least."

"Don't worry, man. It shouldn't be too much longer
before I wrap this up."

Gerald nodded. "Thanks, Watts."

"No problem, G."

Gerald waited until Watts disappeared into the night.
Then he entered the house through the back door. A few
minutes later, a frown marred his face as he moved

through the house searching for Leah. He hadn't smelled anything when he stepped into the kitchen; there hadn't been one pot or pan on the stove nor any signs of a meal in planning. Bounding up the steps, he moved quickly down the hallway. Evidence of Leah's concentration littered the sitting room floor. Gerald saw the balled up sheets as he crossed the bedroom. He stood in the doorway and watched Leah.

It was a few minutes before she felt him and looked up. "G!" She hopped up from the couch.

When Leah leaped into his arms, Gerald returned the hug and voraciously devoured her lips. A couple of minutes later, he set Leah on her feet and chuckled softly. "Looks like the speech writing isn't going too well."

Leah didn't answer because the doorbell chimed. She grabbed some money off the dresser and rushed down the stairs. Gerald followed more slowly.

In the kitchen, Leah scurried around the room. "I know I said I would cook, but I was so busy with the speech the time got away from me. I hope you don't mind."

Gerald crossed his legs, picked up his glass of juice, and continued to watch Leah dump Chinese takeout into serving dishes. "I don't mind, sweetheart."

Ten minutes into the meal, he said, "You have no idea how much I missed you, baby girl." Leah didn't respond and Gerald set his coffee cup in the saucer. For a few moments, he observed the distant stare. She might be looking at him, but her mind was somewhere else. "Leah, I'm talking to you. The least you could do is pay attention."

She blinked her eyes and really looked at him. "I'm sorry, but this speech really has me worried. It's been hard, but I finally managed to get something down on paper. Would you mind if I read it to you?"

So much for their evening, Gerald thought wearily.

"All right, Leah. Get the speech."

She stood in front of him when she returned. "Okay, here goes," she said, taking a deep breath. "Ladies and gentlemen. We are all glad that you could attend the festivities today. Project Spruce is a very worthwhile organization and we've done a lot of things for the community. However, we need your time and we need your money or in a few short weeks Project Spruce will have to close its doors. I'm sure none of you want to see that happen. So please see one of our representatives and ask how you can help. Thank you."

Mortification highlighted her cheeks when Leah heard the deep chuckle. "I'm glad you find this so amusing, Gerald. However, it's not quite the reaction I was going for."

Gerald sucked in his cheeks to stop his laughter. "I'm sorry, baby girl. It's just that—"

The hands went to the hips. "Just that what, Gerald?"

"Well, for one thing, you mentioned that Project Spruce is a very worthwhile organization. Why? And what is Project Spruce? Secondly, you refer to a lot of things PS has done for the community. If I were in the audience, I'd want to know what things specifically. Third, it is evident by your demeanor that you're scared out of your mind and you're in our kitchen. Are you sure you're going to be able to stand in front of a bunch of strangers and give that speech?"

Leah's chagrin turned to anger. "Thank you for your heartfelt criticism, Gerald. It's nice to know that my man has so much faith in me."

Gerald rose from his chair and crossed the floor. He turned Leah to him and rested his arms over her shoulders. "Sweetheart, it sounds like you're taking this on a personal level."

"Isn't that how I was supposed to take it?"

"Baby girl, you don't have put yourself through this."

Gerald paused, recalling how Leah had gone off on him the last time he tried to prohibit her from attending a PS meeting. "Why don't you let me take care of this for you?" he suggested. "I'll write a check for whatever that organization of yours needs right now."

Gray eyes changed to the color of warm smoke. "Gerald, if you would like to make a contribution to Project Spruce, then do it because you believe in what we are trying to accomplish. Not because you think I'm incompetent."

"I never said you were incompetent, Leah, and I wouldn't give money to an organization I didn't believe in. The service Project Spruce provides in this community is unquestionable and needed. What I am trying to do is get you out of...I only want to help."

"I don't want that kind of help, and I don't want you taking care of things for me because you think I can't handle them." Leah turned away and left the kitchen.

Gerald caught up with her at the staircase. "Where are you going?"

"To pack. Since my speech needs so much work, I thought I'd go back to my place where I can give it the uninterrupted devotion it needs."

His face became a mask of stone. She was not going back to that apartment, especially after the rock and the note. "Leah. You are not leaving this house. Now, if you want to work on that speech, then take yourself right back up those stairs and do it."

Leah was so angry, she couldn't speak. When? When was this man going to stop treating her like a child?

Gerald walked away in the direction of his den. A minute later, she heard the faint strains of music. The walls in the house were so thick, Leah knew that if she could hear the music, it was blasting and he was walking the floor. She slowly climbed the staircase. If Gerald wouldn't take her home tonight, in the morning, she'd call a cab.

∽

August 4

The sun rose. The sun set. Leah knew the pattern well because she had counted off the days, and now that the fundraiser was just two days away her misgivings had risen to epidemic proportions. She was no closer to having a speech written than she'd been five days ago.

Pushing the laptop away, she rose from the table. In the kitchen, she filled a copper kettle and set it on the stove. She grabbed a mug, placed a tea bag in it and leaned back against the counter hugging herself while she waited for the water to boil.

Working on the speech and last minute details for the fundraiser didn't leave time for much else and Leah had fooled herself into thinking she was glad she had something to keep her mind off Gerald. Her aching body told a different story. She missed him. She missed his soothing touch and the sound of his voice. She missed Gerald.

Their passion for one another was undeniable; mentally they were on different planes. Staying away from Gerald was the hardest thing she'd ever done, but too much was happening in her life right now to continue the contest of wills with him.

Sighing when the kettle whistled, Leah filled her cup and carried it to the table, grumbling about going with her first effort. It wasn't really that good a speech and while Gerald might have been more diplomatic in his criticism, he was right. Her speech had to grab the attention of the crowd and convince them to reach into their pockets and dole out money by the handfuls.

Pulling the agenda of activities from the PS folder,
Leah sipped at the tea and reviewed the list. The Ashanti
Dance Troupe had agreed to perform. She remembered
the first time she had seen the group on stage. They had
mesmerized the audience and when the show ended, it
had taken a few moments before applause had broken
out in the auditorium. Leah hoped to garner the same
reaction at the festival.

Leah continued to review the list, but her eyes kept
returning to the Ashanti Dance Troupe. Her brow rose
and Leah set her cup down. Pulling the laptop forward,
she began to type. Now that she had hit upon an idea,
her fingers flew over the keyboard.

Four hours and many edits later, Leah was finally satisfied with what she had written. She saved the document and rose from the table. Tomorrow, she'd print a
hard copy and give it to Rachel for the files. She had the
speech firmly in her mind and she would not need a written reminder. She also planned to hit the mall.
Hopefully, she'd find what she wanted and it would not
stretch her budget too far.

Rachel dug her nails into Michael Ray's back and
whimpered delightedly when he grunted and crushed her
body beneath his. Ray had been so happy when she'd
given him the article. And it had been easier than she'd
thought to get her hands on it.

For the last few days, Gerald had been like a raging
bull around the offices of The Path. She had gone to
Susan to find out what was wrong and was told that in
nine years, not once had Gerald Morris ever raised his
voice to her or any of the other employees. That's when
he had appeared in the doorway.

"Where are the revisions on the Mattise contract?"

"I don't have them yet," Susan replied. "Mr. Wilkins said—"

"Save it, Susan! I am not interested in hearing excuses," Gerald rudely interrupted. He tossed a report on her desk. "But I do want an explanation for these cost overruns on the supplies for the stores."

Astounded, Susan lifted her hand to her chest. Gerald never questioned her decisions regarding the stores. "Give me a minute to gather my files and I'll come to your office."

Her brown eyes filled with concern when Gerald stalked away. Shaking her head in confusion, Susan turned to Rachel and shrugged her shoulders, then picked up her keys and moved to the files. Rachel smiled when Susan left her office, leaving the keys hanging in the lock.

Reading the article, she had been stunned to learn that Gerald Morris was co-owner of TyJo Productions and wondered why Leah Ellis hadn't known. Maybe she did, Rachel thought shrewdly. Maybe that innocent act of Leah's was just that. An act. She had her own copy of the article. There had to be a way she could use it to her advantage.

Rachel smiled again as Michael Ray continued to lap at her breast. "Ray. Don't you think it's time you made that proposal?"

As if he hadn't heard her, Michael Ray moved from her body and left the bed. Rachel watched him cross the bedroom and light a joint. He folded one arm across his middle and inhaled deeply. He leaned back against the dresser and studied her. "What proposal?"

Rachel reached for the tray. Ray was joking around, she thought. "You said when I delivered the article, we would get married."

Michael Ray put out the joint, moved to a chair and picked up his trousers. "Rachel, I only said that because you were leaning the wrong way in your decision to help me," he responded, stepping into his pants. He picked up his shirt.

She took several hits from the tiny silver spoon. "But Ray. You said you loved me and that you wanted to get married."

"Love you?" Michael Ray laughed. "Rachel, what makes you think I would tie myself down to a coke head whore like you?"

Stunned, bewildered tears formed in Rachel's eyes. "Ray! You've been coming to see me and have been in my bed for the last year and I thought—"

"You thought what, Rachel? That this was about you?" Michael Ray's chuckle sounded nasty. "Well, just so you know, it's not. And you're not that good in bed; I've had a lot better. But the woman I love is on her way back, which means you're out."

Rachel already knew the answer and didn't understand why she felt the need to torture herself by hearing him say it. "Who are you in love with, Ray?"

Michael Ray sat in the chair. He bent over and slipped his feet into a pair of Italian loafers before responding. "Leah. I've loved Leah since she was sixteen. She is the only woman who has my heart and she'll have it until the day I die." Michael Ray stood up and went to the mirror.

Rachel closed her eyes. When she opened them again, they were a firestorm of pent-up fury. "In case you've forgotten. Leah Ellis has a man!"

Michael Ray gathered his hair back and snapped the rubber band around his ponytail. "Not for long, baby. I spent eight years grooming Leah to be my wife and Morris is an indiscretion I'll forgive her for in time. Besides, he has an appointment with a bullet. And once the deed is done, I'll be there to comfort Leah through her time of grief. She'll be so grateful, don't you think?" Michael Ray checked his image in the mirror one last time and moved to the door. "It won't be long after that and Leah will be right back where she belongs. With me, her man."

"You bastard!" Rachel screamed. She swiped away the tears dripping from her eyes. After snorting so much coke, Rachel's head felt as if it would explode. But she couldn't stop herself from asking the next question. "I gave that article to you yesterday, Ray. Why did you come here tonight?"

Michael Ray stepped through the doorway and turned back. His face displayed a vulgar grin. "To give you one last thrill. By the way, the blow's on the house." His heinous laugh rang out in the hallway, and he never saw the green-flowered tray come flying after him.

Rachel scrambled off the bed and fell to her knees. Her hand moved frantically as she tried to scoop the disappearing white power from the brown carpet and onto the tray. Realizing it was useless, she sat back on her haunches and let the tears fall. Ray had used her again and it was all Leah's fault.

When she finally stopped crying and lifted her head, her features had twisted in grotesque hatred. Rachel picked herself up from the floor and kicked the tray across the room. Stomping to the dresser, she removed the article from a drawer and for a few minutes studied Gerald's picture. Michael Ray had crushed her about as low as she was willing to go. She lifted her head and looked at the shattered woman in the mirror. Rachel didn't know who she hated more: Michael Ray, Leah or herself. What she did know was that the time had finally come to do something about it.

She dropped the picture on the dresser and turned away. She went to her nightstand and picked up the telephone. She dialed a number and waited through several rings before the call was answered. When she heard the familiar deep voice, tears began to roll down her cheeks again. "Daddy," she began. "I'm in trouble and I need to come home."

Twenty-Seven

August 6

L eah picked up the colorful silk material and held it up for examination. She'd been in the store only a few minutes and the outfit was exactly what she wanted. She headed for the fitting room. Dressed, she stood in front of the full-length mirror outside the room.

"You look positively stunning."

The deep voice worked its way through her and Leah turned slowly. The haggard furrows lining his face and guarded pain shining in his eyes told Leah that Gerald hadn't weathered their separation any better than she. Her love for him swelled and she fought to hold her ground. They had some major problems, but she couldn't help feeling a little guilty about the effect her leaving had obviously had on him.

Gerald tried to absorb Leah with his eyes and keep his composure, which for the last few days had been hanging by a thread. When he awakened to find Leah gone, his emotions had run the gamut from disbelief to anguish. Though Gerald had respected her wish not to see him, everyone around him had felt the brunt of his broken heart. "I've been following you," he said in answer to Leah's unasked question. To break the rising tension, he added with dispirited humor. "And it took all of my driving skills to keep up with you on that freeway."

"Following me?"

"Yep. I want to apologize for my behavior the other night. You have every right to be angry with me, Leah. I was wrong to belittle your efforts and to say what I said in the manner that I said it. I was boorish and rude and tried to take away something that is very important to you because I selfishly wanted you to myself. I love you, Leah, and I believe you can do anything you set your heart on. I've also cleared my schedule for the day. I'll do anything you want me to do to help with the fundraiser."

This had to be a humbling experience for him and Gerald looked so forlorn, Leah took pity on him. "That was very nice, G, and I accept your apology."

"You do?" A facetious glimmer entered his eyes when Leah nodded. "Well, in that case, I still think the speech needs work. Now, you've written the bulk of it, but together we can polish it up and you can practice your delivery on me all afternoon."

Leah pursed her lips to keep from smiling. So much for making amends. "Gerald, you were right about that speech and I put it in the trash."

Compunction dimmed the light in his eyes. "Leah, you shouldn't have thrown your speech away because of anything I said."

Her eyes twinkled. "Why not? You were absolutely right. But I've written another speech."

"Then I'll help you with that one."

"No, thank you, Gerald. The speech is done and I think it will be okay." She turned back to the mirror. The outfit was lovely, Leah mused, looking down to check the cost. Her eyes bulged when she saw the ten thousand dollar price tag.

"What's wrong?"

Leah cleared her throat. "Nothing," she replied huskily. "It was an idea I had for the fundraiser." That was her problem: always trying to drink champagne on a beer budget. She moved to another rack and removed a hanger. Having learned her lesson, Leah looked at the price tag first. Four hundred; that was more in the range of her wallet size. She moved back to mirror. Though nice, the outfit didn't come close to the one she had on, but it would do.

When she came out of the dressing room, Gerald was still there. "Leah, I really did clear my day, so what do you want me to do?"

"Nothing," she replied, surveying herself in the mirror. "Everything's done."

His eyes took on an immediate glow. "Good. Then how would you like to spend the evening relaxing by going out with me?"

"Can't, G. Everything's done, but I want to stay by the phone, just in case."

"Leah, you need to relax before your big day and knowing you, if you say everything's done, then I don't think you need to worry. So how about it?" Gerald followed her to the door of the dressing room. "Leah?"

She turned around. "Okay, G."

Later that afternoon, Leah answered the knock at her door and stepped back when she saw the uniformed man. He cleared his throat and held out a white envelope. "Miss Leah Ellis?" She nodded. "This is for you."

With hesitation, she took the envelope and when the man didn't go away, she reached for her purse. She held out a couple of bills. "Not necessary, miss," he said. "I'm supposed to wait."

He stepped back from the door and leaned against the wall. Leah closed the door. She sat on the couch and removed the letter inside the envelope.

Sweetheart,
Go with the driver. He has full instructions. And know-ing how your mind is working right this minute, I'll tell you what is going to happen. I promised you a relaxing evening. It will begin at Roxanne's. She is a friend and knows exactly what I want done, beginning with a full body massage. The driver will take you next to Selena's, also a friend. She'll do your hair and also has a dress and shoes. Then you'll be brought to where I am waiting for you. And that, baby girl, I'm keeping as a surprise. I love you and will see you in a little while.

G.

Leah dropped the letter on the couch and ran back to the door. Leaning against the wall, the uniformed man straightened when he saw her. "You ready, miss?"

Leah retrieved the letter and her purse and returned to the door. "Yes, I am."

Merri was standing outside the apartment building when Leah reached the street. Baffled, Merri looked from the chauffeur to Leah to the silver stretch limousine. "What's going on?"

Leah grinned at her. "Gerald." She handed Merri the note.

She watched the stunned expression on her friend's face as she read the letter. It had turned to concern by the time Merri finished. "Leah, where are you going?"

"To meet Gerald, after all this pampering of course."

"But Leah. Where are you meeting Gerald?"

"You read the letter, Merri. It's a surprise." When Leah saw Merri's frown, she added, "It's all right. This is Gerald and I'll be fine."

"I'm not going to rain on your parade, Leah. But when you arrive at this surprise destination, call me."

"Thanks, Merri," Leah said, giving her a hug, "and I will."

Merri hugged her back. "Promise?"

"Uh-huh. I have to go now. G's waiting for me."

Merri watched the chauffeur open the door and Leah step into the limo. Inside, Leah found a silver, ice-filled bucket, a bottle of sparkling cider and yellow roses. She turned and waved at Merri, then settled back in the seat.

Merri returned the wave, but the trepidation stayed on her face and she watched the car until it rounded the corner. When she turned around, the frown on her face turned to a scowl when she saw Sheila.

"Was Leah in that limo?"

"Yes."

Sheila clenched her hands at her sides. "Where is she going, Merri?"

Merri appraised Sheila from head to toe. "I know you don't expect me to answer that, girlfriend."

"Merri, please! I need to know. Where is Leah going?"

"Then you'll just need to know," Merri replied, crossing the street to her house.

Sheila pulled the red leather skirt over her hips and went into the bathroom. She took out her makeup kit, poured foundation on the sponge and hastily dabbed at her face. Ray would be furious. She was supposed to show up with Leah, but she'd arrived at the apartment too late. The sponge fell from her hand into the sink and Sheila gripped the counter's edge. Her face suffused with foreboding. What would he do to her this time?

Two hours later, Sheila was holding her cheek in an attempt to quiet the pain from the slap just delivered by Michael Ray. "Damnit! Where is she?"

Sheila cowered on the couch. That was the third time Michael Ray had hit her. She used the back of her hand to wipe the blood from her mouth. "I-I don't know. When I got there, Leah was getting into a limo and Merri wouldn't tell me."

Michael Ray was so angry, he rose to his toes. "I told you to bring Leah here, Sheila. That's all I asked you to do."

"I tried, Ray. I really did."

Michael Ray grabbed Sheila by the hair and yanked her up from the couch. "Well, since you couldn't carry out that simple assignment. Maybe you'll do better at this one."

Michael Ray released her hair and grabbed Sheila by the arm when she tried to run. He dragged her through the house and out the front door. He shoved her into a car and drove through the streets like a madman until he pulled up outside a mansion. It sat on several acres of property, secluded by a thick circle of trees for privacy. Although she'd never been inside, Sheila was familiar the place. It was on of Ray's houses, and used to entertain his wealthier, more distinguished clients.

Sheila didn't move from the car until Michael Ray grabbed her by the arm and pulled her out. At the door, he hauled her inside. They entered a mirrored room with red walls and a wooden bar that seemed to dominate the space. Attractive waitresses wandered through the tables spaced throughout, and by the cards and stacks of bills on the table, Sheila knew heavy betting was taking place.

Michael Ray yelled for attention. "This one's on the house," he bellowed, and after jerking her forward, he turned and left.

Aghast, Sheila watched him go. When she turned around, her entire body numbed with fear when she saw several of the men leering at her.

~

The limousine came to a halt beside a silver and red helicopter. Leah glanced at the back of the driver's head, then looked at the helicopter again. She tapped on the glass. The driver lowered the panel.

"Is Mr. Morris here?"

The driver's eyes met hers in the rearview mirror for a moment before he got out of the car. He opened the back door of the limousine and took off his cap.

"But is Gerald Morris here?"

"Miss, I'm to follow my instructions. Will you please step from the car?"

He snapped his boots together and stood holding the door. Leah left the car, and apprehension set in when a man exited the hanger and hurried toward her

"Hello, Leah," he said when he reached her. "My name is Ralph Jenkins. I'm Gerald's personal pilot. If you'll come with me, I'll take you on the last leg of your trip."

Leah took the hand he offered and followed him to the helicopter. Ralph admired the shimmering lavender gown and matching heels as he settled her inside. He sneaked another peek at Leah's face as he adjusted the gears and elevated the craft. Gerald Morris had all the luck.

Some time later, he landed in a field and through the windshield, Leah saw a white cottage. Three chimneys rose to the sky and a white picket fence surrounded the yard. The dirt driveway on the right side of the house continued to the back and a stone path starting at the porch led into a grove of trees where Leah caught a glimpse of large lake. But the curtains on the windows were drawn, the house dark and the dirt drive empty.

Leah took several deep breaths and turned to Ralph.

"Is he here?"

"He's waiting for you down by the lake." Ralph came around to help Leah out of the aircraft. "Just follow the stone path, and have a good evening, Leah."

Leah trembled and pulled the white cape tighter. The chill, she knew, was not from the air. It was her anticipation of seeing Gerald. Once Ralph had taken off again, she started down the stone path. She saw him as soon as she passed through the trees. He was staring out at the lake and he was dressed in lavender, too.

Gerald turned. "Hello, baby girl," he said quietly. "It's about time you showed." He pulled Leah into his arms and kissed her. "I hope you've enjoyed your evening so far."

"I have. But why have you brought me all the way out here? Where are we?"

"I told you I wanted you to spend a relaxing evening," he replied. He took her hand started walking up the stone path.

Leah removed her hand from his. "Gerald, you know the fundraiser is tomorrow. How am I supposed to get back in time? I have to be at the park early to help set up the booth."

He took her hand again and began up the path. "Stop worrying, Leah. I'll get you back to Chicago in time."

"But the festivities start at nine."

Gerald stopped abruptly. "I would appreciate it, if you would refrain from mentioning Project Spruce or the fundraiser for the remainder of the evening."

His brow raised as if daring her to speak. Then he grabbed her hand again and started forward. But the closer they got to the cottage the slower Gerald's steps became. On the porch, he stopped altogether. He turned to Leah and surveyed for so long, her heart began a topsy-turvy spin. Gerald had a strange look in his eyes and she couldn't read it. When his hand lifted and brushed against her cheek, Leah brought hers up to cover his.

"Baby, what is it?"

Gerald turned away and opened the door. He ushered her inside the cottage and hit a panel on the wall, flooding the room with light. Thunderstruck, Leah whirled to face Gerald. He pushed his hands into his pockets and anxious brown eyes met astonished gray ones. Leah turned back to the spectacular sight laid out before her.

Sitting in the middle of a gleaming pinewood floor was a square, white clothed table. Two chairs with red velvet backs were pushed underneath. The table held porcelain china place settings, crystal wineglasses, two silver holders with red candles, and a low cut crystal bowl filled with water and red rose petals. A silver bucket of ice and two bottles sat nearby. And dozens of vases filled with yellow roses were placed in every corner of the room, on the bar, the bookcase, the mantle above the fireplace and on the table in front of a black leather couch.

Gerald removed her wrap, took her hand and led Leah to the table. He seated her, then moved off to the left and stopped in front of an entertainment center. He picked up a remote and when he hit the PLAY button, soft jazz music filled the air. Leah watched, stupefied, as three waiters, dressed in white coats and chef's hats, entered the room carrying silver-plated serving dishes. With a shaking hand at her throat, Leah looked at Gerald again. He smiled and winked.

When they'd served the wilted lettuce salad, stuffed veal steaks, parsley-buttered new potatoes, and lemon flavored broccoli flowers, the waiters left the room and another man, dressed in a black tuxedo, entered. He moved to the table and lit the candles. Then he lifted a bottle of cider from the bucket, popped the cork and filled their wineglasses. When he was done, he bowed in

Gerald's direction. "Will there be anything else, sir?"

At Gerald's dismissal, the man turned off the lights and left the room. A few minutes later, she heard the sound of a vehicle driving away. Gerald moved to the table and stood in front of her. Leah tried to stop the tears from flowing over. Gerald didn't have to do this. His apology this morning had been enough.

Gerald crouched down in front of her. "What's wrong, sweetheart? If you don't like this, then we'll do something else."

Leah dabbed at the tears in her eyes with her fingers. She gave him a trembly smile. "Don't like this? Are you crazy? I love it. But, Gerald. Why?"

Gerald sighed and stood up. He pulled the case with the ruby and diamond bracelet from the inside pocket of his blazer and raised her arm. "This belongs to you," he said, latching the bracelet onto her wrist. He pulled Leah gently from the chair, lifted her from the floor and kissed her. He moaned when he raised his head. Re-seating her, he moved to his chair. "I didn't do this to apologize, Leah. I did it because I love you."

Leah picked up the white linen napkin and spread it in her lap. A seductive smile touched her lips. "Gerald, did you cook this meal?"

"Yes. And don't look at me like that," he requested quietly. "Or we'll be eating it for breakfast."

Picking up his glass, Gerald leaned back and crossed his legs. His features remained expressionless, but thick lashes hooded the heated gaze centered on Leah. In the soft sentimental glow of candlelight, Gerald raised his glass to his mouth and his eyes began a visual exploration over molten gold skin and a full, slightly parted mouth. His eyes lowered to her chest and the optic massage he gave her breasts had Leah releasing whispery pants into the sexually charged air. Gerald adjusted his position in the chair and tried to remember that they had all evening, at the end of which, he hoped Leah would finally agree to become his wife.

Her own eyes wandered over the husky build in the tailored, loose fitting suit. The rich darkness of his skin stood out stark against the collar of the snow white, silk shirt. And when their eyes linked and held, the stare Gerald returned was swelteringly sultry in direct contrast to the cool glint of the inlaid diamond cufflinks at his wrists and the stone in his ear.

Her already warm cheeks flushed hotter as her heart began a rhythmic pounding in response to the provocative messages shooting between them. Totally entranced, Leah clasped fidgety hands in her lap. Then in an attempt to resist his alluring potency, she said, "Gerald is there a telephone I can use. I need to call Merri, and it's not about the fundraiser," she added quickly, when his brow rose.

"On the desk in the library," he replied, "but don't be too long."

Gerald was on the couch when Leah returned and their glasses were on the table. She lowered herself beside him, relaxing against his body and gently rubbed the back of his head as she reflected on the incredibly romantic evening he'd created; one Leah would always remember.

Standing suddenly, Gerald took off his coat and threw it on the chair. He sat on the couch again and took Leah into his arms. He toyed at her mouth until she sighed and wrapped her arms around his neck. Gerald drew her upright and removed the barrette holding her hair. When it tumbled down, he combed his fingers through the silky curls, then buried his hands in the thick tresses.

"So soft," he whispered, lowering her back down to the

couch. His tongue began stroking the underside of her jaw and she gasped. Hot breath teased her neck and she shivered. Gerald's teeth grazed her skin and Leah closed her eyes.

"Gerald." His name was a rasping whisper.

"Not now, baby girl," he murmured, closing his mouth over hers. He siphoned the cider from her mouth; his body quaked with an almost uncontrollable craving. Leah's reaction to his touch had his blood boiling, and only she could douse the heat. Not sure how he did it, Gerald managed to repress his urges. He was not going to make love to Leah on the couch. Standing, he held out his hand. When she took his hand and stood up, Gerald swung her into his arms. He kissed her again and headed for the bedroom, blowing out the candles as he passed by the table.

Twenty-Eight

August 7

A t one in the morning and after hours of lovemaking, Leah climbed on top of Gerald and closed her eyes. She had to get up in a little while and had just drifted off when she heard Gerald's question.

"Leah, will you please marry me?"

All she wanted to do was sleep, which was the reason her response was a little harsher than she intended for it to be. "No, Gerald. And I wish you would stop asking me."

"Why do you keep saying no?"

"Because we're just starting to learn about each other. And for a while, I would like to take this relationship one day at a time. But I do love you, Gerald."

Leah tumbled off his body when Gerald sat up. "You don't love me. If you did, you'd say yes."

Leah raised up on her elbow. "I do love you, Gerald. But there are some things about this relationship that concern me. You cannot continue to treat me like a child or storm around the house when you don't get your way. I'm a grown woman, able to take care of myself and make my own decisions."

Insulted, Gerald scowled. "When have you ever seen me storm around the house?"

She chose to ignore that question. "Gerald. You don't like the time I have to spend away from you and you want to tell me what to do. I need a man who can stand by me and support me as the woman I am. A man who knows that while I might have to take care of business, I can still love and take care of him, too. A successful marriage requires that both people be able to cooperate, understand and communicate with one another. You are a male chauvinist, Gerald, and your views on the role of women are outdated and out of place in this day and age. And I just don't know, Gerald, if the love we share is strong enough to survive the compromises of a marriage."

Gerald reached for Leah. She scooted to her side of the bed. "Tomorrow is a big day not only for PS, but for me. It's been a long night and I'm really tired. I love you, Gerald Tyler Morris."

Gerald rolled to his back. First, Leah refused to marry him. Now she didn't want to make love with him. Resentment fueled the gnashing of teeth. He wasn't a male chauvinist. He had grown up with women. His mother owned a successful real estate business and had single-handedly gotten them out of that ghetto. NayNay owned an interior design firm and had no problems taking care of William and the kids. And without Susan to keep him straight each day, he'd be absolutely lost. Why then did he have such problems letting Leah be the woman she was? He knew the answer: his mother and sister were not in danger; Leah was. He had to make her understand how much he loved her.

Emitting a low growl, Gerald moved across the bed and leaned down over Leah. He covered her face with a flurry of kisses, nudging her from sleep, then moved his lips over her throat, neck and shoulders. His mouth came down on hers. When she resisted, Gerald placed his hands on both sides of her face. "Open up to me, baby girl," he said, insistently stroking her mouth with his tongue until Leah parted her lips.

"I love you, Leah," he stated. "And I can be the man you need; the man you want." His lips moved lower until he encountered her breast. Taking a hardened bud into his mouth, Gerald suckled like a babe nursing its mother's milk.

Leah arched under the assault. "You are, baby. You are," she moaned deep in her throat.

Gerald placed Leah beneath him and rose over her. Holding on to her thighs, his entry was slow and deliberate. Then he stopped. "Tell me you love me," he demanded, setting his hips in motion. "Say it, Leah. Say you love me."

The red-hot blood her heart pumped flowed at an electrified rate, and had Leah so breathless, she couldn't respond. She grabbed his shoulders and held on as he placed kisses all over her face. When he reached her mouth, Gerald sucked her bottom lip. "Say it, Leah."

"I love you, G," she finally gulped as a fire started low in her belly and spread through her limbs. Their passion continued to rise...higher and higher...until it exploded like white lightening scorching the sky. Leah called out his name as both careened and fell off the cliff into a wondrous, rapturous place only those truly in love have ever visited.

When the glinting lights dimmed, Gerald shifted to his side of the bed. Replete, but feeling lonely without him, Leah nestled against his side. Soon, their hushed breathing was the only sound in the room. She slept. He did too, but not before saying a prayer that she loved him enough to spend the rest of her life with him.

❧

Gerald arrived in Adams Park and at the Project

Spruce booth just as the Ashanti Dance Troupe finished their performance. He shouldered his way to the front of the crowd and positioned himself in front of the stage as the last loud pound of the drum reverberated in the air. For a minute, all was strangely quiet; then the uproarious sound of clapping hands, shrill whistles and noisy cat-calls broke the unity of silence.

Spotting Watts, some of the tension left Gerald's body. Watts was on the stage posing as an electrician and he gave Gerald a thumbs up sign to signal that everything had been checked out.

Barefoot, Leah stepped to the microphone. Wearing a gèlèè, the traditional African headdress, and draped in purple cloth of the purest silk imprinted with African designs in gold and red, Leah looked every bit a royal princess. While she waited for the thunderous approval of the dancers to die down, her eyes roamed the sea of faces that varied in hues of ebony, chocolate, cream, cinnamon, ginger, and all the other shades of brown. When she came to the one she sought most, Leah's thoughts took her back to earlier that morning.

Gerald handed Leah a large, white box tied with a red ribbon. "I know how important today is and I hope you will accept this in the spirit in which it is intended," he told her. "It is being given for no other reason than that I love you."

"Thank you, Gerald," Leah replied, taking the box.

He kissed her and walked to the bedroom door. "You need to get a move on, though. Breakfast will be here in a few minutes."

Leah sat on the bed and untied the ribbon. Her eyes grew large when she opened the box and saw the dress she had tried on in the boutique. Tossing the box aside, she ran from the room and threw herself into his arms. "I love you, Gerald Tyler Morris!"

Dressed now in the outfit, Leah smiled at him and tried to ignore the moths spreading their wings in her stomach.

"I love you," Gerald mouthed.

Leah nodded, then took a long draw of air. She looked out over the body of people until the commotion died down and all eyes turned to the stage. Slowly, she raised her arm and pointed out at the crowd. "Back with you people! Back to the jungles whence you came! Back to the jungles to where you belong!"

When a collective gasp rose from the audience, Leah wanted to smile. She'd succeeded in getting the crowd's attention focused solely on her.

"Some look at us and see rundown projects and ghettos, drugs addicts and drunks, fatherless children, senseless crime, black-on-black violence and say we do not belong in America. Some say we are a people without heart. A people without pride. A people without a soul. I say...they are wrong!"

Leah heard the sighs of relief and continued.

"I stand before you today, the proud daughter of exalted African kings and glorified African queens. I stand before you today, the proud descendent of noble African chieftains and valiant African warriors. I stand before you today proud to be African and proud to be an American."

When the crowd began clapping again, Leah took another breath and gripped the microphone. "I also stand here before you today and my heart weeps. It weeps for our ancestors whose tears watered the cotton fields of the South. It weeps for our ancestors whose blood seeped into the streets in the fight for freedom and equality. It weeps for our ancestors, who gladly gave their lives in service for a country that is not ours by choice. It weeps when I look into the faces of my brothers and sisters today and see a lost people. A people who have been divided by those who do not have our best interests at heart. A people so separated, our children have been lost in our despair.

"I look and I ask, why? Why have we allowed others to control the future of our race? Why have slums become our shelters? Why have crime and gang warfare taken away our peace of mind? Why are the fathers of our children not helping to raise them? And why aren't we taking a proactive stand to do something about these problems?

"Ask yourself this question: when was the last time I looked into the face of a child and said, you are a descendent of a proud people? You are the descendent of a people steeped in a glorious history. You come from a people who were not afraid to pave the way for you and we expect you to live up to your heritage. Our ancestors were a people of hope. They were not afraid to stand up for their principles and demand to be heard. They were not afraid to band together and fight for their rights. Look at the person next to you. Do you know this person? Do you acknowledge the proud heritage you share? Join hands with the people next to you."

The PS volunteers sitting on stage came forward to join hands with Leah. She raised them in the air.

"Together, we are a strong people and this is our bond! It is our bond of hope! It is the bond that makes us stand tall…stand proud…stand united. Our vote is our bond for change. And we will use that vote to elect those who truly have the interests of this nation and its people at heart. Together, we will say no to the drugs! Together, we will say no to the slums! Together, we will say no to the crime and gangs! This is the bond of our heritage. It is the bond that holds us together and it is the bond we will pass on to our children!

"For anyone interested in learning more about Project Spruce, what we do, and how you can help shore up this bond with your time and donations, please see our booth representatives for more information. Thank you."

Leah left the stage amid the deafening eruption of applause that continued to grow louder the longer it went on. None clapped more loudly than Gerald. He pushed his way through the crowd and headed for the back of the stage. Leah had been spectacular, her speech bold and dramatic, her delivery emotional and thought pro-voking. Leah was sensational and she was his. He shouldn't have tried to stop her participation in Project Spruce. He should have offered to help her. He could do this. He could let her be Leah. And he would support and share her, as long as she always remained his.

Leah hadn't made it halfway down the backstairs before she was enveloped in a pair of young, hard arms. "Lele. You were absolutely wonderful."

"Thanks, Bobby."

"I'm going back out front. If the way that crowd was rushing the booth when you left the stage is any indica-tion, I can hear the register 'ka-chinking' with money."

Merri rushed forward. "Sister-girl! Didn't I say you could do it?"

"Yes, you did." Leah took hold of Merri's shoulders. "But don't ever ask me to do anything like this again. This had been the worst two months of my life."

Merri leaned back. "You are kidding, right?"

"I am kidding, Merri. Although I wouldn't want to make a habit of this."

Tony pulled Leah away from Merri and swung her around. "You were great, babe!" He set her to her feet.

"Thanks, Tony."

It was then that Leah caught sight of the shining light

brown gaze. Her eyes glowed with happiness when Gerald nodded his head in approval. When the last of her well-wishers stepped away, he came forward. "You were fabulous, Leah, and I'm very proud of you."

"Thank you, G."

"I hope you will accept my donation to this worthy cause."

Leah looked down at the check held in his outstretched hand and counted the zeros until she came to the number four that began the string. Four hundred thousand dollars! Gerald was giving Project Spruce four hundred thousand dollars. Leah took the check reverently. With this much money Project Spruce's doors would be open for a long time. Another crowd of people rushed Leah and Gerald stepped back. By the time she looked up again, he was gone.

Disappointed, she made her way to the trailer. She changed her clothes, pulling on a pair of blue jean shorts, a white blouse and her blue jean high tops. Shadowed by Watts, she delivered the check to Bobby, then wandered the park looking for Gerald. When she didn't find him, she sat at a picnic table feeling decidedly blue. At least Gerald could have said good-bye, or something.

"Hello, gorgeous."

She raised eyes animated with joy. "Were you speaking to me?"

"Since you're the most gorgeous creature here, I guess I am speaking to you." Gerald held out his hand. "And I hope you're hungry, gorgeous, because I'm starving."

The day passed quickly and Gerald and Leah wandered hand in hand through the park. Without her costume, she blended in with the populace, which was fine with Gerald. He wanted her to himself, and he could hardly wait until they were at home. Then he would show her just how much. But Leah wanted to stay and watch the fireworks display.

At twilight, they walked up the incline and stood with the crowd waiting for the show to begin. Gerald curved his arm around Leah's waist and pulled her against his side. It was good to feel her there, but not nearly enough to even begin to satisfy his need to touch her. When the first volley splintered the sky in a burst of red and gold, Gerald looked down into eyes that were wide and child-like.

"It's so pretty," Leah said in awe.

"Yep," he replied, never taking his eyes off her.

"Oh, G, look," Leah said, pointing as more fireworks exploded and another barrage of vivid hues fragmented against the black backdrop.

When she slumped against him, Gerald tightened his hold around her. The sticky dampness on his arm alerted him first. "Sweetheart?"

Gerald removed his arm and Leah crumpled to the ground. He fell to his knees beside her. In the fusillade of rockets lighting the sky, Gerald, crippled by his stupefied emotions, could only stare at the dark stain spreading on her white blouse. A woman next to them screamed and Gerald vaulted into action, yanking the cell phone from his back pocket.

"We need an ambulance now," he barked. "There's been a shooting in Adams Park!"

Twenty-Nine

"**W**hy?"

Gerald mumbled the word as he paced the floor of the waiting room.

"Lele's going to be okay, man," Bobby said, going over to him. "She has to be."

Gerald continued to walk. Merri stepped in front of him. "Gerald, will you please sit down! This constant moving is driving me crazy and it's not helping anyone. Now, Leah is going to be fine. You'll see. Leah will be just fine."

Gerald observed the others in the room. His mother sat on the lumpy sofa next to Mabel Ellis offering what comfort she could, and Malcolm sat next to her. Bobby propped his head in his hands and stared down the long, sterile hallway. Tony was at the window, his back to the room. Danye and Stacia were talking quietly, trying to console each other, and Peter held Ja'Nise, who was sobbing on his chest.

Only one person in the room appeared to be unaffected, and Sheila sat in a corner chair by herself. Her eyes were clear, her face calm. No one would have guessed that as she waited for news of her sister, her mind was occupied with Michael Ray and his callous treatment of her. Her cheeks burned with the humiliation of the previous night, but Sheila also knew that she'd been lucky; for most of the men in that room had left, possibly fearing public reprisals. However, two had stayed, and Sheila was planning her revenge.

She hadn't gone to the festival in the park, but had instead spent the better part of her evening waiting for Michael Ray to leave his office. When he did, she'd entered and removed his stash of joints from the teakwood box, replacing them with others she'd had specially made up. They wouldn't kill him, but if and when he smoked one, it would be a long time before Michael Ray Dupree would be able to think straight again. She'd had time to copy only a few of his accounting books before security began their nightly checks. But she'd get the rest; that Sheila vowed. And when she turned them over to the police, they would think they'd struck gold.

Overwhelmed by anger and grief, Gerald stalked off toward the front doors. Outside, he sat on a bench and bowed his head.

"Son, that young woman in there is not going to die. Leah is strong and she will pull through this. She has a reason to live—and that reason is you."

Gerald stood up. He wanted to believe Malcolm. He wanted to believe anything that would help him get through this.

Malcolm saw the emotions churning in his face. "Sit down, Gerald." He noted the space Gerald put between them on the bench and moved closer.

"Gerald, I know how much you love Leah. I can understand that kind of love. It's the same love I have for your mother."

"Malcolm, if you don't mind, I'd rather not talk about this right now."

Malcolm continued as if Gerald hadn't said anything. "I was wrong to leave your mother, Gerald. I should have been a man and stayed, no matter what. But at the time my failure to provide for her, for Beth and for you, even though you hadn't yet made an appearance, had beaten me to the ground. Your brother's death knocked me so low, I felt I'd never stand up again. I am so deeply sorry that I wasn't there for you, Gerald, and you'll never know how much I regret leaving my family and especially my son. The only thing I can do now is try and make it right. I know that you suspect my motives, but I'm not after your mother's money. I make my living as a financial advisor and I'm pretty good at it. I want only two things: an opportunity to reestablish my ties to the family and maybe to be a friend to you."

Gerald didn't lift his head from his hands. Leah was fighting for her life and nothing was more important to him than that. Besides, he had already read the report from Watts. He knew Malcolm was telling the truth. "Malcolm," Gerald sighed, looking at him, "if that's all you want—a tie to the family—I won't try to stop you. As for me, I can't make any promises. Right now, my woman is the only thing I can think about."

A few minutes later, they reentered the hospital. When Gerald saw the surgeon, his pace quickened. Mabel went to Gerald, who held her hands. They both looked at the doctor.

"Leah came through the surgery just fine," he said. "She's in ICU and is resting comfortably. There was a lot of internal bleeding and she lost a lot of blood, but she has been stabilized. She's sleeping now and the nurses will watch her closely for the next twenty-four to forty-eight hours."

Mabel searched his face. "What about the wounds?"

"We were most concerned about the bullet that entered her upper chest, but it was a clean wound and missed the arteries. The bullets that grazed her shoulder and hit her left arm were flesh wounds, causing only minor tissue damage. Physically, Leah should recover completely from this incident."

"When can we see her?" Gerald asked anxiously.

"Not for a few hours. As I said, Leah is resting and we don't want to disturb her just yet. But when you do see her, don't be surprised if she doesn't remember what happened. Memory loss is common when a person undergoes a traumatic ordeal. I'll keep you posted and let you know when you can go in."

The doctor smiled at them and walked back down the corridor.

"Miss Ellis? Miss Ellis, I need you to wake up now," a woman's soothing voice said.

It was several hours later, and Leah's lids drifted open to the bright light shining in her eyes. She tried to raise her body, but she lay back down and grimaced with pain. Why couldn't she move? She heard movement at her side. A large hand brushed curls back from her forehead.

"Hello, sweetheart. How are you feeling? No. Don't answer that. I imagine you're feeling pretty bad right now."

Leah tried to lift her hand. She wanted to wipe away the tear on his cheek. She groaned when a sharp pain pinched her. "G, why I can't move?"

Gerald looked at the nurse. "It's okay, Miss Ellis. The doctor will be in to see you shortly."

Leah lifted her head and surveyed her surroundings. Why was there a nurse in her room? Why was Gerald crying? She let her head fall and moaned. Everything hurt so badly.

Gerald jumped to his feet. "Give her something."

"I can't, Mr. Morris. Her chart says she was medicated only an hour ago."

"I don't care what that chart says. I said, give her something!"

"G," Leah called, her voice a scarce whisper. When he didn't respond, she tried again. "Gerald?"

He rushed to the bed and knelt again. "Leah, please. Give me a moment and let me deal with this." He looked at the nurse again. "Please help her."

Leah squeezed his arm and grimaced. "Gerald—"

"Leah, I just need a minute. I can fix this. You'll see. I can fix it." Gerald looked at the nurse. "Can't you see how much pain she's in? Help her."

The nurse saw the tears in his eyes and sympathy cramped her heart. She swallowed around the lump in her throat. "Mr. Morris, I can't. But I can go and find the doctor and bring him here right away."

"Thank you." Gerald gazed down at Leah and picked up one of her hands. "See, baby girl," he sighed. "I told you I could fix this. You're going to be okay, Leah. I promise."

∾

August 26

"How are you feeling, sweetheart?" Gerald asked the question as he entered the room carrying a bed table in his hands.

"I'm feeling just fine, Gerald."

In truth, Leah was going crazy. It had been a week since her release from the hospital. Gerald had safely ensconced her at his house and like a bee buzzing at a flower, his hovering had been constant. She knew he blamed himself for not preventing the shooting and that he was trying to be helpful. But Gerald Morris was getting on her nerves. She sat up and swung her legs over the side of the bed.

"What do you need, Leah?"

"Nothing. I'm going to the bathroom."

"Wait right there. Let me set down this tray and I'll carry you."

"Gerald, I do not need to be carried to the bathroom. I can walk." She gasped when the tray hit the dresser top.

"No! I said I would carry you." He strode across the room and lifted her from the bed.

Leah sighed as she put her arms around his neck and laid her head on his shoulder. How was she going to help Gerald get over this? Almost daily, his manner became even more possessive and dictatorial. And he adamantly refused to discuss the subject of her going home. Several times, she had awakened at night with the feeling of being smothered, only to find his arms wrapped around her so tight she could hardly breathe. Leah didn't know what to do. In the bathroom, she shooed him away when he would have lifted the night-gown for her and wasn't surprised to see him in front of the door when she opened it.

She was surprised later that afternoon when she heard familiar voices. Except for her family or his, Gerald didn't allow visitors.

"Merri! Tony!" Leah yelled, attempting to sit up.

"Hey, sister-girl. How are you feeling?"

"Much better, Merri. How are you? And Jimmy and Bobby and Project Spruce? Oh, how much money—?"

"Hey, babe, slow down," Tony said, bending over to kiss her on the cheek. He lifted his head to her ear when he felt the hand on his shoulder. "What's up with the bodyguard?"

"Oh, don't mind, Gerald. He means well. Anyway, both of you sit. I'm so happy to see the two of you."

"When are you coming home?" Merri asked.

"Soon." Leah looked at Gerald. "Probably a couple of days. Today, the doctor said I was making remarkable progress. I still have soreness in my chest, but I can get around pretty well."

"Leah won't be going home until I'm satisfied she can take care of herself," Gerald spoke up from the doorway. "And that's going to be more than a couple of days."

"But if her doctor said—"

"Leah stays here until I say she can go," Gerald interrupted. "You have fifteen minutes, then Leah needs to rest."

At Leah's insistence, Tony and Merri stayed for thirty minutes. When they left, Leah leaned back on the pillows and closed her eyes. She hadn't thought she was tired, but when Leah opened her eyes two hours later, she was surprised to see Sheila sitting in a chair by the bed. She looked around the room expecting to see her mother, too. Though Sheila came to see her each day, she had never come alone. She returned her eyes to her sister, wondering what was going on. "Sheila?"

"Hi, Leah. I just stopped by to see how you were doing."

Leah frowned "You did?"

"Yeah. Gerald let me in. I wanted to—"

Sheila's voice broke then and tears filled her eyes. When they spilled over and ran down her cheeks, Leah sat up in the bed, silenced by shock. Through the years, she'd witnessed many emotions in her sister; crying had never been one of them. Watching Sheila's struggle to compose herself, Leah felt an overwhelming urge to reach out and offer comfort, but she was hesitant, given their past. But this was her sister and Sheila was in pain. She couldn't just sit there and do nothing. Leah opened her arms. When Sheila left the chair, Leah enfolded and hugged her sister for the first time in years.

Holding Sheila in her arms, Leah remembered the happy little girl who used to follow her everywhere. Then, they had been inseparable, and it wasn't until Leah had become a teenager that things had begun to change between them. She remembered striking out on her own, making new friends and finding new interests. She also remembered the many times Sheila had begged to be included, and the harsh way she'd rejected those requests. Then she'd gotten herself involved with Michael Ray Dupree and had cut not only Sheila, but virtually everyone else out of her life.

Leah's mouth dropped open as comprehension dawned. She had abandoned her sister! That had to be the reason behind Sheila's behavior towards her. The more she thought about it, the more she realized that, while always appearing to hate her, Sheila had never tried to harm her physically. Rather, Sheila had been bent on ruining Leah's relationship with anyone she considered close. The revelation astounded her. And made her feel guilty. Still, she didn't want to spend this precious time rehashing the past. This was a chance to renew their bond of sisterhood; it might be the only chance she'd have. First though, she needed to apologize. "Sheila, I think I've finally figured out what went wrong between us and I am sorry. I didn't purposely mean to exclude you from my life. You're my sister and I love you and I want you to know that from now on—"

Sheila sat up. "No, Leah. I'm the one who's sorry. I've acted so hateful towards you and you didn't deserve it, and you certainly didn't deserve what happened to you. But I truly believed that Ray was in love with you. I never thought he'd try to hurt you again." Sheila dried her eyes. Her voice turned bitter. "But this time, Michael Ray Dupree is going to pay for what he's done—to both of us."

Confusion and anger lit Leah's eyes. "Sheila, you said to both of us? Did Michael Ray do something to you, too?" When Sheila shook her head and lowered her eyes, Leah picked up one of her hands. "Sheila. If Ray did something that hurt you, I want to know. I've already talked to the police and anything you can add will help put him back behind bars."

Sheila squeezed Leah's hand, then rose from the bed. "Don't worry. I'm taking care of everything and when I'm through, Ray Dupree won't bother either of us again!" She moved toward the door. "I have to go now."

"Sheila," Leah called. "Don't go. I want to talk to you."

Sheila faced Leah and smiled. It was the first smile she'd offered to her sister in a long time. "Leah, Gerald was very specific about the amount of time I could spend up here, but I'll come back tomorrow. We'll talk then."

Sheila left before Leah could say anything further. Staring at the closed door, Leah had to wonder what Sheila was up to and how she could help her sister.

That night, as Leah and Gerald lay together in bed, she took his face in her hands. "You were very rude to Tony and Merri this afternoon, G."

He looked contrite. "I know. I spoke with Tony before he left and I'll apologize to Merri when she's in a better frame of mind to listen. But I can't help it, Leah. I know you want to go home and I'm not going to let you. This is your home. If you go back to that apartment, I know something else will happen. Marry me and stay here."

Leah kissed both his eyelids and the tip of his nose. "Do you believe that I love you, Gerald?"

"Yeah."

"Then let it go, G. I'm going to be fine and we are together now. Let's just enjoy each other for whatever time we have. We are not guaranteed a tomorrow."

"Don't say that, Leah. You and I are forever."

"Are we, Gerald? How do you know?"

He leaned his head back on the pillow. "I feel it. But I can't ease up anymore. When you gave that speech at

the fundraiser, I was so proud of you and felt bad for trying to stop you from participating. That day, I'd decided
that maybe I had gone a little overboard. I was going to
loosen up and support you in whatever way you needed
me. And look what happened. That decision was wrong,
Leah. You are going to stay here where I can keep my
eye on you."

"And what happens when we go to work? Or what
about when you make a run to the store, or what if we're
out and you have to go to the bathroom?"

His brows furrowed. "I haven't exactly worked out all
the details yet."

Leah chuckled. "G, I love you so much, I can hardly
stand it.   But can't you hear how ridiculous this all
sounds? You cannot possibly protect me twenty-four
hours a day, and even if you could, I would not want it. I
want to love you and be free to live my life the way it is
supposed to be lived, and at the end of the week, I'm
going home."

∽

August 28

"Yes.   Eleven o'clock on the third is fine," Leah
responded, making the notation in her organizer. "Yes.
The fundraiser was a success, and I look forward to
updating Mr. Michaelson on that and other Project
Spruce activities. Good-bye."

Leah hung up the telephone. A frown of puzzlement
creased her face. The president of Maxwell Corp. wanted to meet with her? Why? Bobby and Tony handled the
financial side of Project Spruce and the company had
made it clear that their organization wasn't high on their
list of priorities.

Leah sighed and lifted another piece of mail from the

pile she'd been going through before the call. She was meeting Gerald for lunch and wanted to get the task done. Unfortunately, it had been almost a month and there was a stack of it. When she opened the yellow envelope and an article fell out, Leah picked it up.

"Thought this might be of interest to you, as if you didn't already know, Love Rachel."

Leah reread the note, then looked at the fuzzy picture. Recognizing Gerald, she dropped the article from her hands and her body started to tremble in distress. In desperation, she tried to stop the conclusion her mind was drawing.

Gerald was TyJo Productions! Gerald had lied to her!

Leah squeezed her eyes shut to ward off the tears. No. Not Gerald! No matter what this paper said, she knew it wasn't Gerald. Leah left the table and ran out of her apartment.

"Enter," Gerald said. He glanced up from the note he was making and smiled. "I'll be just a minute, baby girl. Then we can go." He reared back when Leah slapped the article down on the desk in front of him.

"Is this you?"

Gerald stared down at the photograph. The headline leaped off the page at him.

"THE G-MAN OF HIP HOP AND R&B FINALLY CAPTURED ON FILM."

Gerald didn't need to read the rest. He knew what the article said and clearly remembered the night the photograph had been taken. TyJo had collected eight Grammy Awards that evening and leaving the ceremony, Gerald had almost made it to his limo when a man appeared at his side. After the flash went off, his bodyguard had removed the camera from the man's hands and smashed it to the ground. The roll of film had already been slipped inside the photographer's pocket.

Gerald stood up. "Leah, I know what this looks like. But I can explain."

Leah released a furious breath. "You mean you can tell another lie."

"Leah! I have never lied to you."

"You haven't, huh? Well, when I told you about that note from TyJo Productions, why didn't you say anything?"

Gerald ran a distraught hand over his head. This was not about TyJo. This was about trust and looking at Leah, he knew he had made the biggest error of his life by not telling her about his connection. "Leah, it wasn't the only one. The first was in your apartment the day we found it burglarized. Another came the day you fell ill. I didn't tell you because you had enough to deal with and because I wanted to find out who was behind them. This article is seven years old and I haven't been with TyJo for over two years. I don't know what's going on yet, and a good friend of mine, Bill Watson, is trying to get the answers. But, baby girl, I am not the one trying to harm you or Project Spruce."

Leah didn't believe him and complete loathing for his explanation flared in her eyes. She walked around the desk and stabbed her finger in his chest. He could explain all he wanted. She wasn't about to be taken in by his duplicity again. "You were in my apartment around the time it was broken into. You were in my apartment when this supposed other note arrived. You were even with me in Adam's Park when I was shot and you didn't tell me about TyJo Productions, and that was a lie!"

Gerald couldn't believe the venom he heard in Leah's voice or the hatred for him he saw in her eyes. "How can you accuse me of this when you know how much I love you, Leah? Now, maybe I didn't tell you about TyJo, but that does not mean I've been lying to you."

She backed away from him, shaking her head. "Omission is the same thing, Gerald Morris. You're a liar! Just like Michael Ray Dupree. And I'm not listening anymore. I'm leaving and I never want to see you again!"

Gerald was around the desk before Leah took one step. Startled when his hands seized her waist and brought her to eye level, she recoiled from the volatile, copper eyes boring into hers. "We are going to the house and we are going to sit down and talk this out. But the one thing you will never do, Leah Nicole Ellis, is leave me."

Gerald knew what was coming before it happened and his body tensed in preparation for the impact. Leah raised her knee and when he released her, she didn't stick around to see Gerald's arms come around his stomach where she'd landed her blow. She ran until she reached her Jeep. Jumping in, she sped away, scared, but regretful at the same time, knowing she was running away from the man she loved with all her heart.

❦

September 3

With a rueful expression, Gerald lifted the pot and filled his cup. At eight in the morning, he was already on his sixth cup of coffee. Agitated movements took him around the kitchen as he tried to empty his mind. He picked up the plate of scrambled eggs and sat at the kitchen table stirring the food around with his fork.

Leah didn't think he had tried to kill her. She believed he had lied to her and to Leah, that was the unforgivable sin. Nothing he'd said had convinced her otherwise. Still convalescing at home, she had changed the locks on the door, added bolts and a peephole, and his head still rang

from the number of times the phone had been slammed
down in his ear.

Gerald told himself Leah was overwrought. When she
calmed down, she would realize he had only been trying
to protect her. He had already spoken to Watts this
morning and Bill thought he was on to something. He'd
said he'd call back in a couple of hours. Gerald didn't
think he could wait for Watts. He was miserable, empty
and lonely. He needed Leah. Dropping the fork to his
plate, he left the kitchen, went to his den and picked up
the telephone.

"How long are you going to sit in this bed crying over
that man?"

Leah sat up and wiped away the tears she'd been crying for seven days. A full week of trying to forget Gerald
had left her bone weary and exhausted. A full week of
trying to forget him had left her heart crushed. "I don't
know."

Merri studied her friend's face. Leah's eyes were
shadowed and deadened, her posture and movements
discernible signs of her misery. Leah's energy and her
optimistic outlook were slowly being sapped with each
passing day. "You told me that if two people truly loved
each other, they could work out their problems. I know
you love Gerald and that he loves you. Talk to him, Leah,
and this time listen to what he has to say."

Leah refused to consider Merri's suggestion. Twice,
she had walked, eyes open, into a relationship built on
lies. To her, the meaning was clear: she was either the
world's biggest sucker or just a damn fool. Maybe it was
a genetic flaw in her character. "I'm not going to talk to
Gerald, Merri. He's just like Michael Ray." She ignored
the ringing at her side.

Merri picked up the phone. "Hello."

"Merri?"

"Uh-huh. Hi, Gerald."

Leah shook her head from side to side and motioned for Merri to hang up the phone.

"I need to talk to Leah."

"Hold on, Gerald." She turned to Leah with a stern look she might have given Jimmy and held out the telephone. "Talk to him," she commanded.

Leah pushed the hair from her face and reached for the telephone. "Hello."

"Leah, it's G."

Though she had a hard time drawing in air that had suddenly become as thick as pea soup, Leah couldn't stop the elation she felt at hearing his voice. She fought to overcome it. "No, Gerald."

"Leah, please don't hang up. I just want to talk to you. You don't even have to say anything; just listen. Okay?"

"I don't want to listen to someone who tried to kill me."

Merri gasped and Gerald just stopped himself from becoming hysterical. "Are you deliberately trying to hurt me, Leah? You know I had nothing to do with the shooting and if you are trying to hurt me, it's too late. I'm already hurting."

"I don't know," Leah responded, trying to get her over-tired brain to function. "Look, Gerald. I'm sorry for what I said. It was cruel. I know you didn't try to hurt me and I've already told the police it was Michael Ray. However, that does not dismiss the fact that you lied. After what I told you about that man, how could you do that?"

"Leah, I haven't been with TyJo for two years. The notes were written on TyJo Productions stationery, and I thought someone was trying to get to me by using you. The second note was a threat against Project Spruce, the third directed specifically at you. You were worried about the fundraiser, your speech, missing supplies, me and my problems with Malcolm. I couldn't bring myself to tell you that I owned the company you thought was behind all this. And Leah, to be honest, I was just plain scared. But you were being protected, sweetheart. And when I got to the bottom of it, I planned to talk to you."

"That story sounds really good, Gerald. It might even be true. I just don't know."

Gerald thought Leah might be ready to listen to him, but he didn't want to do it over the phone. They needed to hash this out face to face. "Leah, we need to talk. I'll be there shortly."

Despite what she thought he'd done, Leah knew she still loved Gerald. She could feel his pain and didn't want the additional burden. On top of her own misery, it was too much to handle. "I won't be here. I have a meeting at Maxwell Corp. this morning."

His heart stopped pumping as Gerald struggled to deal with his escalating anguish. "Leah, please. We need to resolve this, sweetheart. If you have some time, I can come by now."

Every brain cell in her head screamed yes, but Leah couldn't allow the word to escape her mouth. "Gerald, I can't," she whispered so softly he barely heard her. "And please don't ever call here again."

Leah hung up the phone. Merri sat on the bed. "Leah—"

Leah threw off the covers and left the bed. "Just leave it alone, Merri."

"Where are you going?"

"To get ready for my meeting."

"That meeting isn't until eleven. Why are you in such an all-fired hurry now?"

"Because I know Gerald. He's on his way and I don't plan to be here when he arrives."

"It's eight o'clock, Leah. What are you going to do for three hours?"

"I'll go to the mall and shop."

"The stores open at ten."

"Then I'll look in the windows," Leah said with impatience. "Merri, I need to get dressed now. I'll call you when I get back and let you know how the meeting went."

After seeing Merri to the door, Leah hurried into the bathroom. By the time she came out, twenty minutes had passed. She had to move faster. She wanted to be gone by the time Gerald arrived at her door. Going to her closet, Leah grabbed an indigo business suit and a white blouse. She dressed, threw some makeup in her purse and left the apartment.

Thirty

At the quiet click in his ear, Gerald remained on his back staring at the receiver in his hand. Leah didn't mean it. If she did, that meant it was over. And if it was over...

Heartache hit him hard, right in the gut.

It was not over, Gerald vowed. He wanted to set his mind to finding a solution, but his head was filled with a mire of thoughts he couldn't pull together. He left the couch and headed out of the den. Halfway up the stairs, he heard the ringing telephone. Hoping it was Leah, Gerald ran down the hallway to his bedroom and snatched up the phone.

"G, I have the answers. It is Dupree! He's behind all of it, man: the attempted buyout of TyJo, the shooting in the park, the notes, the burglary and the setup. A company called Maxwell Corp. is his cover. He's back in the business big time and he's added a stable of prostitutes.

"The police found the weapon used in the shooting and the hired thug who fired the shots has been apprehended. His prints were all over that gun, so he's not going anywhere. Wallis Montgomery is the other player. It's been six years since you put him out of business, but the man is still holding that grudge. He hasn't been to Chicago and I don't have anything concrete that ties him to Dupree, but I did find out that his current lady friend

works for TyJo Productions. Now, Leah helped put
Dupree behind bars and that may be the reason he
wants her dead, but I don't believe that it's her he's after.
I think those bullets were meant for you. How do you
want to handle this?"

Gerald's heartbeat revved up. Wallis Montgomery
and Dupree! How in the hell had those two hooked up?
But he couldn't think about that now. He had to get to
Leah and stop her from going to that meeting. "Watts,
ring Pete and let him know what's happening, then both
of you meet me at Maxwell Corp., pronto!"

"I'm on it, G."

Gerald hung up the telephone and raced for the
garage. He was backing out the Jag when a car pulled
into the driveway. Cursing, Gerald jammed the gear into
park and stepped from the car when he saw Malcolm.
"Whatever you have to say, do it in the car because I'm
in a hurry."

Sighing wearily, Leah stepped from the elevator and
headed for the double, maple doors of Maxwell Corp.
Halfway down the corridor, she stopped in the ladies'
room and pulled her makeup from her purse. She could-
n't go into a meeting looking like this. She needed to
project excitement and confidence if she were to convince Maxwell Corp. to continue its support of Project
Spruce. Tony was counting on her. Since the fundraiser, he had lined up other potential supporters, but if
Maxwell Corp. pulled out, it might have negative consequences.

She applied highlighter under her eyes to cover the
dark circles and mascara to enhance her lashes. After
patting her face with a powder puff, she pasted on a
smile and left the bathroom.

The receptionist greeted her. "Go right in, Ms. Ellis. He's expecting you."

Leah walked down the hall and knocked on the door. "Come in."

She entered, and closed the door behind her while her eyes adjusted to the room's dimmed lighting. "Mr. Michaelson, I'm Leah Ellis with Project—"

"One moment please," he interrupted, and she saw the back of a tall leather chair and the extended cord of a telephone.

While she waited for him to end the call, Leah examined the chrome and smoked glass office. She'd just stepped closer to examine a gold framed photograph which sat on a nearby table when blinding lights flashed on and the leather chair swung around. Before Leah had regained her senses, the man was at her side.

Her body jerked back when she recognized his face. "Michael Ray!" The sound was a gasp.

"It's been a long time, Peaches," he said, his voice smooth and low.

"Not long enough," Leah replied hotly. Her eyes quickly scanned the room. "Where is Mr. Michaelson?"

"I'm Mr. Michaelson."

Leah's face held a scowl. "That's not funny, Ray. I'm here to meet with Mr. Michaelson, the president of Maxwell Corp."

"Does it look like I'm joking, Leah?"

Her blood suddenly ran cold and her mind numbed with fear. It wasn't true. It couldn't possibly be true. "You're Maxwell Corp?"

A wicked smile spread across his. "Yes, and I'm surprised you didn't figure it out before now."

Leah took a moment to catch her breath. Michael Ray was a skilled liar, and she didn't trust anything that came out of his mouth. "You're not the president of this company, Michael Ray. I don't know why you're here, but I know you should be in jail."

Michael Ray feigned confusion. "Why would you say that, Leah? Oh, the shooting. Yeah, I was questioned about that. But I have at least twenty people who'll swear I was nowhere near that park. And I am the president of Maxwell Corp."

"I don't believe you," she muttered, attempting to move around him.

Michael Ray grabbed her arm. "Don't."

Panic dilated Leah's eyes. Not again, she thought, and jerking herself from his hand, she ran for the door.

Michael Ray caught her easily and led Leah back into the room. "The door is locked, Leah. Why don't we sit on the couch? I think we'll be more comfortable there."

Once there, he dragged Leah's trembling body into his arms. He closed his eyes and buried his face in her hair, inhaling her fragrance. "Remember how good it was between us, Peaches?" he asked, rubbing his hand across the front of her dress. "Remember?" Michael Ray placed his lips on her cheek and Leah cringed. "Everything is okay now," he whispered in her ear. "We're going to have a fine life together."

Leah's fear escalated. Her stomach revolted from his touch and she whimpered before she could stop the sound. What was Michael Ray going to do to her this time?

He turned Leah toward him. His hands surrounded her face and he kissed her lips. "You are a beautiful woman, Leah, and I'm so sorry I hit you. I swear I'll never lay my hands on you again. I hope you believe me and that it makes you happy. I only want to make you happy. I love you and from now on, it's going to be you and me."

His babble continued, and her heart pounded wildly when his hand moved down her body and underneath her skirt. Leah pushed it away. "What's the matter with you, Ray? You don't love me. You tried to kill me!"

A look of distress crossed his face. "That was a mistake, Leah. I never meant for you to get hurt. Morris was supposed to take that hit in the park. Not you. Never you. But you're okay and the next time, Gerald Morris will—"

Outside the office, a commotion erupted when Gerald and Malcolm charged into the offices of Maxwell Corp. Gerald strode to the receptionist's desk. "Where is Leah Ellis?" he demanded loudly.

"In-in a meeting with—" She froze when two more men rushed into the room.

Hearing Gerald's voice, Leah kicked Michael Ray in the shin. She jumped up and ran for the door. " Gerald! I'm in here!"

Furious, Michael Ray vaulted from the couch and tackled Leah to the floor. Jerking her up, he slapped her across the face, then dragged her back and removed a pistol from a side holster. "Keep you mouth shut, Leah, and no one gets hurt."

Seeing the gun, everything he'd done to her came back to Leah in a rush of anger, and she unleashed all of it on Michael Ray. "No more," Leah screamed vehemently, swinging her arms wildly in an attempt to hit him anywhere. When his grip finally loosened, she twisted in his arms and with her nails left a long, red trail down the side of his face.

Michael Ray shouted in pain and lifted the hand holding the gun into the air. Leah tried to duck the oncoming blow, but tripped and fell to her knees. She tried to crawl away, but Michael Ray grabbed her around the waist and brought her to her feet. She elbowed him in the stomach; the gun dropped to the floor when he doubled over. Leah kicked it away and ran for the door again. Recovering quickly, Michael Ray grabbed the jacket of her suit and pulled her back against his body. She heard a click and stared in horror at the switchblade he brandished in her face.

In the next instant, the door crashed in and four men invaded the room. Gerald headed straight for Leah. Michael Ray's arm clamped her tightly to him and pointed the knife.

"Hold it right there, Morris! The rest of you, too."

Gerald halted. His eyes honed in on Leah's terrified face and his heart began a brutal beat. She looked as if she'd been fighting for her life. Striving to maintain his cool, he tried to will her a message of his love and an assurance that everything would be okay. "Let her go, Dupree."

"I don't think so, man. Leah is mine and she wants to be with me," Michael Ray replied. "Tell him, Leah."

Despite the danger, all Leah could think about was how much she loved Gerald. If she had gone with her heart, they wouldn't be here and if something happened to Gerald she would never forgive herself. Her eyes pleaded with Gerald to cooperate. "G., will you wait for me outside while I talk to Michael Ray?"

Gerald's heart jumped. "No! I'm not leaving you here with a crazy man."

"I'm not crazy, Morris. And you're not getting her back." Michael Ray's eyes glanced around the room as he kissed the top of Leah's head. "How does it feel, G-man, seeing the woman you love with another man? Does it make you jealous? That's how I felt. Are you angry? I was, too. Well, you can't have her. Leah loves me and she's mine!"

Leah saw a blaze ignite in Gerald's eyes. If she were going to act, it had to be now. She twisted her head as far as she could to face Michael Ray. "I don't love you, Ray. I never have."

"That's a lie! You tell him the truth, Leah, or I swear I'll…"

"Leah, please don't do this," Gerald begged, trying to

get her attention.

She paid him no heed. "What are you going to do this time, Ray? You beat me and I lived through that. You trashed my apartment, sent threatening notes. You even tried to have me killed. None of it worked. I'm still here and there is nothing you can do or say to make me love you."

"Leah, I never meant to harm you; I told you that. I ordered that hit for Morris and that stuff in your apartment is not important. I'm going to give you everything, just like before. And the notes were just threats to get you away from that group so that we would have time for each other. Don't you see, Leah? I did those things so that you'll love me again. I understand why you left me and everything's been fixed. There are no other women and I've stashed enough cash for us to live comfortably for the rest of our lives. I can make you happy, Leah, if you'll give me the chance."

Watts, who had inched his way closer, quickly assessed the situation. Michael Ray's agitation was rising and Gerald Morris was about to explode. They needed a plan or someone might just get killed. "G," Watts whispered.

He cocked his head to the right when Gerald looked at him. Understanding, Gerald tried to calm down, but his heart sank as he listened to Leah's response to Michael Ray.

"I'll never love you, Ray! Your love is dirty and manipulative! You use and control people and I'll never let you do that to me again."

Maddened, Michael Ray secured his hold on Leah. With every word she spat at him, his eyes seemed to glaze more and more. Now he really did look crazed, though his voice sounded calm when he spoke. "If you're not going to love me, Leah, then you're not going to love anyone."

"No!" Gerald shouted as Michael Ray placed the knife against Leah's throat.

Michael Ray looked at Gerald and laughed. "What's the matter, Morris? Afraid I'm going to kill her? Well, you're right; I will kill her. If I can't have Leah, you won't either."

"Dupree, if you hurt her, I swear I'll take you apart with my bare hands."

Michael Ray surveyed the four men. When their images blurred, he knew something was wrong. He'd smoke a joint earlier to calm his anticipation of seeing Leah, but dope had never affected him this way before. He tried to think. Only one thought broke through. If they got their hands on him, he was a dead man. The only chance he had of getting out was to take Leah with him. "I want out of here."

"That's not going to happen," Gerald replied quietly, taking a step closer.

"I said I'd kill her and I meant it," Michael Ray yelled.

Leah swallowed and the knife nipped her skin. Seeing the drops of blood pierced Gerald's heart with a gripping terror that spread with speed through his body. He knew he was close to losing it and willed himself to keep his head.

Gerald's eyes flicked in Watts' direction, then returned to Michael Ray. He took a couple of steps to his left. "Okay, Dupree. We won't try to stop you. Just let Leah go," he said, moving again.

Michael Ray's eyes stayed with him. "No way, man. I'm taking Leah with me."

"Can't let you do that, Dupree. You can go, but Leah stays." Gerald continued moving as he spoke.

"Take another step and she's dead."

Gerald stopped.

Watts moved.

Seconds later, all hell broke loose!

Leah spiked Michael Ray's foot with the heel of her shoe at the same time a steel-toed boot connected with his hand, kicking the knife away. Michael Ray screamed in agony and loosened his hold on Leah. Gerald sprang forward, grabbed Leah and flung her behind him. Watts dove for Michael Ray and flipped him to the floor, his boot at his throat. Michael Ray looked up to see his own gun pointed at his face.

"He's Gerald's," Malcolm said.

Two hands lifted Michael Ray into the air and Gerald's first punch plowed into his stomach; the second landed on his jaw and sent Michael Ray flying backwards. Enraged, Gerald went after him again. He jerked Michael Ray to his feet and drew back his fist.

"Gerald!"

Her voice penetrated his rage and Michael Ray dropped to the floor. Gerald rushed to Leah and took her in his arms.

A few minutes later, Watts hung up the telephone. "The cops will be here shortly." He pocketed the gun, and said, "Gotta fly, man. Me and the Chicago vice don't exactly see eye to eye, if you know what I mean."

"Thanks, Bill. I owe you one."

"No problem, homes. You know where to reach me if you need me again. Meanwhile, you take care of this lovely lady. Later, G."

Watts left. Malcolm and Peter grabbed Michael Ray and dragged him into the lobby to await the arrival of the police.

Inside the office, Gerald took Leah's face in his hands. He examined the nick on her neck and the bruises on her face, laying gentle kisses on them before crushing her in his arms. "Do you have any idea how scared I was?"

There was no need for a reply. Reaching up, Leah pulled his head down and pressed their lips together in a deep, long-lasting kiss.

Epilogue

Labor Day

Gerald grabbed the bag and stepped from the car. The heavy aroma of barbecue immediately filled his senses as he made his way up the walk. On the porch he rang the bell and waited. His foot tapped automatically to the sound of Lakeside's "Something About That Woman."

"G! It's about time you showed up," Merri said when she threw open the door. Gerald handed her the bag. "What's this?"

"T-bones," Gerald replied, moving to enter the house.

Merri stepped in front of him. "Where is it?"

"Where is what?"

Merri pursed her lips. "I take it, Leah forgot to mention the music you were supposed to bring."

"Music?" he repeated, obviously perplexed

"Uh-huh. You need an album to get in here. But," Merri said, studying him. "You did bring this bag full of steaks and considering that you belong to one of our officers, I guess I can let you in."

"Oh, no," Tony stated, coming up behind Merri. He put his arms around her and kissed her on the cheek. "What do you think you're doing?"

"Leah forgot to tell Gerald that this was a 'Back to the

Seventies and Eighties' party, and he doesn't have any music."

"Real-ly," Tony replied, winking down at Jimmy. "Well, everyone else had to bring an album to get in here and there will be no exceptions." Tony wiped his hands on the Barbecue King apron he wore, and bent over a chair by the door. "I thought something like this might happen and that's why I brought along some extras," he murmured, flipping through the pile. He rose and handed Gerald an album.

Gerald looked down and shuddered when he saw the best-selling album of the worst music he'd ever heard during Disco's blessedly short era. "Saturday Night Fever!" he cried. "No, no, no. I'd rather skip the party than be caught dead bringing this junk."

"We-ll," Merri said, eyeing him with amusement. "You'll be missing the best bash of the year, but I'll give Leah your regrets."

"All right. All right. Here!" Gerald fairly shoved the offensive record into Merri's hand. "Now may I come in?"

"Of course," Merri replied. She handed the bag of steaks to Tony, who handed it to Jimmy. All three were grinning as they made their way to the kitchen.

Gerald stepped on the patio and searched the yard. The red, black and green balloons were back and the grill smoked by the back fence. Music filled the air and a large banner proclaiming $550,000 as the total collected at the fundraiser hung between two trees.

He spotted Leah sitting in a chair and engaged in a discussion with Danye, Ja'Nise and Stacia. He took off in the opposite direction.

At one card table, a game of spades was the offering. At another, bid whist and poker at a third. Gerald continued through the tables until he came up behind Peter, where a heated game of bones was going down.

He stood back and watched as one of the men let go

with a mighty slap of a domino to the table. "Take that, baby boy," the man said to Peter. He sat back with a wide grin. "I think this game is just about through, bro'er man."

Peter tilted his chair back on two legs and studied his last bone. "I wouldn't be going to the bank just yet, bro'er man," he replied, sitting up. He slapped his domino on the table.

"Shoot," the man said. He slouched back in his seat. "I should have known this yellow brother had som'um up his sleeve. Well, that's it for me, boys. I'm off to get me some of them eats 'fore they's all gone."

Peter rose from his chair. "G! It's about time you showed up. Have you heard the news?"

"Yep. Heard it on the way over."

Peter shook his head. "The media is saying it was sui-cide. I don't believe it. I think someone took Dupree out. It was probably the ones he ratted on when he cut his deal with the Feds the first time he went to prison. What do you think?"

"I think I'm glad Sheila turned over that set of books and that Leah won't have to go through another trial," Gerald replied, as they headed for the drink table on the patio.

"Yeah," Peter agreed. He looked across the yard and frowned. "And if the way those two brothers are sliding their way over there is any indication, I'd better go and stake my claim. I'd suggest you do the same."

Gerald moved to the edge of the patio. He didn't need to stake his claim; Leah already belonged to him. She was dressed in a color block, flounce skirt and matching top with a diamond cut away in the middle. When one of the men stopped by her chair, she leaned back and motioned with her finger for him to come closer. He bent down with a smile. She turned the finger and pointed it in Gerald's direction. The man jumped away from the chair as if he'd been burned. Time to go and get her, Gerald thought, moving across the yard.

He leaned over the back of the chair and kissed Leah. "You are very bad."

"I know," she replied, getting up. "Gerald Morris, I'd like you to meet Danye Taylor and Stacia Waters. Ja'Nise and Merri you already know. Ladies, G."

"I hope you don't mind if I steal this one away," Gerald said after greeting them.

"Do what you gotta do, brother," Danye replied.

Arm in arm, they walked away and for the rest of the day enjoyed the party. After dinner, they moved into the house and sat on the couch holding hands, but anyone looking at them could tell they were two people deeply in love and that they were not interested in the debate raging around them.

"You guys have been singing the same tune ever since Switch hit the street with their album. Just because the brothers were good-looking doesn't mean they couldn't sing," a woman said.

"Yeah right. You name one sissified group of brothers that could blow, or even one that wasn't a pantywaist gigolo and I'll eat my hat," Fred spouted off.

"Well, let's start with Ray, Goodman and Brown and add to that Al Jarreau, Maze, Peabo Bryson, LTD, Teddy Pendergrass. Lord, could that brother sing!"

"Wait a minute. What about the ladies? Klymaxx, the Emotions and Minnie Riperton."

"All y'all need to hush up," a man wearing owl glasses and a baseball cap said, stepping into the foray. "If you really want to know who laid funk back in the day, then let's start with Parliament, the Ohio Players, ConFunkSun, Lakeside and Cameo. Then ya gots the GAP Band and the Bar-Kays, oh and them white boys. What did they call themselves?" He snapped his fingers as he tried to remember. "Wait, wasn't it, The Average

White Band? Now those boys could get down. Hell! We thought them boys was a bunch of brothers when 'Cut the Cake' hit the air waves."

"All of those groups were good," the first woman said. "Well, get to scarfin' that lid, Fred."

"You would think these people could find something else to argue about," Leah said.
"Yeah," Gerald responded. "But they are all right. Those groups they named and many they did not laid some tracks that will transcend time, just like our love."

Merri came into the living room then. "If we're going to be on time for Dance Africa we need to make a move. Everyone find a car and after the show it's back here to party on."

Leah and Gerald didn't join the others. When the last vehicle pulled away, Gerald went to his car and retrieved another bag, then took Leah by the hand and led her across the street, into the apartment and directly to the bedroom.

An hour later, Gerald left the bed. When he returned, he dumped a pile of gaily wrapped packages into Leah's lap. He sat on the bed and lifted her arm. "I know you've been wondering about these keys," he said. He removed the bracelet and dumped the keys on the spread. "Tonight, I'm going to tell you."

Gerald picked up the symbolic key marked 1J and placed it in her palm. "This is the key to the Jaguar." He picked up the next one marked 2P. "This is the key to the Porsche. Three B is for the Bronco. Four is to the front door and five will get you into the house by way of the back door. Six is to my safety deposit box. By the way, remind me to give you the name of that bank." Leah could only stare at her hand. "Seven, eight, nine, and ten are the keys to the print shops. Eleven opens the door to my office at The Path and twelve is the key to my private post office box." He handed Leah a box. Inside, she found a gold key ring and the real keys. He had another package waiting for her when she looked up. Another, larger key was inside. Turn it over, baby," Gerald said.

Leah read the inscription. "This is the key to my heart." With tears in her eyes she climbed into his lap.

"You haven't finished opening your gifts." He gave her a peck on the lips, placed her back in the bed and handed her another box. Inside were three leather binders. When she opened them she saw her name, "Leah Nicole Ellis-Morris," inscribed on the checks and the gold credit cards also inside. She took the next box he held out.

"Oh," she gasped when she saw the huge marquis emerald and diamond ring.

"That, if you accept it, is your engagement ring."

Gerald knelt by the side of the bed and locked their gazes. "I love you, Leah and I want you to be my wife." His own hand trembled when he took hers. "Leah, will you please—"

Leah put her finger to his lips to still his words. Gerald wanted this marriage; she couldn't even remember the number of times he had asked her. To please her, he had finally talked to Malcolm, and while they had made some progress, she knew they had a long way to go before they came anywhere near a resolution. Gerald was still being too protective, but he was operating from a base of fear which Leah hoped would lessen over time. However, he was making an effort and that was a good sign.

Mostly, she thought about the day in Michael Ray's office and how close they had come to being separated permanently. She loved Gerald and she didn't ever want to lose him. Leah stood and walked to the dresser. Returning, she sat on the bed and gazed into his handsome face. "You have asked me to marry you more times than I can count and I've disappointed you by say-

ing no. Gerald, I am not going to say no tonight. If you'll
have me, I would like to ask you to marry me."

He expelled his breath and sat heavily on the floor.
"What?"

Leah opened the box in her hand, uncovering the diamond ring inside. "Gerald Tyler Morris, will you please
marry me?"

His brows furrowed together. It didn't feel right that
she'd asked him, then again, it didn't real wrong either.
Besides what did it matter, as long as they did get married and she spent the rest of her life with him. Gerald
looked up. "Yes," he answered, his voice a faint whisper.

The look on his face added a new meaning to the def-
inition of happiness when he rose to his feet and pulled
Leah up from the bed, kissing her as he swung her
around. He set her down and picked up both rings. After
the exchange, he glanced down at his hand before turning a wide grin on Leah. "Baby girl? Since you proposed
to me, does that mean I'll have to change my name to
Gerald Tyler Morris-Ellis?"

Leah was laughing as she brought his head down.
Some things would never change. As their mouths came
together in a kiss of passion, they both shared the same
thought. Their love would last forever.

Midnight Clear

In the small town of Mystic Ridge it is said that the spirits of the ancestors watch over the townsfolk, causing mischief, setting old wrongs right, and healing wounded hearts. Maybe it's rumor, or maybe it's not. But one very special winter night magic truly comes to pass, and four of romances' richest voices spin the enchanting tales of what happened on a Midnight Clear...

In *Angel's Legacy*, **Carmen Green** tells of Angle Snowden who returns home to Mystic with the intention of changing the town. Little does Angel know that the power to not only change the town but the future has been handed down to her from above. But the key to unlocking the gifts that she has bestowed is to discover love again in the arms of her past...

In **Monica Jackson's** *The Choice*, Evelyn Sweet never thought she'd have a love of her own. Neither did her selfish family. And this holiday season is certain to be no different than any of the others—even though David Douglas has returned to town. When the ancient past and an old family curse clash with the present, Evelyn discovers that all she has ever dreamed of can be hers, if only she believes...

In **Leslie Esdaile's** *Home for the Holidays*, returning to Mystic should be a special time for Colette and Franklin. Instead, their homecoming is filled with sorrow over the loss of Colette's grandmother, and doubt about the future of their marriage. Neither of them is prepared for the magical spirit that will change their lives, heal their family and mend their hearts one snowy winter's night...

In **Gwynne Forster's** *Miracle at Midnight*, being stranded on a mystical dirt road is only the first in a series of inexplicable happenings that begin to take over Page Sutherland's life. Encountering Nelson Pettiford, a mysterious stranger, is the next. And when they find themselves returning again to that special place, they discover that they've both been searching for all along is each other..

Rumor, folklore, town gossip? No one knows for certain. Perhaps you will discover the magic of love for yourself... upon a Midnight Clear!

"Midnight Clear *captures the essence of the holiday season: love, family memoried, laughter and spiritual renewal. Leslie Esdaile, Carmen Green, Gwynne Forster and Monica Jackson have given readers a wonderful gift. Thank you for this collection.*"

— Gwendolyn E. Osborne, The Romance Reader

Cypress Whisperings
By Phyllis Hamilton

Before she even turned around she knew he was there to rescue her. Stranded in the middle of a swamp during a life-threatening storm, the attractive and vivacious widow had reached a turning point in her life. A quiver surged through Sandra's veins as she recalled their smoldering history.

Will she surrender to Jack, the former FBJ agent relentlessly pursuing her? Or will she be seduced by the charisma of New Orleans' haute monde artist in residence, the free-spirited Lee Chienier?

No Commitment Required

By Seressia Glass

When hot chocolate meets vanilla shake, sparks immediately fly, leaving the two very aware of each other. Can a lingerie designer and a sexy business consultant truly have a no-strings-attached relationship?

Yvonne Mitchelson owns a small string of lingerie boutiques. Lately her designs have been lackluster. Her partners have the answer: there's nothing like love to spark creativity, but Yvonne isn't interested. Past scars have left her afraid to love...to feel.

Michael Benjamin is the epitome of the American male: tall, white, affluent, and handsome. He has his own scars, given to him by his ex-wife. Michael has honed his anger into a "love-'em-and-leave-'em" façade. He's one of Atlanta's most eligible bachelors and determined to remain that way.

Their first night of passion leaves them both shaken. Unable to go back to the way things were before, they agree to continue their personal relationship...with no commitment required. But love has a way of obliterating even the best-laid plans.

2000 INDIGO TITLES

Romance, African-American Style.

Soul to Soul	Donna Hill	$8.95
Picture Perfect	Reon Carter	$8.95
Best of Friends	Natalie Dunbar	$8.95
All I Ask	Barbara Keaton	$8.95
Path of Fire	T.T. Henderson	$8.95
Bound by Love	Beverly Clark	$8.95
Sin	Crystal Rhodes	$8.95
Midnight Magic	Gwynne Forster	$8.95
And Then Came You	Dorothy Love	$8.95
So Amazing	Sinclair LeBeau	$8.95
A Dangerous Love	J.M. Jefferies	$8.95
Midnight Clear	Leslie Esdaile	
(Anthology)	Gwynne Forster	
	Carmen Green	
	Monica Jackson	$10.95
Cypress Wisperings	Phyllis Hamilton	$8.95
Forever Love	Wanda Y. Thomas	$8.95
Chances	Pamela Leigh Star	$8.95
The Missing Link	Charlyne Dickerson	$8.95

*You may order on-line at www.genesis-press.com, by phone at
1-888-463-4461, or mail the order-form in the back of this book.*

TANGO 2 ROMANCE

Love Stories with a Latino Touch.

Hearts Remember	M. Louise Quesada	$15.95
Rocky Mountain Romance		
	Kathleen Suzanne	$8.95
Love's Destiny	M. Louise Quezada	$8.95
Playing for Keeps	Stephanie Salinas	$8.95
Finding Isabella	A.J. Garrotto	$8.95
Ties That Bind	Kathleen Suzanne	$8.95
Eden's Garden	Elizabeth Rose	$8.95

You may order on-line at www.genesis-press.com, by phone at 1-888-463-4461, or mail the order-form in the back of this book.

LOVE SPECTRUM ROMANCE

Romance across the culture lines.

INDIGO BACKLIST

A Lighter Shade of Brown	Vicki Andrews	$8.95
A Love to Cherish (Hardcover)	Beverly Clark	$15.95
A Love to Cherish (Paperback)	Beverly Clark	$8.95
Again My Love	Kayla Perrin	$10.95
Breeze	Robin Hampton	$10.95
Cajun Heat	Charlene Berry	$8.95
Carless Whispers	Rochelle Alers	$8.95
Caught in a Trap	Andree Michele	$8.95
Dark Embrace	Crystal Wilson Harris	$8.95
Dark Storm Rising	Chinelu Moore	$10.95
Everlastin' Love	Gay G. Gunn	*OUT*
Gentle Yearning	Rochelle Alers	$10.95
Glory of Love	Sinclair LeBeau	$10.95
Indescretions	Donna Hill	$8.95
Interlude	Donna Hill	$8.95
Kiss or Keep	Debra Phillips	$8.95
Love Always	Mildred E. Kelly	$10.95
Love Unveiled	Gloria Green	$10.95
Love's Decption	Charlene Berry	$10.95
Mae's Promise	Melody Walcott	$8.95
Midnight Peril	Vicki Andrews	$10.95
Naked Soul (Hardcover)	Gwynee Forster	$15.95
Naked Soul (Paperback)	Gwynne Forster	$8.95
No Regrets (Hardcover)	Mildred E. Riley	$15.95
No Regrets (Paperback)	Mildred E. Riley	$8.95
Nowhere to Run	*Gay G. Gunn*	*OUT*
Passion	T.T. Henderson	$10.95
Pride & Joi (Hardcover)	Gay G. Gunn	$15.95
Pride & Joi (Paperback)	Gay G. Gunn	$8.95
Quiet Storm	Donna Hill	$10.95
Reckless Surrender	Rochelle Alers	*OUT*

INDIGO BACKLIST

Rooms of the Heart	Donna Hill	$8.95
Shades of Desire	Monica White	$8.95
Somebody's Someone	Beverly Clark	$8.95
The Price of Love	Sinclair LeBeau	$8.95
Truly Inseparable (Hardcover)	Wanda Y. Thomas	$15.95
Truly Inseparable (Paperback)	Wanda Y. Thomas	$8.95
Unconditional Love	Alicia Wiggins	$8.95
Whispers in the Night	Dorothy Love	$8.95
Whispers in the Sand	LaFlorya Gauthier	$10.95
Yesterday is Gone	Beverly Clark	*OUT*

All books are sold in paperback form, unless otherwise noted.

You may order on-line at www.genesis-press.com, by phone at 1-888-463-4461, or mail the order-form in the back of this book.

Shipping Charge:

$3.00 for 1 or 2 books
$4.00 for 3 or 4 books, etc.

Mississippi residents add 7% sales tax.

ORDER FORM

Mail to: **Genesis Press, Inc.**
315 3rd Avenue North
Columbus, MS 39701

Name _____

Address _____

City/State _____ Zip _____

Telephone _____

Ship to (if different from above)

Name _____

Address _____

Telephone _____ Zip _____

City/State _____

Telephone _____

Qty.	Author	Title		

Total for books	_____
Shipping and handling: $3 first book, $1 each additional book	_____
Total S & H	_____
Total amount enclosed	_____

Use this order
form, or call
1-888-INDIGO-1

MS residents add 7% sales tax

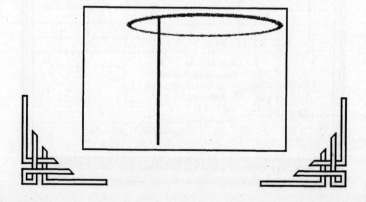